I0784740

Mary Roberts Rinehart

Long Live The King!

OK Publishing 2021

Mary Roberts Rinehart
LONG LIVE THE KING!

Spy Mystery Novel

Published by
MUSAICUM
Books

- Advanced Digital Solutions & High-Quality book Formatting -

musaicumbooks@okpublishing.info

2021 OK Publishing

ISBN 978-80-272-7827-5

Contents

Chapter I. The Crown Prince Runs Away 13

Chapter II. And Sees the World 15

Chapter III. Disgraced 18

Chapter IV. The Terror 21

Chapter V. At the Riding-school 25

Chapter VI. The Chancellor Pays a Visit 30

Chapter VII. Tea in the Schoolroom 33

Chapter VIII. The Letter 35

Chapter IX. A Fine Night 38

Chapter X. The Right to Live and Love 42

Chapter. XI. Rather a Wild Night 46

Chapter XII. Two Prisoners 53

Chapter XIII. In the Park 56

Chapter XIV. Nikky Does a Reckless Thing 61

Chapter XV. Father and Daughter 66

Chapter XVI. On the Mountain Road 70

Chapter XVII. The Fortress 75

Chapter XVIII. Old Adelbert 78

Chapter XIX. The Committee of Ten 83

Chapter XX. The Delegation 90

Chapter XXI. As a Man May Love a Woman 94

Chapter XXII. At Etzel 97

Chapter XXIII. Nikky Makes a Promise 102

Chapter XXIV. The Birthday 105

Chapter XXV. The Gate of the Moon 109

Chapter XXVI. At the Inn 115

Chapter XXVII. The Little Door 119

Chapter XXVIII. Tee Crown Prince's Pilgrimage 125

Chapter XXIX. Old Adelbert the Traitor 129

Chapter XXX. King Karl 134

Chapter XXXI. Let Mettlich Guard His Treasure 140

Chapter XXXII. Nikky and Hedwig 145

Chapter XXXIII. The Day of the Carnival 149

Chapter XXXIV. The Pirate's Den 154

Chapter XXXV. The Paper Crown 158

Chapter XXXVI. The King is Dead 163

Chapter XXXVII. Long Live the King! 165

Chapter XXXVIII. In the Road of the Good Children 168

Chapter XXXIX. The Lincoln Penny 171

Chapter I
The Crown Prince Runs Away

The Crown Prince sat in the royal box and swung his legs. This was hardly princely, but the royal legs did not quite reach the floor from the high crimson-velvet seat of his chair.

Prince Ferdinand William Otto was bored. His royal robes, consisting of a pair of blue serge trousers, a short Eton jacket, and a stiff, rolling collar of white linen, irked him.

He had been brought to the Opera House under a misapprehension. His aunt, the Archduchess Annunciata, had strongly advocated "The Flying Dutchman," and his English governess, Miss Braithwaite, had read him some inspiring literature about it. So here he was, and the Flying Dutchman was not ghostly at all, nor did it fly. It was, from the royal box, only too plainly a ship which had length and height, without thickness. And instead of flying, after dreary aeons of singing, it was moved off on creaky rollers by men whose shadows were thrown grotesquely on the sea backing.

The orchestra, assisted by a bass solo and intermittent thunder in the wings, was making a deafening din. One of the shadows on the sea backing took out its handkerchief and wiped its nose.

Prince Ferdinand William Otto looked across at the other royal box, and caught his Cousin Hedwig's eye. She also had seen the handkerchief; she took out her own scrap of linen, and mimicked the shadow. Then, Her Royal Highness the Archduchess Annunciata being occupied with the storm, she winked across at Prince Ferdinand William Otto.

In the opposite box were his two cousins, the Princesses Hedwig and Hilda, attended by Hedwig's lady in waiting. When a princess of the Court becomes seventeen, she drops governesses and takes to ladies in waiting. Hedwig was eighteen. The Crown Prince liked Hedwig better than Hilda. Although she had been introduced formally to the Court at the Christmas-Eve ball, and had been duly presented by her grandfather, the King, with the usual string of pearls and her own carriage with the spokes of the wheels gilded halfway, only the King and Prince Ferdinand William Otto had all-gold wheels,—she still ran off now and then to have tea with the Crown Prince and Miss Braithwaite in the schoolroom at the Palace; and she could eat a great deal of bread-and-butter.

Prince Ferdinand William Otto winked back at the Princess Hedwig. And just then—"Listen, Otto," said the Archduchess, leaning forward. "The 'Spinning Song'—is it not exquisite?"

"They are only pretending to spin," remarked Prince Ferdinand William Otto.

Nevertheless he listened obediently. He rather liked it. They had not fooled him at all. They were not really spinning,—any one could see that, but they were sticking very closely to their business of each outsinging the other, and collectively of drowning out the orchestra.

The spinning chorus was followed by long and tiresome solos. The Crown Prince yawned again, although it was but the middle of the afternoon. Catching Hedwig's eye, he ran his fingers up through his thick yellow hair and grinned. Hedwig blushed. She had confided to him once, while they were walking in the garden at the summer palace, that, she was thinking of being in love with a young lieutenant who was attached to the King's suite. The Prince who was called Otto, for short, by the family, because he actually had eleven names-the Prince had been much interested. For some time afterward he had bothered Miss Braithwaite to define being in love, but he had had no really satisfactory answer.

In pursuance of his quest for information, he had grown quite friendly with the young officer, whose name was Larisch, and had finally asked to have him ride with him at the royal riding-school. The grim old King had granted the request, but it had been quite fruitless so far after all. Lieutenant Larisch only grew quite red as to the ears, when love was mentioned, although he appeared not unwilling to hear Hedwig's name.

The Crown Prince had developed a strong liking for the young officer. He assured Hedwig one time when she came to tea that when he was king he would see that she married the lieutenant. But Hedwig was much distressed.

"I don't want him that way," she said. "Anyhow, I shall probably have to marry some wretch with ears that stick out and a bad temper. I dare say he's selected already. As to Lieutenant Larisch, I'm sure he's in love with Hilda. You should see the way he stares at her."

"Pish!" said Prince Ferdinand William Otto over his cup. "Hilda is not as pretty as you are. And Nikky and I talk about you frequently."

"Nikky" was the officer. The Crown Prince was very informal with the people he liked.

"Good gracious!" exclaimed the Princess Hedwig, coloring. "And what do you say?"

Miss Braithwaite having left the room, Prince Ferdinand William Otto took another lump of sugar. "Say? Oh, not much, you know. He asks how you are, and I tell him you are well, and that you ate thirteen pieces of bread at tea, or whatever it may have been. The day Miss Braithwaite had the toothache, and you and I ate the fruit-cake her sister had sent from England, he was very anxious. He said we both deserved to be ill."

The Princess Hedwig had been blushing uncomfortably, but now she paled. "He dared to say that?" she stormed. "He dared!" And she had picked up her muff and gone out in a fine temper.

Only-and this was curious-by the next day she had forgiven the lieutenant, and was angry at Ferdinand William Otto. Women are very strange.

So now Ferdinand William Otto ran his fingers through his fair hair; which was a favorite gesture of the lieutenant's, and Hedwig blushed. After that she refused to look across at him, but sat staring fixedly at the stage, where Frau Hugli, in a short skirt, a black velvet bodice, and a white apron, with two yellow braids over her shoulders, was listening with all the coyness of forty years and six children at home to the love-making of a man in a false black beard.

The Archduchess, sitting well back, was nodding. Just outside the royal box, on the red-velvet sofa, General Mettlich, who was the Chancellor, and had come because he had been invited and stayed outside because he said he liked to hear music, not see it, was sound asleep. His martial bosom, with its gold braid, was rising and falling peacefully. Beside him lay the Prince's crown, a small black derby hat.

The Princess Hilda looked across, and smiled and nodded at Ferdinand William Otto. Then she went back to the music; she held the score in her hand and followed it note by note. She was studying music, and her mother, who was the Archduchess, was watching her. But now and then, when her mother's eyes were glued to the stage, Hilda stole a glance at the upper balconies where impecunious young officers leaned over the rail and gazed at her respectfully.

Prince Ferdinand William Otto considered it all very wearisome. If one could only wander around the corridor or buy a sandwich from the stand at the foot of the great staircase-or, better still, if one could only get to the street, alone, and purchase one of the fig women that Miss Braithwaite so despised! The Crown Prince felt in his pocket, where his week's allowance of pocket-money lay comfortably untouched.

The Archduchess, shielded by the velvet hangings with the royal arms on them, was now quite comfortably asleep. From the corridor came sounds indicating that the Chancellor preferred making noises to listening to them. There were signs on the stage that Frau Hugli, braids, six children, and all, was about to go into the arms of the man with the false beard.

The Crown Prince meditated. He could go out quickly, and be back before they knew it. Even if he only wandered about the corridor, it would stretch his short legs. And outside it was a fine day. It looked already like spring.

With the trepidation of a canary who finds his cage door open, and, hopping to the threshold, surveys the world before venturing to explore it, Prince Ferdinand William Otto rose to his feet, tiptoed past the Archduchess Annunciata, who did not move, and looked around him from the doorway.

The Chancellor slept. In the royal dressing-room behind the box a lady in waiting was sitting and crocheting. She did not care for opera. A maid was spreading the royal ladies' wraps before the fire. The princesses had shed their furred carriage boots just inside the door. They were in a row, very small and dainty.

Prince Ferdinand William Otto picked up his hat and concealed it by his side. Then nonchalantly, as if to stretch his legs by walking ten feet up the corridor and back, he passed the dressing-room door. Another moment, and he was out of sight around a bend of the passageway, and before him lay liberty.

Not quite! At the top of the private staircase reserved for the royal family a guard commonly stood. He had moved a few feet from his post, however, and was watching the stage through the half-open door of a private loge. His rifle, with its fixed bayonet, leaned against the stair-rail.

Prince Ferdinand William Otto passed behind him with outward calmness. At the top of the public staircase, however, he hesitated. Here, everywhere, were brass-buttoned officials of the Opera House. A garderobe woman stared at him curiously. There was a noise from the house, too,—a sound of clapping hands and "bravos." The little Prince looked at the woman with appeal in his eyes. Then, with his heart thumping, he ran past her, down the white marble staircase, to where the great doors promised liberty.

Olga, the wardrobe woman, came out from behind her counter, and stood looking down the marble staircase after the small flying figure.

"Blessed Saints!" she said, wondering. "How much that child resembled His Royal Highness!"

The old soldier who rented opera glasses at the second landing, and who had left a leg in Bosnia, leaned over the railing. "Look at that!" he exclaimed. "He will break a leg, the young rascal! Once I could have-but there, he is safe! The good God watches over fools and children."

"It looked like the little Prince," said the wardrobe woman. "I have seen him often-he has the same bright hair."

But the opera-glass man was not listening. He had drawn a long sausage from one pocket and a roll from the other, and now, retiring to a far window, he stood placidly eating —a bite of sausage, a bite of bread. His mind was in Bosnia, with his leg. And because old Adelbert's mind was in Bosnia, and because one hears with the mind, and not with the ear, he did not hear the sharp question of the sentry who ran down the stairs and paused for a second at the cloak-room. Well for Olga, too, that old Adelbert did not hear her reply.

"He has not passed here," she said, with wide and honest eyes; but with an ear toward old Adelbert. "An old gentleman came a moment ago and got a sandwich, which he had left in his overcoat. Perhaps this is whom you are seeking?"

The sentry cursed, and ran down the staircase, the nails in his shoes striking sharply on the marble.

At the window, old Adelbert cut off another slice of sausage with his pocket-knife and sauntered back to his table of opera glasses at the angle of the balustrade. The hurrying figure of the sentry below caught his eye. "Another fool!" he grumbled, looking down. "One would think new legs grew in place of old ones, like the claws of the sea-creatures!"

But Olga of the cloak-room leaned over her checks, with her lips curved up in a smile. "The little one!" she thought. "And such courage! He will make a great king! Let him have his prank like the other children, and-God bless him and keep him!"

Chapter II
And Sees the World

The Crown Prince was just a trifle dazzled by the brilliance of his success. He paused for one breathless moment under the porte-cochere of the opera house; then he took a long breath and turned to the left. For he knew that at the right, just around the corner; were the royal carriages, with his own drawn up before the door, and Beppo and Hans erect on the box, their haughty noses red in the wind, for the early spring air was biting.

So he turned to the left, and was at once swallowed up in the street crowd. It seemed very strange to him. Not that he was unaccustomed to crowds. Had he not, that very Christmas, gone shopping in the city, accompanied only by one of his tutors and Miss Braithwaite, and bought for his grandfather, the King, a burnt-wood box, which might hold either neckties or gloves, and for his cousins silver photograph frames?

But this was different, and for a rather peculiar reason. Prince Ferdinand William Otto had never seen the back of a crowd! The public was always lined up, facing him, smiling and bowing and God-blessing him. Small wonder he thought of most of his future subjects as being much like the ship in the opera, meant only to be viewed from the front. Also, it was surprising to see how stiff and straight their backs were. Prince Ferdinand William Otto had never known that backs could be so rigid. Those with which he was familiar had a way of drooping forward from the middle of the spine up. It was most interesting.

The next hour was full of remarkable things. For one, he dodged behind a street-car and was almost run over by a taxicab. The policeman on the corner came out, and taking Ferdinand William Otto by the shoulder, gave him a talking-to and a shaking. Ferdinand William Otto was furious, but policy kept him silent; which proves conclusively that the Crown Prince had not only initiative-witness his flight-but self-control and diplomacy. Lucky country, to have in prospect such a king!

But even royalty has its weaknesses. At the next corner Ferdinand William Otto stopped and invested part of his allowance in the forbidden fig lady, with arms and legs of dates, and eyes of cloves. He had wanted one of these ever since he could remember, but Miss Braithwaite had sternly refused to authorize the purchase. In fact, she had had one of the dates placed under a microscope, and had shown His Royal Highness a number of interesting and highly active creatures who made their homes therein.

His Royal Highness recalled all this with great distinctness, and, immediately dismissing it from his mind, ate the legs and arms of the fig woman with enjoyment. Which-not the eating of the legs and arms, of course, but to be able to dismiss what is unpleasant-is another highly desirable royal trait.

So far his movements had been swift and entirely objective. But success rather went to his head. He had never been out alone before. Even at the summer palace there were always tutors, or Miss Braithwaite, or an aide-de-camp, or something. He hesitated, took out his small hand-kerchief, dusted his shoes with it, and then wiped his face. Behind was the Opera, looming and gray. Ahead was-the park.

Note the long allee between rows of trees trimmed to resemble walls of green in summer, and curiously distorted skeletons in winter; note the coffee-houses, where young officers in uniforms sat under the trees, reading the papers, and rising to bow with great clanking and much ceremony as a gold-wheeled carriage or a pretty girl went by.

Prince Ferdinand William Otto had the fulfillment of a great desire in his small, active mind. This was nothing less than a ride on the American scenic railroad, which had secured a concession in a far corner of the park. Hedwig's lieutenant had described it to him-how one was taken in a small car to a dizzy height, and then turned loose on a track which dropped giddily and rose again, which hurled one through sheet-iron tunnels of incredible blackness, thrust one out over a gorge, whirled one in mad curves around corners of precipitous heights, and finally landed one, panting, breathless, shocked, and reeling; but safe, at the very platform where one had purchased one's ticket three eternities, which were only minutes, before.

Prince Ferdinand William Otto had put this proposition, like the fig woman, to Miss Braith-waite. Miss Braithwaite replied with the sad history of an English child who had clutched at his cap during a crucial moment on a similar track at the Crystal Palace in London.

"When they picked him up," she finished, "every bone in his body was broken."

"Every bone?"

"Every bone," said Miss Braithwaite solemnly.

"The little ones in his ears, and all?"

"Every one," said Miss Braithwaite, refusing to weaken.

The Crown Prince had pondered. "He must have felt like jelly," he remarked, and Miss Braithwaite had dropped the subject.

So now, with freedom and his week's allowance, except the outlay for the fig woman, in his pocket, Prince Ferdinand William Otto started for the Land of Desire. The allee was almost deserted. It was the sacred hour of coffee. The terraces were empty, but from the coffee-houses along the drive there came a cheerful rattle of cups, a hum of conversation.

As the early spring twilight fell, the gas-lamps along the allee, always burning, made a twin row of pale stars ahead. At the end, even as the wanderer gazed, he saw myriads of tiny red, white, and blue lights, rising high in the air, outlining the crags and peaks of the sheet-iron mountain which was his destination. The Land of Desire was very near!

There came to his ears, too, the occasional rumble that told of some palpitating soul being at that moment hurled and twisted and joyously thrilled, as per the lieutenant's description.

Now it is a strange thing, but true, that one does not reach the Land of Desire alone; because the half of pleasure is the sharing of it with someone else, and the Land of Desire, alone, is not the Land of Desire at all. Quite suddenly, Prince Ferdinand William Otto discovered that he was lonely. He sat down on the curb under the gas-lamp and ate the fig woman's head, taking out the cloves, because he did not like cloves. At that moment there was a soft whirring off to one side of him, and a yellow bird, rising and failing erratically on the breeze, careened suddenly and fell at his feet.

Prince Ferdinand William Otto bent down and picked it up. It was a small toy aeroplane, with yellow silk planes, guy-ropes of waxed thread, and a wooden rudder, its motive power vested in a tightly twisted rubber. One of the wings was bent. Ferdinand William Otto straightened it, and looked around for the owner.

A small boy was standing under the next gas-lamp. "Gee!" he said in English. "Did you see it go that time?"

Prince Ferdinand William Otto eyed the stranger. He was about his own age, and was dressed in a short pair of corduroy trousers, much bloomed at the knee, a pair of yellow Russia-leather shoes that reached well to his calves, and, over all, a shaggy white sweater, rolling almost to his chin. On the very back of his head he had the smallest cap that Prince Ferdinand William Otto had ever seen.

Now, this was exactly the way in which the Crown Prince had always wished to dress. He was suddenly conscious of the long trousers on his own small legs, of the ignominy of his tailless Eton jacket and stiff, rolling collar, of the crowning disgrace of his derby hat. But the lonely feeling had gone from him.

"This is the best time for flying," he said, in his perfect English. "All the exhibition flights are at sundown."

The boy walked slowly over and stood looking down at him. "You ought to see it fly from the top of Pike's Peak!" he remarked. He had caught sight of the despised derby, and his eyes widened, but with instinctive good-breeding he ignored it. "That's Pike's Peak up there."

He indicated the very top of the Land of Desire. The Prince stared up.

"How does one get up?" he queried.

"Ladders. My father's the manager. He lets me up sometimes."

Prince Ferdinand William Otto stared with new awe at the boy. He found the fact much more remarkable than if the stranger had stated that his father was the King of England. Kings were, as you may say, directly in Prince Ferdinand William Otto's line, but scenic railroads —

"I had thought of taking a journey on it," he said, after a second's reflection. "Do you think your father will sell me a ticket?"

"Billy Grimm will. I'll go with you."

The Prince rose with alacrity. Then he stopped. He must, of course, ask the strange boy to be his guest. But two tickets! Perhaps his allowance was not sufficient.

"I must see first how much it costs," he said with dignity.

The other boy laughed. "Oh, gee! You come with me. It won't cost anything," he said, and led the way toward the towering lights.

For Bobby Thorpe to bring a small boy to ride with him was an everyday affair. Billy Grimm, at the ticket-window, hardly glanced at the boy who stood, trembling with anticipation, in the shadow of the booth.

The car came, and they climbed in. Perhaps, as they moved off, Prince Ferdinand William Otto had a qualm, occasioned by the remembrance of the English child who had met an untimely end; but if he did, he pluckily hid it.

"Put your lid on the floor of the car," said Bobby Thorpe' depositing his own atom there. "Father says, if you do that; you're perfectly safe."

Prince Ferdinand William Otto divined that this referred to his hat, and drew a small breath of relief. And then they were off, up an endless, clicking roadway, where at the top the car hung for a breathless second over the gulf below; then, fairly launched, out on a trestle, with the city far beneath them, and only the red, white, and blue lights for company; and into a tunnel, filled with roaring noises and swift moving shadows. Then came the end of all things a flying leap down, a heart-breaking, delirious thrill, an upward sweep just as the strain was too great for endurance.

"Isn't it bully?" shouted the American boy against the onrush of the wind.

"Fine!" shrieked His Royal Highness, and braced himself for another dip into the gulf.

Above the roaring of the wind in their ears, neither child had heard the flying feet of a dozen horses coming down the allee. They never knew that a hatless young lieutenant, white-lipped with fear, had checked his horse to its haunches at the ticket-booth, and demanded to know who was in the Land of Desire.

"Only the son of the manager, and a boy friend of his," replied Billy Grimm, in what he called the lingo of the country. "What's wrong? Lost anybody?"

But Hedwig's lieutenant had wheeled his horse without a word, and, jumping him aver the hedge of the allee, was off in a despairing search of the outskirts of the park, followed by his cavalrymen.

As the last horse leaped the hedge and disappeared, the car came to a stop at the platform. Quivering, Prince Ferdinand William Otto reached down for the despised hat.

"Would you like to go around again?" asked Bobby, quite casually.

His Highness gasped with joy. "If-if you would be so kind!" he said.

And at the lordly wave of Bobby's hand, the car moved on.

Chapter III
Disgraced

At eight o'clock that evening the Crown Prince Ferdinand William Otto approached the Palace through the public square. He approached it slowly, for two reasons. First, he did not want to go back. Second, he was rather frightened. He had an idea that they would be disagreeable.

There seemed to be a great deal going on at the palace. Carriages were rolling in under the stone archway and, having discharged their contents, mostly gentlemen in uniform, were moving off with a thundering of hoofs that reechoed from the vaulted roof of the entrance. All the lights were on in the wing where his grandfather, the King, lived alone. As his grandfather hated lights, and went to bed early, Prince Ferdinand William Otto was slightly puzzled.

He stood in the square and waited for a chance to slip in unobserved.

He was very dirty. His august face was streaked with soot, and his august hands likewise. His small derby hat was carefully placed on the very back of his head at the angle of the American boy's cap. As his collar had scratched his neck, he had, at Bobby's suggestion, taken it off and rolled it up. He decided, as he waited in the square, to put it on again. Miss Braithwaite was very peculiar about collars.

Came a lull in the line of carriages. Prince Ferdinand William Otto took a long breath and started forward. As he advanced he stuck his hands in his pockets and swaggered a trifle. It was, as nearly as possible, an exact imitation of Bobby Thorpe's walk. And to keep up his courage, he quoted that young gentleman's farewell speech to himself: "What d' you care? They won't eat you, will they?"

At the entrance to the archway stood two sentries. They stood as if they were carved out of wood. Only their eyes moved. And within, in the court around which the Palace was built, were the King's bodyguards. Mostly they sat on a long bench and exchanged conversation, while one of them paced back and forth, his gun over his shoulder, in front of them. Prince Ferdinand William Otto knew them all. More than once he had secured cigarettes from Lieutenant Larisch and dropped them from one of his windows, which were just overhead. They would look straight ahead and not see them, until the officer's back was turned. Then one would be lighted and passed along the line. Each man would take one puff and pass it on behind his back. It was great fun.

Prince Ferdinand William Otto stood in the shadows and glanced across. The sentries stood like wooden men, but something was wrong in the courtyard inside. The guards were all standing, and there seemed to be a great many of them. And just as he had made up his mind to take the plunge, so to speak, a part of his own regiment of cavalry came out from the courtyard with a thundering of hoofs, wheeled at the street, and clattered off.

Very unusual, all of it.

The Crown Prince Ferdinand William Otto felt in his pocket for his handkerchief, and, moistening a corner with his tongue, wiped his face. Then he wiped his shoes. Then, with his hands in his trousers pockets, he sauntered into the light.

Now sentries are trained to be impassive. The model of a sentry is a wooden soldier. A really good sentry does not sneeze or cough on duty. Did any one ever see a sentry, for instance, wipe his nose? Or twirl his thumbs? Or buy a newspaper? Certainly not.

Therefore the two sentries made no sign when they saw Ferdinand William Otto approaching. But one of them forgot to bring his musket to salute. He crossed himself instead. And something strained around the other sentry's lower jaw suddenly relaxed into a smile as His Royal Highness drew a hand from its refuge and saluted. He glanced first at one, then at the other, rather sheepishly, hesitated between them, clapped his hat on more securely, and marched in.

"The young rascal!" said the second sentry to himself. And by turning his head slightly-for a sentry learns to see all around like a horse, without twisting his neck-he watched the runaway into the palace.

Prince Ferdinand William Otto went up the stone staircase. Here and there he passed guards who stared and saluted. Had he not been obsessed with the vision of Miss Braithwaite, he would have known that relief followed in his wake. Messengers clattered down the staircase to the courtyard. Other messengers, breathless and eager, flew to that lighted wing where the Council sat, and where the old King, propped up in bed, waited and fought terror.

The Archduchess Annunciata was with her father. Across the corridor the Council debated in low tones.

"Tell me again," said the King. "How in God's name could it have happened? In daylight, and with all of you there!"

"I have told you all I know," said the Archduchess impatiently. "One moment he was there. Hedwig and he were making gestures, and I reproved him. The next he was gone. Hedwig saw him get up and go out. She thought —"

"Send for Hedwig."

"She has retired. She was devoted to him, and —"

"Send for her," said the King shortly.

The Archduchess Annunciata went out. The old King lay back, and his eyes, weary with many years of ruling, of disappointments and bitterness, roved the room. They came to rest at last on the photograph of a young man, which stood on his bedside, table.

He was a very young man, in a uniform. He was boyish, and smiling. There was a dog beside him, and its head was on his knee. Wherever one stood in the room, the eyes of the photograph gazed at one. The King knew this, and because he was quite old, and because there were few people to whom a king dares to speak his inmost thoughts, he frequently spoke to the photograph.

The older he grew, the more he felt, sometimes, as though it knew what he said. He had begun to think that death, after all, is not the end, but only the beginning of things. This rather worried him, too, at times. What he wanted was to lay things down, not to take them up.

"If they've got him," he said to the picture, "it is out of my hands, and into yours, my boy."

Much of his life had been spent in waiting, in waiting for a son, in waiting for that son to grow to be a man, in waiting while that son in his turn loved and married and begot a man-child, in waiting, when that son had died a violent death, for the time when his tired hands could relinquish the scepter to his grandchild.

He folded his old hands and waited. From across the corridor came the low tones of the Council. A silent group of his gentlemen stood in the vestibule outside the door. The King lay on his bed and waited.

Quite suddenly the door opened. The old man turned his head. Just inside stood a very dirty small boy.

The Crown Prince Ferdinand William Otto was most terribly frightened. Everything was at sixes and sevens. Miss Braithwaite had been crying her head off, and on seeing him had fallen in a faint. Not that he thought it was a real faint. He had unmistakably seen her eyelids quiver. And when she came to she had ordered him no supper, and four pages of German translation, and to go to bed at seven o'clock instead of seven-thirty for a week. All the time crying, too. And then she had sent him to his grandfather, and taken aromatic ammonia.

His grandfather said nothing, but looked at him.

"Here-here I am, sir," said the Crown Prince from the door.

The King drew a long breath. But the silence persisted. Prince Ferdinand William Otto furtively rubbed a dusty shoe against the back of a trousers leg.

"I'm afraid I'm not very neat, sir," said Prince Ferdinand William Otto, and took a step forward. Until his grandfather commanded him, he could not advance into the room.

"Come here," said the King.

He went to the side of the bed.

"Where have you been?"

"I'm afraid —I ran away, sir."

"Why?"

Prince Ferdinand William Otto considered. It was rather an awful moment. "I don't exactly know. I just thought I would."

You see, it was really extremely difficult. To say that he was tired of things as they were would sound ungrateful. Would, indeed, be most impolite. And then, exactly why had he run away?

"Suppose," said the King, "you draw up a chair and tell me about it. We'd better talk it over, I think."

His Royal Highness drew up a chair, and sat on it. His feet not reaching the floor, he hooked them around the chair-rung. This was permissible because, first, the King could not see them from his bed. Second, it kept his knees from shaking.

"Probably you are aware," said the King, "that you have alarmed a great many people."

"I'm sorry, sir. I didn't think —"

"A prince's duty is to think."

"Although," observed His Royal Highness, "I don't really believe Miss Braithwaite fainted. She may have thought she fainted, but her eyelids moved."

"Where did you go?"

"To the park, sir. I —I thought I'd like to see the park by myself."

"Go on."

"It's very hard to enjoy things with Miss Braithwaite, sir. She does not really enjoy the things I like. Nikky and I —"

"By 'Nikky' you mean Lieutenant Larisch?"

"Yes, sir."

"Go on."

"We like the same things, sir-the Pike's-Peak-or-Bust, and all that."

The King raised himself on his elbow. "What was that?" he demanded.

Prince Ferdinand William Otto blushed, and explained. It was Bobby's name for the peak at the top of the Scenic Railway. He had been on the railway. He had been-his enthusiasm carried him away. His cheeks flushed. He sat forward on the edge of his chair, and gesticulated. He had never had such a good time in his life.

"I was awfully happy, sir," he ended. "It feels like flying, only safer. And the lights are pretty. It's like fairyland. There were two or three times when it seemed as if we'd turn over, or leap the track. But we didn't."

The King lay back and thought. More than anything in the world he loved this boy. But the occasion demanded a strong hand. "You were happy," he said. "You were disobedient, you were causing grave anxiety and distress-and you were happy! The first duty of a prince is to his country. His first lesson is to obey laws. He must always obey certain laws. A king is but the servant of his people."

"Yes, sir," said Prince Ferdinand William Otto.

The old King's voice was stern. "Some day you will be the King. You are being trained for that high office now. And yet you would set the example of insubordination, disobedience, and reckless disregard of the feelings of others."

"Yes, sir," said prince Ferdinand William Otto, feeling very small and ashamed.

"Not only that. You slipped away. You did not go openly. You sneaked off, like a thief. Are you proud of it?"

"No, sir."

"I shall," said the King, "require no promise from you. Promises are poor things to hold to. I leave this matter in your own hands, Otto. You will be punished by Miss Braithwaite, and for the next ten days you will not visit me. You may go now."

Otto got off his chair. He was feeling exceedingly crushed. "Good-night, sir," he said. And waited for his grandfather to extend his hand. But the old King lay looking straight ahead, with his mouth set in grim lines, and his hands folded over his breast.

At the door the Crown Prince turned and bowed. His grandfather's eyes were fixed on the two gold eagles over the door, but the photograph on the table appeared to be smiling at him.

Chapter IV
The Terror

Until late that night General Mettlich and the King talked together. The King had been lifted from his bed and sat propped in a great chair. Above his shabby dressing-gown his face showed gaunt and old. In a straight chair facing him sat his old friend and Chancellor.

"What it has shown is not entirely bad," said the King, after a pause. "The boy has initiative. And he made no attempt at evasion. He is essentially truthful."

"What it has also shown, sire, is that no protection is enough. When I, who love the lad, and would-when I could sleep, and let him get away, as I did —"

"The truth is," said the King, "we are both of us getting old." He tapped with his gnarled fingers on the blanket that lay over his knees. "The truth is also," he observed a moment later, "that the boy has very few pleasures. He is alone a great deal."

General Mettlich raised his shaggy head. Many years of wearing a soldier's cap had not injured his heavy gray hair. He had bristling eyebrows, white new, and a short, fighting mustache. When he was irritated, or disagreed with any one, his eyebrows came down and the mustache went up.

Many years of association with his king had given him the right to talk to him as man to man. They even quarreled now and then. It was a brave man who would quarrel with old Ferdinand II.

So now his eyebrows came down and his mustache went up. "How-alone, sire?"

"You do not regard that bigoted Englishwoman as a companion, do you?"

"He is attached to her."

"I'm damned if I know why," observed the old King. "She doesn't appear to have a single human quality."

Human quality! General Mettlich eyed his king with concern. Since when had the reigning family demanded human qualities in their governesses? "She is a thoughtful and conscientious woman, sire," he said stiffly. It happened that he had selected her. "She does her duty. And as to the boy being lonely, he has no time to be lonely. His tutors —"

"How old is he?"

"Ten next month."

The King said nothing for a time. Then —"It is hard," he said at last, "for seventy-four to see with the eyes of ten. As for this afternoon-why in the name of a thousand devils did they take him to see the 'Flying Dutchman'? I detest it."

"Her Royal Highness —"

"Annunciata is a fool," said His Majesty. Then dismissing his daughter with a gesture, "We don't know how to raise our children here," he said impatiently. "The English do better. And even the Germans —"

It is not etiquette to lower one's eyebrows at a king, and glare. But General Mettlich did it. He was rather a poor subject. "The Germans have not our problem, sire," he said, and stuck up his mustache.

"I'm not going to raise the boy a prisoner," insisted the King stubbornly. Kings have to be very stubborn about things. So many people disapprove of the things they want to do.

Suddenly General Mettlich bent forward and placed a hand on the old man's knee. "We shall do well, sire," he said gravely, "to raise the boy at all."

There was a short silence, which the King broke. "What is new?"

"We have broken up the University meetings, but I fancy they go on, in small groups. I was gratified, however, to observe that a group of students cheered His Royal Highness yesterday as he rode past the University buildings."

"Socialism at twenty," said the King, "is only a symptom of the unrest of early adolescence. Even Hubert" —he glanced at the picture —"was touched with it. He accused me, I recall, of being merely an accident, a sort of stumbling-block in the way of advanced thought!"

He smiled faintly. Then he sighed. "And the others?" he asked.

"The outlying districts are quiet. So, too, is the city. Too quiet, sire."

"They are waiting, of course, for my death," said the King quietly. "If only, you were twenty years younger than I am, it would be better." He fixed the General with shrewd eyes. "What do those asses of doctors say about me?"

"With care, sire —"

"Come, now. This is no time for evasion."

"Even at the best, sire —" He looked very ferocious, and cleared his throat. He was terribly ashamed that his voice was breaking.. "Even at the best, but of course they can only give an opinion —"

"Six months?"

"A year, sire."

"And at the worst!" said the King, with a grim smile. Then; following his own line of, thought: "But the people love the boy, I think."

"They do. It is for that reason, sire, that I advise particular caution." He hesitated. Then, "Sire," he said earnestly, "there is something of which I must speak. The Committee of Ten has organized again."

Involuntarily the King glanced at the photograph on the table.

"Forgive me, sire, if I waken bitter memories. But I fear —"

"You fear!" said the King. "Since when have you taken to fearing?"

"Nevertheless," maintained General Mettlich doggedly, "I fear. This quiet of the last few months alarms me. Dangerous dogs do not bark. I trust no one. The very air is full of sedition."

The King twisted his blue-veined old hands together, but his voice was quiet. "But why?" he demanded, almost fretfully. "If the people are fond of the boy, and I think they are, to-to carry him off, or injure him, would hurt the cause. Even the Terrorists, in the name of a republic, can do nothing without the people."

"The mob is a curious thing, sire. You have ruled with a strong hand. Our people know nothing but to obey the dominant voice. The boy out of the way, the prospect of the Princess Hedwig on the throne, a few demagogues in the public squares-it would be the end."

The King leaned back and closed his eyes. His thin, arched nose looked pinched. His face was gray.

"All this," he said, "means what? To make the boy a prisoner, to cut off his few pleasures, and even then, at any time —"

"Yes, sire," said Mettlich doggedly. "At any time."

Outside in the anteroom Lieutenant Nikky Larisch roused himself, yawned, and looked at his watch. It was after twelve, and he had had a hard day. He put a velvet cushion behind his head, and resolutely composed himself to slumber, a slumber in which were various rosy dreams, all centered about the Princess Hedwig. Dreams are beyond our control.

Therefore a young lieutenant running into debt on his pay may without presumption dream of a princess.

All through the Palace people were sleeping. Prince Ferdinand William Otto was asleep, and riding again the little car in the Land of Delight. So that, turning a corner sharply, he almost fell out of bed.

On the other side of the city the little American boy was asleep also. At that exact time he was being tucked up by an entirely efficient and placid-eyed American mother, who felt under his head to see that his ear was not turned forward. She liked close-fitting ears.

Nobody, naturally, was tucking up Prince Ferdinand William Otto. Or attending to his ears. But, of course, there were sentries outside his door, and a valet de chambre to be rung for, and a number of embroidered eagles scattered about on the curtains and things, and a country surrounding him which would one day be his, unless —

"At any time," said General Mettlich, and was grimly silent.

It was really no time for such a speech. But there is never a good time for bad news.

"Well?" inquired the King, after a time. "You have something to suggest, I take it."

The old soldier cleared his throat. "Sire," he began, "it is said that a chancellor should have but one passion-his King. I have two: my King and my country."

The King nodded gravely. He knew both passions, relied on both. And found them both a bit troublesome at times!

"Once, some years ago, sire, I came to you with a plan. The Princess Hedwig was a child then, and his late Royal Highness was-still with us. For that, and for other reasons, Your Majesty refused to listen. But things have changed. Between us and revolution there stand only the frail life of a boy and an army none too large, and already, perhaps, affected. There is much discontent, and the offspring of discontent is anarchy."

The King snarled. But Mettlich had taken his courage in his hands, and went on. Their neighbor and hereditary foe was Karnia. Could they any longer afford the enmity of Karnia? One cause of discontent was the expense of the army, and of the fortifications along the Karnian border. If Karnia were allied with them, there would be no need of so great an army. They had the mineral wealth, and Karnia the seaports. The old dream of the Empire, of a railway to the sea, would be realized.

He pleaded well. The idea was not new. To place the little King Otto IX on the throne and keep him there in the face of opposition would require support from outside. Karnia would furnish this support. For a price.

The price was the Princess Hedwig.

Outside, Nikky Larisch rose, stretched, and fell to pacing the floor. It was one o'clock, and the palace slept. He lighted a cigarette, and stepping out into a small balcony which overlooked the Square, faced the quiet night.

"That is my plea, sire," Mettlich finished. "Karl of Karnia is anxious to marry, and looks this way. To allay discontent and growing insurrection, to insure the boy's safety and his throne, to beat our swords into ploughshares"—here he caught the King's scowl; and added—"to a certain extent, and to make us a commercial as well as a military nation, surely, sire, it gains much for us, and loses us nothing."

"But our independence!" said the King sourly.

However, he did not dismiss the idea. The fright of the afternoon had weakened him, and if Mettlich were right-he had what the King considered a perfectly damnable habit of being right-the Royalist party would need outside help to maintain the throne.

"Karnia!" he said. "The lion and the lamb, with the lamb inside the lion! And in, the mean time the boy—"

"He should be watched always."

"The old she-dragon, the governess—I suppose she is trustworthy?"

"Perfectly. But she is a woman."

"He has Lussin." Count Lussin was the Crown Prince's aide-de-camp.

"He needs a man, sire," observed the Chancellor rather tartly.

The King cleared his throat. "This youngster he is so fond of, young Larisch, would he please you better?" he asked, with ironic deference.

"A good boy, sire. You may recall that his mother—" He stopped.

Perhaps the old King's memory was good. Perhaps there was a change in Mettlich's voice.

"A good boy?"

"None better, sire. He is devoted to His Royal Highness. He is still much of a lad himself. I have listened to them talking. It is a question which is the older! He is outside now."

"Bring him in. I'll have a look at him."

Nikky, summoned by a chamberlain, stopped inside the doorway and bowed deeply.

"Come here," said the King.

He advanced.

"How old are you?"

"Twenty-three, sire."

"In the Grenadiers, I believe."

Nikky bowed.

"Like horses?" said the King suddenly.

"Very much, sire."

"And boys?"

"I—some boys, sire."

"Humph! Quite right, too. Little devils, most of them." He drew himself tap in his chair. "Lieutenant Larisch," he said, "His Royal Highness the Crown Prince has taken a liking to you. I believe it is to you that our fright to-day is due."

Nikky's heart thumped. He went rather pale.

"It is my intention, Lieutenant Larisch, to place the Crown Prince in your personal charge. For reasons I need not go into, it is imperative that he take no more excursions alone. These are strange times, when sedition struts in Court garments, and kings may trust neither their armies nor their subjects. I want," he said, his tone losing its bitterness, "a real friend for the little Crown Prince. One who is both brave and loyal."

Afterward, in his small room, Nikky composed a neat, well-rounded speech, in which he expressed his loyalty, gratitude, and undying devotion to the Crown Prince. It was an elegant little speech. Unluckily, the occasion for it had gone by two hours.

"I —I am grateful, sire," was what he said. "I —" And there he stopped and choked up. It was rather dreadful.

"I depend on you, Captain Larisch," said the King gravely, and nodded his head in a gesture of dismissal. Nikky backed toward the door, struck a hassock, all but went down, bowed again at the door, and fled.

"A fine lad," said General Mettlich, "but no talker."

"All the better," replied His Majesty. "I am tired of men who talk well. And" —he smiled faintly —"I am tired of you. You talk too well. You make me think. I don't want to think. I've been thinking all my life. It is time to rest, my friend."

Chapter V
At the Riding-school

His Royal Highness the Crown Prince Ferdinand William Otto was in disgrace.

He had risen at six, bathed, dressed, and gone to Mass, in disgrace. He had breakfasted at seven-thirty on fruit, cereal, and one egg, in disgrace. He had gone to his study at eight o'clock for lessons, in disgrace. A long line of tutors came and went all morning, and he worked diligently, but he was still in disgrace. All morning long and in the intervals between tutors he had tried to catch Miss Braithwaite's eye.

Except for the most ordinary civilities, she had refused to look in his direction. She was correcting an essay in English on Mr. Gladstone, with a blue pencil, and putting in blue commas every here and there. The Crown Prince was amazingly weak in commas. When she was all through, she piled the sheets together and wrote a word on the first page. It might have been "good." On the other hand, it could easily have been "poor." The motions of the hand are similar.

At last; in desperation, the Crown Prince deliberately broke off the point of his pencil, and went to the desk where Miss Braithwaite sat, monarch of the American pencil-sharpener which was the beloved of his heart.

"Again!" said Miss Braithwaite shortly. And raised her eyebrows.

"It's a very soft pencil," explained the Crown Prince. "When I press down on it, it-it busts."

"It what?"

"It busts-breaks." Evidently the English people were not familiar with this new and fascinating American word.

He cast a casual glance toward Mr. Gladstone. The word was certainly "poor." Suddenly a sense of injustice began to rise in him. He had worked rather hard over Mr. Gladstone. He had done so because he knew that Miss Braithwaite considered him the greatest man since Jesus Christ, and even the Christ had not written "The Influence of Authority in Matters of Opinion."

The injustice went to his eyes and made him blink. He had apologized for yesterday, and explained fully. It was not fair. As to commas, anybody could put in enough commas.

The French tutor was standing near a photograph of Hedwig, and pretending not to look at it. Prince Ferdinand William Otto had a suspicion that the tutor was in love with Hedwig. On one occasion, when she had entered unexpectedly, he had certainly given out the sentence, "Ce dragon etait le vieux serpent, la princesse," instead of "Ce dragon etait le vieux serpent, le roi."

Prince Ferdinand William Otto did not like the French tutor. His being silly about Hedwig was not the reason. Even Nikky had that trouble, and once, when they were all riding together, had said, "Canter on the snaffle, trot on the curb," when he meant exactly the opposite. It was not that. Part of it was because of his legs, which were inclined to knock at the knees. Mostly it was his eyes, which protruded. "When he reads my French exercises," he complained once to Hedwig, "he waves them around like an ant's."

He and Hedwig usually spoke English together. Like most royalties, they had been raised on languages. It was as much as one's brains were worth, sometimes, to try to follow them as they leaped from grammar to grammar.

"Like an aunt's?" inquired Hedwig, mystified.

"An ant's. They have eyes on the ends of their feelers, you know."

But Miss Braithwaite, overhearing, had said that ants have no eyes at all. She had no imagination.

His taste of liberty had spoiled the Crown Prince for work. Instead of conjugating a French verb, he made a sketch of the Scenic Railway. He drew the little car, and two heads looking over the edge, with a sort of porcupine effect of hairs standing straight up.

"Otto!" said Miss Braithwaite sternly.

Miss Braithwaite did not say "sir" to him or "Your Royal Highness," like the tutors. She had taken him from the arms of his mother when he was a baby, and had taught a succession of nurses how to fix his bottles, and made them raise the windows when he slept-which was heresy in that country, and was brought up for discussion in the Parliament. When it came time for his first tooth, and he was wickedly fretful, and the doctors had a consultation over him, it was Miss Braithwaite who had ignored everything they said, and rubbed the tooth through with her silver thimble. Boiled first, of course.

And when one has cut a Royal Highness's first tooth, and broken him of sucking his thumb, and held a cold buttered knife against his bruises to prevent their discoloring, one does get out of the way of being very formal with him.

"Otto!" said Miss Braithwaite sternly.

So he went to work in earnest. He worked at a big desk, which had been his father's. As a matter of fact, everything in the room was too big for him. It had not occurred to any one to make any concessions to his size. He went through life, one may say, with his legs dangling, or standing on tiptoe to see things.

The suite had been his father's before him. Even the heavy old rug had been worn shabby by the scuffing of his father's feet. On the wall there hung a picture his father had drawn. It was of a yacht in full sail. Prince Hubert had been fifteen when he drew it, and was contemplating abandoning his princely career and running away to be a pirate. As a matter of fact, the yacht boasted the black flag, as Otto knew quite well. Nikky had discover it. But none of the grown-ups had recognized the damning fact. Nikky was not, strictly speaking a grown-up.

The sun came through the deep embrasures of the window and set Prince Ferdinand William Otto's feet to wriggling. It penetrated the gloomy fastnesses of the old room and showed its dingy furniture, its great desk, its dark velvet portieres, and the old cabinet in which the Crown Prince kept his toys on the top shelf. He had arranged them there himself, the ones he was fondest of in the front row, so he could look up and see them; a drum which he still dearly loved, but which made Miss Braithwaite's headache; a locomotive with a broken spring; a steam-engine which Hedwig had given him, but which the King considered dangerous, and which had never, therefore, had its baptism of fire; and a dilapidated and lop-eared cloth dog.

He was exceedingly fond of the dog. For quite a long time he had taken it to bed with him at night, and put its head on his pillow. It was the most comforting thing, when the lights were all out. Until he was seven he had been allowed a bit of glimmer, a tiny wick floating in a silver dish of lard-oil, for a night-light. But after his eighth birthday that had been done away with, Miss Braithwaite considering it babyish.

The sun shone in on the substantial but cheerless room; on the picture of the Duchess Hedwig, untouched by tragedy or grief; on the heavy, paneled old doors through which, once on a time, Prince Hubert had made his joyous exits into a world that had so early cast him out;

on his swords, crossed over the fireplace; his light rapier, his heavy cavalry saber; on the bright head of his little son, around whom already so many plots and counterplots were centering.

The Crown Prince Ferdinand William Otto found the sun unsettling. Besides, he hated verbs. Nouns were different. One could do something with nouns, although even they had a way of having genders. Into his head popped a recollection of a delightful pastime of the day before-nothing more nor less than flipping paper wads at the guard on the Scenic Railway as the car went past him.

Prince Ferdinand William Otto tore off the corner of a piece of paper, chewed it deliberately, rounded and hardened it with his royal fingers, and aimed it at M. Puaux. It struck him in the eye.

Instantly things happened. M. Puaux yelled, and clapped a hand to his eye. Miss Braithwaite rose. His Royal Highness wrote a rather shaky French verb, with the wrong termination. And on to this scene came Nikky for the riding-lesson. Nikky, smiling and tidy, and very shiny as to riding-boots and things, and wearing white kid gloves. Every one about a palace wears white kid gloves, except the royalties themselves. It is extremely expensive.

Nikky surveyed the scene. He had, of course, bowed inside the door, and all that sort of thing. But Nikky was an informal person, and was quite apt to bow deeply before his future sovereign, and then poke him in the chest.

"Well!" said Nikky.

"Good-morning," said Prince Ferdinand William Otto, in a small and nervous voice.

"Nothing wrong, is there?" demanded Nikky.

M. Puaux got out his handkerchief and said nothing violently.

"Otto!" said Miss Braithwaite. "What did you do?"

"Nothing." He looked about. He was quite convinced that M. Puaux was what Bobby would have termed a poor sport, and had not played the game fairly. The guard at the railway, he felt, would not have yelled and wept. "Oh, well, I threw a piece of paper. That's all. I didn't think it would hurt."

Miss Braithwaite rose and glanced at the carpet. But Nikky was quick. Quick and understanding. He put his shiny foot over the paper wad.

"Paper!" said Miss Braithwaite. "Why did you throw paper? And at M. Puaux?"

"I —just felt like throwing something," explained His Royal Highness. "I guess it's the sun, or something."

Nikky dropped his glove, and miraculously, when he had picked it up the little wad was gone.

"For throwing paper, five marks," said Miss Braithwaite, and put it down in the book she carried in her pocket. It was rather an awful book. On Saturdays the King looked it over, and demanded explanations. "For untidy nails, five marks! A gentleman never has untidy nails, Otto. For objecting to winter flannels, two marks. Humph! For pocketing sugar from the tea-tray, ten marks! Humph! For lack of attention during religious instruction, five marks. Ten off for the sugar, and only five for inattention to religious instruction! What have you to say, sir?"

Prince Ferdinand William Otto looked at Nikky and Nikky looked back. Then Ferdinand William Otto's left eyelid drooped. Nikky was astounded. How was he to know the treasury of strange things that the Crown Prince had tapped the previous afternoon? But, after a glance around the room, Nikky's eyelid drooped also. He slid the paper wad into his pocket.

"I am afraid His Royal Highness has hurt your eye, M. Puaux," said Miss Braithwaite. Not with sympathy. She hated tutors.

"Not at all," said the unhappy young man, testing the eye to discover if he could see through it. "I am sure His Royal Highness meant no harm." M. Puaux went out, with his handkerchief to his eye. He turned at the door and bowed, but as no one was paying any attention to him, he made two bows. One was to Hedwig's picture.

While Oskar, his valet, put the Crown Prince into riding-clothes, Nikky and Miss Braithwaite had a talk. Nikky was the only person to whom Miss Braithwaite really unbent. Once he had written to a friend of his in China, and secured for her a large box of the best China tea. Miss

Braithwaite only brewed it when the Archduchess made one of her rare visits to the Crown Prince's apartment.

But just now their talk was very serious. It began by Nikky's stating that she was likely to see him a great deal now, and he hoped she would not find him in the way. He had been made aide-de-camp to the Crown Prince, vice Count Lussin, who had resigned on account of illness, having been roused at daybreak out of a healthy sleep to do it.

Not that Nikky said just that. What he really observed was: "The King sent for me last night, Miss Braithwaite, and-and asked me to hang around."

Thus Nikky, of his sacred trust! None the less sacred to him, either, that he spoke lightly. He glanced up at the crossed swords, and his eyes were hard.

And Miss Braithwaite knew. She reached over and put a hand on his arm. "You and I," she said. "Out of all the people in this palace, only you and I! The Archduchess hates him. I see it in her eyes. She can never forgive him for keeping the throne from Hedwig. The Court? Do they ever think of the boy, except to dread his minority, with Mettlich in control? A long period of mourning, a regency, no balls, no gayety that is all they think of. And whom can we trust? The very guards down below, the sentries at our doors, how do we know they are loyal?"

"The people love him," said Nikky doggedly.

"The people! Sheep. I do not trust the people. I do not trust any one. I watch, but what can I do? The very food we eat —"

"He is coming," said Nikky softly. And fell to whistling under his breath.

Together Nikky and Prince Ferdinand William Otto went out and down the great marble staircase. Sentries saluted. Two flunkies in scarlet and gold threw open the doors. A stray dog that had wandered into the courtyard watched them gravely.

"I wish," said Prince Ferdinand William Otto, "that I might have a dog."

"A dog! Why?"

"Well, it would be company. Dogs are very friendly. Yesterday I met a boy who has a dog. It sleeps on his bed at night."

"You have a good many things, you know," Nikky argued. "You've got a dozen horses, for one thing."

"But a dog's different." He felt the difference, but he could not put it into words. "And I'd rather have only one horse. I'd get better acquainted with it."

Nikky looked back. Although it had been the boast of the royal family for a century that it could go about unattended, that its only danger was from the overzeal of the people in showing their loyalty, not since the death of Prince Hubert had this been true in fact. No guards or soldiers accompanied them, but the secret police were always near at hand. So Nikky looked, made sure that a man in civilian clothing was close at their heels, and led the way across the Square to the riding-school.

A small crowd lined up and watched the passing of the little Prince. As he passed, men lifted their hats and women bowed. He smiled right and left, and, took two short steps to one of Nikky's long ones.

"I have a great many friends," he said with a sigh of content, as they neared the riding-school. "I suppose I don't really need a dog."

"Look here," said Nikky, after a pause. He was not very quick in thinking things out. He placed, as a fact, more reliance on his right arm than on his brain. But once he had thought a thing out, it stuck. "Look here, Highness, you didn't treat your friends very well yesterday."

"I know;" said Prince Ferdinand William Otto meekly. But Prince Ferdinand William Otto had thought out a defense. "I got back all right, didn't I?" He considered. "It was worth it. A policeman shook me!"

"Which policeman?" demanded Nikky in a terrible tone, and in his fury quite forgot the ragging he had prepared for Otto.

"I think I'll not tell you, if you don't mind. And I bought a fig lady. I've saved the legs for you."

Fortune smiled on Nikky that day. Had, indeed, been smiling daily for some three weeks. Singularly enough, the Princess Hedwig, who had been placed on a pony at the early age of two, and who had been wont to boast that she could ride any horse in her grandfather's stables, was taking riding-lessons. From twelve to one-which was, also singularly, the time Prince Ferdinand William Otto and Nikky rode in the ring-the Princess Hedwig rode also. Rode divinely. Rode saucily. Rode, when Nikky was ahead, tenderly.

To tell the truth, Prince Ferdinand William Otto rather hoped, this morning, that Hedwig would not be there. There was a difference in Nikky when Hedwig was around. When she was not there he would do all sorts of things, like jumping on his horse while it was going, and riding backward in the saddle, and so on. He had once even tried jumping on his horse as it galloped past him, and missed, and had been awfully ashamed about it. But when Hedwig was there, there was no skylarking. They rode around, and the riding-master put up jumps and they took them. And finally Hedwig would get tired, and ask Nikky please to be amusing while she rested. And he would not be amusing at all. The Crown Prince felt that she never really saw Nikky at his best.

Hedwig was there. She had on a new habit, and a gardenia in her buttonhole, and she gave Nikky her hand to kiss, but only nodded to the Crown Prince.

"Hello, Otto!" she said. "I thought you'd have a ball and chain on your leg to-day."

"There's nothing wrong with my legs," said Prince Ferdinand William Otto, staring at the nets habit. "But yours look rather queer."

Hedwig flushed. The truth was that she was wearing, for the first time, a cross-saddle habit of coat and trousers. And coat and trousers were forbidden to the royal women. She eyed Otto with defiance, and turned an appealing glance to Nikky. But her voice was very dignified.

"I bought them myself," she said. "I consider it a perfectly modest costume, and much safer than the other."

"It is quite lovely-on you, Highness," said Nikky.

In a stiff chair at the edge of the ring Hedwig's lady in waiting sat resignedly. She was an elderly woman, and did not ride. Just now she was absorbed in wondering what would happen to her when the Archduchess discovered this new freak of Hedwig's. Perhaps she would better ask permission to go into retreat for a time. The Archduchess, who had no religion herself, approved of it in others. She took a soft rubber from her pocket, and tried to erase a spot from her white kid gloves.

The discovery that Hedwig had two perfectly good legs rather astounded Prince Ferdinand William Otto. He felt something like consternation.

"I've never seen any one else dressed like that," he observed, as the horses were brought up.

Hedwig colored again. She looked like an absurdly pretty boy. "Don't be a silly," she replied, rather sharply. "Every one does it, except here, where old fossils refuse to think that anything new can be proper. If you're going to be that sort of a king when you grow up, I'll go somewhere else to live."

Nikky looked gloomy. The prospect, although remote, was dreary. But, as the horses were led out, and he helped Hedwig to her saddle, he brightened. After all, the future was the future, and now was now.

"Catch me!" said Hedwig, and dug her royal heels into her horse's flanks. The Crown Prince climbed into his saddle and followed. They were off.

The riding-school had been built for officers of the army, but was now used by the Court only. Here the King had ridden as a lad with young Mettlich, his close friend even then. The favorite mare of his later years, now old and almost blind, still had a stall in the adjacent royal stables. One of the King's last excursions abroad had been to visit her.

Overhead, up a great runway, were the state chariots, gilt coaches of inconceivable weight, traveling carriages of the post-chaise periods, sleighs in which four horses drove abreast, their panels painted by the great artists of the time; and one plain little vehicle, very shabby, in which the royal children of long ago had fled from a Karnian invasion.

In one corner, black and gold and forbidding, was the imposing hearse in which the dead sovereigns of the country were taken to their long sleep in the vaults under the cathedral. Good, bad, and indifferent, one after the other, as their hour came, they had taken this last journey in the old catafalque, and had joined their forbears. Many they had been: men of iron, men of blood, men of flesh, men of water. And now they lay in stone crypts, and of all the line only two remained.

One and all, the royal vehicles were shrouded in sheets, except on one day of each month when the sheets were removed and the public admitted. But on that morning the great hearse was uncovered, and two men were working, one at the upholstery, which he was brushing. The other was carefully oiling the wood of the body. Save for them, the wide and dusky loft was empty.

One was a boy, newly come from the country. The other was an elderly man. It was he who oiled.

"Many a king has this carried," said the man. "My father, who was here before me, oiled it for the last one."

"May it be long before it carries another!" commented the boy fervently.

"It will not be long. The old King fails hourly. And this happening of yesterday —"

"What happened yesterday?" queried the boy.

"It was a matter of the Crown Prince."

"Was he ill?"

"He ran away," said the man shortly.

"Ran away?" The boy stopped his dusting, and stared, open-mouthed.

"Aye, ran away. Grew weary of back-bending, perhaps. I do not know. I do not believe in kings."

"Not believe in kings?" The boy stopped his brushing.

"You do, of course," sneered the man. "Because a thing is, it is right. But I think. I use my brains. I reason. And I do not believe in kings."

Up the runway came sounds from the ring, the thudding of hoofs, followed by a child's shrill, joyous laughter. The man scowled.

"Listen!" he said. "We labor and they play."

"It has always been so. I do not begrudge happiness."

But the man was not listening.

"I do not believe in kings," he said sullenly.

Chapter VI
The Chancellor Pays a Visit

The Archduchess was having tea. Her boudoir was a crowded little room. Nikky had once observed confidentially to Miss Braithwaite that it was exactly like her, all hung and furnished with things that were not needed. The Archduchess liked it because it was warm. The palace rooms were mostly large and chilly. She lad a fire there on the warmest days in spring, and liked to put the coals on, herself. She wrapped them in pieces of paper so she would not soil her hands.

This afternoon she was not alone. Lounging at a window was the lady who was in waiting at the time, the Countess Loschek. Just now she was getting rather a wigging, but she was remarkably calm.

"The last three times," the Archduchess said, stirring her tea, "you have had a sore throat."

"It is such a dull book," explained the Countess.

"Not at all. It is an improving book. If you would put your mind on it when you are reading, Olga, you would enjoy it. And you would learn something, besides. In my opinion," went on the Archduchess, tasting her tea, "you smoke too many cigarettes."

The Countess yawned, but silently, at her window.

Then she consulted a thermometer. "Eighty!" she said briefly, and, coming over, sat down by the tea-table.

The Countess Loschek was thirty, and very handsome, in an insolent way. She was supposed to be the best-dressed woman at the Court, and to rule Annunciata with an iron hand, although it was known that they quarreled a great deal over small things, especially over the coal fire.

Some said that the real thing that held them together was resentment that the little Crown Prince stood between the Princess Hedwig and the throne. Annunciata was not young, but she was younger than her dead brother, Hubert. And others said it was because the Countess gathered up and brought in the news of the Court-the small intrigues and the scandals that constitute life in the restricted walls of a palace. There is a great deal of gossip in a palace where the king is old and everything rather stupid and dull.

The Countess yawned again.

"Where is Hedwig?" demanded the Archduchess.

"Her Royal Highness is in the nursery, probably."

"Why probably?"

"She goes there a great deal."

The Archduchess eyed her. "Well, out with it," she said. "There is something seething in that wicked brain of yours."

The Countess shrugged her shoulders. Not that she resented having a wicked brain. She rather fancied the idea. "She and young Lieutenant Larisch have tea quite frequently with His Royal Highness."

"How frequently?"

"Three times this last week, madame."

"Little fool!" said Annunciata. But she frowned, and sat tapping her teacup with her spoon. She was just a trifle afraid of Hedwig, and she was more anxious than she would have cared to acknowledge. "It is being talked about, of course?"

The Countess shrugged her shoulders.

"Don't do that!" commanded the Archduchess sharply. "How far do you think the thing has gone?"

"He is quite mad about her."

"And Hedwig-but she is silly enough for anything. Do they meet anywhere else?"

"At the riding-school, I believe. At least, I —"

Here a maid entered and stood waiting at the end of the screen. The Archduchess Annunciata would have none of the palace flunkies about her when she could help it. She had had enough of men, she maintained, in the person of her late husband, whom she had detested. So except at dinner she was attended by tidy little maids, in gray Quaker costumes, who could carry tea-trays into her crowded boudoir without breaking things.

"His Excellency, General Mettlich," said the maid.

The Archduchess nodded her august head, and the maid retired. "Go away, Olga," said the Archduchess. "And you might," she suggested grimly, "gargle your throat."

The Chancellor had passed a troubled night. Being old, like the King, he required little sleep. And for most of the time between one o'clock and his rising hour of five he had lain in his narrow camp-bed and thought. He had not confided all his worries to the King.

Evidences of renewed activity on the part of the Terrorists were many. In the past month two of his best secret agents had disappeared. One had been found the day before, stabbed in the back. The Chancellor had seen the body-an unpleasant sight. But it was not of the dead man that General Mettlich thought. It was of the other. The dead tell nothing. But the living, under torture, tell many things. And this man Haeckel, young as he was, knew much that was vital. Knew the working of the Secret Service, the names of the outer circle of twelve, knew the codes and passwords, knew, too the ways of the palace, the hidden room always ready for emergency, even the passage that led by devious ways, underground, to a distant part of the great park.

At five General Mettlich had risen, exercised before an open window with an old pair of iron dumbbells, had followed this with a cold bath and hot coffee, and had gone to early Mass at the Cathedral.

And there, on his knees, he had prayed for a little help. He was, he said, getting old and infirm, and he had been too apt all his life to rely on his own right arm. But things were getting rather difficult. He prayed to Our Lady for intercession for the little Prince. He felt, in his old heart, that the Mother would understand the situation, and how he felt about it. And he asked in a general supplication, and very humbly, for a few years more of life. Not that life meant anything to him personally. He had outlived most of those he loved. But that he might serve the King, and after him the boy who would be Otto IX. He added, for fear they might not understand, having a great deal to look after, that he had earned all this by many years of loyalty, and besides, that he knew the situation better than any one else.

He felt much better after that. Especially as, at the moment he rose from his knees, the cathedral clock had chimed and then struck seven. He had found seven a very lucky number, So now he entered the boudoir of the Archduchess Annunciata, and the Countess went out another door, and closed it behind her, immediately opening it about an inch.

The Chancellor strode around the screen, scratching two tables with his sword as he advanced, and kissed the hand of the Princess Annunciata. They were old enemies and therefore always very polite to each other. The Archduchess offered him a cup of tea, which he took, although she always made very bad tea. And for a few moments they discussed things. Thus: the King's condition; the replanting of the Place with trees; and the date of bringing out the Princess Hilda, who was still in the schoolroom.

But the Archduchess suddenly came to business. She was an abrupt person. "And now, General," she said, "what is it?"

"I am in trouble, Highness," replied the Chancellor simply.

"We are most of us in that condition at all times. I suppose you mean this absurd affair of yesterday. Why such a turmoil about it? The boy ran away. When he was ready he returned. It was absurd, and I dare say you and I both are being held for our sins. But he is here now, and safe."

"I am afraid he is not as safe as you think, madame."

"Why?"

He sat forward on the edge of his chair, and told her of the students at the University, who were being fired by some powerful voice; of the disappearance of the two spies; of the evidence that the Committee of Ten was meeting again, and the failure to discover their meeting-place; of disaffection among the people, according to the reports of his agents. And then to the real purpose of his visit. Karl of Karnia had, unofficially, proposed for the Princess Hedwig. He had himself broached the matter to the King, who had at least taken it under advisement. The Archduchess listened, rather pale. There was no mistaking the urgency in the Chancellor's voice.

"Madame after centuries of independence we now face a crisis which we cannot meet alone. Believe me, I know of what I speak. United, we could stand against the world. But a divided kingdom, a disloyal and discontented people, spells the end."

And at last he convinced her. But, because she was built of a contrary mould, she voiced an objection, not to the scheme, but to Karl himself. "I dislike him. He is arrogant and stupid."

"But powerful, madame. And-what else is there to do?"

There was nothing else, and she knew it. But she refused to broach the matter to Hedwig.

She stated, and perhaps not without reason, that such a move was to damn the whole thing at once. She did not use exactly these words, but their royal equivalent. And it ended with the Chancellor, looking most ferocious but inwardly uneasy, undertaking to put, as one may say, a flea into the Princess Hedwig's small ear.

As he strode out, the door into the next room closed quietly.

Chapter VII
Tea in the Schoolroom

Tea at the Palace, until the old King had taken to his bed, had been the one cheerful hour of the day. The entire suite gathered in one of the salons, and remained standing until the King's entrance. After that, formality ceased. Groups formed, footmen in plush with white wigs passed trays of cakes and sandwiches and tiny gilt cups of exquisite tea. The Court, so to speak, removed its white gloves, and was noisy and informal. True, at dinner again ceremony and etiquette would reign. The march into the dining-hall between rows of bowing servants, the set conversation, led by the King, the long and tedious courses, the careful watch for precedence that was dinner at the Palace.

But now all that was changed. The King did not leave his apartment. Annunciata occasionally took tea with the suite, but glad for an excuse, left the Court to dine without her. Sometimes for a half-hour she lent her royal if somewhat indifferently attired presence to the salon afterward, where for thirty minutes or so she moved from group to group, exchanging a few more or less gracious words. But such times were rare. The Archduchess, according to Court gossip, had "slumped."

To Hedwig the change had been a relief. The entourage, with its gossip, its small talk, its liaisons, excited in her only indifference and occasional loathing. Not that her short life had been without its affairs. She was too lovely for that. But they had touched her only faintly.

On the day of the Chancellor's visit to her mother she went to tea in the schoolroom. She came in glowing from a walk, with the jacket of her dark velvet suit thrown open, and a bunch of lilies-of-the-valley tucked in her belt.

Tea had already come, and Captain Larisch, holding his cup, was standing by the table. The Crown Prince, who was allowed only one cup, was having a second of hot water and milk, equal parts, and sweetened.

Hedwig slipped out of her jacket and drew off her gloves. She had hardly glanced at Nikky, although she knew quite well every motion he had made since she entered. "I am famished!" she said, and proceeded to eat very little and barely touch the tea. "Please don't go, Miss Braithwaite. And now, how is everything?"

Followed a long half-hour, in which the Crown Prince talked mostly of the Land of Desire and the American boy. Miss Braithwaite, much indulged by long years of service, crocheted, and Nikky Larisch, from the embrasure of a window, watched the little group. In reality he watched Hedwig, all his humble, boyish heart in his eyes.

After a time Hedwig slipped the lilies out of her belt and placed them in a glass of water.

"They are thirsty, poor things," she said to Otto. Only-and here was a strange thing, if she were really sorry for them-one of the stalks fell to the floor, and she did not trouble to pick it up. Nikky retrieved it, and pretended to place it with the others. But in reality he had palmed it quite neatly, and a little later he pocketed it. Still later, he placed it in his prayer-book.

The tea-table became rather noisy. The room echoed with laughter. Even Miss Braithwaite was compelled to wipe her eyes over some of Nikky's sallies, and the Crown Prince was left quite gasping. Nikky was really in his best form, being most unreasonably happy, and Hedwig, looking much taller than in her boyish riding-clothes —Hedwig was fairly palpitating with excitement.

Nikky was a born mimic. First he took off the King's Council, one by one. Then in an instant he was Napoleon, which was easy, of course; and the next second, with one of the fur tails which had come unfastened from Hedwig's muff, he had become a pirate, with the tail for a great mustache. One of the very best things he did, however, was to make a widow's cap out of a tea-napkin, and surmount it with a tiny coronet, which was really Hedwig's bracelet.

He put it on, drew down his upper lip, and puffed his cheeks, and there was Queen Victoria of England to the life.

Hedwig was so delighted with this, that she made him sit down, and draped one of Miss Braithwaite's shawls about his shoulders. It was difficult to look like Queen Victoria under the circumstances, with her small hands deftly draping and smoothing. But Nikky did very well.

It was just as Hedwig was tucking the shawl about his neck to hide the collar of his tunic, and Miss Braithwaite was looking a trifle offended, because she considered the memory of Queen Victoria not to be trifled with, and just as Nikky took a fresh breath and puffed out leis cheeks again, that the Archduchess came in.

She entered unannounced, save by a jingle of chains, and surveyed the room with a single furious glance. Queen Victoria's cheeks collapsed and the coronet slid slightly to one side. Then Nikky rose and jerked off the shawl and bowed. Every one looked rather frightened, except the Crown Prince. In a sort of horrible silence he advanced and kissed Annunciata's hand.

"So-this is what you are doing," observed Her Royal Highness to Hedwig. "In this-this undignified manner you spend your time!"

"It is very innocent fun, mother."

For that matter, there was nothing very dignified in the scene that followed. The Archduchess dismissed the governess and the Crown Prince, quite as if he had been an ordinary child, and naughty at that. Miss Braithwaite looked truculent. After all, the heir to the throne is the heir to the throne and should have the privilege of his own study. But Hedwig gave her an appealing glance, and she went out, closing the door with what came dangerously near being a slam.

The Archduchess surveyed the two remaining culprits with a terrible gaze. "Now," she said, "how long have these ridiculous performances been going on?"

"Mother!" said Hedwig.

"Answer me."

"The question is absurd. There was no harm in what we were doing. It amused Otto. He has few enough pleasures. Thanks to all of us, he is very lonely."

"And since when have you assumed the responsibility for his upbringing?"

"I remember my own dreary childhood," said Hedwig stiffly.

The Archduchess turned on her furiously. "More and more," she said, "as you grow up, Hedwig, you remind me of your unfortunate father. You have the same lack of dignity, the same" —she glanced at Nikky —"the same common tastes, the same habit of choosing strange society, of forgetting your rank."

Hedwig was scarlet, but Nikky had gone pale. As for the Archduchesss, her cameos were rising and falling stormily. With hands that shook; Hedwig picked up her jacket and hat. Then she moved toward the door.

"Perhaps you are right, mother," she said, "but I hope I shall never have the bad taste to speak ill of the dead." Then she went out.

The scene between the Archduchess and Nikky began in a storm and ended in a sort of hopeless quiet. Miss Braithwaite had withdrawn to her sitting-room, but even there she could hear the voice of Annunciata, rasping and angry.

It was very clear to Nikky from the beginning that the Archduchess's wrath was not for that afternoon alone. And in his guilty young mind rose various memories, all infinitely dear, all infinitely, incredibly reckless-other frolics around the tea-table, rides in the park, lessons in the riding-school. Very soon he was confessing them all, in reply to sharp questions. When the tablet of his sins was finally uncovered, the Archduchess was less angry and a great deal more anxious. Hedwig free was a problem. Hedwig in love with this dashing boy was a greater one.

"Of one thing I must assure Your Highness," said Nikky. "These-these meetings have been of my seeking."

"The Princess requires no defense, Captain Larisch."

That put him back where he belonged, and Annunciata did a little thinking, while Nikky went on, in his troubled way, running his fingers through his hair until he looked rather like an uneasy but ardent-eyed porcupine. He acknowledged that these meetings had meant much to him, everything to him, he would confess, but he had never dared to hope. He had always thought of Her Royal Highness as the granddaughter of his King. He had never spoken a word that he need regret. Annunciata listened, and took his measure shrewdly. He was the sort of young fool, she told herself, who would sacrifice himself and crucify his happiness for his country. It was on just such shoulders as his that the throne was upheld. His loyalty was more to be counted on than his heart.

She changed her tactics adroitly, sat down, even softened her voice. "I have been emphatic, Captain Larisch," she said, "because, as I think you know, things are not going too well with us. To help the situation, certain plans are being made. I will be more explicit. A marriage is planned for the Princess Hedwig, which will assist us all. It is" —she hesitated imperceptibly — "the King's dearest wish."

Horror froze on Nikky's face. But he bowed.

"After what you have told me, I shall ask your cooperation," said Annunciata smoothly. "While there are some of us who deplore the necessity, still-it exists. And an alliance with Karnia —"

"Karnia!" cried Nikky, violating all ceremonial, of course. "But surely —!"

The Archduchess rose and drew herself to her full height. "I have given you confidence for confidence, Captain Larisch," she said coldly. "The Princess Hedwig has not yet been, told. We shall be glad of your assistance when that time comes. It is possible, that it will not come. In case it does, we shall count on you."

Nikky bowed deeply as she went out; bowed, with death in his eyes.

And thus it happened that Captain Nicholas Larisch aide-de-camp to his Royal Highness the Crown Prince Ferdinand William Otto, and of no other particular importance, was informed of the Princess Hedwig's projected marriage before she was. And not only informed of it, but committed to forward it, if he could!

Chapter VIII
The Letter

The Countess Loschek was alone. Alone and storming. She had sent her maid away with a sharp word, and now she was pacing the floor.

Hedwig, of all people!

She hated her. She had always hated her. For her youth, first; later, when she saw how things were going, for the accident that had made her a granddaughter to the King.

And Karl.

Even this last June, when Karl had made his looked-for visit to the summer palace where the Court had been in, residence, he had already had the thing in mind. Even when his arms had been about her, Olga Loschek, he had been looking over her shoulder, as it were, at Hedwig. He had had it all in his wicked head, even then. For Karl was wicked. None would know it better than she, who was risking everything, life itself, for him. Wicked; ungrateful, and unscrupulous. She loathed him while she loved him.

The thing would happen. This was the way things were done in Courts. An intimation from one side that a certain thing would be agreeable and profitable. A discussion behind closed doors. A reply that the intimation had been well received. Then the formal proposal, and its acceptance.

Hedwig would marry Karl. She might be troublesome, would indeed almost certainly be troublesome. Strangely enough, the Countess hated her the more for that. To value so lightly the thing for which Olga Loschek would have given her soul, this in itself was hateful. But there was more. The Countess saw much with her curiously wide, almost childishly bland eyes; it was only now that it occurred to her to turn what she knew of Hedwig and Nikky to account.

She stopped pacing the floor, and sat down. Suppose Hedwig and Nikky Larisch went away together? Hedwig, she felt, would have the courage even for that. That would stop things. But Hedwig did not trust her. And there was about Nikky a dog-like quality of devotion, which warned her that, the deeper his love for Hedwig, the more unlikely he would be to bring her to disgrace. Nikky might be difficult.

"The fool!" said the Countess, between her clenched teeth. To both the Archduchess Annunciata and her henchwoman, people were chiefly divided into three classes, fools, knaves, and themselves.

She must try for Hedwig's confidence, then. But Karl! How to reach him? Not with reproaches, not with anger. She knew her man well. To hold him off was the first thing. To postpone the formal proposal, and gain time. If the Chancellor had been right, and things were as bad as they appeared, the King's death would precipitate a crisis. Might, indeed, overturn the throne.

And Karl had changed. The old days when he loved trouble were gone. His thoughts, like all thoughts these days, she reflected contemptuously, were turned to peace, not to war. He was for beating his swords into ploughshares, with a vengeance.

To hold him off, then. To gain time.

The King was very feeble. This affair of yesterday had told on him. The gossip of the Court was that the day had seen a change for the worse. His heart was centered on the Crown Prince.

Ah, here was another viewpoint. Suppose the Crown Prince had not come back? What would happen, with the King dead, and no king? Chaos, of course. A free hand to revolution. Hedwig fighting for her throne, and inevitably losing it. Then what about Karl and his dreams of peace?

But that was further than she cared to go just then. She would finish certain work that she had set out to do, and then she was through. No longer would dread and terror grip her in the night hours.

But she would finish. Karl should never say she had failed him. In her new rage against him she was for cleaning the slate at once. She had in her possession papers for which he waited or pretended to wait; data secured by means she did not care to remember; plans and figures carefully compiled —a thousand deaths in one, if, they were found on her. She would get them out of her hands at once.

It was still but little after five. She brought her papers together on her small mahogany desk, from such hiding places as women know-the linings of perfumed sachets, the toes of small slippers, the secret pocket in a muff; and having locked her doors, put them in order. Her hands were trembling, but she worked skillfully. She was free until the dinner hour, but she had a great deal to do. The papers in order, she went to a panel in the wall of her dressing-room; and, sliding it aside, revealed the safe in which her jewels were kept. Not that her jewels were very valuable, but the safe was there, and she used it.

The palace, for that matter, was full of cunningly contrived hiding-places. Some, in times of stress, had held jewels. Others-rooms these, built in the stone walls and carefully mapped-had held even royal refugees themselves. The map was in the King's possession, and descended from father to son, a curious old paper, with two of the hidden rooms marked off in colored inks as closed. Closed, with strange secrets beyond, quite certainly.

The Countess took out a jewel-case, emptied it, lifted its chamois cushions, and took out a small book. It was an indifferent hiding-place, but long immunity had made her careless. Referring to the book, she wrote a letter in code. It was, to all appearances a friendly letter referring to a family in her native town, and asking that the recipient see that assistance be sent them before Thursday of the following week. The assistance was specified with much detail-at her expense to send so many blankets, so many loaves of bread, a long list. Having finished, she destroyed, by burning, a number of papers watching until the last ash had turned from dull red to smoking gray. The code-book she hesitated over, but at last, with a shrug of her shoulders, she returned it to its hiding-place in the jewel case.

Coupled with her bitterness was a sense of relief. Only when the papers were destroyed had she realized the weight they had been. She summoned Minna, her maid, and dressed for the street. Then, Minna accompanying her, she summoned her carriage and went shopping.

She reached the palace again in time to dress for dinner. Somewhere on that excursion she had left the letter, to be sent to its destination over the border by special messenger that night.

Prince Ferdinand William Otto, at the moment of her return, was preparing for bed. At a quarter to seven he had risen, bowed to Miss Braithwaite, said good-night, and disappeared toward his bedroom and his waiting valet. But a moment later he reappeared.

"I beg your pardon," he said, "but I think your watch is fast."

Miss Braithwaite consulted it. Then, rising she went to the window and compared at with the moonlike face of the cathedral clock.

"There is a difference of five minutes," she conceded. "But I have no confidence in the cathedral clock. It needs oiling, probably. Besides, there are always pigeons sitting on the hands."

"May I wait for five minutes?"

"What could you do in five minutes?"

"Well," he suggested, rather pleadingly, "we might have a little conversation, if you axe not too tired."

Miss Braithwaite sighed. It had been a long day and not a calm one, and conversation with His Highness meant questions, mostly.

"Very well," she said.

"I'm not at all sleepy," Prince Ferdinand William Otto observed, climbing on a chair. "I thought you might tell me about America. I'm awfully curious about America."

"I suppose you mean the United States."

"I'm not sure. It has New York, in it, anyhow. They don't have kings, do they?"

"No," said Miss Braithwaite, shortly. She hated republics.

"What I wondered was," said Ferdinand William Otto, swinging his legs, "how they managed without a king. Who tells them what to do? I'm interested, because I met a boy yesterday who came from there, and he talked quite a lot about it. He was a very interesting boy."

Miss Braithwaite waived the matter of yesterday. "In a republic," she said, "the people think they can govern themselves. But they do it very badly. The average intelligence among people in the mass is always rather low."

"He said," went on His Royal Highness, pursuing a line of thought, "that the greatest man in the world was a man named Lincoln. But that he is dead. And he said that kings were nuisances, and didn't earn their bread-and-butter. Of course," Otto hastened to explain, "he didn't know that my grandfather is a king. After that, I didn't exactly like to tell him. It would have made him very uncomfortable." Here he yawned, but covered it with a polite hand, and Oskar, his valet, came to the doorway and stood waiting. He was a dignified person in a plum-colored livery, because the King considered black gloomy for a child.

The Crown Prince slipped to the floor, and stood with his feet rather wide apart, looking steadfastly at Miss Braithwaite. "I would like very much to see that boy again," he observed. "He was a nice boy, and very kind-hearted. If we could go to the Scenic Railway when we are out in the carriage, I —I'd enjoy it." He saw refusal in her face, for he added hurriedly, "Not to ride. I just want to look at it."

Miss Braithwaite was touched, but firm. She explained that it would be better if the Crown Prince did not see the boy again; and to soften the refusal, she reminded him that the American child did not like royalties, and that even to wave from his carriage with the gold wheels would therefore be a tactical error.

Prince Ferdinand William Otto listened, and Oskar waited. And something that had been joyous and singing in a small boy's heart was suddenly still.

"I had forgotten about that," he said.

Then Miss Braithwaite rose, and the Prince put his heels together with a click, and bowed, as he had been taught to do.

"Good-night," he said.

"Good-night, Your Highness," replied Miss Braithwaite.

At the door Prince Ferdinand William Otto turned and bowed again. Then he went out, and the door closed behind him.

He washed himself, with Oskar standing by, holding a great soft towel. Even the towels were too large. And he brushed his teeth, and had two drinks of water, because a stiffish feeling in his throat persisted. And at last he crawled up into the high bed that was so much too big for him, and had to crawl out again, because he had forgotten his prayers.

When everything was done, and the hour of putting out the light could no longer be delayed, he said goodnight to Oskar, who bowed. There was a great deal of, bowing in Otto's world. Then, whisk! it was dark, with only the moon face of the cathedral clock for company. And as it was now twenty minutes past seven, the two hands drooped until it looked like a face with a cruel mouth and was really very poor company.

Oskar, having bowed himself into the corridor and past the two sentries, reported to a very great dignitary across the hall that His Royal Highness the Crown Prince Ferdinand William Otto was in bed. And the dignitary had a chance to go away and get his dinner.

But alone in his great bed, the Crown Prince was shedding a few shamefaced tears. He was extremely ashamed of them. He felt that under no circumstances would his soldier father have behaved so. He reached out and secured one of the two clean folded handkerchiefs that were always placed on the bedside stand at night, and blew his nose very loudly. But he could not sleep.

He gave Miss Braithwaite time to go to her sitting-room, and for eight o'clock to pass, because once every hour, all night, a young gentleman of the Court, appointed for this purpose and dubbed a "wet-nurse" by jealous comrades, cautiously opened his door and made a stealthy circuit of the room, to see that all was well.

The Crown Prince got up. He neglected to put on his bedroom slippers, of course, and in his bare feet be padded across the room to the study door. It was not entirely dark. A night-light burned there. It stood on a table directly under the two crossed swords. Beneath the swords, in a burnt-wood frame, were the pictures of his father and mother. Hedwig had given him a wood-burning outfit at Christmas, and he had done the work himself. It consisted of the royal arms, somewhat out of drawing and not exactly in the center of the frame, and a floral border of daisies, extremely geometrical, because he had drawn them in first with a compass.

The boy, however, gave the pictures only a hasty glance and proceeded, in a business-like manner, to carry a straight chair to the cabinet. On the top shelf sat the old cloth dog. Its shoe-button eyes looked glazed with sleep, but its ears were quite alert. Very cautiously the Crown Prince unlocked the door, stepped precariously to the lower shelf of the cabinet, hung there by one royal hand, and lifted the dog down.

At nine o'clock the wet-nurse took off his sword in another room and leaned it against a chair. Then he examined his revolver, in accordance with a formula prescribed by the old King. Then he went in and examined the room with a flashlight, and listened to the Crown Prince's breathing. He had been a croupy baby. And, at last, he turned the flashlight on to the bed. A pair of shoe-button eyes stared at him from the pillow.

"Well, I'm damned," said the wet-nurse And went out, looking thoughtful.

Chapter IX
A Fine Night

In a shop where, that afternoon, the Countess had purchased some Lyons silks, one of the clerks, Peter Niburg, was free at last. At seven o'clock, having put away the last rolls of silk on the shelves behind him, and covered them with calico to keep off the dust; having given a final glance of disdain at the clerk in the linens, across; having reached under the counter for his stiff black hat of good quality and his silver-topped cane; having donned the hat and hung the stick to his arm with two swaggering gestures; having prepared his offensive, so to speak, he advanced.

Between Peter Niburg and Herman Spier of the linens, was a feud. Its source, in the person of a pretty cashier, had gone, but the feud remained. It was of the sort that smiles with the lips and scowls with the eyes, that speaks pleasantly quite awful things, although it was Peter Niburg who did most of the talking. Herman Spier was a moody individual, given to brooding. A man who stood behind his linens, and hated with his head down.

And he hated Peter. God, how he hated him! The cashier was gone, having married a restaurant keeper, and already she waxed fat. But Herman's hatred grew with the days. And business being bad, much of the time he stood behind his linens and thought about a certain matter, which was this:

How did Peter Niburg do it?

They were paid the same scant wage. Each Monday they stood together, Peter smiling and he frowning, and received into open palms exactly enough to live on, without extras. And each Monday Peter pocketed his cheerfully, and went back to his post, twirling his mustache as though all the money of the realm jingled in his trousers.

To accept the inevitable, to smile over one's poverty, that is one thing. But there was more to it. Peter made his money go amazingly far. It was Peter, for instance, who on name-days had been able to present the little cashier with a nosegay. Which had, by the way, availed him nothing against the delicatessen offerings of the outside rival. When, the summer before, the American Scenic Railway had opened to the public, with much crossing of flags, the national emblem and the Stars and Stripes, it was Peter who had invited the lady to an evening of thrills on that same railway at a definite sum per thrill. Nay, more, as Herman had seen with his own eyes, taken her afterward to a coffee-house, and shared with her a litre of white wine. A litre, no less.

Herman himself had been to the Scenic Railway, but only because he occupied a small room in the house where the American manager lived. The manager had given tickets to Black Humbert, the concierge, but Humbert was busy with other thing, and was, besides, chary of foreign deviltries. So he had passed the tickets on.

It was Peter, then, who made the impossible possible, who wore good clothes and did not have his boots patched, who went, rumor said, to the Opera now and then, and followed the score on his own battered copy.

How?

Herman Spier had suspected him of many things; had secretly audited his cash slips; had watched him for surreptitious parcels of silk. Once he had thought he had him. But the package of Lyons silk, opened by the proprietor at Herman's suggestion, proved to be material for a fancy waistcoat, and paid for by Peter Niburg's own hand.

With what? Herman stood confused, even confounded, but still suspicious. And now, this very day, he had stumbled on something. A great lady from the Court had made a purchase, and had left, under a roll of silk, a letter. There was no mistake. And Peter Niburg had put away the silk, and pocketed the letter, after a swift glance over the little shop.

An intrigue, then, with Peter Niburg as the go-between, or-something else. Something vastly more important, the discovery of which would bring Herman prominence beyond his fellows in a certain secret order to which he belonged.

In a way, he was a stupid man, this pale-eyed clerk who sold the quaint red and yellow cottons of the common people side by side with the heavy linens that furnished forth the tables of the rich. But hatred gave him wits. Gave him speed, too. He was only thirty feet behind Peter Niburg when that foppish gentleman reached the corner.

Herman was skilled in certain matters. He knew, for instance, that a glance into a shop window, a halt to tie a shoe, may be a ruse for passing a paper to other hands. But Peter did not stop. He went, not more swiftly than usual, to his customary restaurant, one which faced over the Square and commanded a view of the Palace. And there he settled himself in a window and ordered his dinner.

From the outside Herman stared in. He did not dine there. It was, for one thing, a matter of bitterness to see sitting at the cashier's high desk, the little Marie, grown somewhat with flesh, it is true, but still lovely in his eyes. It made Herman wince, even now, to see through the window that her husband patted her hand as he brought her money to be changed.

He lurked in the shadows outside, and watched. Peter sat alone. He had bowed very stiffly to Marie, and had passed the desk with his chest out. She had told him once that he had a fine figure.

Peter sat alone, and stared out. Herman took shelter, and watched. But Peter Niburg did not see him. His eyes were fixed on the gloomy mass across, shot with small lights from deep windows, which was the Palace.

Peter was calm. He had carried many such letters as the one now hidden in his breast pocket. No conscience stirred in him. If he did not do this work, others would. He shrugged his shoulders. He drank his brandy, and glanced at Marie. He found her eyes on him. Pretty eyes they still were, and just now speculative. He smiled at her, but she averted her head, and colored. Many things filled Peter Niburg's mind. If now she was not happy, what then? Her husband adored her. It was fatal. A woman should not be too sure of a husband. And probably he bored her. Another six months, and perhaps she would not turn away her head.

He had until midnight. At that hour a messenger would receive the letter from him in the colonnade of the cathedral. On this night, each week, the messenger waited. Sometimes there was a letter, sometimes none. That was all. It was amazingly simple, and for it one received the difference between penury and comfort.

Seeing Peter settled, a steaming platter before him, Herman turned and hurried through the night. This which he had happened on was a big thing, too big for him alone. Two heads were better than one. He would take advice.

Off the main avenue he fell into a smart trot. The color came to his pale cheeks. A cold sweat broke out over him. He was short of wind from many cigarettes. But at last he reached the house. It was near the park. Although the season was early spring and there was more than a hint of winter in the air, the Scenic Railway, he perceived, was already open for business. Certainly the Americans were enterprising.

The double doors of the tall, gloomy house on the Road of Good Children were already closed for the evening. As he stood panting, after he had rung the bell, Herman Spier could look across to that remote and unfashionable end of the great park where the people played on pleasant evenings, and where even now, on the heels of winter, the Scenic Railway made a pretense at summer.

The sight recalled that other vision of Marie and Peter Niburg, snugly settled in a car, Marie a trifle pale and apprehensive. Herman swore softly; and opened the doors.

Black Humbert was not in his bureau, behind the grating. With easy familiarity Herman turned to a door beyond and entered. A dirty little room, it was littered now with the preparations for a meal. On the bare table were a loaf, a jug of beer, and a dish of fried veal. The concierge was at the stove making gravy in a frying-pan —a huge man, bearded and heavy of girth, yet stepping lightly, like a cat. A dark man and called "the Black," he yet revealed, on full glance, eyes curiously pale and flat.

No greeting passed between them. Humbert gave his visitor a quick glance. Herman closed the door, and wiped out the band of his hat. The concierge poured the gravy over the meat.

"I have discovered something, something," Herman said. "As to its value, I know nothing, or its use to us."

"Let me judge that." But the concierge was unmoved, by Herman's excitement. He dealt in sensations. His daily tools were men less clever than himself, men who constantly made worthless discoveries. And it was the dinner hour. His huge body was crying for food.

"It is a matter of a letter."

"Sit down, man, and tell it. Or do you wish me to draw the information, like bad teeth?"

"A letter from the Palace," said Herman. And explained.

Black Humbert listened. He was skeptical, but not entirely incredulous. He knew the Court-none better. The women of the Court wrote many letters. He saw a number of them, through one of his men in the post office. There were many intrigues. After all, who could blame them? The Court was dreary enough these days, and if they chose to amuse themselves as best they could-one must make allowances.

"A liaison!" he said at last, with his mouth full. "The Countess is handsome, and bored. Annunciata is driving her to wickedness, as she drove her husband. But it is worth consideration. Even the knowledge of an intrigue is often helpful. Of what size was the letter?"

"A small envelope. I saw no more."

The concierge reflected. "The Countess uses a gray paper with a coronet."

"This was white."

Black Humbert reflected. "There is, of course, a chance that he has already passed this on. But even if so, there will be others. The Countess comes often to the shop?"

"Once in a week, perhaps."

"So." The big man rose, and untied his soiled apron. "Go back," he said, "and enter the restaurant. Order a small meal, that you may have finished when he does. Leave with him and suggest the Hungaria."

"Hungaria! I have no money."

"You will need no money. Now, mark this. At a certain corner you will be attacked and robbed. A mere form," he added, as he saw Herman's pallid face go whiter. "For the real envelope will be substituted another. In his breast-pocket, you said. Well, then suggest going to his room. He may," added the concierge grimly, "require your assistance. Leave him at his lodging, but watch the house. It is important to know to whom he delivers these letters."

As the man stood, he seemed to the cowering Herman to swell until he dominated the room. He took on authority. To Herman came suddenly the memory of a hidden room, and many men, and one, huge and towering, who held the others in the hollow of his hand. Herman turned to go, but at the door the concierge stopped him.

"A moment," he said. "We will select first the shape and fashion of this envelope you saw. These matters require finesse."

He disappeared, returning shortly with a wooden box, filled to the top with old envelopes. Each had been neatly opened and its contents extracted. And on each was neatly penned in a corner the name of the sender. Herman watched while the concierge dug through it.

"Here it is," he said at last. "The Countess, to her aunt in a nunnery and relating to wool knitting. See, is this the sort of envelope?"

"That is gray," Herman Spier said sullenly.

"But in size?"

"It is similar."

"Good." He held the envelope to the light and inspected it. "It would be interesting to know," he said, "whether the Countess has an aunt in this nunnery, or whether-but go, man. And hurry."

Left alone, he got together pens, ink, and carbon paper. He worked awkwardly, his hands too large for the pen, his elbows spread wide over the table. But the result was fair. He surveyed it with satisfaction.

Meanwhile, back went Herman over his earlier route. But now he did not run. His craven knees shook beneath him. Fresh sweat, not of haste but of fear, broke out over him. He who was brave enough of tongue in the meetings, who was capable of rising to heights of cruelty that amounted to ferocity when one of a mob, was a coward alone.

However, the sight of the restaurant, and of his fellow clerk eating calmly, quieted him. Peter Niburg was still alone. Herman took a table near him, and ordered a bowl of soup. His hands shook, but the hot food revived him. After all, it was simple enough. But, of course, it hinged entirely on his fellow-clerk's agreeing to accompany him.

He glanced across. Peter Niburg was eating, but his eyes were fixed on Madame Marie, at her high desk. There was speculation in them, and something else. Triumph, perhaps.

Suddenly Herman became calm. Calm with hate.

And, after all, it was very easy. Peter Niburg was lonely. The burden of the letter oppressed him. He wanted the comfort of human conversation and the reassurance of a familiar face. When the two met at-the rack by the door which contained their hats, his expression was almost friendly. They went out together.

"A fine night," said Herman, and cast an eye at the sky.

"Fine enough."

"Too good to waste in sleep. I was thinking," observed Herman, "of an hour or two at the Hungaria."

The Hungaria! Something in Peter's pleasure-hungry heart leaped, but he mocked his fellow-clerk.

"Since when," he inquired, "have you frequented the Hungaria?

"I feel in the mood," was the somewhat sullen reply. "I work hard enough, God knows, to have a little pleasure now and then." Danger was making him shrewd. He turned away from Peter Niburg, then faced him again. "If you care to come," he suggested. "Not a supper, you understand; but a glass of wine, Italian champagne," he added.

Peter Niburg was fond of sweet champagne.

Peter Niburg pushed his hat to the back of his head, and hung his stick over his forearm. After all, why not? Marie was gone. Let the past die. If Herman could make the first move, let him, Peter, make the second. He linked arms with his old enemy.

"A fine night," he said.

Chapter X
The Right to Live and Love

Dinner was over in the dull old dining-room. The Archduchess Annunciata lighted a cigarette, and glanced across the table at Hedwig.

Hedwig had been very silent during the meal. She had replied civilly when spoken to, but that was all. Her mother, who had caught the Countess's trick of narrowing her eyes, inspected her from under lowered lids.

"Well?" she said. "Are you still sulky?"

"I? Not at all, mother." Her head went up, and she confronted her mother squarely.

"I should like to inquire, if I may," observed the Archduchess, "just how you have spent the day until the little divertissement on which I stumbled. This morning, for instance?"

Hedwig shrugged her shoulders, but her color rose. It came in a soft wave over her neck and mounted higher and higher. "Very quietly, mother," she said.

"Naturally. It is always quiet here. But how?"

"I rode."

"Where?"

"At the riding-school, with Otto."

"Only with Otto?"

"Captain Larisch was there."

"Of course! Then you have practically spent the day with him!"

"I have spent most of the day with Otto."

"This devotion to Otto-it is new, I think. You were eager to get out of the nursery. Now, it appears, you must fly back to schoolroom teas and other absurdities. I should like to know why."

"I think Otto is lonely, mother."

Hilda took advantage of her mother's preoccupation to select another peach. She was permitted only one, being of the age when fruit caused her, colloquially speaking, to "break out." She was only faintly interested in the conversation. She dreaded these family meals, with her mother's sharp voice and the Countess Loschek's almost too soft one. But now a restrained irritability in the tones of the Archduchess made her glance up. The Archduchess was in one of her sudden moods of irritation. Hedwig's remark about Otto's loneliness, the second that day, struck home. In her anger she forgot her refusal to the Chancellor.

"I have something to say that will put an end to this sentimental nonsense of yours, Hedwig. I should forbid your seeing this boy, this young Larisch, if I felt it necessary. I do not. You would probably see him anyhow, for that matter. Which, as I observed this afternoon, also reminds me unpleasantly of your father." She rose, and threw her bolt out of a clear sky. She had had, as a matter of fact, no previous intention of launching any bolt. It was wholly a result of irritation. "It is unnecessary to remind you not to make a fool of yourself. But it may not be out of place to say that your grandfather has certain plans for you that will take your mind away from this-this silly boy, soon enough."

Hedwig had risen, and was standing, very white, with her hands on the table. "What plans, mother?"

"He will tell you."

"Not —I am not to be married?"

The Archduchess Annunciata was not all hard. She could never forgive her children their father. They reminded her daily of a part of her life that she would have put behind her. But they were her children, and Hedwig was all that she was not, gentle and round and young. Suddenly something almost like regret stirred in her.

"Don't look like that, child," she said. "It is not settled. And, after all, one marriage or another what difference does it make! Men are men. If one does not care, it makes the things they do unimportant."

"But surely," Hedwig gasped, "surely I shall be consulted?"

Annunciata shook her head. They had all risen and Hilda was standing, the peach forgotten, her mouth a little open. As for Olga Loschek, she was very still, but her eyes burned. The Archduchess remembered her presence no more than that of the flowers on the table.

"Mother, you cannot look back, and-and remember your own life, and allow me to be wretched. You cannot!"

Hilda picked up her peach. It was all very exciting, but Hedwig was being rather silly. Besides, why was she so distracted when she did not know who the man was? It might be some quite handsome person. For Hilda was also at the age when men were handsome or not handsome, and nothing else.

Unexpectedly Hedwig began to cry. This Hilda considered going much too far, and bad taste into the bargain. She slipped the peach into the waist of her frock.

The Archduchess hated tears, and her softer moments were only moments. "Dry your eyes, and don't be silly," she said coldly. "You have always known that something of the sort was inevitable."

She moved toward the door. The two princesses and her lady in waiting remained still until she had left the table. Then they fell in behind her, and the little procession moved to the stuffy, boudoir, for coffee. But Hilda slipped her arm around her sister's waist, and the touch comforted Hedwig.

"He may be very nice," Hilda volunteered cautiously. "Perhaps it is Karl. I am quite mad about Karl, myself."

Hedwig, however, was beyond listening. She went slowly to a window, and stood gazing out. Looming against the sky-line, in the very center of the Place, was the heroic figure of her dead grandmother. She fell to wondering about these royal women who had preceded her. Her mother, frankly unhappy in her marriage, permanently embittered; her grandmother. Hedwig had never seen the King young. She could not picture him as a lover. To her he was a fine and lonely figure. But romantic? Had he ever been romantic?

He had made her mother's marriage, and had lived to regret it. He would make hers. But what about the time when he himself had taken a wife? Hedwig gazed at the statue. Had she too come with unwilling arms? And if she had, was it true that after all, in a year or a lifetime, it made no difference.

She slipped out on to the balcony and closed the curtains behind her. As her eyes grew accustomed to the darkness she saw that there was some one below, under the trees. Her heart beat rapidly. In a moment she was certain. It was Nikky down there, Nikky, gazing up at her as a child may look at a star. With a quick gesture Hedwig drew the curtain back. A thin ray of light fell on her, on her slim bare arms, on her light draperies, on her young face. He had wanted to see her, and he should see her. Then she dropped the curtain, and twisted her hands together lest, in spite of her, they reach out toward him.

Did she fancy it, or did the figure salute her? Then came the quick ring of heels on the old stone pavement. She knew his footsteps, even as she knew every vibrant, eager inflection of his voice. He went away, across the Square, like one who, having bent his knee to a saint, turns back to the business of the world.

In the boudoir the Archduchess had picked up some knitting to soothe her jangled nerves. "You may play now, Hilda," she said.

Into Hilda's care-free young life came two bad hours each day. One was the dinner hour, when she ate under her mother's pitiless eyes. The other was the hour after dinner, when, alone in the white drawing-room beyond the boudoir, with the sliding doors open, she sat at the grand piano, which was white and gold, like the room, and as cold, and played to her mother's pitiless ears.

She went slowly into the drawing-room. Empty, it was a dreary place. The heavy chandeliers of gold and cut glass were unlighted. The crimson and gilt chairs were covered with white linen. Only the piano, a gleaming oasis in a desert of polished floor, was lighted, and that by two tall candles in gilt candlesticks that reached from the floor. Hilda, going reluctantly to her post, was the only bit of life and color in the room.

At last Annunciata dozed, and Hilda played softly. Played now, not for her mother, but for herself. And as she played she dreamed: of Hedwig's wedding, of her own debut, of Karl, who had fed her romantic heart by treating her like a woman grown.

The Countess's opportunity had come. She put down the dreary embroidery with which she filled the drearier evenings, and moved to the window. She walked quietly, like a cat.

Her first words to Hedwig were those of Peter Niburg as he linked arms with his enemy and started down the street. "A fine night, Highness," she said.

Hedwig raised her eyes to the stars. "It is very lovely."

"A night to spend out-of-doors, instead of being shut up —" She finished her, sentence with a shrug of the shoulders.

Hedwig was not fond of the Countess. She did not know why. The truth being, of course, that between them lay the barrier of her own innocence. Hedwig could not have put this into words, would not, indeed, if she could. But when the Countess's arm touched hers, she drew aside.

"To-night," said the lady in waiting dreamily, "I should like to be in a motor, speeding over mountain roads. I come from the mountains, you know. And I miss them."

Hedwig said nothing; she wished to be alone with her trouble.

"In my home, at this time of the year," the Countess went on, still softly, "they are driving the cattle up into the mountains for the summer. At night one hears them going —a bell far off, up the mountainside, and sometimes one sees the light of a lantern."

Hedwig moved, a little impatiently, but as the Countess went on, she listened. After all, Nikky, too, came from the mountains. She saw it all-the great herds moving with deliberate eagerness already sniffing the green slopes above, and the star of the distant lantern. She could even hear the thin note of the bell. And because she was sorry for the Countess, who was homesick, and perhaps because just then she had to speak to some one, she turned to her at last with the thing that filled her mind.

"This marriage," she said bitterly. "Is it talked about? Am I the only one in the palace who has not known about it?"

"No, Highness, I had heard nothing."

"But you knew about it?"

"Only what I heard to-night. Of course, there are always rumors."

"As to the other, the matter my mother referred to," Hedwig held her head very high, "I — she was unjust. Am I never to have any friends?"

The Countess turned and, separating the curtains, surveyed the room within. Annunciata was asleep, and beyond, Hilda was playing dreamily, and very softly, as behooves one whose bedtime is long past. When the Countess dropped the curtain, she turned abruptly to Hedwig.

"Friends, Highness? One may have friends, of course. It is not friendship they fear."

"What then?"

"A lover," said the Countess softly. "It is impossible to see Captain Larisch in your presence, and not realize —"

"Go on."

"And not realize, Highness, that he is in love with you."

"How silly!" said the Princess Hedwig, with glowing eyes.

"But Highness!" implored the Countess. "If only you would use a little caution. Open defiance is its own defeat."

"I am not ashamed of what I do," said Hedwig hotly.

"Ashamed! Of course not. But things that are harmless in others, in your position-you are young. You should have friends, gayety. I am," she smiled grimly in the darkness, "not so old myself but that I can understand."

"Who told my mother that I was having tea with-with Prince Otto?"

"These things get about. Where there is no gossip, there are plenty to invent it. And-pardon, Highness-frankness, openness, are not always understood."

Hedwig stood still. The old city was preparing for sleep. In the Place a few lovers loitered, standing close, and the faint tinkling of a bell told of the Blessed Sacrament being carried through the streets to some bedside of the dying. Soon the priest came into view, walking rapidly, with his skirts flapping around his legs. Before him marched a boy, ringing a bell and carrying a lighted lamp. The priest bent his steps through the Place, and the lovers kneeled as he passed by. The Princess Hedwig bowed her head.

It seemed to her, all at once, that the world was full of wretchedness and death, and of separation, which might be worse than death. The lamp, passing behind trees, shone out fitfully. The bell tinkled —a thin, silvery sound that made her heart ache.

"I wish I could help you, Highness," said the Countess. "I should like to see you happy. But happiness does not come of itself. We must fight for it."

"Fight? What chance have I to fight?" Hedwig asked scornfully.

"One thing, of course, I could do," pursued the Countess. "On those days when you wish to have tea with-His Royal Highness, I could arrange, perhaps, to let you know if any member of the family intended going to his apartments."

It was a moment before Hedwig comprehended. Then she turned to her haughtily. "When I wish to have tea with my cousin," she said coldly, "I shall do it openly, Countess."

She left the balcony abruptly, abandoning the Countess to solitary fury, the greater because triumph had seemed so near. Alone, she went red and white, bit her lips, behaved according to all the time-honored traditions. And even swore-in a polite, lady-in-waiting fashion, to be sure-to get even.

Royalties, as she knew well, were difficult to manage. They would go along perfectly well, and act like human beings, and rage and fuss and grieve, and even weep. And then, quite unexpectedly, the royal streak would show. But royalties in love were rather rare in her experience. Love was, generally speaking, not a royal attribute. Apparently it required a new set of rules.

Altogether, the Countess Loschek worked herself to quite as great a fury as if her motives had been purely altruistic, and not both selfish and wicked.

That night, while the Prince Ferdinand William Otto hugged the woolen dog in his sleep; while the Duchess Hilda, in front of her dressing-table, was having her hair brushed; while Nikky roamed the streets and saw nothing but the vision of a girl on a balcony, a girl who was lost to him, although she had never been anything else, Hedwig on her knees at the prie-dieu in her dressing-room followed the example of the Chancellor, who, too, had felt himself in a tight corner, as one may say, and was growing tired of putting his trust in princes. So Hedwig prayed for many things: for the softening of hard hearts; for Nikky's love; and, perhaps a trifle tardily, for the welfare and recovery of her grandfather, the King. But mostly she prayed for happiness, for a bit of light and warmth in her gray days-to be allowed to live and love.

Chapter. XI
Rather a Wild Night

Things were going very wrong for Nikky Larisch.

Not handsome, in any exact sense, was Nikky, but tall and straight, with a thatch of bright hair not unlike that of the Crown Prince, and as unruly. Tall and straight, and occasionally truculent, with a narrow rapier scar on his left cheek to tell the story of wild student days, and with two clear young eyes that had looked out humorously at the world until lately. But Nikky was not smiling at the world these days.

Perhaps, at the very first, he had been in love with the princess, not the woman. It had been rather like him to fix on the unattainable and worship it from afar. Because, for all the friendliness of their growing intimacy, Hedwig was still a star, whose light touched him, but whose warmth was not for him. He would have died fighting for her with a smile on his lips. There had been times when he almost wished he might. He used to figure out pleasant little dramas, in which, fallen on the battlefield, his last word, uttered in all reverence, was her name. But he had no hope of living for her, unless, of course, she should happen to need him, which was most unlikely. He had no vanity whatever, although in parade dress, with white gloves, he hoped he cut a decent figure.

So she had been his star, and as cold and remote. And then, that very morning, whether it was the new cross-saddle suit or whatever it was, Hedwig had been thrown. Not badly-she was too expert for that. As a matter of fact, feeling herself going, she had flung two strong young arms around her horse's neck, and had almost succeeded in lighting on her feet. It was not at all dramatic.

But Nikky's heart had stopped beating. He had lifted her up from where she sat, half vexed and wholly ashamed, and carried her to a chair. That was all. But when it was all over, and Hedwig was only a trifle wobbly and horribly humiliated, Nikky Larisch knew the truth about himself, knew that he was in love with the granddaughter of his King, and that under no conceivable circumstances would he ever be able to tell her so. Knew, then, that happiness and he had said a long farewell, and would thereafter travel different roads.

It had stunned him. He had stood quite still and thought about it. And Prince Ferdinand William Otto had caught him in the act of thinking; and had stood before him and surveyed him anxiously.

"You needn't look so worried, you know," he protested. "She's not really hurt."

Nikky came back, but slowly. He had in a few seconds already traveled a long way along the lonely road. But he smiled down at the little Prince.

"But she might have been, you know. It-it rather alarmed me."

Prince Ferdinand William Otto was for continuing the subject. He blamed the accident on the new riding-suit, and was royally outspoken about it. "And anyhow," he finished, "I don't like her in boy's clothes. Half of her looks like a girl, and the rest doesn't."

Nikky, letting his eyes rest on her, realized that all of her to him was wonderful, and forever beyond reach.

So that night he started out to think things over. Probably never before in his life had he deliberately done such a thing. He had never, as a fact, thought much at all. It had been his comfortable habit to let the day take care of itself. Beyond minor problems of finance-minor because his income was trifling-he had considered little. In the last border war he had distinguished himself only when it was a matter of doing, not of thinking.

He was very humble about himself. His young swagger was a sort of defiance. And he was not subtle. Taken suddenly, through the Chancellor's favor, into the circles of the Court, its intrigues and poisoned whispers passed him by. He did not know they existed. And he had one creed, and only one: to love God, honor the King, and live like a gentleman.

On this boy, then, with the capacity for suffering of his single-minded type, had fallen the mantle of trouble. It puzzled him. He did not exactly know what to do about it. And it hurt. It hurt horribly.

That night, following the Archduchess's confidence, he had stood under the Palace windows, in the Place, and looked up. Not that he expected to see Hedwig. He did it instinctively, turning toward her hidden presence with a sort of bewildered yearning. Across his path, as he turned away, had passed the little procession of the priest and the Sacrament. He knelt, as did the lovers and the passers-by, and when he got up he followed the small flame of the lamp with his eyes as far as he could see it.

This was life, then. One lived and suffered and yearned, and then came death. Were there barriers of rank over there? Or were all equal, so that those who had loved on earth without hope might meet face to face? The tinkle of the bell grew fainter. This weight that he carried, it would be his all his life. And then, one day, he too would hear the bell coming nearer and nearer, and he would die, without having lived.

But he was young, and the night was crisp and beautiful. He took a long breath, and looked up at the stars. After all, things might not be so bad. Hedwig might refuse this marriage. They were afraid that she would, or why have asked his help? When he thought of King Karl, he drew himself up; and his heels rang hard on the pavement. Karl! A hard man and a good king-that was Karl. And old. From the full manhood of his twenty-three years Nikky surveyed Karl's almost forty, and considered it age.

But soon he was bitter again, bitter and jealous. Back there in the palace they were plotting their own safety, and making a young girl pay for it. He swore softly.

It was typical of Nikky to decide that he needed a hard walk. He translated most of his emotions into motion. So he set off briskly, turning into the crowded part of the city. Here were narrow, winding streets; old houses that overhung above and almost touched, shutting out all but a thin line of sky; mediaeval doorways of heavy oak and iron that opened into courtyards, where once armed men had lounged, but where now broken wagons and other riffraff were stored.

And here it was that Nikky happened on the thing that was to take him far that night, and bring about many curious things. Not far ahead of him two men were talking. They went slowly, arm in arm. One was talking loquaciously, using his free arm, on which hung a cane, to gesticulate. The other walked with bent head.

Nikky, pausing to light a cigarette, fell behind. But the wind was tricky, and with his third match he stepped into a stone archway, lighted his cigarette, buttoned his tunic high against the chill, and emerged to a silent but violent struggle just ahead. The two men had been attacked by three others, and as he stared, the loquacious one went down. Instantly a huge figure of a man outlined against the light from a street-lamp, crouched over the prostrate form of the fallen man. Even in the imperceptible second before he started to run toward the group, Nikky saw that the silent one, unmolested, was looking on.

A moment later he was in the thick of things and fighting gloriously. His soldierly cap fell off. His fair hair bristled with excitement. He flung out arms that were both furious and strong, and with each blow the group assumed a new formation. Unluckily, a great deal of the fighting was done over the prostrate form of Peter Niburg.

Suddenly one of the group broke away, and ran down the street. He ran rather like a kangaroo, gathering his feet under him and proceeding by a series of leaps, almost as if he were being shamefully pricked from behind. At a corner he turned pale, terror-stricken eyes back on that sinister group, and went on into the labyrinth of small streets.

But disaster, inglorious disaster, waited for Nikky. Peter Niburg, face down on the pavement, was groaning, and Nikky had felled one man and was starting on a second with the fighting appetite of twenty-three, when something happened. One moment Nikky was smiling, with a cut lip, and hair in his eyes, and the next he was dropped like an ox, by a blow from behind. Landing between his shoulder-blades, it jerked his head back with a snap, and sent him reeling. A second followed, delivered by a huge fist.

Down went Nikky, and lay still.

The town slept on. Street brawls were not uncommon, especially in the neighborhood of the Hungaria. Those who roused grumbled about quarrelsome students, and slept again.

Perhaps two minutes later, Nikky got up. He was another minute in locating himself. His cap lay in the gutter. Beside him, on his back, lay a sprawling and stertorous figure, with, so quick the downfall, a cane still hooked to his arm.

Nikky bent over Peter Niburg. Bending over made his head ache abominably.

"Here, man!" he said. "Get up! Rouse yourself!"

Peter Niburg made an inarticulate reference to a piece of silk of certain quality, and lay still. But his eyes opened slowly, and he stared up at the stars. "A fine night," he said thickly. "A very fine —" Suddenly he raised himself to a sitting posture. Terror gave him strength. "I've been robbed," he said. "Robbed. I am ruined. I am dead."

"Tut," said Nikky, mopping his cut lip. "If you are dead, your spirit speaks with an uncommonly lusty voice! Come, get up. We present together a shameful picture of defeat."

But he raised Peter Niburg gently from the ground and, finding his knees unstable, from fright or weakness, stood him against a house wall. Peter Niburg, with rolling eyes, felt for his letter, and, the saints be praised, found it.

"Ah!" he said, and straightened up. "After all it is not so bad as I feared. They got nothing."

He made a manful effort to walk, but tottered reeled. Nikky caught him.

"Careful!" he said. "The colossus was doubtless the one who got us boxy, and we are likely to feel his weight for some time. Where do you live?"

Peter Niburg was not for saying. He would have preferred to pursue his solitary if uncertain way. But Nikky was no half Samaritan. Toward Peter Niburg's lodging, then, they made a slow progress.

"These recent gentlemen," said Nikky, as they rent along, "they are, perhaps, personal enemies?"

"I do not know. I saw nothing."

"One was very large, a giant of a man. Do you now such a man?"

Peter Niburg reflected. He thought not. "But I know why they came," he said unguard-edly. "Some early morning, my friend, you will hear of man lying dead in the street, That man will be I."

"The thought has a moral," observed Nikky. "Do not trust yourself out-of-doors at night."

But he saw that Peter Niburg kept his hand over breast-pocket.

Never having dealt in mysteries, Nikky was slow recognizing one. But, he reflected, many things were going on in the old city in these troubled days.

Came to Nikky, all at once; that this man on his arm might be one of the hidden eyes of Government.

"These are difficult times," he ventured, "for those who are loyal."

Peter Niburg gave him a sidelong glance. "Difficult indeed," he said briefly.

"But," said Nikky, "perhaps we fear too much. The people love the boy Prince. And without the people revolution can accomplish nothing."

"Nothing at all," assented Peter Niburg.

"I think," Nikky observed, finding his companion unresponsive, "that, after I see you safely home, I shall report this small matter to the police. Surely there cannot be in the city many such gorillas as our friend with the beard and the huge body."

But here Peter Niburg turned even paler. "Not-not the police!" he stammered.

"But why? You and I, my friend, will carry their insignia for some days. I have a mind to pay our debts."

Peter Niburg considered. He stopped and faced Nikky. "I do not wish the police," he said. "Perhaps I have said too little. This is a private matter. An affair of jealousy."

"I see!"

"Naturally, not a matter for publicity."

"Very well," Nikky assented. But in his mind was rising, dark suspicion. He had stumbled on something. He cursed his stupidity that it meant, so far, nothing more than a mystery to him. He did not pride himself on his intelligence.

"You were not alone, I think?"

Peter Niburg suddenly remembered Herman, and stopped.

"Your friend must have escaped."

"He would escape," said Peter Niburg scornfully. "He is of the type that runs."

He lapsed into sullen silence. Soon he paused before a quiet house, one of the many which housed in cavernous depths uncounted clerks and other small fry of the city. "Good-night to you," said Peter Niburg. Then, rather tardily. "And my thanks. But for you I should now —" he shrugged his shoulders.

"Good-night, friend," said Nikky. "And better keep your bed to-morrow."

He had turned away, and Peter Niburg entered the house.

Nikky inspected himself in the glow of a street lamp. Save for some dust, and a swollen lip, which he could not see, he was not unpresentable. Well enough, anyhow, for the empty streets. But before he started he looked the house and the neighborhood over carefully. He might wish to return to that house.

For two hours he walked, and resumed his interrupted train of thought-past the gloomy University buildings, past the quay, where sailed the vessels that during peaceful times went along the Ar through the low lands of Karnia to the sea. At last, having almost circled the city, he came to the Cathedral. It was nearly midnight by the clock in the high tower. He stopped and consulted his watch. The fancy took him to go up the high steps, and look out over the city from the colonnade.

Once there, he stood leaning against a column, looking out. The sleeping town appealed to him. Just so had it lain in old feudal times, clustered about the church and the Palace, and looking to both for protection. It had grown since then, had extended beyond the walls which sheltered it, had now destroyed those walls and, filling in the moat, had built thereon its circling parks. And other things had changed. No longer, he reflected gloomily, did it look to the palace, save with tolerance and occasional disloyalty. The old order was changing. And, with all his hot young heart, Nikky was for the old order.

There was some one coming along the quiet streets, with a stealthy, shuffling gait that caught his attention. So, for instance, might a weary or a wounded man drag along. Exactly so, indeed, had Peter Niburg shambled into his house but two hours gone.

The footsteps paused, hesitated, commenced a painful struggle up the ascent. Nikky moved behind his column, and waited. Up and up, weary step after weary step. The shadowy figure, coming close, took a form, became a man—became Peter Niburg.

Now, indeed, Nikky roused. Beaten and sorely bruised, Peter Niburg should have been in bed. What stealthy business of the night brought him out?

Fortunately for Nikky's hiding-place, the last step or two proved too much for the spy. He groaned, and sat down painfully, near the top. His head lolled forward, and he supported it on two shaking hands. Thus he sat, huddled and miserable, for five minutes or thereabouts. The chime rang out overhead the old hymn which the little Crown Prince so often sang to it:

> "Draw me also, Mary mild,
> To adore Thee and thy Child!
> Mary mild,
> Star in desert drear and wild."

Time had gone since the old church stood in a desert drear and wild, but still its chimes rang the old petition, hour after hour.

At ten minutes past the hour, Nikky heard the engine of an automobile. No machine came in sight, but the throbbing kept on, from which he judged that a car had been stopped around the corner. Peter Niburg heard it, and rose. A moment later a man, with the springiness of youth, mounted the steps and confronted the messenger.

Nikky saw a great light. When Peter Niburg put his hand to his breast-pocket, there was no longer room for doubt, nor, for that matter, time for thinking. As a matter of fact, never afterward could Nikky recall thinking at all. He moved away quietly, hidden by the shadows of the colonnade. Behind him, on the steps, the two men were talking. Peter Niburg's nasal voice had taken on a whining note. Short, gruff syllables replied. Absorbed in themselves and their business, they neither heard nor saw the figure that slipped through the colonnade, and dropped, a bloodcurdling drop, from the high end of it to the street below.

Nikky's first impulse, beside the car, was to cut a tire. By getting his opponent into a stooping position; over the damaged wheel, it would be easier to overcome him. But a hasty search revealed that he had lost his knife in the melee. And second thought gave him a better plan. After all, to get the letter was not everything. To know its destination would be important. He had no time to think further. The messenger was coming down the steps, not stealthily, but clattering, with the ring of nails in the heels of heavy boots.

Nikky flung his long length into the tonneau, and there crouched. It was dark enough to conceal him, but Nikky's was a large body in a small place. However, the chauffeur only glanced at the car, kicked a tire with a practiced foot, and got in.

He headed for the open country. Very soon his passenger knew that he was in for a long ride possibly, a cold ride certainly. Within the city limits the car moved decorously, but when the suburbs were reached, the driver put on all his power. He drove carefully, too, as one who must make haste but cannot afford accident.

Nikky grew very uncomfortable. His long legs ached. The place between the shoulders where the concierge had landed his powerful blows throbbed and beat. Also he was puzzled, and he hated being puzzled. He was unarmed, too. He disliked that most of all. Generally speaking, he felt his position humiliating. He was a soldier, not a spy. His training had been to fight, not to hide and watch.

After a time he raised his head. He made out that they were going east, toward the mountains, and he cursed the luck that had left his revolver at home. Still he had no plan but to watch. Two hours' ride, at their present rate, would take them over the border and into Karnia.

Nikky, although no thinker, was not a fool, and he knew rather better than most what dangers threatened the country from outside as well. Also, in the back of his impulsive head was a sort of dogged quality that was near to obstinacy. He had started this thing and he would see it through. And as the car approached the border, he began to realize that this was not of the Terrorists at home, but something sinister, abroad.

With a squealing of brakes the machine drew up at the frontier. Here was a chain across the highway, with two sets of guards. Long before they reached it, a sentry stepped into the road and waved his lantern.

Nikky burrowed lower into the car, and attempted to look like a rug. In the silence, while the sentry evidently examined a passport and flashed a lantern over the chauffeur, Nikky cursed the ticking of his watch, the beating of his own heart.

Then came a clanking as the chain dropped in the road. The car bumped over it, and halted again. The same formalities, this time by Karnian sentries. A bit more danger, too, for the captain in charge of the guard asked for matches, and dangled a careless hand over the side, within a few inches of Nikky's head. Then the jerk following a hasty letting-in of the clutch, and they were off again.

For some time they climbed steadily. But Nikky, who knew the road, bided his time. Then at last, at two o'clock, came the steep ascent to the very crest of the mountain, and a falling-back, gear by gear, until they climbed slowly in the lowest.

Nikky unfolded his length quietly. The gears were grinding, the driver bent low over his wheel. Very deliberately, now that he knew what he was going to do, Nikky unbuttoned his tunic and slipped it off. It was a rash thing, this plan he had in mind, rash under any circumstances, in a moving car particularly rash here, where between the cliff and a precipice that fell far away below, was only a winding ribbon of uneven road.

Here, at the crucial moment, undoubtedly he should have given a last thought to Hedwig. But alas for romance! As a matter of honesty, he had completely forgotten Hedwig. This was his work, and with even the hottest of lovers, work and love are things apart.

So he waited his moment, loveless, as one may say, and then, with one singularly efficient gesture, he flung his tunic over the chauffeur's head. He drove a car himself, did Nikky-not his own, of course; he was far too poor-and he counted on one thing: an automobile driver acts from the spinal cord, and not from the brain. Therefore his brain may be seething with a thousand frenzies, but he will shove out clutch and brake feet in an emergency, and hold them out.

So it happened. The man's hands left the wheel, but he stopped his car. Not too soon. Not before it had struck the cliff, and then taken a sickening curve out toward the edge of the precipice. But stop it did, on the very edge of eternity, and the chauffeur held it there.

"Set the hand brake!" Nikky said. The lamps were near enough the edge to make him dizzy.

The chauffeur ceased struggling, and set the hand brake. His head was still covered. But having done that, he commenced a struggle more furious than forceful, for both of them were handicapped. But Nikky had steel-like young arms from which escape was impossible.

And now Nikky was forced to an unsoldier-like thing that he afterward tried to forget. For the driver developed unexpected strength, refused to submit, got the tunic off his head, and, seeing himself attacked by one man only, took courage and fell to. He picked up a wrench from the seat beside him, and made a furious pass at Nikky's head. Nikky ducked and, after a struggle, secured the weapon. All this in the car, over the seat back.

It was then that Nikky raised the wrench and stunned his man with it. It was hateful. The very dull thud of it was sickening. And there was a bad minute or two when he thought he had killed his opponent. The man had sunk down in his seat, a sodden lump of inanimate human flesh. And Nikky, whose business, in a way, was killing; was horrified.

He tried to find the pulse, but failed-which was not surprising, since he had the wrong side of the wrist. Then the unconscious man groaned. For a moment, as he stood over him, Nikky reflected that he was having rather a murderous night of it.

The chauffeur wakened, ten minutes later, to find himself securely tied with his own towing rope, and lying extremely close to the edge of death. Beside him on the ground sat a steady-eyed young man with a cut lip. The young man had lighted a cigarette, and was placing it carefully in the uninjured side of his mouth.

"Just as soon as you are up to it," said Nikky, "we shall have a little talk."

The chauffeur muttered something in the peasant patois of Karnia.

"Come, come!" Nikky observed. "Speak up. No hiding behind strange tongues. But first, I have the letter. That saves your worrying about it. You can clear your mind for action." Suddenly Nikky dropped his mocking tone. To be quite frank, now that the man was not dead, and Nikky had the letter, he rather fancied himself. But make no mistake-he was in earnest, grim and deadly earnest.

"I have a fancy, my friend," he said, "to take that letter of yours on to its destination. But what that destination is, you are to tell me."

The man on the ground grinned sardonically. "You know better than to ask that," he said. "I will never tell you."

Nikky had thought things out fairly well, for him, in that ten minutes. In a business-like fashion he turned the prostrate prisoner on his side, so that he faced toward the chasm. A late moon showed its depth, and the valley in which the Ar flowed swiftly. And having thus faced him toward the next world, Nikky, throwing away his cigarette because it hurt his lip, put a stone or two from the roadway behind his prisoner, and anchored him there. Then he sat down and waited. Except that his ears were burning, he was very calm.

"Any news?" he asked, at the end of ten minutes' unbroken silence.

His-prisoner said nothing. He was thinking, doubtless. Weighing things, too,—perhaps life against betrayal, a family against separation.

Nikky examined the letter again. It was addressed to a border town in Livonia. But the town lay far behind them. The address, then, was a false one. He whistled softly. He was not, as a fact, as calm as he looked. He had never thrown a man over a precipice before, and he disliked the idea. Fortunately, his prisoner did not know this. Besides, suppose he did push him over? Dead men are extremely useless about telling things. It would, as a fact, leave matters no better than before. Rather worse.

Half an hour.

"Come, come," said Nikky fiercely. "We are losing time." He looked fierce, too. His swollen lip did that. And he was nervous. It occurred to him that his prisoner, in desperation, might roll over the edge himself, which would be most uncomfortable.

But the precipice, and Nikky's fierce lip, and other things, had got in their work. The man on the ground stopped muttering in his patois, and turned on Nikky eyes full of hate.

"I will tell you," he said. "And you will free me. And after that —"

"Certainly," Nikky replied equably. "You will follow me to the ends of the earth-although that will not be necessary, because I don't intend to go there-and finish me off." Then, sternly: "Now, where does the letter go? I have a fancy for delivering it myself."

"If I tell you, what then?"

"This: If you tell me properly, and all goes well, I will return and release you. If I do not return, naturally you will not be released. And, for fear you meditate a treachery, I shall gag you and leave you, not here, but back a short distance, in the wood we just passed. And, because you are a brave man, and this thing may be less serious than I think it is, I give you my word of honor that, if you advise me correctly, I shall return and liberate you."

He was very proud of his plan. He had thought it out carefully. He had everything to gain and nothing to lose by it-except, perhaps, his life. The point was, that he knew he could not take a citizen of Karnia prisoner, because too many things would follow, possibly a war.

"It's a reasonable proposition," he observed. "If I come back, you are all right. If I do not, there are a number of disagreeable possibilities for you."

"I have only your word."

"And I yours," said Nikky.

The chauffeur took a final glance around; as far as he could see, and a final shuddering look at the valley of the Ar, far below. "I will tell you," he said sullenly.

Chapter XII
Two Prisoners

Herman Spier had made his escape with the letter. He ran through tortuous byways of the old city, under arches into courtyards, out again by doorway set in walls, twisted, doubled like a rabbit. And all this with no pursuit, save the pricking one of terror.

But at last he halted, looked about, perceived that only his own guilty conscience accused him, and took breath. He made his way to the house in the Road of the Good Children, the letter now buttoned inside his coat, and, finding the doors closed, lurked in the shadow of the park until, an hour later, Black Humbert himself appeared.

He eyed his creature with cold anger. "It is a marvel," he sneered, "that such flight as yours has not brought the police in a pack at your heels."

"I had the letter," Herman replied sulkily. "It was necessary to save it."

"You were to see where Niburg took the substitute."

But here Herman was the one to sneer. "Niburg!" he said. "You know well enough that he will take no substitute to-night, or any night, You strike hard, my friend."

The concierge growled, and together they entered the house across the street.

In the absence of Humbert, his niece, daughter of a milk-seller near, kept the bureau, answered the bell, and after nine o'clock, when the doors were bolted, admitted the various occupants of the house and gave them the tiny tapers with which to light themselves upstairs. She was sewing and singing softly when they entered. Herman Spier's pale face colored. He suspected the girl of a softness for him, not entirely borne out by the facts. So he straightened his ready-made tie, which hooked to his collar button, and ogled her.

"All right, girl. You may go," said Humbert. His huge bulk seemed to fill the little room.

"Good-night to you both," the girl said, and gave Herman Spier a nod. When she was gone, the concierge locked the door behind her.

"And now," he said, "for a look at the treasure."

He rubbed his hands together as Herman produced the letter. Heads close, they examined it under the lamp. Then they glanced at each other.

"A cipher," said the concierge shortly. "It tells nothing."

It was a moment of intense disappointment. In Humbert's mind had been forming, for the past hour or two, a plan-nothing less than to go himself before the Council and, with the letter in hand, to point out certain things which would be valuable. In this way he would serve both the party and him-self. Preferment would follow. He could demand, under the corning republic, some high office. Already, of course, he was known to the Committee, and known well, but rather for brawn than brain. They used him. Now — "Code!" he said. And struck the paper with a hairy fist. "Everything goes wrong. That blond devil interferes, and now this letter speaks but of blankets and loaves!"

The bell rang, and, taking care to thrust the letter out of sight, the concierge disappeared. Then ensued, in the hall, a short colloquy, followed by a thumping on the staircase. The concierge returned.

"Old Adelbert, from the Opera," he said. "He has lost his position, and would have spent the night airing his grievance. But I sent him off!"

Herman turned his pale eyes toward the giant. "So!" he said. And after a pause, "He has some influence among the veterans."

"And is Royalist to his marrow," sneered the concierge. He took the letter out again and, bringing a lamp, went over it carefully. It was signed merely "Olga." "Blankets and loaves!" he fumed.

Now, as between the two, Black Humbert furnished evil and strength, but it was the pallid clerk who furnished the cunning. And now he made a suggestion.

"It is possible," he said, "that he-upstairs-could help."

"Adelbert? Are you mad?"

"The other. He knows codes. It was by means of one we caught him. I have heard that all these things have one basis, and a simple one."

The concierge considered. Then he rose. "It is worth trying," he observed.

He thrust the letter into his pocket, and the two conspirators went out into the gloomy hall. There, on a ledge, lay the white tapers, and one he lighted, shielding it from the draft in the hollow of his great hand. Then he led the way to the top of the house.

Here were three rooms. One, the best, was Herman Spier's, a poor thing at that. Next to it was old Adelbert's. As they passed the door they could hear him within, muttering to himself. At the extreme end of the narrow corridor, in a passage almost blocked by old furniture, was another room, a sort of attic, with a slanting roof.

Making sure that old Adelbert did not hear them, they went back to this door, which the concierge unlocked. Inside the room was dark. The taper showed little. As their eyes became accustomed to the darkness, the outlines of the attic stood revealed, a junk-room, piled high with old trunks, and in one corner a bed.

Black Humbert, taper in hand, approached the bed. Herman remained near the door. Now, with the candle near, the bed revealed a man lying on it, and tied with knotted ropes; a young man, with sunken cheeks and weary, desperate eyes. Beside him, on a chair, were the fragments of a meal, a bit of broken bread, some cold soup, on which grease had formed a firm coating.

Lying there, sleeping and waking and sleeping again, young Haeckel, one time of His Majesty's secret service and student in the University, had lost track of the days. He knew not how long he had been a prisoner, except that it had been eternities. Twice a day, morning and evening, came his jailer and loosened his bonds, brought food, of a sort, and allowed him, not out of mercy, but because it was the Committee's pleasure that for a time he should live, to move about the room and bring the blood again to his numbed limbs.

He was to live because he knew many things which the Committee would know. But, as the concierge daily reminded him, there was a limit to mercy and to patience.

In the mean time they held him, a hostage against certain contingencies. Held him and kept him barely alive. Already he tottered about the room when his bonds were removed; but his eyes did not falter, or his courage. Those whom he had served so well, he felt, would not forget him. And meanwhile, knowing what he knew, he would die before he became the tool of these workers in the dark.

So he lay and thought, and slept when thinking became unbearable, and thus went his days and the long nights.

The concierge untied him, and stood back. "Now," he said.

But the boy-he was no more-lay still. He made one effort to rise, and fell back.

"Up with you!" said the concierge, and jerked him to his feet. He caught the rail of the bed, or he would have fallen. "Now-stand like a man."

He stood then, facing his captors without defiance. He had worn all that out in the first days of his imprisonment. He was in shirt and trousers only, his feet bare, his face unshaven-the thin first beard of early manhood.

"Well?" he said at last. "I thought-you've been here once to-night."

"Right, my cuckoo. But to-night I do you double honor."

But seeing that Haeckel was swaying, he turned to Herman Spier. "Go down," he said, "and bring up some brandy. He can do nothing for us in this state."

He drank the brandy eagerly when it came, and the concierge poured him a second quantity. What with weakness and slow starvation, it did what no threat of personal danger would have done. It broke down his resistance. Not immediately. He fought hard, when the matter was first broached to him. But in the end he took the letter and, holding it close to the candle, he examined it closely. His hands shook, his eyes burned. The two Terrorists watched him narrowly.

Brandy or no brandy, however, he had not lost his wits. He glanced up suddenly. "Tell me something about this," he said. "And what will you do for me if I decode it?"

The concierge would promise anything, and did. Haeckel listened, and knew the offer of liberty was a lie. But there was something about the story of the letter itself that bore the hall-marks of truth.

"You see," finished Black Humbert cunningly, "she-this-lady of the Court-is plotting with some one, or so we suspect. If it is only a liaison —!" He spread his hands. "If, as is possible, she betrays us to Karnia, that we should find out. It is not," he added, "among our plans that Karnia should know too much of us."

"Who is it?"

"I cannot betray a lady," said Black Humbert, and leered.

The brandy was still working, but the spy's mind was clear. He asked for a pencil, and set to work. After all, if there was a spy of Karl's in the Palace, it were well to know it. He tried complicated methods first, to find that the body of the letter, after all, was simple enough. By reading every tenth word, he got a consistent message, save that certain supplies, over which the concierge had railed, were special code words for certain regiments. These he could not decipher.

"Whoever was to receive this," he said at last, "would have been in possession of complete data of the army, equipment and all, and the location of various regiments. Probably you and your band of murderers have that already."

The concierge nodded, no whit ruffled. "And for whom was it intended?"

"I cannot say. The address is fictitious, of course."

Black Humbert scowled. "So!" he said. "You tell us only a part!"

"There is nothing else to tell. Save, as I have written here, the writer ends: 'I must see you at once. Let me know where.'"

The brandy was getting in its work well by that time. He was feeling strong, his own man again, and reckless. But he was cunning, too. He yawned. "And in return for all this, what?" he demanded. "I have done you a service, friend cut-throat."

The concierge stuffed letter and translation into his pocket. "What would you have, short of liberty?"

"Air, for one thing." He stood up and stretched again. God, how strong he felt! "If you would open that accursed window for an hour-the place reeks."

Humbert was in high good humor in spite of his protests. In his pocket he held the key to favor, aye, to a plan which he meant to lay before the Committee of Ten, a plan breath-taking in its audacity and yet potential of success. He went to the window and put his great shoulder against it.

Instantly Haeckel overturned the candle and, picking up the chair, hurled it at Herman Spier. He heard the clerk go down as he leaped for the door. Herman had not locked it. He was in the passage before the concierge had stumbled past the bed.

On the stairs his lightness counted. His bare feet made no sound. He could hear behind him the great mass of Humbert, hurling itself down. Haeckel ran as he had never run before. The last flight now, with the concierge well behind, and liberty two seconds away.

He flung himself against the doors to the street. But they were fastened by a chain, and the key was not in the lock.

He crumpled up in a heap as the concierge fell on him with fists like flails.

Some time later, old Adelbert heard a sound in the corridor, and peered out. Humbert, assisted by the lodger, Spier, was carrying to the attic what appeared to be an old mattress, rolled up and covered with rags. In the morning, outside the door, there was a darkish stain, however, which might have been blood.

Chapter XIII
In the Park

At nine o'clock the next morning the Chancellor visited the Crown Prince. He came without ceremony. Lately he had been coming often. He liked to come in quietly, and sit for an hour in the schoolroom, saying nothing. Prince Ferdinand William Otto found these occasions rather trying.

"I should think," he protested once to his governess, "that he would have something else to do. He's the Chancellor, he?"

But on this occasion the Chancellor had an errand, the product of careful thought. Early as it was, already he had read his morning mail in his study, had dictated his replies, had eaten a frugal breakfast of fruit and sausage, and in the small inner room which had heard so many secrets, had listened to the reports of his agents, and of the King's physicians. Neither had been reassuring.

The King had passed a bad night, and Haeckel was still missing. The Chancellor's heart was heavy.

The Chancellor watched the Crown Prince, as he sat at the high desk, laboriously writing. It was the hour of English composition, and Prince Ferdinand William Otto was writing a theme.

"About dogs," he explained. "I've seen a great many, you know. I could do it better with a pencil. My pen sticks in the paper."

He wrote on, and Mettlich sat and watched. From the boy his gaze wandered over the room. He knew it well. Not so many years ago he had visited in this very room another bright-haired lad, whose pen had also stuck in the paper. The Chancellor looked up at the crossed swords, and something like a mist came into his keen old eyes.

He caught Miss Braithwaite's glance, and he knew what was in her mind. For nine years now had come, once a year, the painful anniversary, of the death of the late Crown Prince and his young wife. For nine years had the city mourned, with flags at half-mast and the bronze statue of the old queen draped in black. And for nine years had the day of grief passed unnoticed by the lad on whom hung the destinies of the kingdom.

Now they confronted a new situation. The next day but one was the anniversary again. The boy was older, and observant. It would not be possible to conceal from him the significance of the procession marching through the streets with muffled drums. Even the previous year he had demanded the reason for crape on his grandmother's statue, and had been put off, at the cost of Miss Braithwaite's strong feeling for the truth. Also he had not been allowed to see the morning paper, which was, on these anniversaries, bordered with black. This had annoyed him. The Crown Prince always read the morning paper-especially the weather forecast.

They could not continue to lie to the boy. Truthfulness had been one of the rules of his rigorous upbringing. And he was now of an age to remember. So the Chancellor sat and waited, and, fingered, his heavy watch-chain.

Suddenly the Crown Prince looked up. "Have you ever been on a scenic railway?", he inquired politely.

The Chancellor regretted that he had not.

"It's very remarkable," said Prince Ferdinand William Otto. "But unless you like excitement, perhaps you would not care for it."

The Chancellor observed that he had had his share of excitement, in his, time, and was now for the ways of quiet.

Prince Ferdinand William Otto had a great many things to say, but thought better of it. Miss Braithwaite disliked Americans, for instance, and it was quite possible that the Chancellor did also. It seemed strange about Americans. Either one liked them a great deal, or not at all. He put his attention to the theme, and finished it. Then, flushed with authorship, he looked up. "May I read you the last line of it?" he demanded of the Chancellor.

"I shall be honored, Highness." not often did the Chancellor say "Highness." Generally he said "Otto" or "my child."

Prince Ferdinand William Otto read aloud, with dancing eyes, his last line: " 'I should like to own a dog.' I thought," he said wistfully, "that I might ask my grandfather for one."

"I see no reason why you should not have a dog," the Chancellor observed.

"Not one to be kept at the stables," Otto explained. "One to stay with me all the time. One to sleep on the foot of the bed."

But here the Chancellor threw up his hands. Instantly he visualized all the objections to dogs, from fleas to rabies. And he put the difficulties into words. No mean speaker was the Chancellor when so minded. He was a master of style, of arrangement, of logic and reasoning. He spoke at length, even, at the end, rising and pacing a few steps up and down the room. But when he had concluded, when the dog, so to speak, had fled yelping to the country of dead hopes, Prince Ferdinand William Otto merely gulped, and said:

"Well, I wish I could have a dog!"

The Chancellor changed his tactics by changing the subject. "I was wondering this morning, as I crossed the park, if you would enjoy an excursion soon. Could it be managed, Miss Braithwaite?"

"I dare say," said Miss Braithwaite dryly. "Although I must say, if there is no improvement in punctuation and capital letters —"

"What sort of excursion?" asked His Royal Highness, guardedly. He did not care for picture galleries.

"Out-of-doors, to see something interesting."

But Prince Ferdinand William Otto was cautious with the caution of one who, by hoping little, may be agreeably disappointed. "A corner-stone, I suppose," he said.

"Not a corner-stone," said the Chancellor, with eyes that began to twinkle under ferocious brows. "No, Otto. A real excursion, up the river."

"To the fort? I do want to see the new fort."

As a matter of truth, the Chancellor had not thought of the fort. But like many another before him, he accepted the suggestion and made it his own. "To the fort, of course," said he.

"And take luncheon along, and eat it there, and have Hedwig and Nikky? And see the guns?"

But this was going too fast. Nikky, of course, would go, and if the Princess cared to, she too. But luncheon! It was necessary to remind the Crown Prince that the officers at the fort would expect to have him join their mess. There was a short parley over this, and it was finally settled that the officers should serve luncheon, but that there should be no speeches. The Crown Prince had already learned that his presence was a sort of rod of Aaron, to unloose floods of speeches. Through what outpourings of oratory he had sat or stood, in his almost ten years!

"Then that's settled," he said at last. "I'm very happy. This morning I shall apologize to M. Puaux."

During the remainder of the morning the Crown Prince made various excursions to the window to see if the weather was holding good. Also he asked, during his half-hour's intermission, for the great box of lead soldiers that was locked away in the cabinet. "I shall pretend that the desk is a fort, Miss Braithwaite," he said. "Do you mind being the enemy, and pretending to be shot now and then?"

But Miss Braithwaite was correcting papers. She was willing to be a passive enemy and be potted at, but she drew the line at falling over. Prince Ferdinand William Otto did not persist.

He was far too polite. But he wished in all his soul that Nikky would come. Nikky, he felt, would die often and hard.

But Nikky did not come.

Came German and French, mathematics and music and no Nikky. Came at last the riding-hour—and still no Nikky.

At twelve o'clock, Prince Ferdinand William Otto, clad in his riding-garments of tweed knickers, puttees, and a belted jacket, stood by the schoolroom window and looked out. The inner windows of his suite faced the courtyard, but the schoolroom opened over the Place—a bad arrangement surely, seeing what distractions to lessons may take place in a public square, what pigeons feeding in the sun, what bands with drums and drum-majors, what children flying kites.

"I don't understand it," the Crown Prince said plaintively. "He is generally very punctual. Perhaps —"

But he loyally refused to finish the sentence. The "perhaps" was a grievous thought, nothing less than that Nikky and Hedwig were at that moment riding in the ring together, and had both forgotten him. He was rather used to being forgotten. With the exception of Miss Braithwaite, he was nobody's business, really. His aunt forgot him frequently. On Wednesdays it was his privilege-or not; as you think of it-to take luncheon with the Archduchess; and once in so often she would forget and go out. Or be in, and not expecting him, which was as bad.

"Bless us, I forgot the child," she would say on these occasions.

But until now, Nikky had never forgotten. He had been the soul of remembering, indeed, and rather more than punctual. Prince Ferdinand William Otto consulted his watch. It was of gold, and on the inside was engraved:

"To Ferdinand William Otto from his grandfather, on the occasion of his taking his first communion."

"It's getting rather late," he observed.

Miss Braithwaite looked troubled. "No doubt something has detained him," she said, with unusual gentleness. "You might work at the frame for your Cousin Hedwig. Then, if Captain Larisch comes, you can still have a part of your lesson."

Prince Ferdinand William Otto brightened. The burntwood photograph frame for Hedwig was his delight. And yesterday, as a punishment for the escapade of the day before, it had been put away with an alarming air of finality. He had traced the design himself, from a Christmas card, and it had originally consisted of a ring and small Cupids, alternating with hearts. He liked it very much. The Cupids were engagingly fat. However, Miss Braithwaite had not approved of their state of nature, and it had been necessary to drape them with sashes tied in neat bows.

The pyrography outfit was produced, and for fifteen minutes Prince Ferdinand William Otto labored, his head on one side, his royal tongue slightly protruded. But, above the thin blue smoke of burning, his face remained wistful. He was afraid, terribly afraid, that he had been forgotten again.

"I hope Nikky is not ill," he said once. "He smokes a great many cigarettes. He says he knows they are bad for him."

"Certainly they are bad for him," said Miss Braithwaite. "They contain nicotine, which is a violent poison. A drop of nicotine on the tongue of a dog will kill it."

The reference was unfortunate.

"I wish I might have a dog," observed Prince Ferdinand William Otto.

Fortunately, at that moment, Hedwig came in. She came in a trifle defiantly, although that passed unnoticed, and she also came unannounced, as was her cousinly privilege. And she stood inside the door and stared at the Prince. "Well!" she said.

Prince Ferdinand William Otto was equal to the occasion. He hastily drew out his pocket-handkerchief and spread it over the frame. But his face was rather red. A palace is a most difficult place to have a secret in.

"Well?" she repeated; with a rising inflection. It was clear that she had not noticed the handkerchief incident. "Is there to be no riding-lesson to-day?"

"I don't know. Nikky has not come."

"Where is he?"

Here the drop of nicotine got in its deadly work. "I'm afraid he is ill," said Prince Ferdinand William Otto. "He said he smoked too many cigarettes, and —"

"Is Captain Larisch ill?" Hedwig looked at the governess, and lost some of her bright color.

Miss Braithwaite did not know, and said so. "At the very least," she went on, "he should have sent some word. I do not know what things are coming to. Since His Majesty's illness, no one seems to have any responsibility, or to take any."

"But of course he would have sent word," said Hedwig, frowning: "I don't understand it. He has never been so late before, has he?"

"He has never been late at all," Prince Ferdinand William Otto spoke up quickly.

After a time Hedwig went away, and the Crown Prince took off his riding-clothes. He ate a very small luncheon, swallowing mostly a glass of milk and a lump in his throat. And afterward he worked at the frame, for an hour, shading the hearts carefully. At three o'clock he went for his drive.

There were two variations to the daily drive: One day they went up the river-almost as far as the monastery; the next day they went through the park. There was always an excitement about the park drive, because the people who spied the gold-wheeled carriage always came as close as possible, to see if it was really the Crown Prince. And when, as sometimes happened, it was only Hedwig, or Hilda, and Ferdinand William Otto had been kept at home by a cold, they always looked disappointed.

This was the park day. The horses moved sedately. Beppo looked severe and haughty. A strange man, in the place of Hans, beside Beppo, watched the crowd with keen and vigilant eyes. On the box between them, under his hand, the new footman had placed a revolver. Beppo sat as far away from it as he dared. The crowd lined up, and smiled and cheered. And Prince Ferdinand William Otto sat very straight; and bowed right and left, smiling.

Old Adelbert, limping across the park to, the Opera, paused and looked. Then he shook his head. The country was indeed come to a strange pass, with only that boy and the feeble old King to stand between it and the things of which men whispered behind their hands. He went on, with his head down. A strange pass indeed, with revolution abroad in quiet places, and a cabal among the governors of the Opera to sell the opera-glass privilege to the highest bidder.

He went on, full of trouble.

Olga, the wardrobe woman, was also on her way to the Opera, which faced the park. She also saw the carriage, and at first her eyes twinkled. It was he, of course. The daring of him! But, as the carriage drew nearer, she bent forward. He looked pale, and there was a wistful droop to his mouth. "They have punished him for the little prank," she muttered. "That tight-faced Englishwoman, of course. The English are a hard race." She, too, went on.

As they drew near the end of the park, where the Land of Desire towered, Prince Ferdinand William Otto searched it with eager eyes. How wonderful it was! How steep and high, and alluring! He glanced sideways at Miss Braithwaite, but it was clear that to her it was only a monstrous heap of sheet-iron and steel, adorned with dejected greenery that had manifestly been out too soon in the chill air of very early spring.

A wonderful possibility presented itself. "If I see Bobby," he asked, "may I stop the carriage and speak to him?"

"Certainly not."

"Well, may I call to him?"

"Think it over," suggested Miss Braithwaite. "Would your grandfather like to know that you had done anything so undignified?"

He turned to her a rather desperate pair of eyes. "But I could explain to him," he said. "I was in such a hurry when I left, that I'm afraid I forgot to thank him. I ought to thank him, really. He was very polite to me."

Miss Braithwaite sat still in her seat and said nothing. The novelty of riding in a royal carriage had long since passed away, but she was aware that her position was most unusual. Not often did a governess, even of good family, as she was, ride daily in the park with a crown prince. In a way, on these occasions, she was more royal than royalty. She had, now and then, an inclination to bow right and left herself. And she guarded the dignity of these occasions with a watchful eye. So she said nothing just then. But later on something occurred to her. "You must remember, Otto," she said, "that this American child dislikes kings, and our sort of government." Shades of Mr. Gladstone-our sort of government! "It is possible, isn't it, that he would resent your being of the ruling family? Why not let things be as they are?"

"We were very friendly," said Ferdinand William Otto in a small voice. "I don't think it would make any difference."

But the seed was sown in the fertile ground of his young mind, to bear quick fruit.

It was the Crown Prince who saw Bobby first.

He was standing on a bench, peering over the shoulders of the crowd. Prince Ferdinand William Otto saw him, and bent forward. "There he is!" he said, in a tense tone. "There on the —"

"Sit up straight," commanded Miss Braithwaite.

"May I just wave once? I —"

"Otto!" said Miss Braithwaite, in a terrible voice.

But a dreadful thing was happening. Bobby was looking directly at him, and making no sign. His mouth was a trifle open, but that was all. Otto had a momentary glimpse of him, of the small cap set far back, of the white sweater, of two coolly critical eyes. Then the crowd closed up, and the carriage moved on.

Prince Ferdinand William Otto sat back in his seat, very pale. Clearly Bobby was through with him. First Nikky had forgotten him, and now the American boy had learned his unfortunate position as one of the detested order, and would have none of him.

"You see," said Miss Braithwaite, with an air of relief, "he did not know you."

Up on the box the man beside Beppo kept his hand on the revolver. The carriage turned back toward the Palace.

Late that afternoon the Chancellor had a visitor. Old Mathilde, his servant and housekeeper, showed some curiosity but little excitement over it. 'She was, in fact, faintly resentful. The Chancellor had eaten little all day, and now, when she had an omelet ready to turn smoking out of the pan, must come the Princess Hedwig on foot like the common people, and demand to see him.

Mathilde admitted her, and surveyed her uncompromisingly. Royalties were quite as much in her line as they were in the Crown Prince's.

"He is about to have supper, Highness."

"Please, Mathilde," begged Hedwig. "It is very important."

Mathilde sighed. "As Your Highness wishes," she agreed, and went grumblingly back to the study overlooking the walled garden.

"You may bring his supper when it is ready," Hedwig called to her.

Mathilde was mollified, but she knew what was fitting, if the Princess did not. The omelet spoiled in the pan.

The Chancellor was in his old smoking-coat and slippers. He made an effort to don his tunic, but Hedwig, on Mathilde's heels, caught him in the act. And, after a glance at her face, he relinquished the idea, bowed over her hand, and drew up a chair for her.

And that was how the Chancellor of the kingdom learned that Captain Larisch, aide-de-camp to His Royal Highness the Crown Prince, had disappeared.

"I am afraid it is serious," she said, watching him with wide, terrified eyes. "I know more than you think I do. I—we hear things, even in the Palace."

Irony here, but unconscious. "I know that there is trouble. And it is not like Captain Larisch to desert his post."

"A boyish escapade, Highness," said the Chancellor. But, in the twilight, he gripped hard at the arms of his chair. "He will turn up, very much ashamed of himself, to-night or to-morrow."

"That is what you want to believe. You know better."

He leaned back in his chair and considered her from under his heavy brows. So this was how things were; another, and an unlooked-for complication. Outside he could hear Mathilde's heavy footstep as she waited impatiently for the Princess to go. The odor of a fresh omelet filled the little house. Nikky gone, perhaps to join the others who, one by one, had felt the steel of the Terrorists. And this girl, on whom so much hung, sitting there, a figure of young tragedy.

"Highness," he said at last, "if the worst has happened, —and that I do not believe, —it will be because there is trouble, as you have said. Sooner or later, we who love our country must make sacrifices for it. Most of all, those in high places will be called upon. And among them you may be asked to help."

"I? What can I do?" But she knew, and the Chancellor saw that she knew.

"It is Karl, then?"

"It may be King Karl, Hedwig."

Hedwig rose, and the Chancellor got heavily to his feet. She was fighting for calmness, and she succeeded very well. After all, if Nikky were gone, what did it matter? Only—"There are so many of you," she said, rather pitifully. "And you are all so powerful. And against you there is only-me."

"Why against us, Highness?"

"Because," said Hedwig, "because I care for some one else, and I shall care for him all the rest of my life, even if he never comes back. You may marry me to whom you please, but I shall go on caring. I shall never forget. And I shall make Karl the worst wife in the world, because I hate him."

She opened the door and went out without ceremony, because she was hard-driven and on the edge of tears. In the corridor she almost ran over the irritated Mathilde, and she wept all the way back to the Palace, much to the dismay of her lady in waiting, who had disapproved of the excursion anyhow.

That night, the city was searched for Nikky Larisch, but without result.

Chapter XIV
Nikky Does a Reckless Thing

Nikky Larisch had been having an exciting time. First of all, he exchanged garments with the chauffeur, and cursed his own long legs, which proved difficult to cover adequately. But the chauffeur's long fur ulster helped considerably. The exchange was rather a ticklish matter, and would have been more so had he not found a revolver in the fur coat pocket. It is always hard to remove a coat from a man whose arms are tied, and trousers are even more difficult. To remove trousers from a refractory prisoner offers problems. They must be dragged off, and a good thrust from a heavy boot, or two boots, has been known to change the fate of nations.

However, Nikky's luck stood. His prisoner kicked, but owing to Nikky's wise precaution of having straddled him, nothing untoward happened.

Behold, then, Nikky of the brave heart standing over his prostrate prisoner, and rolling him, mummy fashion, in his own tunic and a rug from the machine.

"It is cold, my friend," he said briefly; "but I am a kindly soul, and if you have told me the truth, you will not have so much as a snuffle to remind you of this to-morrow."

"I have told the truth."

"As a soldier, of course," Nikky went on, "I think you have made a mistake. You should have chosen the precipice. But as a private gentleman, I thank you."

Having examined the knots in the rope, which were very well done, indeed, and having gagged the chauffeur securely, Nikky prepared to go. In his goggles, with the low-visored cap and fur coat, he looked not unlike his late companion. But he had a jaunty step as he walked toward the car, a bit of swagger that covered, perhaps, just a trifle of uneasiness.

For Nikky now knew his destination, knew that he was bound on perilous work, and that the chances of his returning were about fifty-fifty, or rather less.

Nevertheless, he was apparently quite calm as he examined the car. He would have chosen, perhaps, a less perilous place to attempt its mysteries, but needs must. He climbed in, and released the brakes. Then, with great caution, and considerable noise, he worked it away from the brink of the chasm, and started off.

He did not know his way. Over the mountains it was plain enough, for there was but one road. After he descended into the plain of Karnia, however, it became difficult. Sign-posts were few and not explicit. But at last he found the railroad, which he knew well-that railroad without objective, save as it would serve to move troops toward the border. After that Nikky found it easier.

But, with his course assured, other difficulties presented themselves. To take the letter to those who would receive it was one thing. But to deliver it, with all that it might contain, was another. He was not brilliant, was Nikky. Only brave and simple of heart, and unversed in the ways of darkness.

If, now, he could open the letter and remove it, substituting-well, what could he substitute? There were cigarette papers in his pocket. Trust Nikky for that. But how to make the exchange?

Nikky pondered. To cut the side of the envelope presented itself. But it was not good enough. The best is none too good when one's life is at stake.

The engine was boiling hard, a dull roaring under the hood that threatened trouble. He drew up beside the road and took off the water-cap. Then he whistled. Why, of course! Had it not been done from time immemorial, this steaming of letters? He examined it. It bore no incriminating seal.

He held the envelope over the water-cap, and was boyishly pleased to feel the flap loosen. After all, things were easy enough if one used one's brains. He rather regretted using almost all of his cigarette papers, of course. He had, perhaps, never heard of the drop of nicotine on the tongue of a dog.

As for the letter itself, he put it, without even glancing at it, into his cap, under the lining. Then he sealed the envelope again and dried it against one of the lamps. It looked, he reflected, as good as new.

He was extremely pleased with himself.

Before he returned to the machine he consulted his watch. It was three o'clock. True, the long early spring night gave him four more hours of darkness. But the messenger was due at three, at the hunting-lodge in, the mountains which was his destination. He would be, at the best, late by an hour.

He pushed the car to its limit. The fine hard road, with its border of trees, stretched ahead. Nikky surveyed it with a soldier's eye. A military road, or he knew nothing-one along which motor-lorries could make express time. A marvelous road, in that sparsely settled place. Then he entered the forest, that kingly reserve in which Karl ran deer for pastime.

He was nearing his destination.

On what the messenger had told him Nikky hung his hope of success. This was, briefly, that he should go to the royal shooting-box at Wedeling, and should go, not to the house itself, but to the gate-keeper's lodge. Here he was to leave his machine, and tap at the door. On its being opened, he was to say nothing, but to give the letter to him who opened the door. After that he was to take the machine away to the capital, some sixty miles farther on.

The message, then, was to the King himself. For Nikky, as all the world, knew that Karl, with some kindred spirits, was at Wedeling, shooting. That is, if the messenger told the truth. Nikky intended to find out. He was nothing if not thorough.

Nikky had lost much of his jaunty air by that time. On the surface he was his usual debonair self; but his mouth was grim and rather contemptuous. This was Karl's way: to propose marriage with a Princess of Livonia, and yet line the country with his spies! Let him but return, God willing, with his report, and after that, let them continue negotiations with Karl if they dared.

When at last the lights of the lodge at the gate of Wedeling gleamed out through the trees, it was half-pass three, and a wet spring snow was falling softly. In an open place Nikky looked up. The stars were gone.

The lodge now, and the gate-keeper's house. Nikky's heart hammered as he left the car—hammered with nervousness, not terror. But he went boldly to the door, and knocked.

So far all was well. There were footsteps within, and a man stepped out into the darkness, closing the door behind him. Nikky, who had come so far to see this very agent, and to take back a description of him, felt thwarted. Things were not being done, he felt, according to specification. And the man spoke, which was also unexpected.

"You have the letter?" he asked.

"It is here." Luckily he did not speak the patois.

"I will take it."

Nikky held it out. The man fumbled for it, took it.

"Orders have come," said the voice, "that you remain here for the night. In the morning you are to carry dispatches to the city."

Poor Nikky! With his car facing toward the lodge, and under necessity, in order to escape, to back it out into the highway! He thought quickly. There was no chance of overpowering his man quickly and silently. And the house was not empty. From beyond the door came the sounds of men's voices, and the thud of drinking-mugs on a bare table.

"You will take me up to the house, and then put the car away until morning."

Nikky breathed again. It was going to be easy, after all. If only the road went straight to the shooting-box itself, the rest was simple. But he prayed that he make no false turning, to betray his ignorance.

"Very well," —he said.

His companion opened the door behind him. "Ready, now," he called. "The car is here."

Two men rose from a table where they had been sitting, and put on greatcoats of fur. The lamplight within quivered in the wind from the open door. Nikky was quite calm now. His heart beat its regular seventy-two, and he even reflected, with a sort of grim humor, that the Chancellor would find the recital of this escapade much to his taste. In a modest way Nikky felt that he was making history.

The man who had received the letter got into the machine beside him. The other two climbed into the tonneau. And, as if to make the denouement doubly ridiculous, the road led straight. Nikky, growing extremely cheerful behind his goggles, wondered how much petrol remained in the car.

The men behind talked in low tones. Of the shooting, mostly, and the effect of the snow on it. They had been after pheasants that day, it appeared.

"They are late to-night," grumbled one of them, as the house appeared, full lighted. "A tardy start to-morrow again!"

"The King must have his sleep," commented the other, rather mockingly.

With a masterly sweep, Nikky drew up his machine before the entrance. Let them once alight, let him but start his car down the road again, and all the devils of the night might follow. He feared nothing.

But here again Nikky planned too fast. The servant who came out to open the doors of the motor had brought a message. "His Majesty desires that the messenger come in," was the bomb-shell which exploded in Nikky's ears.

Nikky hesitated. And then some imp of recklessness in him prompted him not to run away, but to see the thing through. It was, after all, a chance either way. These men beside the car were doubtless armed-one at least, nearest him, was certainly one of Karl's own secret agents. And, as Nikky paused, he was not certain, but it seemed to him that the man took, a step toward him.

"Very well," said Nikky, grumbling. "But I have had a long ride, and a cold one. I need sleep."

Even then he had a faint hope that the others would precede him, and that it would be possible to leap back to the car, and escape. But, whether by accident or design, the group closed about him. Flight was out of the question.

A little high was Nikky's head as he went in. He had done a stupid thing now, and he knew it. He should have taken his letter and gone back with it. But, fool or not, he was a soldier. Danger made him calm.

So he kept his eyes open. The shooting-box was a simple one, built, after the fashion of the mountains, of logs, and wood-lined. The walls of the hall were hung with skins and the mounted heads of animals, boar and deer, and even an American mountain sheep, testifying to the range of its royal owner's activities as a hunter. Great pelts lay on the floor, and the candelabra were horns cunningly arranged to hold candles. The hall extended to the roof, and a gallery half-way up showed the doors of the sleeping-apartments.

The lodge was noisy. Loud talking, the coming and going of servants with trays, the crackle of wood fires in which whole logs were burning, and, as Nikky and his escort entered, the roaring chorus of a hunting-song filled the ears.

Two of the men flung off their heavy coats, and proceeded without ceremony into the room whence the sounds issued. The third, however, still holding the letter, ushered Nikky into a small side room, a sort of study, since it contained a desk. For kings must pursue their clerical occupations even on holiday. A plain little room it was, containing an American typewriter, and beside the desk only a chair or two upholstered in red morocco.

Nikky had reluctantly removed his cap. His goggles, however, he ventured to retain. He was conscious that his guide was studying him intently. But not with suspicion, he thought: Rather as one who would gauge the caliber of the man before him. He seemed satisfied, too, for his voice, which had been curt, grew more friendly.

"You had no trouble?" he asked.

"None, sir."

"Did Niburg say anything?"

Niburg, then, was the spy of the cathedral. Nikky reflected. Suddenly he saw a way out. It was, he afterward proclaimed, not his own thought. It came to him like a message. He burned a candle to his patron saint, sometime later, for it.

"The man Niburg had had an unfortunate experience, sir. He reported that, during an evening stroll, before he met me, he was attacked by three men, with the evident intention of securing the letter. He was badly beaten up."

His companion started. "Niburg," he said. "Then —" He glanced at the letter he held. "We must find some one else," he muttered. "I never trusted the fellow. A clerk, nothing else. For this work it takes wit."

Nikky, sweating with strain; felt that it did, indeed. "He was badly used up, sir," he offered. "Could hardly walk, and was still trembling with excitement when I met him."

The man reflected. A serious matter, he felt. Not so serious as it might have been, since he held the letter. But it showed many things, and threatened others. He touched a bell. "Tell his, Majesty," he said to the servant who appeared, "that his messenger is here."

The servant bowed and withdrew.

Nikky found the wait that followed trying. He thought of Hedwig, and of the little Crown Prince. Suddenly he knew that he had had, no right to attempt this thing. He had given his word, almost, his oath, to the King, to protect and watch over the boy. And here he was, knowing now that mischief was afoot, and powerless. He cursed himself for his folly.

Then Karl came in. He came alone, closing the door behind him. Nikky and his companion bowed, and Nikky surveyed him through his goggles. The same mocking face he remembered, from Karl's visit to the summer palace, the same easy, graceful carriage, the same small mustache. He was in evening dress, and the bosom of his shirt was slightly rumpled. He had been drinking, but he was not intoxicated. He was slightly flushed, his eyes were abnormally bright. He looked, for the moment; rather amiable. Nikky was to learn, later on, how easily his smile hardened to a terrifying grin. The long, rather delicate nose of his family, fine hair growing a trifle thin, and a thin, straight body this was Karl, King of Karnia, and long-time enemy to Nikky's own land.

He ignored Nikky's companion. "You brought a letter?"

Nikky bowed, and the other man held it out. Karl took it.

"The trip was uneventful?"

"Yes, sire."

"A bad night for it," Karl observed, and glanced at the letter in his hand. "Was there any difficulty at the frontier?"

"None, sire."

Karl tore the end off the envelope. "You will remain here to-night," he said. "To-morrow morning I shall send dispatches to the city. I hope you have petrol. These fellows here —" He did not complete the sentence. He inserted two royal fingers into the envelope and drew out-Nikky's cigarette papers!

For a moment there was complete silence in the room. Karl turned the papers over.

It was then that his face hardened into a horrible grin. He looked up, raising his head slowly.

"What is this?" he demanded, very quietly.

"The letter, sire," said Nikky.

"The letter! Do you call these a letter?"

Nikky drew himself up. "I have brought the envelope which was given me."

Without a word Karl held out papers and envelope to the other man, who took them. Then he turned to Nikky, and now he raised his voice. "Where did you get this-hoax?" he demanded.

"At the cathedral, from the man Niburg."

"You lie!" said Karl. Then, for a moment, he left Nikky and turned on his companion in a fury. He let his royal rage beat on that unlucky individual while the agent stood, white and still. Not until it was over, and Karl, spent with passion, was pacing the floor, did Nikky venture a word.

"If this is not what Your Majesty expected," he said, "there is perhaps an explanation."

Karl wheeled on him. "Explanation!"

"The man Niburg was attacked, early last evening, by three men. They beat him badly, and attempted to rob him. His story to me, sire. He believed that they were after the letter, but that he had preserved it. It is, of course, a possibility that, while he lay stunned, they substituted another envelope for the one he carried."

Karl tore the envelope from the agent's hands and inspected it carefully. Evidently, as with the agent, the story started a new train of thought. Nikky drew a long breath. After all, there was still hope that the early morning shooting would have another target than himself.

Karl sat down, and his face relaxed. It was stern, but no longer horrible. "Tell me this Niburg's story," he commanded.

"He was walking through the old city," Nikky commenced, "when three men fell on him. One, a large one, knocked him insensible and then went through his pockets. The others —"

"Strange!" said Karl. "If he was insensible, how does he know all this?"

"It was his story, sire," Nikky explained. But he colored. "A companion, who was with him, ran away."

"This companion," Karl queried. "A dark, heavy fellow, was it?"

"No. Rather a pale man, blond. A —" Nikky checked himself.

But Karl was all suavity. "So," he said, "while Niburg was unconscious the large man took the letter, which was sealed, magically opened it, extracted its contents, replaced them with-this, and then sealed it again!"

The King turned without haste to a drawer in his desk, and opened it. He was smiling. When he faced about again, Nikky saw that he held a revolver in =his hand. Save that the agent had taken a step forward, nothing in the room had changed. And yet; for Nikky everything had changed.

Nikky had been a reckless fool, but he was brave enough. He smiled, a better smile than Karl's twisted one.

"I have a fancy," said King Karl, "to manage this matter for myself. Keep back, Kaiser. Now, my friend, you will give me the packet of cigarette papers you carry."

Resistance would do no good. Nikky brought them out, and Karl's twisted smile grew broader as he compared them with the ones the envelope had contained.

"You see," he said, "you show the hand of the novice. You should have thrown these away. But, of course, all your methods are wrong. Why, for instance, have you come here at all? You have my man-but that I shall take up later. We will first have the letter."

But here Nikky stood firm. Let them find the letter. He would not help them. But again he cursed himself. There had been a thousand hiding-places along the road-but he must bring the incriminating thing with him, and thus condemn himself!

Now commenced a curious scene, curious because one of the actors was Karl of Karnia himself. He seemed curiously loath to bring in assistance, did Karl. Or perhaps the novelty of the affair appealed to him. And Nikky's resistance to search, with that revolver so close, was short-lived.

Even while he was struggling, Nikky was thinking. Let them get the letter, if they must. Things would at least be no worse than before. But he resolved that no violence would tear from him the place where the messenger was hidden. Until they had got that, he had a chance for life.

They searched his cap last. Nikky, panting after that strange struggle, saw Kaiser take it from the lining of his cap, and pass it to the King.

Karl took it. The smile was gone now, and something ugly and terrible had taken its place. But that, too, faded as he looked at the letter.

It was a blank piece of note-paper.

Chapter XV
Father and Daughter

With the approach of the anniversary of his son's death, the King grew increasingly restless. Each year he determined to put away this old grief, and each year, as his bodily weakness increased, he found it harder to do so. In vain he filled his weary days with the routine of his kingdom. In vain he told himself that there were worse things than to be cut off in one's prime, that the tragedy of old age is a long tragedy, with but one end. To have out-lived all that one loves, he felt, was worse by far. To have driven, in one gloomy procession after another, to the old Capuchin church and there to have left, prayerfully, some dearly beloved body-that had been his life. His son had escaped that. But it was poor comfort to him.

On other years he had had the Crown Prince with him as much as possible on this dreary day of days. But the Crown Prince was exiled, in disgrace. Not even for the comfort of his small presence could stern discipline be relaxed.

Annunciata was not much comfort to him. They had always differed, more or less, the truth being, perhaps, that she was too much like the King ever to sympathize fully with him. Both were arrogant, determined, obstinate. And those qualities, which age was beginning to soften in the King, were now, in Annunciata, in full strength and blooming.

But there was more than fundamental similarity at fault. Against her father the Archduchess held her unhappy marriage.

"You did this," she had said once, when an unusually flagrant escapade had come to the ears of the Palace. "You did it. I told you I hated him. I told you what he was, too. But you had some plan in mind. The plan never materialized, but the marriage did. And here I am." She had turned on him then, not angrily, but with cold hostility. "I shall never forgive you for it," she said.

She never had. She made her daily visit to her father, and, as he grew more feeble, she was moved now and then to pity for him. But it was pity, nothing more. The very hands with which she sometimes changed his pillows were coldly efficient. She had not kissed him in years.

And now, secretly willing that Hedwig should marry Karl, she was ready to annoy him by objecting to it.

On the day after her conversation with General Mettlich, she visited the King. It was afternoon. The King had spent the morning in his study, propped with pillows as was always the case now, working with a secretary. The secretary was gone when she entered, and he sat alone. Over his knees was spread one of the brilliant rugs that the peasants wove in winter evenings, when the snow beat about their small houses and the cattle were snug in barns. Above it his thin old face looked pinched and pale.

He had passed a trying day. Once having broken down the Chancellor's barrier of silence, the King had insisted on full knowledge; with the result that he had sat, aghast, amid the ruins of his former complacency. The country and the smaller cities were comparatively quiet, so far as demonstrations against the Government were concerned. But unquestionably they plotted. As for the capital, it was a seething riot of sedition, from the reports. A copy of a newspaper, secretly printed and more secretly circulated, had brought fire to the King's eyes. It lay on his knees as his daughter entered.

Annunciata touched her lips to his hand. Absorbed as he was in other matters, it struck him, as she bent, that Annunciata was no longer young, and that Time w as touching her with an unloving finger. He viewed her graying hair, her ugly clothes, with the detached eye of age. And he sighed.

"Well, father," she said, looking down at him, "how do you feel?"

"Sit down," he said. The question as to his health was too perfunctory to require reply. Besides, he anticipated trouble, and it was an age-long habit of his to meet it halfway.

Annunciata sat, with a jingling of chains. She chose a straight chair, and faced him, very erect.

"How old is Hedwig?" demanded the King

"Nineteen."

"And Hilda?"

"Sixteen."

He knew their ages quite well. It was merely the bugle before the attack.

"Hedwig is old enough to marry. Her grandmother was not nineteen when I married her."

"It would be better," said Annunciata, "to marry her while she is young, before she knows any better."

"Any better than what?" inquired the King testily.

"Any better than to marry at all."

The King eyed her. She was not, then, even attempting to hide her claws. But he was an old bird, and not to be caught in an argumentative cage.

"There are several possibilities for Hedwig," he said. "I have gone into the matter pretty thoroughly. As you know, I have had this on my mind for some time. It is necessary to arrange things before I —go."

The King, of course, was neither asking nor expecting sympathy from her, but mentally, and somewhat grimly, he compared her unmoved face with that of his old friend and Chancellor, only a few nights before.

"It is a regrettable fact," he went on, "that I must leave, as I shall, a sadly troubled country. But for that —" he paused. But for that, he meant, he would go gladly. He needed rest. His spirit, still so alive, chafed daily more and more against its worn body. He believed in another life, did the old King. He wanted the hearty handclasp of his boy again. Even the wife who had married him against her will had grown close to him in later years. He needed her too. A little rest, then, and after that a new life, with those who had gone ahead.

"A sadly troubled country," he repeated.

"All countries are troubled. We are no worse than others."

"Perhaps not. But things are changing. The old order is changing. The spirit of unrest —I shall not live to see it. You may, Annunciata. But the day is coming when all thrones will totter. Like this one."

Now at last he had pierced her armor. "Like this one!"

"That is what I said. Rouse yourself, Annunciata. Leave that little boudoir of yours, with its accursed clocks and its heat and its flub-dubbery, and see what is about you! Discontent! Revolution! We are hardly safe from day to day. Do you think that what happened nine years ago was a flash that died as it came? Nonsense. Read this!"

He held out the paper and she put on her pince-nez and read its headings, a trifle disdainfully. But the next moment she rose, and stood in front of him, almost as pale as he was. "You allow this sort of thing to be published?"

"No. But it is published."

"And they dare to say things like this? Why, it-it is —"

"Exactly. It is, undoubtedly." He was very calm. "I would not have troubled you with it. But the situation is bad. We are rather helpless."

"Not-the army too?"

"What can we tell? These things spread like fires. Nothing may happen for years. On the other hand, tomorrow —!"

The Archduchess was terrified. She had known that there was disaffection about. She knew that in the last few years precautions at the Palace had been increased. Sentries were doubled. Men in the uniforms of lackeys, but doing no labor, were everywhere. But with time and safety she had felt secure.

"Of course," the King resumed, "things are not as bad as that paper indicates. It is the voice of the few, rather than the many. Still, it is a voice."

Annunciata looked more than her age now. She glanced around the room as though, already, she heard the mob at the doors.

"It is not safe to stay here, is it?" she asked. "We could go to the summer palace. That, at least, is isolated."

"Too isolated," said the King dryly. "And flight! The very spark, perhaps, to start a blaze. Besides," he remind her, "I could not make the journey. If you would like to go, however, probably it can be arranged."

But Annunciata was not minded to go without the Court. And she reflected, not unwisely, that if things were really as bad as they appeared, to isolate herself, helpless in the mountains, would be but to play into the enemy's hand.

"To return to the matter of Hedwig's marriage," said the King. "I —"

"Marriage! When our very lives are threatened!"

"I would be greatly honored," said the King, "if I might be permitted to finish what I was saying."

She had the grace to flush.

"Under the circumstances," the King resumed, "Hedwig's marriage takes on great significance-great political significance."

For a half-hour then, he talked to her. More than for years, he unbosomed himself. He had tried. His ministers had tried. Taxes had been lightened; the representation of the people increased, until; as he said, he was only nominally a ruler. But discontent remained. Some who had gone to America and returned with savings enough to set themselves up in business, had brought back with them the American idea.

He spoke without bitterness. They refused to allow for the difference between a new country and an old land, tilled for many generations. They forgot their struggles across the sea and brought back only stories of prosperity. Emigration had increased, and those who remained whispered of a new order, where each man was the government, and no man a king.

Annunciata listened to the end. She felt no pity for those who would better themselves by discontent and its product, revolt. She felt only resentment that her peace was being threatened, her position assailed. And in her resentment she included the King himself. He should have done better. These things, taken early enough, could have been arranged.

And something of this she did not hesitate to say. "Karnia is quiet enough," she finished, a final thrust.

"Karnia is better off. A lowland, most of it, and fertile." But a spot of color showed in his old cheeks. "I am glad you spoke of Karnia. Whatever plans we make, Karnia must be considered."

"Why? Karnia does not consider us."

He raised his hand. "You are wrong. Just now, Karnia is doing us the honor of asking an alliance with us. A matrimonial alliance."

The Archduchess was hardly surprised, as one may believe. But she was not minded to yield too easily. The old resentment against her father flamed. Indifferent mother though she was, she made capital of a fear for Hedwig's happiness. In a cold and quiet voice she reminded him of her own wretchedness, and of Karl's reputation.

At last she succeeded in irritating the King —a more difficult thing now than in earlier times, but not so hard a matter at that. He listened quietly until she had finished, and then sent her away. When she had got part way to the door, however, he called her back. And since a king is a king, even if he is one's father and very old, she came.

"Just one word more," he said, in his thin, old, highbred voice. "Much of your unhappiness was of your own making. You, and you only, know how much. But nothing that you have said can change the situation. I am merely compelled to make the decision alone, and soon. I have not much time."

So, after all, was the matter of the Duchess Hedwig's marriage arranged, a composite outgrowth of expediency and obstinacy, of defiance and anger. And so was it hastened.

Irritation gave the King strength. That afternoon were summoned in haste the members of his Council: fat old Friese, young Marschall with the rat face, austere Bayerl with the white skin and burning eyes, and others. And to them all the King disclosed his royal will. There was some demur. Friese, who sweated with displeasure, ranted about old enemies and broken pledges. But, after all, the King's will was dominant. Friese could but voice his protest and relapse into greasy silence.

The Chancellor sat silent during the conclave, silent, but intent. On each speaker he turned his eyes, and waited until at last Karl's proposal, with its promises, was laid before them in full. Then, and only then, the Chancellor rose. His speech was short. He told them of what they all knew, their own insecurity. He spoke but a word of the Crown Prince, but that softly. And he drew for them a pictures of the future that set their hearts to glowing —a throne secure, a greater kingdom, freedom from the cost of war, a harbor by the sea.

And if, as he spoke, he saw not the rat eyes of Marschall, the greedy ones of some of the others, but instead a girl's wide and pleading ones, he resolutely went on. Life was a sacrifice. Youth would pass, and love with it, but the country must survive.

The battle, which was no battle at all, was won. He had won. The country had won. The Crown Prince had won. Only Hedwig had lost. And only Mettlich knew just how she had lost.

When the Council, bowing deep, had gone away, the Chancellor remained standing by a window. He was feeling old and very tired. All that day, until the Council met with the King, he had sat in the little office on a back street, which was the headquarters of the secret service. All that day men had come and gone, bringing false clues which led nowhere. The earth had swallowed up Nikky Larisch.

"I hope you are satisfied," said the King grimly, from behind him. "It was your arrangement."

"It was my hope, sire," replied the Chancellor dryly.

The necessity for work brought the King the strength to do it. Mettlich remained with him. Boxes were brought from vaults, unlocked and examined. Secretaries came and went. At eight o'clock a frugal dinner was spread in the study, and they ate it almost literally over state documents.

On and on, until midnight or thereabouts. Then they stopped. The thing was arranged. Nothing was left now but to carry the word to Karl.

Two things were necessary: Haste. The King, having determined it, would lose no time. And dignity. The granddaughter of the King must be offered with ceremony. No ordinary King's messenger, then, but some dignitary of the Court.

To this emergency Mettlich rose like the doughty old warrior and statesman that he was. "If you are willing, sire," he said, as he rose, "I will go myself."

"When?"

"Since it must be done, the sooner the better. To-night, sire."

The King smiled. "You were always impatient!" he commented. But he looked almost wistfully at the sturdy and competent old figure before him. Thus was he, not so long ago. Cold nights and spring storms had had no terrors for him. And something else he felt, although he said nothing-the stress of a situation which would send his Chancellor out at midnight, into a driving storm, to secure Karl's support. Things must be bad indeed!

"To the capital?" he asked.

"Not so far. Karl is hunting. He is at Wedeling." He went almost immediately, and the King summoned his valets, and was got to bed. But long after the automobile containing Mettlich and two secret agents was on the road toward the mountains, he tossed on his narrow bed. To what straits had they come indeed! He closed his eyes wearily. Something had gone out of his life. He did not realize at first what it was. When he did, he smiled his old grim smile in the darkness.

He had lost a foe. More than anything perhaps, he had dearly loved a foe.

Chapter XVI
On the Mountain Road

The low gray car which carried the Chancellor was on its way through the mountains. It moved deliberately, for two reasons. First, the Chancellor was afraid of motors. He had a horseman's hatred and fear of machines. Second, he was not of a mind to rouse King Karl from a night's sleep, even to bring the hand of the Princess Hedwig. His intention was to put up at some inn in a village not far from the lodge and to reach Karl by messenger early in the morning, before the hunters left for the day.

Then, all being prepared duly and in order, Mettlich himself would arrive, and things would go forward with dignity and dispatch.

In the mean time he sat back among his furs and thought of many things. He had won a victory which was, after all, but a compromise. He had chosen the safe way, but it led over the body of a young girl, and he loathed it. Also, he thought of Nikky, and what might be. But the car was closed and comfortable. The motion soothed him. After a time he dropped asleep.

The valley of the Ar deepened. The cliff rose above them, a wall broken here and there by the offtake of narrow ravines, filled with forest trees. There was a pause while the chains on the rear wheels were supplemented by others in front, for there must be no danger of a skid. And another pause, where the road slanted perilously toward the brink of the chasm, and caution dictated that the Chancellor alight, and make a hundred feet or so of dangerous curve afoot.

It required diplomacy to get him out. But it was finally done, and his heavy figure, draped in its military cape, went on ahead, outlined by the lamps of the car behind him. The snow was hardly more than a coating, but wet and slippery. Mettlich stalked on, as one who would defy the elements, or anything else, to hinder him that night.

He was well around the curve, and the cliff was broken by a wedge of timber, when a curiously shaped object projected itself over the edge of the bank, and rolling down, lay almost at his feet. The lamps brought it into sharp relief—a man, gagged and tied, and rolled, cigar shaped, in an automobile robe.

The Chancellor turned, and called to his men. Then he bent over the bundle. The others ran up, and cut the bonds. What with cold and long inaction, and his recent drop over the bank, the man could not speak. One of the secret-service men had a flask, and held it to his lips. An amazing situation, indeed, increased by the discovery that under the robe he wore only his undergarments, with a soldier's tunic wrapped around his shoulders. They carried him into the car, where he lay with head lolling back, and his swollen tongue protruding. Half dead he was, with cold and long anxiety. The brandy cleared his mind long before he could speak, and he saw by the uniforms that he was in the hands of the enemy. He turned sulkily silent then, convinced that he had escaped one death but to meet another. Twenty-four hours now he had faced eternity, and he was ready.

He preferred, however, to die fully clothed, and when, in response to his pointing up the bank and to his inarticulate mouthings, one of the secret police examined the bit of woodland with his pocket flash, he found a pair of trousers where Nikky had left them, neatly folded and hung over the branch of a tree. The brandy being supplemented by hot coffee from a patent bottle, the man revived further, made an effort, and sat up. His tongue was still swollen, but they made out what he said. He had been there since the night before. People had passed, a few peasants, a man with a cart, but he could not cry out, and he had hesitated to risk the plunge to the road. But at last he had made it. He was of Karnia, and a King's messenger.

"I was coming back from the barrier," he said thickly, "where I had carried dispatches to the officer in charge. On my return a man hailed me from the side of, the road, near where you found me. I thought that he desired to be taken on, and stopped my car. But he attacked me. He was armed and I was not. He knocked me senseless, and when I awakened I was above the road, among trees. I gave myself up when the snow commenced. Few pass this way. But I heard your car coming and made a desperate effort."

"Then," asked one of the agents, "these are not your clothes?"

"They are his; sir."

The agent produced a flash-light and inspected the garments. Before the Chancellor's eyes, button by button, strap on the sleeve, star on the cuff, came into view the uniform of a captain of his own regiment, the Grenadiers. Then one of his own men had done this infamous thing, one of his own officers, indeed.

"Go through the pockets," he continued sternly.

Came, into view under the flash a pair of gloves, a box of matches, a silk handkerchief, a card-case. The agent said nothing, but passed a card to the Chancellor, who read it without comment.

There was silence in the car.

At last the Chancellor stirred. "This man-he took your car on?"

"Yes. And he has not returned. No other machine has passed."

The secret-service men exchanged glances. There was more to this than appeared. Somewhere ahead, then, was Nikky Larisch, with a motor that did got belong to him, and wearing clothing which his victim described as a chauffeur's coat of leather, breeches and puttees, and a fur greatcoat over all.

"Had the snow commenced when this happened?"

"Not then; sir. Shortly after."

"Go out with the driver," the Chancellor ordered one of his men, "and watch the road for the tracks of another car. Go slowly."

So it was that, after an hour or so, they picked up Nikky's trail, now twenty-four hours old but still clear, and followed it. The Chancellor was awake enough by this time, and bending forward. The man they had rescued slept heavily. As the road descended into the foothills, there were other tracks in the thin snow, and more than once they roused Nikky's victim to pick out his own tire marks. He obeyed dully. When at last the trail turned from the highway toward the shooting-box at Wedeling, Mettlich fell back with something between a curse and a groan.

"The fool!" he muttered. "The young fool! It was madness."

At last they drew up at an inn in the village on the royal preserve, and the Chancellor, looking rather gray, alighted. He directed that the man they had rescued be brought in. The Chancellor was not for losing him just yet. He took a room for him at the inn, and rather cavalierly locked him in it.

The dull-eyed landlord, yawning as he lighted the party upstairs with candles, apparently neither noticed nor cared that the three of them surrounded a fourth, and that the fourth looked both sullen and ill.

The car, with one of the secret-service men, Mettlich sent on to follow Nikky's trail, and to report it to him. The other man was assigned to custody of the chauffeur. The Chancellor, more relieved than he would have acknowledged, reflected before a fire and over a glass of hot milk that he was rather unpropitiously bringing Karl a bride!

It was almost four in the morning when the police agent returned. The track he had followed apparently led into the grounds of Wedeling, but was there lost in many others. It did not, so far as he could discover, lead beyond the lodge gates.

The Chancellor sipped his hot milk and considered. Nikky Larisch a prisoner in Karl's hands caused him less anxiety than it would have a month before. But what was behind it all?

The inn, grumbling at its broken rest, settled down to sleep again. The two secret-service agents took turns on chairs outside their prisoner's door, glancing in occasionally to see that he still slept in his built-in bed.

At a little before five the man outside the prisoner's door heard something inside the room. He glanced in. All was quiet. The prisoner slept heavily, genuine sleep. There was no mistaking it, the sleep of a man warm after long cold and exhaustion, weary after violent effort. The agent went out again, and locked the door behind him.

And as the door closed, a trap-door from the kitchen below opened softly under the sleeping man's bed. With great caution came the landlord, head first, then shoulders. The space was cramped. He crawled up, like a snake out of a hole, and ducked behind the curtains of the bed. All was still quiet, save that the man outside struck a match and lighted a pipe.

Half an hour later, the Chancellor's prisoner, still stiff and weak, was making his way toward the hunting-lodge.

Kaiser saw him first, and found the story unenlightening. Nor could Karl, roused by a terrified valet, make much more of it. When the man had gone, Karl lay back among his pillows and eyed his agent.

"So Mettlich is here!" he said. "A hasty journey. They must be eager."

"They must be in trouble," Kaiser observed dryly. And on that uncomplimentary comment King Karl slept, his face drawn into a wry smile.

But he received the Chancellor of Livonia cordially the next morning, going himself to the lodge doorstep to meet his visitor, and there shaking hands with him.

"I am greatly honored, Excellency," he said, with his twisted smile.

"And I, sire."

But the Chancellor watched him from under his shaggy brows. The messenger had escaped. By now Karl knew the story, knew of his midnight ride over the mountains; and the haste it indicated. He sheathed himself in dignity; did the Chancellor, held his head high and moved ponderously, as became one who came to talk of important matters, but not to ask a boon.

Karl himself led the way to his study, ignoring the chamberlain, and stood aside to let Mettlich enter. Then he followed and closed the door.

"It is a long time since you have honored Karnia with a visit," Karl observed. "Will you sit down?"

Karl himself did not sit. He stood negligently beside the mantel, an arm stretched along it.

"Not since the battle of the Ar, sire," replied the Chancellor dryly. He had headed an army of invasion then.

Karl smiled. "I hope that now your errand is more peaceful."

For answer the Chancellor opened a portfolio he carried, and fumbled among its papers. But, having found the right one, he held it without opening it. "Before we come to that, sire, you have here, I believe, detained for some strange reason, a Captain Larisch, aide-de-camp" —he paused for effect —"to His Royal Highness, the Crown Prince of Livonia."

Karl glanced up quickly. "Perhaps, if you will describe this-gentleman —"

"Nonsense," said the Chancellor testily, "you have him. We have traced him here. Although by what authority you hold him I fail to understand. I am here to find out what you have done with him." The paper trembled in the old man's hand. He knew very well Karl's quick anger, and he feared for Nikky feared horribly.

"Done with him?" echoed Karl. "If as Captain Larisch you refer to a madman who the night before last —"

"I do, sire. Madman is the word."

Of course, it is not etiquette to interrupt a king. But kings were no novelty to the Chancellor. And quite often, for reasons of state, he had found interruptions necessary.

"He is a prisoner," Karl said, in a new tone, stern enough now. "He assaulted and robbed one of my men. He stole certain documents. That he has not suffered for it already was because-well, because I believed that the unfortunate distrust between your country and mine, Excellency, was about to end."

A threat that, undoubtedly. Let the arrangement between Karnia and Livonia be made, with Hedwig to seal the bargain, and Nikky was safe enough. But let Livonia demand too much, or not agree at all, and Nikky was lost. Thus did Nikky Larisch play his small part in the game of nations.

"Suppose," said Karl unctuously, "that we discuss first another more important matter. I confess to a certain impatience." He bowed slightly.

The Chancellor hesitated. Then he glanced thoughtfully at the paper in his hand.

Through a long luncheon, the two alone and even the servants dismissed, through a longer afternoon, negotiations went on. Mettlich fought hard on some points, only to meet defeat. Karl stood firm. The great fortresses on the border must hereafter contain only nominal garrisons. For the seaport strip he had almost doubled his price. The railroad must be completed within two years.

"Since I made my tentative proposal," Karl said, "certain things have come to my ears which must be considered. A certain amount of unrest we all have. It is a part of the times we live in. But strange stories have reached us here, that your revolutionary party is again active, and threatening. This proposal was made to avoid wars, not to marry them. And civil war —" He shrugged his shoulders.

"You have said yourself, sire, that we all have a certain discontent."

"The Princess Hedwig," Karl said suddenly. "She has been told, of course?"

"Not officially. She knows, however."

"How does she regard it?"

The Chancellor hesitated. "Like most young women, she would prefer making her own choice. But that," he added hastily, "is but a whim. She is a lovable and amiable girl. When the time comes she will be willing enough."

Karl stared out through one of the heavily curtained windows. He was not so sure. And the time had gone by when he would have enjoyed the taming of a girl. Now he wanted peace-was he not paying a price for it? —and children to inherit his well-managed kingdom. And perhaps-who knows? —a little love. His passionate young days were behind him, but he craved something that his unruly life had not brought him. Before him rose a vision of Hedwig her frank eyes, her color that rose and fell, her soft, round body.

"You have no reason to believe that she has looked elsewhere?"

"None, sire," said the Chancellor stoutly.

By late afternoon all was arranged, papers signed and witnessed, and the two signatures affixed, the one small and cramped —a soldier's hand; the other bold and flowing-the scrawl of a king. And Hedwig, save for the ceremony, was the bride of Karl of Karnia.

It was then that the Chancellor rose and stretched his legs. "And now, sire," he said, "since we are friends and no longer enemies, you will, I know, release that mad boy of mine."

"When do you start back?"

"Within an hour."

"Before that time," said Karl, "you shall have him, Chancellor."

And with that Mettlich was forced to be content. He trusted Karl no more now than he ever had. But he made his adieus with no hint of trouble in his face.

Karl waited until the machine drove away. He had gone to the doorstep with the Chancellor, desiring to do him all possible honor. But Mettlich unaccustomed to democratic ways, disapproved of the proceeding, and was indeed extremely uncomfortable, and drew a sigh of relief when it was all over. He was of the old order which would keep its royalties on gilded thrones and, having isolated there in grandeur, have gone about the business of the kingdom without them.

Karl stood for a moment in the open air. It was done, then, and well done. It was hard to realize. He turned to the west, where for so long behind the mountains had lurked an enemy. A new era was opening; peace, disarmament, a quiet and prosperous land. He had spent his years of war and women. That was over.

From far away in the forest he heard the baying of the hounds. The crisp air filled his lungs. And even as he watched, a young doe, with rolling eyes, leaped across the drive. Karl watched it with coolly speculative eyes.

When he returned to the study the agent Kaiser was already there. In the democracy of the lodge men came and went almost at will. But Karl, big with plans for the future, would have been alone, and eyed the agent with disfavor.

"Well?" he demanded.

"We have been able to search the Chancellor's rooms, sire," the agent said, "for the articles mentioned last night —a card-case, gloves, and a silk handkerchief, belonging to the prisoner upstairs. He is Captain Larisch, aide-de-camp to the Crown Prince of Livonia."

He had, expected Karl to be, impressed. But Karl only looked at him. "I know that," he said coldly. "You are always just a little late with your information, Kaiser."

Something like malice showed in the agent's face. "Then you also know, sire, that it is this Captain Larisch with whom rumor couples the name of the Princess Hedwig." He stepped back a pace or two at sight of Karl's face. "You requested such information, sire."

For answer, Karl pointed to the door.

For some time after he had dismissed the agent, Karl paced his library alone. Kaiser brought no unverified information. Therefore the thing was true. Therefore he had had his enemy in his hand, and now was pledged to let him go. For a time, then, Karl paid the penalty of many misdeeds. His triumph was ashes in his mouth.

What if this boy, infatuated with Hedwig, had hidden somewhere on the road Olga Loschek's letter? What, then, if he recovered it and took it to Hedwig? What if — But at last he sent for the prisoner upstairs, and waited for him with both jealousy and fear in his eyes.

Five minutes later Nikky Larisch was ushered into the red study, and having bowed, an insolent young bow at that, stood and eyed the King.

"I have sent for you to release you," said Karl. Nikky drew a long breath. "I am grateful, sire."

"You have been interceded for by the Chancellor of Livonia, General Mettlich, who has just gone."

Nikky bowed.

"Naturally, since you said nothing, of your identity, we could not know that you belonged to His Majesty's household. Under the circumstances, it is a pleasure to give you your freedom."

Nikky, bowed again.

Karl fixed him with cold eyes. "But before you take leave of us," he said ironically, "I should like the true story of the night before last. Somehow, somewhere, a letter intended for me was exchanged for a blank paper. I want that letter."

"I know no more than you, sire. It is not reasonable that I would have taken the risk I took for an envelope containing nothing."

"For that matter," said His Majesty, "there was nothing reasonable about anything you did!"

And now Karl played his trump card, played it with watchful eyes on Nikky's face. He would see if report spoke the truth, if this blue-eyed boy was in love with Hedwig. He was a jealous man, this Karl of the cold eyes, jealous and passionate. Not as a king, then, watching a humble soldier of Livonia, but as man to man, he gazed at Nikky.

"For fear that loyalty keeps you silent, I may say to you that the old troubles between Karnia and Livonia are over."

"I do not understand, sire."

Karl hesitated. Then, with his twisted smile, he cast the rigid etiquette of such matters to the winds. "It is very simple," he said. "There will be no more trouble between these two neighboring countries, because a marriage has to-day been arranged —a marriage between the Princess Hedwig, His Majesty's granddaughter, and myself."

For a moment Nikky Larisch closed his eyes.

Chapter XVII
The Fortress

The anniversary of the death of Prince Hubert dawned bright and sunny. The Place showed a thin covering of snow, which clung, wet and sticky, to the trees; but by nine o'clock most of it had disappeared, and Prince Ferdinand William Otto was informed that the excursion would take place.

Two motors took the party, by back streets, to the landing-stage. In the first were Annunciata, Hedwig, and the Countess, and at the last moment Otto had salvaged Miss Braithwaite from the second car, and begged a place for her with him. A police agent sat beside the chauffeur. Also another car, just ahead, contained other agents, by Mettlich's order before his departure —a plain black motor, without the royal arms.

In the second machine followed a part of the suite, Hedwig's lady in waiting, two gentlemen of the Court, in parade dress, and Father Gregory, come from his monastery at Etzel to visit his old friend, the King.

At the landing-stage a small crowd had gathered on seeing the red carpet laid and the gilt ropes put up, which indicated a royal visit. A small girl, with a hastily secured bouquet in her hot hands, stood nervously waiting. In deference to the anniversary, the flowers were tied with a black ribbon!

Annunciata grumbled when she saw the crowd, and the occupants of the first car looked them over carefully. It remained for Hedwig to spy the black ribbon. In the confusion, she slipped over to the little girl, who went quite white with excitement. "They are lovely," Hedwig whispered, "but please take off the black ribbon." The child eyed her anxiously. "It will come to pieces, Highness."

"Take the ribbon from your hair. It will be beautiful."

Which was done! But, as was not unnatural, the child forgot her speech, and merely thrust the bouquet, tied with a large pink bow, into the hands of Prince Ferdinand William Otto.

"Here," she said. It was, perhaps, the briefest, and therefore the most agreeable presentation speech the Crown Prince had ever heard.

Red carpet and gold ropes and white gloves these last on the waiting officers-made the scene rather gay. The spring sun shone on the gleaming river, on the white launch with its red velvet cushions, on the deck chairs, its striped awnings and glittering brass, on the Crown Prince, in uniform, on the bouquet and the ribbon. But somewhere, back of the quay, a band struck up a funeral march, and a beggar, sitting in the sun, put his hand to his ear.

"Of course," he said, to no one in particular. "It is the day. I had forgotten."

The quay receded, red carpet and all. Only the blare of the band followed them, and with the persistence of sound over water, followed them for some time. The Crown Prince put down the bouquet, and proceeded to stand near the steersman.

"When I am grown up," he observed to that embarrassed sailor, "I hope I shall be able to steer a boat."

The steersman looked about cautiously. The royal guests were settling themselves in chairs; with rugs over their knees. "It is very easy, Your Royal Highness," he said. "See, a turn like this, and what happens? And the other way the same."

Followed a five minutes during which the white launch went on a strange and devious course, and the Crown Prince grew quite hot and at least two inches taller. It was, of course, the Archduchess who discovered what was happening. She was very disagreeable about it.

The Archduchess was very disagreeable about everything that day. She was afraid to stay in the Palace, and afraid to leave it. And just when she had begun to feel calm, and the sun and fresh air were getting in their work, that wretched funeral band had brought back everything she was trying to forget.

The Countess was very gay. She said brilliant, rather heartless things that set the group to laughing, and in the intervals she eyed Hedwig with narrowed eyes and hate in her heart. Hedwig herself was very quiet. The bouquet had contained lilies-of-the-valley, for one thing.

Miss Braithwaite knitted, and watched that the Crown Prince kept his white gloves clean.

Just before they left the Palace the Archduchesss had had a moment of weakening, but the Countess had laughed away her fears.

"I really think I shall not go, after all," Annunciata had said nervously. "There are reasons."

The Countess had smiled mockingly. "Reasons!" she said. "I know that many things are being said. But I also know that General Mettlich is an alarmist;" purred the Countess. "And that the King is old and ill, and sees through gray glasses."

So the Archduchess had submitted to having a plumed and inappropriate hat set high on her head, regardless of the fashion, and had pinned on two watches and gone.

It was Hedwig who showed the most depression on the trip, after all. Early that morning she had attended mass in the royal chapel. All the household had been there, and the King had been wheeled in, and had sat in his box, high in the wall, the door of which opened from his private suite.

Looking up, Hedwig had seen his gray old face set and rigid. The Court had worn black, and the chapel was draped in crepe. She had fallen on her knees and had tried dutifully to pray for the dead Hubert. But her whole soul was crying out for help for herself.

So now she sat very quiet, and wondered about things.

Prince Ferdinand William Otto sat by the rail and watched the green banks flying by. In one place a group of children were sailing a tiny boat from the bank. It was only a plank, with a crazy cotton sail. They shoved it off and watched while the current seized it and carried it along. Then they cheered, and called good-bye to it.

The Crown Prince leaned over the rail, and when the current caught it, he cheered too, and waved his cap. He was reproved, of course, and some officious person insisted on tucking the rug around his royal legs. But when no one was looking, he broke a flower from the bouquet and flung it overboard. He pretended that it was a boat, and was going down to Karnia, filled with soldiers ready to fight.

But the thought of soldiers brought Nikky to his mind. His face clouded. "It's very strange about Nikky," he said. "He is away somewhere. I wish he had sent word he was going."

Hedwig looked out over the river.

The Archduchess glanced at Miss Braithwaite. "There is no news?" she asked, in an undertone.

"None," said Miss Braithwaite.

A sudden suspicion rose in Hedwig's mind, and made her turn pale. What if they had sent him away? Perhaps they feared him enough for that! If that were true, she would never know. She knew the ways of the Palace well enough for that. In a sort of terror she glanced around the group, so comfortably disposed. Her mother was looking out, with her cool, impassive gaze. Miss Braithwaite knitted. The Countess, however, met her eyes, and there was something strange in them: triumph and a bit of terror, too, had she but read them. For the Countess had put in her plea for a holiday and had been refused.

The launch drew up near the fort, and the Crown Prince's salute of a certain number of guns was fired. The garrison was drawn up in line, and looked newly shaved and very, very neat. And the officers came out and stood on the usual red carpet, and bowed deeply, after which they saluted the Crown Prince and he saluted them. Then the Colonel in charge shook hands all round, and the band played. It was all very ceremonious and took a lot of tine.

The new fortress faced the highroad some five miles from the Karnian border. It stood on a bluff over the river, and was, as the Crown Prince decided, not so unlike the desk, after all, except that it had a moat around it.

Hedwig and the Countess went with the party around the fortifications. The Archduchess and Miss Braithwaite had sought a fire. Only the Countess, however, seemed really interested. Hedwig seemed more intent on the distant line of the border than on anything else. She stood on a rampart and stared out at it, looking very sad. Even the drill-when at a word all the great guns rose and peeped over the edge at the valley below, and then dropped back again as if they had seen enough-even this failed to rouse her.

"I wish you would listen, Hedwig," said the Crown Prince, almost fretfully. "It's so interesting. The enemy's soldiers would come up the river in boats, and along that road on foot. And then we would raise the guns and shoot at them. And the guns would drop back again, before the enemy had time to aim at them."

But Hedwig's interest was so evidently assumed that he turned to the Countess. The Countess professed smiling terror, and stood a little way back from the guns, looking on. But Prince Ferdinand William Otto at last coaxed her to the top of the emplacement.

"There's a fine view up there," he urged. "And the guns won't hurt you. There's nothing in them."

To get up it was necessary to climb an iron ladder. Hedwig was already there. About a dozen young officers had helped her up, and ruined as many pairs of white gloves, although Hedwig could climb like a cat, and really needed no help at all.

"You go up," said the Crown Prince eagerly. "I'll hold your bag, so you can climb."

He caught her handbag from her, and instantly something snapped in it. The Countess was climbing up the ladder. Rather dismayed, Prince Ferdinand William Otto surveyed the bag. Something had broken, he feared. And in another moment he saw what it was. The little watch which was set in one side of it had slipped away, leaving a round black hole. His heart beat a trifle faster.

"I'm awfully worried," he called up to her, as he climbed. "I'm afraid I've broken your bag. Something clicked, and the watch is gone. It is not on the ground."

It was well for the Countess that the Colonel was talking to Hedwig. Well for her, too, that the other officers were standing behind with their eyes worshipfully on the Princess. The Countess turned gray-white.

"Don't worry, Highness," she said, with stiff lips, "The watch falls back sometimes. I must have it repaired."

But long after the tour of the ramparts was over, after ammunition-rooms had been visited, with their long lines of waiting shells, after the switchboard which controlled the river mines had been inspected and explained, she was still trembling.

Prince Ferdinand William Otto, looking at the bag later on, saw the watch in place and drew a long breath of relief.

Chapter XVIII
Old Adelbert

Old Adelbert of the Opera had lost his position. No longer, a sausage in his pocket for refreshment, did he leave his little room daily for the Opera. A young man, who made ogling eyes at Olga, of the garde-robe, and who was not careful to keep the lenses clean, had taken his place.

He was hurt in his soldier's soul. There was no longer a place in the kingdom for those who had fought for it. The cry was for the young. And even in the first twenty-four hours a subtle change went on in him. His loyalty, on which he had built his creed of life, turned to bitterness.

The first day of his idleness he wandered into the back room of the cobbler's shop near by, where the butter-seller from the corner, the maker of artificial flowers for graves, and the cobbler himself were gathered, and listened without protest to such talk as would have roused him once to white anger.

But the iron had not yet gone very deep, and one thing he would not permit. It was when, in the conversation, one of them attacked the King. Then indeed he was roused to fury.

"A soldier and a gentleman," he said. "For him I lost this leg of mine, and lost it without grieving. When I lay in the hospital he himself came, and —"

A burst of jeering laughter greeted this, for he had told it many times. Told it, because it was all he had instead of a leg, and although he could not walk on it, certainly it had supported him through many years.

"As for the little Crown Prince," he went on firmly, "I have seen him often. He came frequently to the Opera. He has a fine head and a bright smile. He will be a good king."

But this was met with silence.

Once upon a time a student named Haeckel had occasionally backed him up in his defense of the royal family. But for some reason or other Haeckel came no more, and old Adelbert missed him. He had inquired for him frequently.

"Where is the boy Haeckle?" he had asked one day. "I have not seen him lately."

No one had replied. But a sort of grim silence settled over the little room. Old Adelbert, however, was not discerning.

"Perhaps, as a student, he worked too hard" he had answered his own question. "They must both work and play hard, these students. A fine lot of young men. I have watched them at the Opera. Most of them preferred Italian to German music."

But, that first day of idleness, when he had left the cobbler's, he resolved not to return. They had not been unfriendly, but he had seen at once there was a difference. He was no longer old Adelbert of the Opera. He was an old man only, and out of work.

He spent hours that first free afternoon repairing his frayed linen and his shabby uniform, with his wooden leg stretched out before him and his pipe clutched firmly in his teeth. Then, freshly shaved and brushed, he started on a painful search after work. With no result. And, indeed, he was hopeless before he began. He was old and infirm. There was little that he had even the courage to apply for.

True, he had his small pension, but it came only twice a year, and was sent, intact, to take care of an invalid daughter in the country. That was not his. He never used a penny of it. And he had saved a trifle, by living on air; as the concierge declared. But misfortunes come in threes, like fires and other calamities. The afternoon of that very day brought a letter, saying that the daughter was worse and must have an operation. Old Adelbert went to church and burned a candle for her recovery, and from there to the bank, to send by registered mail the surgeon's fee.

He was bankrupt in twenty-four hours.

That evening in his extremity he did a reckless thing. He wrote a letter to the King. He spent hours over it, first composing it in pencil and then copying it with ink borrowed from the concierge. It began "Sire," as he had learned was the form, and went on to remind His Majesty, first, of the hospital incident, which, having been forty years ago, might have slipped the royal memory. Then came the facts-his lost position, his daughter, the handicap of his wooden leg. It ended with a plea for reinstatement or, failing that, for any sort of work.

He sent it, unfolded, in a large flat envelope, which also he had learned was the correct thing with kings, who for some reason or other do not like folded communications. Then he waited. He considered that a few hours should bring a return.

No answer came. No answer ever came. For the King was ill, and secretaries carefully sifted the royal mail.

He waited all of the next day, and out of the mixed emotions of his soul confided the incident of the letter to Humbert, in his bureau below.

The concierge smiled in his beard. "What does the King care?" he demanded. "He will never see that letter. And if he did-you have lived long, my friend. Have you ever known the King to give, or to do anything but take? Name me but one instance."

And that night, in the concierge's bureau, he was treated to many incidents, all alike. The Government took, but gave nothing. As well expect blood out of a stone. Instances were given, heartlessness piled on heartlessness, one sordid story on another.

And as he listened there died in old Adelbert's soul his flaming love for his sovereign and his belief in him. His eyes took on a hard and haunted look. That night he walked past the Palace and shook his fist at it. He was greatly ashamed of that, however, and never repeated it. But his soul was now an open sore, ready for infection.

And Black Humbert bided his time.

On the day of the excursion to the fortress old Adelbert decided to appeal to his fellow lodger, Herman Spier. Now and then, when he was affluent, he had paid small tribute to Herman by means of the camp cookery on which he prided himself.

"A soldier's mess!" he would say, and bring in a bowl of soup, or a slice of deer meat, broiled over hot coals in his tiny stove. "Eat it, man. These restaurants know nothing of food."

To Herman now he turned for advice and help. It was difficult to find the clerk. He left early, and often came home after midnight in a curious frame of mind, a drunkenness of excitement that was worse than that of liquor.

Herman could not help him. But he eyed the old soldier appraisingly. He guessed shrewdly the growing uneasiness behind Adelbert's brave front. If now one could enlist such a man for the Cause, that would be worth doing. He had talked it over with the concierge. Among the veterans the old man was influential, and by this new policy of substituting fresh blood for stale, the Government had made many enemies among them.

"In a shop!" he said coldly. "With that leg? No, my friend. Two legs are hardly enough for what we have to do."

"Then, for any sort of work. I could sweep and clean."

"I shall inquire," said Herman Spier. But he did not intend to. He had other plans.

The old man's bitterness had been increased by two things. First, although he had been dismissed without notice, in the middle of the week, he had been paid only up to the hour of leaving. That was a grievance. Second, being slow on his feet, one of the royal motorcars had almost run him down, and the police had cursed him roundly for being in the way.

"Why be angry?" observed the concierge, on this being reported to him. "The streets are the King's. Who are the dogs of pedestrians but those that pay the taxes to build them?"

At last he determined to find Haeckel, the student. He did not know his Christian name, nor where he lodged. But he knew the corps he belonged to, by his small gray cap with a red band.

He was very nervous when he made this final effort. Corps houses were curious places, he had heard, and full of secrets. Even the great professors from the University might not enter without invitation. And his experience had been that students paid small respect to uniforms or to age. In truth, he passed the building twice before he could summon courage to touch the great brass knocker. And the arrogance of its clamor, when at last he rapped, startled him again. But here at least he need not have feared.

The student who was also doorkeeper eyed him kindly. "Well, comrade?" he said.

"I am seeking a student named Haeckel, of this corps," said old Adelbert stoutly.

And had violated all etiquette, too, had he but known it!

"Haeckle?" repeated the doorkeeper. "I think-come in, comrade. I will inquire."

For the name of Haeckel was, just then, one curiously significant.

He disappeared, and old Adelbert waited. When the doorkeeper returned, it was to tell him to follow him, and to lead the way downstairs.

There dawned on the old man's eyes a curious sight. In a long basement room were perhaps thirty students, each armed with a foil, and wearing a wire mask. A half dozen lay figures on springs stood in the center in a low row, and before these perspiring youths thrust and parried. Some of them, already much scarred, stood and watched. This, then, was where the students prepared themselves for duels. Here they fought the mimic battles that were later on to lead to the much-prized scars.

Old Adelbert stared with curious, rather scornful eyes. The rapier he detested. Give him a saber, and a free field, and he would show them. Even yet, he felt, he had not lost his cunning. And the saber requires cunning as well as strength.

Two or three students came toward him at once. "You are seeking Haeckle?" one of them asked.

"I am. I knew him, but not well. Lately, however, I have thought-is he here?"

The students exchanged glances. "He is not here," one said. "Where did you know him?"

"He came frequently to a shop I know of—a cobbler's shop, a neighborhood meeting-place. A fine lad. I liked him. But recently he has not come, and knowing his corps, I came here to find him."

They had hoped to learn something from him, and he knew nothing. "He has disappeared," they told him. "He is not at his lodging, and he has left his classes. He went away suddenly, leaving everything. That is all we know."

It sounded sinister. Old Adelbert, heavy-hearted, turned away and climbed again to the street. That gateway was closed, too. And he felt a pang of uneasiness. What could have happened to the boy? Was the world, after all, only a place of trouble?

But now came good fortune, and, like evil, it came not singly. The operation was over, and his daughter on the mend. The fee was paid also. And the second followed on the heels of the first.

He did not like Americans. Too often, in better days, had he heard the merits of the American republic compared with the shortcomings of his own government. When, as happened now and then, he met the American family on the staircase, he drew sharply aside that no touch of republicanism might contaminate his uniform.

On that day, however, things changed.

First of all, he met the American lad in the hallway, and was pleased to see him doff his bit of a cap. Not many, nowadays, uncovered a head to him. The American lad was going down; Adelbert was climbing, one step at a time, and carrying a small basket of provisions.

The American boy, having passed, turned, hesitated, went back. "I'd like to carry that for you, if you don't mind."

"Carry it?"

"I am very strong," said the American boy stoutly.

So Adelbert gave up his basket, and the two went up. Four long flights of stone stairs led to Adelbert's room. The ascent took time and patience.

At the door Adelbert paused. Then, loneliness overcoming prejudice, "Come in," he said.

The bare little room appealed to the boy. "It's very nice, it?" he said. "There's nothing to fall over."

"And but little to sit on," old Adelbert added dryly. "However, two people require but two chairs. Here is one."

But the boy would not sit down. He ranged the room, frankly curious, exclaimed at the pair of ring doves who lived in a box tied to the window-sill, and asked for crumbs for them. Adelbert brought bread from his small store.

The boy cheered him. His interest in the old saber, the intentness with which he listened to its history, the politeness with which he ignored his host's infirmity, all won the old man's heart.

These Americans downstairs were not all bad, then. They were too rich, of course. No one should have meat three times a day, as the meat-seller reported they did. And they were paying double rent for the apartment below. But that, of course, they could not avoid, not knowing the real charge.

The boy was frankly delighted. And when old Adelbert brought forth from his basket a sausage and, boiling it lightly, served him a slice between two pieces of bread, an odd friendship was begun that was to have unforeseen consequences. They had broken bread together.

Between the very old and the very young come sometimes these strong affections. Perhaps it is that age harkens back to the days of its youth, and by being very old, becomes young again. Or is it that children are born old, with the withered, small faces of all the past, and must, year by year, until their maturity, shed this mantle of age?

Gradually, over the meal, and the pigeons, and what not, old Adelbert unburdened his heart. He told of his years at the Opera, where he had kept his glasses clean and listened to the music until he knew by heart even the most difficult passages. He told of the Crown Prince, who always wished opera-glasses, not because he needed them, but because he liked to turn them wrong end before, and thus make the audience appear at a great distance. And then he told of the loss of his position.

The American lad listened politely, but his mind was on the Crown Prince. "Does he wear a crown?" he demanded. "I saw him once in a carriage, but I think he had a hat."

"At the coronation he will wear a crown."

"Do people do exactly what he tells them?"

Old Adelbert was not certain. He hedged, rather. "Probably, whenever it is good for him."

"Huh! What's the use of being a prince?" observed the boy, who had heard of privileges being given that way before. "When will he be a king?"

"When the old King dies. He is very old now. I was in a hospital once, after a battle. And he came in. He put his hand on my shoulder, like this" he illustrated it on the child's small one-and said — Considering that old Adelbert no longer loved his King, it is strange to record that his voice broke.

"Will he die soon?" Bobby put in. He found kings as much of a novelty as to Prince Ferdinand William Otto they were the usual thing. Bobby's idea of kings, however, was of the "off with his head" order.

"Who knows? But when he does, the city will learn at once. The great bell of the Cathedral, which never rings save at such times, will toll. They say it is a sound never to be forgotten. I, of course, have never heard it. When it tolls, all in the city will fall on their knees and pray. It is the custom." Bobby, reared to strict Presbyterianism and accustomed to kneeling but once a day, and that at night beside his bed, in the strict privacy of his own apartment, looked rather startled. "What will they pray for?" he said.

And old Adelbert, with a new bitterness, replied that the sons of kings needed much prayer. Sometimes they were hard and did cruel things.

"And then the Crown Prince will be a king," Bobby reflected. "If I were a king, I'd make people stand around. And I'd have an automobile and run it myself. But has the Crown Prince only a grandfather, and no father?"

"He died-the boy's father. He was murdered, and the Princess his mother also."

Bobby's eyes opened wide. "Who did it?"

"Terrorists," said old Adelbert. And would not be persuaded to say more.

That night at dinner Bobby Thorpe delivered himself of quite a speech. He sat at the table, and now and then, when the sour-faced governess looked at her plate, he slipped a bit of food to his dog, which waited beside him.

"There's a very nice old man upstairs," he said. "He has a fine sword, and ring-doves, and a wooden leg. And he used to rent opera-glasses to the Crown Prince, only he turned them around. I'm going to try that with yours, mother. We had sausage together, and he has lost his position, and he's never been on the Scenic Railway, father. I'd like some tickets for him. He would like riding, I'm sure, because walking must be pretty hard. And what I want to know is this: Why can't you give him a job, father?"

Bobby being usually taciturn at the table, and entirely occupied with food, the family stared at him.

"What sort of a job, son? A man with one leg!"

"He doesn't need legs to chop tickets with."

The governess listened. She did not like Americans. Barbarians they were, and these were of the middle class, being in trade. For a scenic railway is trade, naturally. Except that they paid a fat salary, with an extra month at Christmas, she would not be there. She and Pepy, the maid, had many disputes about this. But Pepy was a Dalmatian, and did not matter.

"He means the old soldier upstairs," said Bobby's mother softly. She was a gentle person. Her eyes were wide and childlike, and it was a sort of religion of the family to keep them full of happiness.

This also the governess could not understand.

"So the old soldier is out of work," mused the head of the family. Head, thought the governess! When they wound him about their fingers! She liked men of sterner stuff. In her mountain country the men did as they wished, and sometimes beat their wives by way of showing their authority. Under no circumstances, she felt, would this young man ever beat his wife. He was a weakling.

The weakling smiled across the table at the wife with the soft eyes. "How about it, mother?" he asked. "Shall the firm of 'Bobby and I' offer him a job?"

"I would like it very much," said the weakling's wife, dropping her eyes to hide the pride in them.

"Suppose," said the weakling, "that you run up after dinner, Bob, and bring him down. Now sit still, young man, and finish. There's no such hurry as that."

And in this fashion did old Adelbert become ticket-chopper of the American Scenic Railway.

And in this fashion, too, commenced that odd friendship between him and the American lad that was to have so vital an effect on the very life itself of the Crown Prince Ferdinand William Otto of Livonia.

Late that evening, old Adelbert's problem having been solved, Pepy the maid and Bobby had a long talk. It concerned itself mainly with kings. Pepy sat in a low chair by the tiled stove in the kitchen, and knitted a stocking with a very large foot.

"What I want to know is this," said Bobby, swinging his legs on the table: "What are the Terrorists?"

Pepy dropping her knitting, and stared with open mouth. "What know you of such things?" she demanded.

"Well, Terrorists killed the Crown Prince's father, and —"

Quite suddenly Pepy leaped from her chair, and covered Bobby's mouth with her hand. "Hush!" she said, and stared about her with frightened eyes. The door into the dining-room was open, and the governess sat there with a book. Then, in a whisper: "They are everywhere. No one knows who they are, nor where they meet." The superstition of her mountains crept into her voice. "It is said that they have the assistance of the evil one, and that the reason the police cannot find them is because they take the form of cats. I myself," she went on impressively, "crossing the Place one night late, after spending the evening with a friend, saw a line of cats moving in the shadows. One of them stopped and looked at me." Pepy crossed herself. "It had a face like the Fraulein in there."

Bobby stared with interest through the doorway. The governess did look like a cat. She had staring eyes, and a short, wide face. "Maybe's she's one of them," he reflected aloud.

"Oh, for God's sake, hush!" cried Pepy, and fell to knitting rapidly. Nor could Bobby elicit anything further from her. But that night, in his sleep, he saw a Crown Prince, dressed in velvet and ermine, being surrounded and attacked by an army of cats, and went, shivering, to crawl into his mother's bed.

Chapter XIX
The Committee of Ten

On the evening of the annual day of mourning, the party returned from the fortress. The Archduchess slept. The Crown Prince talked, mostly to Hedwig, and even she said little. After a time the silence affected the boy's high spirits. He leaned back in his chair on the deck of the launch, and watched the flying landscape. He counted the riverside shrines to himself. There were, he discovered, just thirteen between the fortress and the city limits.

Old Father Gregory sat beside him. He had taken off his flat black hat, and it lay on his knee. The ends of his black woolen sash fluttered in the wind, and he sat, benevolent hands folded, looking out.

From guns to shrines is rather a jump, and the Crown Prince found it difficult.

"Do you consider fighting the duty of a Christian?" inquired the Crown Prince suddenly.

Father Gregory, whose mind had been far away, with his boys' school at Etzel, started.

"Fighting? That depends. To defend his home is the Christian duty of every man."

"But during the last war," persisted Otto, "we went across the mountains and killed a lot of people. Was that a Christian duty?"

Father Gregory coughed. He had himself tucked up his soutane and walked forty miles to join the army of invasion, where he had held services, cared for the wounded, and fired a rifle, all with equal spirit. He changed the subject to the big guns at the fortress.

"I think," observed the Crown Prince, forgetting his scruples, "that if you have a pencil and an old envelope to draw on, I'll invent a big gun myself."

Which he proceeded to do, putting in a great many wheels and levers, and adding, a folding-table at the side on which the gunners might have afternoon tea-this last prompted by the arrival just then of cups and saucers and a tea service.

It was almost dark when the launch arrived at the quay. The red carpet was still there, and another crowd. Had Prince Ferdinand William Otto been less taken up with finding one of his kid gloves, which he had lost, he would have noticed that there was a scuffle going on at the very edge of the red carpet, and that the beggar of the morning was being led away, between two policemen, while a third, running up the river bank, gingerly deposited a small round object in the water, and stood back. It was merely one of the small incidents of a royal outing, and was never published in the papers. But Father Gregory, whose old eyes were far-sighted, had seen it all. His hand-the hand of the Church-was on the shoulder of the Crown Prince as they landed.

The boy looked around for the little girl of the bouquet. He took an immense interest in little girls, partly because he seldom saw any. But she was gone.

When the motor which had taken them from the quay reached the Palace, Hedwig roused the Archduchess, whose head had dropped forward on her chest. "Here we are, mother," she said. "You have had a nice sleep."

But Annunciata muttered something about being glad the wretched day was over, and every one save Prince Ferdinand William Otto seemed glad to get back. The boy was depressed. He felt, somehow, that they should have enjoyed it, and that, having merely endured it, they had failed him again.

He kissed his aunt's hand dutifully when he left her, and went with a lagging step to his own apartments. His request to have Hedwig share his supper had met with a curt negative.

The Countess, having left her royal mistress in the hands of her maids, went also to her own apartment. She was not surprised, on looking into her mirror, to find herself haggard and worn. It had been a terrible day. Only a second had separated that gaping lens in her bag from the eyes of the officers about. Never, in an adventurous life, had she felt so near to death. Even now its cold breath chilled her.

However, that was over, well over. She had done well, too. A dozen pictures of the fortress, of its guns, of even its mine chart as it hung on a wall, were in the bag. Its secrets, so securely held, were hers, and would be Karl's.

It was a cunningly devised scheme. Two bags, exactly alike as to appearance, had been made. One, which she carried daily, was what it appeared to be. The other contained a camera, tiny but accurate, with a fine lens. When a knob of the fastening was pressed, the watch slid aside and the shutter snapped. The pictures when enlarged had proved themselves perfect.

Pleading fatigue, she dismissed her maid and locked the doors. Then she opened the sliding panel, and unfastened the safe. The roll of film was in her hand, ready to be deposited under the false bottom of her jewel-case.

Within the security of her room, the Countess felt at ease. The chill of the day left her, to be followed by a glow of achievement. She even sang a little, a bit of a ballad from her native mountains:

He has gone to the mountains, The far green mountains. (Hear the cattle lowing as they drive them up the hill!) When he comes down he'll love me; When he comes down he'll marry me. (But what is this that touches me with fingers dead and chill?)

Still singing, she carried the jewel-case to her table, and sat down before it. Then she put a hand to her throat.

The lock had been forced.

A glance about showed her that her code-book was gone. In the tray above, her jewels remained untouched; her pearl collar, the diamond knickknacks the Archduchess had given her on successive Christmases, even a handful of gold coins, all were safe enough. But the code-book was gone.

Then indeed did the Countess look death in the face and found it terrible. For a moment she could not so much as stand without support. It was then that she saw a paper folded under her jewels and took it out with shaking fingers. In fine, copperplate script she read:

> MADAME, —To-night at one o'clock a closed fiacre will await
> you in the Street of the Wise Virgins, near the church. You
> will go in it, without fail, to wherever it takes you.
> (Signed) THE COMMITTEE OF TEN

The Committee of Ten! This thing had happened to her. Then it was true that the half-mythical Committee of Ten existed, that this terror of Livonia was a real terror, which had her by the throat. For there was no escape. None. Now indeed she knew that rumor spoke the truth, and that the Terrorists were everywhere. In daylight they had entered her room. They had known of the safe, known of the code. Known how much else?

Wild ideas of flight crossed her mind, to be as instantly abandoned for their futility. Where could she go that they would not follow her? When she had reacted from her first shock she fell to pondering the matter, pro and con. What could they want of her? If she was an enemy to the country, so were they. But even that led nowhere, for after all, the Terrorists were not enemies to Livonia. They claimed indeed to be its friends, to hold in their hands its future and its betterment. Enemies of the royal house they were, of course.

She was nearly distracted by that time. She was a brave woman, physically and mentally of hard fiber, but the very name signed to the paper set her nerves to twitching. It was the Committee of Ten which had murdered Prince Hubert and his young wife; the Committee of Ten which had exploded a bomb in the very Palace itself, and killed old Breidau, of the King's Council; the Committee of Ten which had burned the Government House, and had led the mob in the student riots a year or so before.

Led them, themselves hidden. For none knew their identity. It was said that they did not even know each other, wearing masks and long cloaks at their meetings, and being designated by numbers only.

In this dread presence, then, she would find herself that night! For she would go. There was no way out.

She sent a request to be excused from dinner on the ground of illness, and was, as a result, visited by her royal mistress at nine o'clock. The honor was unexpected. Not often did the Archduchess Annunciata so favor any one. The Countess, lying across her bed in a perfect agony of apprehension, staggered into her sitting-room and knelt to kiss her lady's hand.

But the Archduchess, who had come to scoff, believing not at all in the illness, took one shrewd glance at her, and put her hands behind her.

"It may be, as you say, contagious, Olga," she said. "You would better go to bed and stay there. I shall send Doctor Wiederman to you."

When she had gone the Countess rang for her maid. She was cool enough now, and white, with a cruel line about her mouth that Minna knew well. She went to the door into the corridor, and locked it.

Then she turned on the maid. "I am ready for you, now."

"Madame will retire?"

"You little fool! You know what I am ready for!"

The maid stood still. Her wide, bovine eyes, filled with alarm, watched the Countess as she moved swiftly across the room to her wardrobe. When she turned about again, she held in her hand a thin black riding-crop. Minna's ruddy color faded. She knew the Loscheks, knew their furies. Strange stories of unbridled passion had oozed from the old ruined castle where for so long they had held feudal sway over the countryside.

"Madame!" she cried, and fell on her knees. "What have I done? Oh, what have I done?"

"That is what you will tell me," said the Countess, and brought down the crop. A livid stripe across the girl's face turned slowly to red.

"I have done nothing, I swear it. Mother of Pity, help me! I have done nothing."

The crop descended again, this time on one of the great sleeves of her peasant costume. So thin it was, so brutal the blow, that it cut into the muslin. Groaning, the girl fell forward on her face. The Countess continued to strike pitiless blows into which she put all her fury, her terror, her frayed and ragged nerves.

The girl on the floor, from whimpering, fell to crying hard, with great noiseless sobs of pain and bewilderment. When at last the blows ceased, she lay still.

The Countess prodded her with her foot. "Get up," she commanded.

But she was startled when she saw the girl's face. It was she who was the fool. The welt would tell its own story, and the other servants would talk. It was already a deep purple, and swollen. Both women were trembling. The Countess, still holding the crop, sat down.

"Now!" she said. "You will tell me to whom you gave a certain small book of which you know."

"I, madame?"

"You."

"But what book? I have given nothing, madame. I swear it."

"Then you admitted some one to this room?"

"No one, madame, except —" She hesitated.

"Well?"

"There came this afternoon the men who clean madame's windows. No one else, madame."

She put her hand to her cheek, and looked furtively to see if her fingers were stained with blood. The Countess, muttering, fell to furious pacing of the room. So that was it, of course. The girl was telling the truth. She was too stupid to lie. Then the Committee of Ten indeed knew everything-had known that she would be away, had known of the window cleaners, had known of the safe, and her possession of the code.

Cold and calculating rage filled her. Niburg had played her false, of course. But Niburg was only a go-between. He had known nothing of the codebook. He had given the Committee the letter, and by now they knew all that it told. What did it not know?

She dismissed the girl and put away the riding-crop, then she smoothed the disorder of her hair and dress. The court physician, calling a half hour later, found her reading on a chaise longue in her boudoir, looking pale and handsome; and spent what he considered a pleasant half-hour with her. He loved gossip, and there was plenty just now. Indications were that they would have a wedding soon. An unwilling bride, perhaps, eh? But a lovely one. For him, he was glad that Karnia was to be an ally, and not an enemy. He had seen enough of wars. And so on and on, while the Countess smiled and nodded, and shivered in her very heart.

At eleven o'clock he went away, kissing her hand rather more fervently than professionally, although his instinct to place his fingers over the pulse rather spoiled the effect. One thing, however, the Countess had gained by his visit. He was to urge on the Archduchess the necessity for an immediate vacation for her favorite.

"Our loss, Countess," he said, with heavy gallantry.. "But we cannot allow beauty to languish for need of mountain air."

Then at last he was gone, and she went about her heavy-hearted preparations for the night. From a corner of her wardrobe she drew a long peasant's cape, such a cape as Minna might wear. Over her head, instead of a hat, she threw a gray veil. A careless disguise, but all that was necessary. The sentries through and about the Palace were not unaccustomed to such shrouded figures slipping out from its gloom to light, and perhaps to love.

Before she left, she looked about the room. What assurance had she that this very excursion was not a trap, and that in her absence the vault would not he looted again? It contained now something infinitely valuable-valuable and incriminating-the roll of film. She glanced about, and seeing a silver vase of roses, hurriedly emptied the water out, wrapped the film in oiled paper, and dropped it down among the stems.

The Street of the Wise Virgins was not near the Palace. Even by walking briskly she was in danger of being late. The wind kept her back, too. The cloak twisted about her, the veil whipped. She turned once or twice to see if she were being followed, but the quiet streets were empty. Then, at last, the Street of the Wise Virgins and the fiacre, standing at the curb, with a driver wrapped in rugs against the cold of the February night, and his hat pulled down over his eyes. The Countess stopped beside him.

"You are expecting a passenger?"

"Yes, madame."

With her hand on the door, the Countess realized that the fiacre was already occupied. As she peered into its darkened interior, the shadow resolved itself into a cloaked and masked figure. She shrank back.

"Enter, madame," said a voice.

The figure appalled her. It was not sufficient to know that behind the horrifying mask which covered the entire face and head, there was a human figure, human pulses that beat, human eyes that appraised her. She hesitated.

"Quickly," said the voice.

She got in, shrinking into a corner of the carriage.

Her lips were dry, the roaring of terror was in her ears. The door closed.

Then commenced a drive of which afterward the Countess dared not think. The figure neither moved nor spoke. Inside the carriage reigned the most complete silence. The horse's feet clattered over rough stones, they turned through narrow, unfamiliar streets, so that she knew not even the direction they took. After a time the noise grew less. The horse padded along dirt roads, in darkness. Then the carriage stopped, and at last the shrouded figure moved and spoke.

"I regret, Countess, that my orders are to blindfold you."

She drew herself up haughtily.

"That is not necessary, I think."

"Very necessary, madame."

She submitted ungracefully, while he bound a black cloth over her eyes. He drew it very close and knotted it behind. In the act his fingers touched her face, and she felt them cold and clammy. The contact sickened her.

"Your hand, madame."

She was led out of the carriage, and across soft earth, a devious course again, as though they avoided small obstacles. Once her foot touched something low and hard, like marble. Again, in the darkness, they stumbled over a mound. She knew where she was, then-in a graveyard. But which? There were many about the city.

An open space, the opening of a gate or door that squealed softly, a flight of steps that led downward, and a breath of musty, cold air, damp and cellar-like.

She was calmer now. Had they meant to kill her, there had been already a hundred chances. It was not death, then, that awaited her-at least, not immediate death. These precautions, too, could only mean that she was to be freed again, and must not know where she had been.

At last, still in unbroken silence, she knew that they had entered a large space. Their footsteps no longer echoed and re-echoed. Her guide walked more slowly, and at last paused, releasing her hand. She felt again the touch of his clammy fingers as he untied the knots of her bandage. He took it off.

At first she could see little. The silence remained unbroken, and only the center of the room was lighted. When her eyes grew accustomed, she made out the scene slowly.

A great stone vault, its walls broken into crypts which had contained caskets of the dead. But the caskets had been removed; and were piled in a corner, and in the niches were rifles. In the center was a pine table, curiously incongruous, and on it writing materials, a cheap clock, and a pile of documents. There were two candles only, and these were stuck in skulls-old brown skulls so infinitely removed from all semblance to the human that they were not even horrible. It was as if they had been used, not to inspire terror, but because they were at hand and convenient for the purpose. In the shadow, ranged in a semicircle, were nine figures, all motionless, all masked, and cloaked in black. They sat, another incongruity, on plain wooden chairs. But in spite of that they were figures of dread. The one who had brought her made the tenth.

Still the silence, broken only by the drip of water from the ceiling into a tin pail.

Had she not known the past record of the men before her, the rather opera bouffe setting with which they chose to surround themselves might have aroused her scorn. But Olga Loschek knew too much. She guessed shrewdly that, with the class of men with whom they dealt, it was not enough that their name spelled terror. They must visualize it. They had taken their cue from that very church, indeed, beneath which they hid. The church, with its shrines and images, appealed to the eye. They, too, appealed to the eye. Their masks, the carefully constructed and upheld mystery of their identity, the trappings of death about them-it was skillfully done.

Not that she was thinking consecutively just then. It was a mental flash, even as her eyes, growing accustomed to the darkness made out the white numeral, from one to ten, on the front of each shroud-like cloak.

Still no one spoke. The Countess faced them.

Only her eyes showed her nervousness; she stood haughtily, her head held high. But like most women, she could not endure silence for long, at least the silence of shrouded figures and intent eyes.

"Now that I am here," she demanded, "may I ask why I have been summoned?"

It was Number Seven who replied. It was Number Seven who, during the hour that followed, spoke for the others. None moved, or but slightly. There was no putting together of heads, no consulting. Evidently all had been carefully prearranged.

"Look on the table, Countess. You will find there some papers you will perhaps recognize."

She took a step toward the table and glanced down. The code-book lay there. Also the letter she had sent by Peter Niburg. She made no effort to disclaim them.

"I recognize them," she said clearly.

"You acknowledge, then, that they are yours?"

"I acknowledge nothing."

"They bear certain indications, madame."

"Possibly."

"Do you realize what will happen, madame, if these papers are turned over to the authorities?"

She shrugged her shoulders. And now Number Seven rose, a tall figure of mystery, and spoke at length in a cultivated, softly intoned voice. The Countess, listening, felt the voice vaguely familiar, as were the burning eyes behind the mask.

"It is our hope, madame," he said, "that you will make it unnecessary for the Committee of Ten to use those papers. We have no quarrel with women. We wish rather a friend than an enemy. There be those, many of them, who call us poor patriots, who would tear down without building up. They are wrong. The Committee of Ten, to those who know its motives, has the highest and most loyal of ideals-to the country."

His voice took on a new, almost a fanatic note. He spoke as well to the other shrouded figures as to his comrades. No mean orator this. He seldom raised his voice, he made no gestures. Almost, while she listened, the Countess understood.

They had watched the gradual decay of the country, he said. Its burden of taxation grew greater each year. The masses sweated and toiled, to carry on their backs the dead weight of the aristocracy and the throne. The iron hand of the Chancellor held everything; an old King who would die, was dying now, and after that a boy, nominal ruler only, while the Chancellor continued his hard rule. And now, as if that were not enough, there was talk of an alliance with Karnia, an alliance which, carried through, would destroy the hope of a republic.

The Countess stared.

"No wall is too thick for our ears," he continued. "Our eyes see everywhere. And as we grow in strength, they fear us. Well they may."

He grew scornful then. To gain support for the tottering throne the Chancellor would unite the two countries, that Karl's army, since he could not trust his own, might be called on for help. And here he touched the Countess's raw nerves with a brutal finger.

"The price of the alliance, madame, is the Princess Hedwig in marriage. The Committee, which knows all things, believes that you have reason to dislike this marriage."

Save that she clutched her cloak more closely, the Countess made no move. But there was a soft stir among the figures. Perhaps, after all, the Committee as a whole did not know all things.

"To prevent this alliance, madame, is our first aim. There are others to follow. But" —he bent forward —"the King will not live many days. It is our hope that that marriage will not occur before his death."

By this time Olga Loschek knew very well where she stood. The Committee was propitiatory. She was not in danger, save as it might develop. They were, in a measure, putting their case.

She had followed the speaker closely. When he paused, she was ready for him. "But, even without a marriage, at any time now a treaty based on the marriage may be signed. A treaty for a mutually defensive alliance. Austria encroaches daily, and has Germany behind her. We are small fry, here and in Karnia, and we stand in the way."

"King Karl has broken faith before. He will not support Livonia until he has received his price. He is determined on the marriage."

"A marriage of expediency," said the Countess, impatiently.

The speaker for the Committee shrugged his shoulders. "Perhaps," he replied. "Although there are those of us who think that in this matter of expediency, Karl gives more than he receives. He is to-day better prepared than we are for war. He is more prosperous. As to the treaty, it is probably already signed, or about to be. And here, madame, is the reason for our invitation to you to come here.

"I have no access to state papers," the Countess said impatiently.

"You are too modest," said Number Seven suavely, and glanced at the letter on the table.

"The matter lies thus, madame. The Chancellor is now in Karnia. Doubtless he will return with the agreement signed. We shall learn that in a day or so. We do not approve of this alliance for various reasons, and we intend to take steps to prevent it. The paper itself is nothing. But plainly, Countess, the need a friend in the Palace, one who is in the confidence of the royal family."

"And for such friendship, I am to secure safety?"

"Yes, madame. But that is not all. Let me tell you briefly how things stand with us. We have, supporting us, certain bodies, workingmen's guilds, a part of the student body, not so much of the army as we would wish. Dissatisfied folk, madame, who would exchange the emblem of tyranny for freedom. On the announcement of the King's death, in every part of the kingdom will go up the cry of liberty. But the movement must start here. The city must rise against the throne. And against that there are two obstacles." He paused. The clock ticked, and water dripped into the tin pail with metallic splashes. "The first is this marriage. The second-is the Crown Prince Ferdinand William Otto."

The Countess recoiled. "No!"

"A moment, madame. You think badly of us." Under his mask the Countess divined a cold smile. "It is not necessary to contemplate violence. There are other methods. The boy could be taken over the border, and hidden until the Republic is firmly established. After that, he is unimportant."

The Countess, still pale, looked at him scornfully. "You do my intelligence small honor."

"Where peaceful methods will avail, our methods are peaceful, madame."

"It was, then, in peace that you murdered Prince Hubert?"

"The errors of the past are past." Then, with a new sternness: "Make no mistake. Whether through your agency or another, Countess, when the Cathedral bell rouses the city to the King's death, and the people wait in the Place for their new King to come out on the balcony, he will not come."

The Countess was not entirely bad. Standing swaying and white-faced before the tribunal, she saw suddenly the golden head of the little Crown Prince, saw him smiling as he had smiled that day in the sunlight, saw him troubled and forlorn as he had been when, that very evening, he had left them to go to his lonely rooms. Perhaps she reached the biggest moment of her life then, when she folded her arms and stared proudly at the shrouded figures before her.

"I will not do it," she said.

Then indeed the tribunal stirred, and sat forward. Perhaps never before had it been defied.

"I will not," repeated the Countess.

But Number Seven remained impassive. "A new idea, Countess!" he said suavely. "I can understand that your heart recoils. But this thing is inevitable, as I have said. Whether you or another but perhaps with time to think you may come to another conclusion. We make no threats. Our position is, however, one of responsibility. We are compelled to place the future of the Republic before every other consideration."

"That is a threat."

"We remember both our friends and our enemies, madame. And we have only friends and enemies. There is no middle course. If you would like time to think it over —"

"How much time?" She clutched at the words.

With time all things were possible. The King might die soon, that night, the next day. Better than any one, save his daughter Annunciata and the physicians, she knew his condition.

The Revolutionists might boast, but they were not all the people. Once let the boy be crowned, and it would take more than these posing plotters in their theatrical setting to overthrow him.

"How much time may I have?"

"Women vary," said Number Seven mockingly. "Some determine quickly. Others —"

"May I have a month?"

"During which the King may die! Alas, madame, it is now you who do us too little honor!"

"A week?" begged the Countess desperately.

The leader glanced along the line. One head after another nodded slowly.

"A week it is, madame. Comrade Five!"

The one who had brought her came forward with the bandage.

"At the end of one week, madame, a fiacre will, as to-night, be waiting in the Street of the Wise Virgins."

"And these papers?"

"On the day the Republic of Livonia is established, madame, they will be returned to you."

He bowed, and returned to his chair. Save for the movements of the man who placed the bandage over her eyes; there was absolute silence in the room.

Chapter XX
The Delegation

Prince Ferdinand William Otto was supremely happy. Three quite delightful things had happened. First, Nikky had returned. He said he felt perfectly well, but the Crown Prince thought he looked as though he had been ill, and glanced frequently at Nikky's cigarette during the riding-hour. Second, Hedwig did not come to the riding-lesson, and he had Nikky to himself. Third, he, Prince Ferdinand William Otto, was on the eve of a birthday.

This last, however, was not unmixed happiness. For the one day the sentence of exile was to be removed so that he might lunch with the King, and he was to have strawberry jam with his tea, some that Miss Braithwaite's sister had sent from England. But to offset all this, he was to receive a delegation of citizens.

He had been well drilled for it. As a matter of fact, on the morning of Nikky's return, they took a few minutes to go over the ceremony, Nikky being the delegation. The way they did it was simple.

Nikky went out into the corridor, and became the Chamberlain. He stepped inside, bowed, and announced: "The delegation from the city, Highness," standing very stiff, and a trifle bow-legged, as the Chamberlain was. Then he bowed again, and waddled out-the Chamberlain was fat-and became the delegation.

This time he tried to look like a number of people, and was not so successful. But he looked nervous, as delegations always do when they visit a Royal Highness. He bowed inside the door, and then came forward and bowed again.

"I am, of course, standing in a row," said Nikky, sotto voce. "Now, what comes next?"

"I am to shake hands with every one."

So they shook hands nine times, because there were to be nine members of the delegation. And Nikky picked up a brass inkwell from the desk and held it out before him.

"Your Highness," he said, after clearing his throat, for all the world as Prince Ferdinand William Otto had heard it done frequently at cornerstones and openings of hospitals, "Your Highness-we are here to-day to felicitate Your Highness on reaching the mature age of ten. In testimonial of our-our affection and-er loyalty, we bring to you a casket of gold, containing the congratulations of the city, which we beg that Your Highness may see fit to accept. It will be of no earthly use to you, and will have to be stuck away in a vault and locked up. But it is the custom on these occasions, and far be it from us to give you a decent present that you can use or enjoy!"

Prince Ferdinand William Otto had to cover his mouth with his hand to preserve the necessary dignity. He stepped forward and took the ink-well. "I thank you very much. Please give my thanks to all the people. I am very grateful. It is beautiful. Thank you."

Whereupon he placed the ink-well on the desk, and he and Nikky again shook hands nine times, counting, to be sure it was right. Then Nikky backed to the door, getting all tangled up in his sword, bowed again and retired.

When he reentered, the boy's face was glowing.

"Gee!" he said, remembering this favorite word of the American boy's. "It's splendid to have you back again, Nikky. You're going to stay now, aren't you?"

"I am." Nikky's voice was fervent.

"Where did you go when you went away?"

"I took a short and foolish excursion, Highness. You see, while I look grown-up I dare say I am really not. Not quite, anyhow. And now and then, like other small boys I have heard of, I—well, I run away. And am sorry afterward, of course."

Miss Braithwaite was not in the study. The Prince looked about, and drew close-to Nikky. "Did you, really?"

"I did. Some day, when you are older, I'll tell you about it. I—has the Princess Hedwig been having tea with you, as usual?"

Carelessly spoken as it was, there was a change in Nikky's voice. And the Crown Prince was sensitive to voices. Something similar happened to Monsieur Puaux, the French tutor, when he mentioned Hedwig.

"Not yesterday. We went to the fortress. Nikky, what is it to be in love?"

Nikky looked startled, "Well," he said reflectively, "it's to like some one, a lady in your case or mine, of course; to-to like them very much, and want to see them often."

"Is that all?"

"It's enough, sometimes. But it's more than that. It's being dreadfully unhappy if the other person isn't around, for one thing. It isn't really a rational condition. People in love do mad things quite often."

"I know some one who is in love with Hedwig."

Nikky looked extremely conscious. There was, too, something the Crown Prince was too small to see, something bitter and hard in his eyes. "Probably a great many are," he said. "But I'm not sure she would care to have us discuss it."

"It is my French tutor."

Nikky laughed suddenly, and flung the boy to his shoulder. "Of course he is!" he cried gayly. "And you are, and the Chancellor. And I am, of course." He stood the boy on the desk.

"Do you think she is in love, with you?" demanded the Crown Prince, very seriously.

"Not a bit of it, young man!"

"But I think she is," he persisted. "She's always around when you are."

"Not this morning."

"But she is, when she can be. She never used to take riding-lessons. She doesn't need them." This was a grievance, but he passed it over. "And she always asks where you are. And yesterday, when you were away, she looked very sad."

Nikky stood with his hand on the boy's shoulder, and stared out through the window. If it were so, if this child, with his uncanny sensitiveness, had hit on the truth! If Hedwig felt even a fraction of what he felt, what a tragedy it all was!

He forced himself to smile, however. "If she only likes me just a little," he said lightly, "it is more than I dare to hope, or deserve. Come, now, we have spent too much time over love and delegations. Suppose we go and ride."

But on the way across the Place Prince Ferdinand William Otto resumed the subject for a moment. "If you would marry Hedwig," he suggested, an anxious thrill in his voice, "you would live at the Palace always, wouldn't you? And never have to go back to your regiment?" For the bugaboo of losing Nikky to his regiment was always in the back of his small head.

"Now, listen, Otto, and remember," said Nikky, almost sternly. "It may be difficult for you to understand now, but some day you will. The granddaughter of the King must marry some one of her own rank. No matter how hard you and I may wish things to be different, we cannot change that. And it would be much better never to mention this conversation to your cousin. Girls," said Nikky, "are peculiar."

"Very well," said the Crown Prince humbly. But he made careful note of one thing. He was not to talk of this plan to Hedwig, but there was no other restriction. He could, for instance, take it up with the Chancellor, or even with the King to-morrow, if he was in an approachable humor.

Hedwig was not at the riding-school. This relieved Prince Ferdinand William Otto, whose views as to Nikky were entirely selfish, but Nikky himself had unaccountably lost his high spirits of the morning. He played, of course, as he always did. And even taught the Crown Prince how to hang over the edge of his saddle, while his horse was cantering, so that bullets would not strike him.

They rode and frolicked, yelled a bit, got two ponies and whacked a polo ball over the tan-bark, until the Crown Prince was sweating royally and was gloriously flushed.

"I don't know when I have been so happy," he said, dragging out his handkerchief and mopping his face. "It's a great deal pleasanter without Hedwig, isn't it?"

While they played, overhead the great hearse was ready at last. Its woodwork shone. Its gold crosses gleamed. No fleck of dust disturbed its austere magnificence.

The man and the boy who had been working on it stood back and surveyed it.

"All ready," said the man, leaning on the handle of his long brush. "Now it may happen any time."

"It is very handsome. But I am glad I am not the old King." The boy picked up pails and brushes. "Nothing to look forward to but-that."

"But much to look back on," the man observed grimly, "and little that is good."

The boy glanced through a window, below which the riding-ring stretched its brown surface, scarred by nervous hoofs. "I would change places with the Crown Prince," he said enviously. "Listen to him! Always laughing. Never to labor, nor worry, nor think of the next day's food —"

"Young fool!" The man came to his shoulder and glanced down also. "Would like to be a princeling, then! No worry. No trouble. Always play, play!" He gripped the boy's shoulder. "Look, lad, at the windows about. That is what it is to be a prince. Wherever you look, what do you see? Stablemen? Grooms? Bah, secret agents, watching that no assassin, such perhaps as you and I, lurk about."

The boy opened wide, incredulous eyes. "But who would attack a child?" he asked.

"There be those, nevertheless," said the man mockingly. "Even a child may stand in the way of great changes."

He stopped and stared, wiping the glass clear that he might see better. Nikky without his cap, disheveled and flushed with exertion, was making a frantic shot at the white ball, rolling past him. Where had he seen such a head, such a flying mop of hair? Ah! He remembered. It was the flying young devil who had attacked him and the others that night in the by-street, when Peter Niburg lay stunned!

Miss Braithwaite had a bad headache that afternoon, and the Crown Prince drove out with his aunt. The Archduchess Annunciata went shopping. Soon enough she would have Hedwig's trousseau on her mind, so that day she bought for Hilda-Hilda whose long legs had a way of growing out of skirts, and who was developing a taste of her own in clothes.

So Hilda and her mother shopped endlessly, and the Crown Prince sat in the carriage and watched the people. The man beside the coachman sat with alert eyes, and there were others who scanned the crowd intently. But it was a quiet, almost an adoring crowd, and there was even a dog, to Prince Ferdinand William Otto's huge delight.

The man who owned the dog, seeing the child's eyes on him, put him through his tricks. Truly a wonderful dog, that would catch things on its nose and lie dead, rousing only to a whistle which its owner called Gabriel's trumpet.

Prince Ferdinand William Otto, growing excited, leaned quite out of the window. "What is your dog's name?" he inquired, in his clear treble.

The man took off his hat and bowed. "Toto, Highness. He is of French origin."

"He is a very nice dog. I have always wanted a dog like that. He must be a great friend."

"A great friend, Highness." He would have expatiated on the dog, but he was uncertain of the etiquette of the procedure. His face beamed with pleasure, however. Then a splendid impulse came to him. This dog, his boon companion, he would present to the Crown Prince. It was all he had, and he would give it, freely, even though it left him friendless.

But here again he was at a loss. Was it the proper thing? Did one do such things in this fashion, or was there a procedure? He cocked an eye at the box of the carriage, but the two men sat impressive, immobile.

Finally he made up his mind. Hat in hand, he stepped forward. "Highness," he said nervously, "since the dog pleases you, I —I would present him to you."

"To me?" The Crown Prince's voice was full of incredulous joy.

"Yes, Highness. If such a thing be permissible."

"Are you sure you don't mind?"

"He is the best I have, Highness. I wish to offer my best."

Prince, Ferdinand William Otto almost choked with excitement. "I have always wanted one," he cried. "If you are certain you can spare him, I'll be very good to him. No one," he said, "ever gave me a dog before. I'd like to have him now, if I may."

The crowd was growing. It pressed closer, pleased at the boy's delight. Truly they were participating in great things. A small cheer and many smiles followed the lifting of the dog through the open window of the carriage. And the dog was surely a dog to be proud of. Already it shook hands with the Crown Prince.

Perhaps, in that motley gathering, there were some who viewed the scene with hostile eyes, some who saw, not a child glowing with delight over a gift, but one of the hated ruling family, a barrier, an obstacle in the way of freedom. But if such there were, they were few. It was, indeed, as the Terrorists feared. The city loved the boy.

Annunciata, followed by an irritated Hilda, came out of the shop. Hilda's wardrobe had been purchased, and was not to her taste.

The crowd opened, hats were doffed, backs bent. The Archduchess moved haughtily, looking neither to the right nor left. Her coming brought no enthusiasm. Perhaps the curious imagination of the mob found her disappointing. She did not look like an Archduchess. She looked, indeed, like an unnamiable spinster of the middle class. Hilda, too, was shy and shrinking, and wore an unbecoming hat. Of the three, only the Crown Prince looked royal and as he should have looked.

"Good Heavens," cried the Archduchess, and stared into the carriage. "Otto!"

"He is mine," said the Crown Prince fondly. "He is the cleverest dog. He can do all sorts of things."

"Put him out."

"But he is mine," protested Ferdinand William Otto. "He is a gift. That gentleman there, in the corduroy jacket —"

"Put him out," said the Archduchess Annunciata.

There was nothing else to do. The Crown Prince did not cry. He was much too proud. He thanked the donor again carefully, and regretted that he could not accept the dog. He said it was a wonderful dog, and just the sort he liked. And the carriage drove away.

He went back to the Palace, and finding that the governess still had a headache, settled down to the burnt-wood frame. Once he glanced up at the woolen dog on its shelf at the top of the cabinet. "Well, anyhow," he said sturdily, "I still have you."

Chapter XXI
As a Man May Love a Woman

Hedwig came to tea that afternoon. She came in softly, and defiantly, for she was doing a forbidden thing, but Prince Ferdinand William Otto had put away the frame against such a contingency. He had, as a matter of fact, been putting cold cloths on Miss Braithwaite's forehead.

"I always do it," he informed Hedwig. "I like doing it. It gives me something to do. She likes them rather dry, so the water doesn't run down her neck."

Hedwig made a short call on the governess, prostrate on the couch in her sitting-room. The informality of the family relationship had, during her long service, been extended to include the Englishwoman, who in her turn found nothing incongruous in the small and kindly services of the little Prince. So Hedwig sat beside her for a moment, and turned the cold bandage over to freshen it.

Had Miss Braithwaite not been ill, Hedwig would have talked things over with her then. There was no one else to whom she could go. Hilda refused to consider the prospect of marriage as anything but pleasurable, and between her mother and Hedwig there had never been any close relationship.

But Miss Braithwaite lay motionless, her face set in lines of suffering, and after a time Hedwig rose and tiptoed out of the room.

Prince Ferdinand William Otto was excited. Tea had already come, and on the rare occasions when the governess was ill, it was his privilege to pour the tea.

"Nikky is coming," he said rapidly, "and the three of us will have a party. Please don't tell me how you like your tea, and see if I can remember."

"Very well, dear," Hedwig said gently, and went to the window.

Behind her Prince Ferdinand William Otto was in a bustle of preparation. Tea in the study was an informal function, served in the English manner, without servants to bother. The Crown Prince drew up a chair before the tea service, and put a cushion on it. He made a final excursion to Miss Braithwaite and, returning, climbed on to his chair.

"Now, when Nikky comes, we are all ready," he observed.

Nikky entered almost immediately.

As a matter of fact, although he showed no trace of it, Nikky had been having an extremely bad time since his return; the Chancellor, who may or may not have known that his heart was breaking, had given him a very severe scolding on the way back from Wedeling. It did Nikky good, too, for it roused him to his own defense, and made him forget, for a few minutes anyhow, that life was over for him, and that the Chancellor carried his death sentence in his old leather dispatch case.

After that, arriving in the capital, they had driven to the little office in a back street, and there Nikky had roused himself again enough to give a description of Peter Niburg, and to give the location of the house where he lived. But he slumped again after that, ate no dinner, and spent a longish time in the Place, staring up at Annunciata's windows, where he had once seen Hedwig on the balcony.

But of course Hedwig had not learned of his return, and was sitting inside, exactly as despairing as he was, but obliged to converse with her mother in the absence of the Countess. The Archduchess insisted on talking French, for practice, and they got into quite a wrangle over a verb. And as if to add to the general depression, Hilda had been reminded of what anniversary it was, and was told to play hymns only. True, now and then, hearing her mother occupied, she played them in dotted time, which was a bit more cheerful.

Then, late in the evening, Nikky was summoned to the King's bedroom, and came out pale, with his shoulders very square. He had received a real wigging this time, and even contemplated throwing himself in the river. Only he could swim so damnably well!

But he had the natural elasticity of youth, and a sort of persistent belief in his own luck, rather like the Chancellor's confidence in seven as a number—a confidence, by the way, which the Countess could easily have shaken. So he had wakened the next morning rather cheerful than otherwise, and over a breakfast of broiled ham had refused to look ahead farther than the day.

That afternoon, in the study, Nikky hesitated when he saw Hedwig. Then he came and bent low over her hand. And Hedwig, because every instinct yearned to touch his shining, bent head, spoke to him very calmly, was rather distant, a little cold.

"You have been away, I think?" she said.

"For a day or two, Highness."

The Crown Prince put a small napkin around the handle of the silver teapot. He knew from experience that it was very hot. His face was quite screwed up with exertion.

"And to-day," said Nikky reproachfully, "to-day you did not ride."

"I did not feel like riding," Hedwig responded listlessly. "I am tired. I think I am always tired."

"Lemon and two lumps," muttered the Crown Prince. "That's Nikky's, Hedwig. Give it to him, please."

Nikky went a trifle pale as their fingers touched. But he tasted his tea, and pronounced it excellent.

Prince Ferdinand William Otto chattered excitedly. He told of the dog, dilating on its cleverness, but passing politely over the manner of its return. Now and then Hedwig glanced at Nikky, when he was not looking, and always, when they dared, the young soldier's eyes were on her.

"She will take some tea without sugar," announced the Crown Prince.

While he poured it, Hedwig was thinking. Was it possible that Nikky, of every one, should have been chosen to carry to Karl the marriage arrangements? What an irony! What a jest! It was true there was a change in him. He looked subdued, almost sad.

"To Karnia?" she asked, when Prince Ferdinand William Otto had again left the room. "Officially?"

"Not-exactly."

"Where, in Karnia?"

"I ended," Nikky confessed, "at Wedeling."

Hedwig gazed at him, her elbows propped on the tea-table. "Then," she said, "I think you know."

"I know, Highness."

"And you have nothing to say?"

Nikky looked at her with desperate eyes. "What can I say, Highness? Only that-it is very terrible to me-that I—" He rose abruptly and stood looking down at her.

"That you—" said Hedwig softly.

"Highness," Nikky began huskily, "you know what I would say. And that I cannot. To take advantage of Otto's fancy for me, a child's liking, to violate the confidence of those who placed me here—I am doing that, every moment."

"What about me?" Hedwig asked. "Do I count for nothing? Does it not matter at all how I feel, whether I am happy or wretched? Isn't that as important as honor?"

Nikky flung out his hands. "You know," he said rapidly. "What can I tell you that you do not know a thousand times? I love you. Not as a subject may adore his princess, but as a man loves a woman."

"I too!" said Hedwig. And held out her hands.

But he did not take them. Almost it was as though he would protect her from herself. But he closed his eyes for a moment, that he might not see that appealing gesture. "I, who love you more than life, who would, God help me, forfeit eternity for you —I dare not take you in my arms."

Hedwig's arms fell. She drew herself up. "Love!" she said. "I do not call that love."

"It is greater love than you know," said poor Nikky. But all his courage died a moment later, and his resolution with it, for without warning Hedwig dropped her head on her hands and, crouching forlornly, fell to sobbing.

"I counted on you," she said wildly. "And you are like the others. No one cares how wretched I am. I wish I might die."

Then indeed Nikky was lost. In an instant he was on his knees beside her, his arms close about her, his head bowed against her breast. And Hedwig relaxed to his embrace. When at last he turned and looked up at her, it was Hedwig who bent and kissed him.

"At least," she whispered, "we have had this, We can always remember, whatever comes, that we have had this."

But Nikky was of very human stuff, and not the sort that may live by memories. He was very haggard when he rose to his feet-haggard, and his mouth was doggedly set. "I will never give you up, now," he said.

Brave words, of course. But as he said them he realized their futility. The eyes he turned on her were, as he claimed her, without hope. For there was no escape. He had given his word to stay near the Crown Prince, always to watch him, to guard him with his life, if necessary. And he had promised, at least, not to block the plans for the new alliance.

Hedwig, with shining eyes, was already planning.

"We will go away, Nikky," she said. "And it, must be soon, because otherwise —"

Nikky dared not touch her again, knowing what he had to say. "Dearest," he said, bending toward her, "that is what we cannot do."

"No?" She looked up, puzzled, but still confident dent. "And why, cowardly one?"

"Because I have given my word to remain with the Crown Prince." Then, seeing that she still did not comprehend, he explained, swiftly. After all, she had a right to know, and he was desperately anxious that she should understand. He stood, as many a man has stood before, between love and loyalty to his king, and he was a soldier. He had no choice.

It was terrible to him to see the light die out of her eyes. But even as he told her of the dangers that compassed the child and possibly others of the family, he saw that they touched her remotely, if at all. What she saw, and what he saw, through her eyes, was not riot and anarchy, a threatened throne, death itself. She saw only a vista of dreadful years, herself their victim. She saw her mother's bitter past. She saw the austere face of her grandmother, hiding behind that mask her disappointments.

But all she said, when Nikky finished, was: "I might have known it. Of course they would get me, as they did the others." But a moment later she rose and threw out her arms. "How skillful they are! They knew about it. It is all a part of the plot. I do not believe there is danger. All my life I have heard them talk. That is all they do-talk and plan and plot, and do things in secret. They made you promise never to desert Otto, so that their arrangements need not be interfered with. Oh, I know them, better than you do. They are all cruel. It is the blood."

What Nikky would have said to this was lost by the return of Prince Ferdinand William Otto. He came in, carrying the empty cup carefully. "She took it all," he said, "and she feels much better. I hope you didn't eat all the bread and butter."

Reassured as to this by a glance, he climbed to his chair. "We're all very happy, aren't we?" he observed. "It's quite a party. When I grow up I shall ask you both to tea every day."

That evening the Princess Hedwig went unannounced to her grandfather's apartment, and demanded to be allowed to enter.

A gentleman-in-waiting bowed deeply, but stood before the door. "Your Highness must pardon my reminding Your Highness," he said firmly, "that no one may enter His Majesty's presence without permission."

"Then go in," said Hedwig, in a white rage, "and get the permission."

The gentleman-in-waiting went in, very deliberately, because his dignity was outraged. The moment he had gone, however, Hedwig flung the door open, and followed, standing, a figure of tragic defiance, inside the heavy curtains of the King's bedroom.

"There is no use saying you won't see me, grandfather. For here I am."

They eyed each other, the one, it must be told, a trifle uneasily, the other desperately. Then into the King's eyes came a flash of admiration, and just a gleam of amusement.

"So I perceive," he said. "Come here, Hedwig."

The gentleman-in-waiting bowed himself out. His hands, in their tidy white gloves, would have liked to box Hedwig's ears. He was very upset. If this sort of thing went on, why not a republic at once and be done with it?

A Sister of Charity was standing by the King's bed. She had cared for him through many illnesses. In the intervals she retired to her cloister and read holy books and sewed for the poor. Even now, in her little chamber off the bedroom, where bottles sat in neat rows, covered with fresh towels, there lay a small gray flannel petticoat to warm the legs of one of the poor.

The sister went out, her black habit dragging, but she did not sew. She was reading a book on the miracles accomplished by pilgrimages to the shrine of Our Lady of the Angels, in the mountains. Could the old King but go there, she felt, he would be cured. Or failing that, if there should go for him some emissary, pure in heart and of high purpose, it might avail. Over this little book she prayed for courage to make the suggestion. Had she thought of it sooner, she would have spoken to Father Gregory. But the old priest had gone back to his people, to his boys' school, to his thousand duties in the hills.

Sometime later she heard bitter crying in the royal bedchamber, and the King's tones, soothing now and very sad.

"There is a higher duty than happiness," he said. "There are greater things than love. And one day you will know this."

When she went in Hedwig had gone, and the old King, lying in his bed, was looking at the portrait a his dead son.

Chapter XXII
At Etzel

The following morning the Countess Loschek left for a holiday. Minna, silent and wretched, had packed her things for her, moving about the room like a broken thing. And the Countess had sat in a chair by a window, and said nothing. She sent away food untasted, took no notice of the packing, and stared, hour after hour, ahead of her.

Certain things were clear enough. Karl could not now be reached by the old methods. She had, casting caution to the winds, visited the shop where Peter Niburg was employed. But he was not there, and the proprietor, bowing deeply, disclaimed all knowledge of his whereabouts. She would have to go to Karl herself, a difficult matter now. She would surely be watched. And the thousand desperate plans that she thought of for escaping from the country and hiding herself, —in America, perhaps, —those were impossible for the same reason. She was helpless.

She had the choice of but two alternatives, to do as she had been commanded, for it amounted to that, or to die. The Committee would not kill her, in case she failed them. It would be unnecessary. Enough that they place the letter and the code in the hands of the authorities, by some anonymous means. Well enough she knew the Chancellor's inflexible anger, and the Archduchess Annunciata's cold rage. They would sweep her away with a gesture, and she would die the death of all traitors.

A week! Time had been when a week of the dragging days at the Palace had seemed eternity. Now the hours flew. The gold clock on her dressing-table, a gift from the Archduchess, marked them with flying hands.

She was, for the first time, cut off from the gossip of the Palace. The Archduchess let her severely alone. She disliked having anything interfere with her own comfort, disliked having her routine disturbed. But the Countess surmised a great deal. She guessed that Hedwig would defy them, and that they would break her spirit with high words. She surmised preparations for a hasty marriage-how hasty she dared not think. And she guessed, too, the hopeless predicament of Nikky Larisch.

She sat and stared ahead.

During the afternoon came a package, rather unskillfully tied with a gilt cord. Opening it, the Countess disclosed a glove-box of wood, with a design of rather shaky violets burnt into the cover. Inside was a note:

> I am very sorry you are sick. This is to put your gloves in when you travel. Please excuse the work. I have done it in a hurry.
> FERDINAND WILLIAM OTTO.

Suddenly the Countess laughed, choking hysterical laughter that alarmed Minna; horrible laughter, which left her paler than ever, and gasping.

The old castle of the Loscheks looked grim and inhospitable when she reached it that, night. Built during the years when the unbeliever overran southern Europe, it stood in a commanding position over a valley, and a steep, walled road led up to it. The narrow windows of its turrets were built, in defiance of the Moslem hordes, in the shape of the cross. Its walls had been hospitable enough, however, when the crusaders had thronged by to redeem the Holy Sepulcher from the grasp of the infidel. Here, in its stone hall, they had slept in weary rows on the floor. From its battlements they had stared south and east along the road their feet must follow.

But now, its ancient glory and good repute departed, its garrison gone, its drawbridge and moat things of the past, its very hangings and furnishings mouldering from long neglect, it hung over the valley, a past menace, an empty threat.

To this dreary refuge the Countess had fled. She wanted the silence of its still rooms in which to think. Wretched herself, its wretchedness called her. As the carriage which had brought her from, the railway turned into its woods; and she breathed the pungent odor of pine and balsam, she relaxed for the first time.

Why was she so hopeless? She could escape.

She knew the woods well. None who followed her could know them so well. She would get away, and somewhere, in a new world, make a fresh start. Surely, after all, peace was the greatest thing in the world.

Peace! The word attracted her. There were religious houses where one would be safe enough, refuges high-walled and secure, into which no alien foot ever penetrated. And, as if to answer the thought, she saw at that moment across the valley the lights of Etzel, the tower of the church, with its thirteen bells, the monastery buildings behind it, and set at its feet, like pilgrims come to pray, the low houses of the peasants. For the church at Etzel contained a celebrated shrine, none other than that of Our Lady of the Angels, and here came, from all over the kingdom, long lines of footsore and weary pilgrims, seeking peace and sanctity, and some a miracle.

The carriage drove on; Minna, on the box, crossed herself at sight of the church, and chatted with the driver, a great figure who crowded her to the very edge of the seat.

"I am glad to be here," she said. "I am sick of grandeur. My home is in Etzel." She turned and inspected the man beside her. "You are a newcomer, I think?"

"I have but just come to Etzel."

"Then you cannot tell me about my people." She was disappointed.

"And you," inquired the driver, —"you will stay for a visit?"

"A week only. But better than nothing."

"After that, you return to the city?"

"Yes. Madame the Countess-you would know, if you were Etzel-born —Madame the Countess is lady-in-waiting to Her Royal Highness, the Archduchess Annunciata."

"So!" said the driver. But he was not curious, and the broken road demanded his attention. He was but newly come, so very newly that he did not know his way, and once made a wrong turning.

The Countess relaxed. She had not been followed. None but themselves had left the train. She was sure of that. And looking back, she satisfied herself that no stealthy foot-traveler dogged their slow progress. She breathed quietly, for the first time.

She slept that night. She had wired ahead of her coming, and the old caretaker and his wife had opened a few rooms, her boudoir and dressing-room, and a breakfast-room on the first floor. They had swept the hall too, and built a fire there, but it had been built for a great household, and its emptiness chilled her.

At four o'clock in the morning she roused at the ringing of a bell, telling that masses had already begun at the church. For with the approach of Lent pilgrimages had greatly increased in numbers. But she slept again, to waken to full sunlight, greatly refreshed.

When she had breakfasted and dressed, she went out on a balcony, and looked down at the valley. It was late. Already the peasants of Etzel had gone out to their fields. Children played along its single streets. A few women on the steps of the church made rosaries of beads which they strung with deft fingers. A band of pilgrims struggled up the valley, the men carrying their coats, for the sun was warm, and the women holding their skirts from the dust.

As they neared the church, however, coats were donned. The procession took on order and dignity. The sight was a familiar one to the Countess. Her eyes dropped to the old wall below, where in the sunshine the caretaker was beating a rug. Close to him, in intimate and cautious conversation, was the driver of the night before. Glancing up, they saw her and at once separated.

Gone was peace, then. The Countess knew knew certainly. "Our eyes see everywhere." Eyes, indeed, eyes that even now the caretaker raised furtively from his rug.

Nevertheless, the Countess was minded to experiment, to be certain. For none is so suspicious, she knew, as one who fears suspicion. None so guilty as the guilty. During the forenoon she walked through the woods, going briskly, with vigorous, mountainbred feet. No crackle of underbrush disturbed her. Swift turnings revealed no lurking figures skulking behind the trunks of trees. But where an ancient stone bridge crossed a mountain stream, she came on the huge driver of the night before reflectively fishing.

He saluted her gravely, and the Countess paused and looked at him. "You have caught no fish, my friend?" she said.

"No, madame. But one plays about my hook."

She turned back. Eyes everywhere, and arms, great hairy arms. And feet that, for all their size, must step lightly!

Restlessness followed her. She was a virtual Prisoner, free only in name. And the vigilance of the Terrorists obsessed her. She found a day gone, and no plan made. She had come here to think, and consecutive thought was impossible. She went to vespers at the church, and sat huddled in a corner. She suspected every eye that turned on her in frank curiosity. When, during the "Salve Regina," the fathers, followed by their pupils, went slowly down the aisle, in reverent procession between rows of Pilgrims, she saw in their habits only a grim reminder of the black disguises of the Terrorists.

On the second day she made a desperate resolve, and characteristically put it into execution at once. She sent for the caretaker. When he came, uneasy, for the Loscheks were justly feared in the country side, and even the thing of which he knew gave him small courage, she lost no time in evasion.

"Go," she said; "and bring here your accomplice —"

"My accomplice, madame! I do not —"

"You heard me," she said.

He turned, half sullen, half terrified, and paused. "Which do you refer to, madame?"

She had seen only the one. Then there were others. Who could tell how many others?

"The one who drove here."

So he went, leaving her to desperate reflection. When he returned, it was to usher in the heavy figure of the spy.

"Which of you is in authority?" she demanded.

"I, madame." It was the spy who spoke.

She dismissed the caretaker with a gesture.

"Have you any discretion over me? Or must you refer matters to those who sent you?"

"I must refer to them."

"How long will it take to send a message and receive a reply?"

He considered. "Until to-morrow night, madame."

Another day gone, then, and nothing determined!

"Now, listen," she said, "and listen carefully. I have come here to decide a certain question. Whether you know what that question is or not, does not matter. But before I decide it I must take a certain journey. I wish to make that journey. It is into Karnia."

She watched him. "It is impossible. My instructions —"

"I am not asking your permission. I wish to send a letter to the Committee. They, and they alone, will determine this thing. Will you send the letter?"

When he hesitated, perplexed, she got up and moved to her writing-table.

"I shall write the letter," she said haughtily. "See that it is sent. When I report at the end of the time that I have sent such a letter, you can judge better than I the result if it has not been received."

He was still dubious, but she wrote the letter and gave it to him, her face proud and scornful. But she was not easy, for all that, and she watched from her balcony to see if any messenger left the castle and descended the mountain road. She was rewarded, an hour later, by seeing a figure leave the old gateway and start afoot toward the village, a pale-faced man with colorless hair. A part of the hidden guard that surrounded her, she knew, and somehow familiar. But, although she racked her brains, she could not remember where she had seen him.

For the next twenty-four hours she waited. Life became one long endurance. She hated the forest, since she might not visit it alone. She hated the castle, because it was her prison. She stood for hours that first day on her balcony, surveying with scornful eyes the procession of the devout, weary women, perspiring men, lines of children going to something they did not comprehend, and carrying clenched in small, warm hands drooping bunches of early mountain flowers.

And always, calling her to something she scorned, rang the bells for mass or for vespers. The very tower below beckoned her to peace-her, for whom there would never again be peace. She cursed the bell savagely, put her fingers in her ears, to be wakened at dawn the next morning to its insistent call.

There was no more sleep for her. She lay there in her bare room and gave herself to bitter reflection. Here, in this very castle, she had met Karl. That was eleven years before. Prince Hubert was living. During a period of peace between the two countries a truce had been arranged, treaties signed, with every prospect of permanence. During that time Karl and Hubert, glad of peace, had come here for the hunting. She remembered the stir about their coming, her father's hurried efforts to get things in order, the cleaning and refurbishing, the peasants called in to serve the royal guests, and stripped of their quaint costumes to be put into ill-fitting livery.

They had bought her a new frock for evening wear, the father who was now dead, and the old aunt who had raised her-an ugly black satin, too mature for her. She had put it on in that very room, and wept in very despair.

Then came the arrival, her father on the doorstep, she and her aunt behind him, and in the hall, lines of uneasy and shuffling peasants. How awkward and ill at ease they must have seemed! Then came the carriage, Hubert alighting first, then Karl. Karl had seen her instantly, over her father's bent back.

Lying there, seeing things with the clear vision of the dawn, she wondered whether, had she met Karl later, in her sophisticated maturity, she would have fallen in love with him. There was no way to know. He had dawned on her then, almost the first man of rank she had ever seen. She saw him, not only with fresh eyes, but through the halo of his position. He was the Crown Prince of Karnia then, more dashing than Hubert, who was already married and had always been a serious youth, handsomer, a blond in a country of few blond men. His joyous smile had not taken on the mocking twist it acquired later. His blue eyes were gay and joyous.

When she had bowed and would have kissed his hand, it had been Karl who kissed hers, and straightened to smile down at her.

"This is a very happy day, Countess," he had said.

Then the old aunt had hustled forward, and the peasants had bowed nervously, and bustle and noise had filled the old place.

For four days the royal hunters had stayed. On the third day Karl had pleaded fatigue, and they had walked through the pine woods. On that very devil's bridge he had kissed her. They had had serious talks, too. Karl was ambitious, even then. The two countries were at peace, but for how long? Contrary to opinion, he said, it was not rulers who led their people into war. It was the people who forced those wars. He spoke of long antagonisms, old jealousies, trade relations.

She had listened, flattered, had been an intelligent audience. Even now, she felt that it was her intelligence as much as her beauty that had ensnared Karl. For ensnared he had been. She had dreamed wild dreams that night after he kissed her, dreams of being his wife. She was not too young to know passion in a man's eyes, and Karl's had burned with it.

Then, the next day, while the hunters were away, her aunt had come to her, ugly, dowdy, and alarmed. "Little fool!" she had said. "They play, these princes. But they are evil with women, and dangerous. I have seen your eyes on him, sick with love. And Karl will amuse himself-it is the blood-and go away, laughing."

She had been working with the satin dress, trying to make it lovely for him. Over it her eyes had met her aunt's, small and twitching with anxiety. "But suppose he cares for me?" she had asked. "Sometimes I think-Why should you say he is evil?"

"Bah!"

She had grown angry then and, flinging the dress on the floor, had risen haughtily. "I think he will marry me," she had announced, to be met with blank surprise, followed by cackling old laughter.

Karl had gone away, kissing her passionately, before he left her, in the dark hall. And many things had followed. A cousin, married into Karnia became lady-in-waiting to the old Queen. Olga Loschek had visited her. No accident all this, but a carefully thought-out plan of Karl's. She had met Karl again. She was no longer the ill-dressed, awkward girl of the mountains, and his passion grew, rather than died.

He had made further love to her then, urged her to go away with him on a journey to the eastern end of the kingdom, would, indeed, have compromised her hopelessly. But, young as she was, she had had courage and strength; perhaps shrewdness too. Few women could have resisted him. He was gentleness itself with her, kindly, considerate, passionate. But she had kept her head.

And because she had kept her head, she had kept him. Through his many lapses, his occasional mad adventures, he had always come back to her. Having never possessed her, he had always wanted her. But not enough, she said drearily to herself, to pay the price of marriage.

She was fair enough to him. Nothing but a morganatic marriage would be possible, and this would deprive his children of the throne. But less than marriage she would not have.

The old Queen died. Her cousin retired to the country, and raised pheasants for gayety. Olga Loschek's visits to Karnia ceased. In time a place was made for her at the Court of Livonia and a brilliant marriage for her was predicted. But she did not marry. Now and then she retired to the castle near the border, and Karl visited her there. And, at last, after years, the inevitable happened.

She was deeply in love, and the years were passing. The burden of resistance had always been on her, and marriage was out of the question. She was alone now. Her father had died, and the old aunt was in seclusion in a nunnery, where she pottered around a garden and knitted endless garments for the poor.

For a time Olga had been very happy. Karl's motor crossed the mountains, and he came on foot through the woods. No breath of scandal touched her. And, outwardly, Karl did not change. He was still her ardent lover. But the times when they could meet were few.

And the Court of Livonia heard rumors —a gamekeeper's daughter, an actress in his own capital, these were but two of the many. Olga Loschek was clever. She never reproached him or brought him to task. She had felt that, whatever his lapses, the years had made her necessary to him.

The war that followed the truce had seen her Karl's spy in Livonia. She had undertaken it that the burden of gratitude should be on him —a false step, for men chafe under the necessity for gratitude.

Then had come another peace, and his visit to the summer palace. There he had seen Hedwig, grown since his last visit to lovely girlhood, and having what Olga Loschek could never again possess, youth.

And now he would marry her, and Olga Loschek, his tool and spy, was in danger of her life.

That day, toward evening, the huge man presented himself. He brought no letter, but an oral message. "Permission is given, madame," he said. "I myself shall accompany you."

Chapter XXIII
Nikky Makes a Promise

The Chancellor lived alone, in his little house near the Palace, a house that looked strangely like him, overhanging eyebrows and all, with windows that were like his eyes, clear and concealing many secrets. A grim, gray little old house, which concealed behind it a walled garden full of unexpected charm. And that, too, was like the Chancellor.

In his study on the ground floor, overlooking the garden, the Chancellor spent his leisure hours. Here, on the broad, desk-like arm of his chair, where so many state documents had lain for signature, most of his meals were served. Here, free from the ghosts that haunted the upper rooms, he dreamed his dream of a greater kingdom.

Mathilde kept his house for him, mended and pressed his uniforms, washed and starched his linen, quarreled with the orderly who attended him, and drove him to bed at night.

"It is midnight," she would say firmly-or one o'clock, or even later, for the Chancellor was old, and needed little sleep. "Give me the book." Because, if she did not take it, he would carry it off to bed, and reading in bed is bad for the eyes.

"Just a moment, Mathilde," he would say, and finish a paragraph. Sometimes he went on reading, and forgot about her, to look up, a half-hour later, perhaps, and find her still standing there, immobile, firm.

Then he would sigh, and close the book.

At his elbow every evening Mathilde placed a glass of milk. If he had forgotten it, now he sipped it slowly, and the two talked-of homely things, mostly, the garden, or moths in the closed rooms which had lost, one by one, their beloved occupants, or of a loose tile on the roof. But now and then their conversation was more serious.

Mathilde, haunting the market with its gayly striped booths, its rabbits hung in pairs by the ears, its strings of dried vegetables, its lace bazaars Mathilde was in touch with the people. It was Mathilde, and not one of his agents, who had brought word of the approaching revolt of the coppersmiths' guild, and enabled him to check it almost before it began. A stoic, this Mathilde, with her tall, spare figure and glowing eyes, stoic and patriot. Once every month she burned four candles before the shrine of Our Lady of Sorrows in the cathedral, because of four sons she had given to her country.

On the evening of the day Hedwig had made her futile appeal to the King, the Chancellor sat alone. His dinner, almost untasted, lay at his elbow. It was nine o'clock. At something after seven he had paid his evening visit to the King, and had found him uneasy and restless.

"Sit down;" the King had said. "I need steadying, old friend."

"Steadying, sire?"

"I have had a visit from Hedwig. Rather a stormy one, poor child." He turned and fixed on his Chancellor his faded eyes. "In this course that you have laid out, and that I am following, as I always have," irony this, but some truth, too, —"have you no misgivings? You still think it is the best thing?"

"It is the only thing."

"But all this haste," put in the King querulously.

"Is that so necessary? Hedwig begs for time. She hardly knows the man."

"Time! But I thought —" He hesitated. How say to a dying man that time was the one thing he did not have?

"Another thing. She was incoherent, but I gathered that there was some one else. The whole interview was cyclonic. It seems, however, that this young protege of yours, Larisch, has been making love to her over Otto's head."

Mettlich's face hardened, a gradual process, as the news penetrated in all its significance.

"I should judge," the King went on relentlessly, "that this vaunted affection of his for the boy is largely assumed, a cover for other matters. But," he added, with a flicker of humor, "my granddaughter assures me that it is she who has made the advances. I believe she asked him to elope with her, and he refused!"

"A boy-and-girl affair, sire. He is loyal. And in all of this, you and I are reckoning without Karl. The Princess hardly knows him, and naturally she is terrified. But his approaching visit will make many changes. He is a fine figure of a man, and women —"

"Exactly;" said the King dryly. What the Chancellor meant was that women always had loved Karl, and the King understood.

"His wild days are over," bluntly observed the Chancellor. "He is forty, sire."

"Aye," said the King. "And at forty, a bad man changes his nature, and purifies himself in marriage! Nonsense, Karl will be as he has always been. But we have gone into this before. Only, I am sorry for Hedwig. Hilda would have stood it better. She is like her father. However" —his voice hardened "the thing is arranged, and we must carry out our contract. Get rid of this young Larisch."

The Chancellor sat reflecting, his chin dropped forward on his breast. "Otto will miss him."

"Well, out with it. I may not dismiss him. What, then?"

"It is always easy to send men away. But it is sometimes better to retain them, and force them to your will. We have here an arrangement that is satisfactory. Larisch is keen, young, and loyal. Hedwig has thrown herself at him. For that, sire, she is responsible, not he."

"Then get rid of her," growled the King.

The Chancellor rose. "If the situation is left to me, sire," he said, "I will promise two things. That Otto will keep his friend, and that the Princess Hedwig will bow to your wishes without further argument."

"Do it, and God help you!" said the King, again with the flicker of amusement.

The Chancellor had gone home, walking heavily along the darkening streets. Once again he had conquered. The reins remained in his gnarled old hands. And he was about to put the honor of the country into the keeping of the son of Maria Menrad, whom he had once loved.

So now he sat in his study, and waited. A great meerschaum pipe, a stag's head with branching antlers and colored dark with years of use, lay on his tray; and on his knee, but no longer distinguishable in the dusk, lay an old daguerreotype of Maria Menrad.

When he heard Nikky's quick step as he came along the tiled passage, he slipped the case into the pocket of his shabby house-coat, and picked up the pipe.

Nikky saluted, and made his way across the room in the twilight, with the ease of familiarity. "I am late, sir," he apologized. "We found our man and he is safely jailed. He made no resistance."

"Sit down," said the Chancellor. And, touching a bell, he asked Mathilde for coffee. "So we have him," he reflected. "The next thing is to discover if he knows who his assailants were. That, and the person for whom he acted-However, I sent for you for another reason. What is this about the Princess Hedwig?"

"The Princess Hedwig!"

"What folly, boy! A young girl who cannot know her own mind! And for such a bit of romantic trifling you would ruin yourself. It is ruin. You know that."

"I am sorry," Nikky said simply. "As far as my career goes, it does not matter. But I am thinking of her."

"A trifle late."

"But," Nikky spoke up valiantly, "it is not romantic folly, in the way you mean, sir. As long as I live, I shall-It is hopeless, of course, sir."

"Madness," commented the Chancellor. "Sheer spring madness. You would carry her off, I dare say, and hide yourselves at the end of a rainbow! Folly!"

Nikky remained silent, a little sullen.

"The Princess went to the King with her story this evening." The boy started. "A cruel proceeding, but the young are always cruel. The expected result has followed: the King wishes you sent away."

"I am at his command, sir."

The Chancellor filled his pipe from a bowl near by, working deliberately. Nikky sat still, rather rigid.

"May I ask," he said at last, "that you say to the King that the responsibility is mine? No possible blame can attach to the Princess Hedwig. I love her, and —I am not clever. I show what I feel."

He was showing it then, both hurt and terror, not for himself, but for her. His voice shook in spite of his efforts to be every inch a soldier.

"The immediate result," said the Chancellor cruelly, "will doubtless be a putting forward of the date for her marriage." Nikky's hands clenched. "A further result would be your dismissal from the army. One does not do such things as you have done, lightly."

"Lightly!" said Nikky Larisch. "God!"

"But," continued the Chancellor, "I have a better way. I have faith, for one thing, in your blood. The son of Maria Menrad must be-his mother's son. And the Crown Prince is attached to you. Not for your sake, but for his, I am inclined to be lenient. What I shall demand for that leniency is that no word of love again pass between you and the Princess Hedwig."

"It would be easier to go away."

"Aye, of course. But 'easier' is not your word nor mine." But Nikky's misery touched him. He rose and placed a heavy hand on the boy's shoulder. "It is not as simple as that. I know, boy. But you are young, and these things grow less with time. You need not see her. She will be forbidden to visit Otto or to go to the riding-school. You see, I know about the riding-school! And, in a short time now, the marriage will solve many difficulties."

Nikky closed his eyes. It was getting to be a habit, just as some people crack their knuckles.

"We need our friends about us," the Chancellor continued. "The Carnival is coming, —always a dangerous time for us. The King grows weaker day by day. A crisis is impending for all of us, and we need you."

Nikky rose, steady enough now, but white to the lips.

"I give my word, sir," he said. "I shall say no word of-of how I feel to Hedwig. Not again. She knows and I think," he added proudly, "that she knows I shall not change. That I shall always —"

"Exactly!" said the Chancellor. It was the very, pitch of the King's dry old voice. "Of course she knows, being a woman. And now, good-night."

But long after Nikky had gone he sat in the darkness. He felt old and tired and a hypocrite. The boy would not forget, as he himself had not forgotten. His hand, thrust into his pocket, rested on the faded daguerreotype there.

Peter Niburg was shot at dawn the next morning. He went, a coward, to his death, held between two guards and crying piteously. But he died a brave man. Not once in the long hours of his interrogation had he betrayed the name of the Countess Loschek.

Chapter XXIV
The Birthday

The Crown Prince Ferdinand William Otto of Livonia was having a birthday. Now, a birthday for a Crown Prince of Livonia is not a matter of a cake with candles on it; and having his ears pulled, once for each year and an extra one to grow on. Nor of a holiday from lessons, and a picnic in spring woods. Nor of a party, with children frolicking and scratching the best furniture.

In the first place, he was wakened at dawn and taken to early service in the chapel, a solemn function, with the Court assembled and slightly sleepy. The Crown Prince, who was trying to look his additional dignity of years, sat and stood as erect as possible, and yawned only once.

After breakfast he was visited by the chaplain who had his religious instruction in hand, and interrogated. He did not make more than about sixty per cent in this, however, and the chaplain departed looking slightly discouraged.

Lessons followed, and in each case the tutor reminded him that, having now reached his tenth birthday, he should be doing better than in the past. Especially the French tutor, who had just heard a rumor of Hedwig's marriage.

At eleven o'clock came word that the King was too ill to have him to luncheon, but that he would see him for a few moments that afternoon. Prince Ferdinand William Otto, who was diagramming the sentence, "Abraham Lincoln freed the slaves in America," and doing it wrong, looked up in dismay.

"I'd like to know what's the use of having a birthday," he declared rebelliously.

The substitution of luncheon with the Archduchess Annunciata hardly thrilled him. Unluckily he made an observation to that effect, and got five off in Miss Braithwaite's little book.

The King did not approve of birthday gifts. The expensive toys which the Court would have offered the child were out of key with the simplicity of his rearing. As a matter of fact, the Crown Prince had never heard of a birthday gift, and had, indeed, small experience of gifts of any kind, except as he made them himself. For that he had a great fondness. His small pocket allowance generally dissipated itself in this way.

So there were no gifts. None, that is, until the riding-hour came, and Nikky, subverter of all discipline. He had brought a fig lady, wrapped in paper.

"It's quite fresh," he said, as they walked together across the Place. "I'll give it to you when we get to the riding-school. I saw the woman myself take it out of her basket. So it has no germs on it."

But, although he spoke bravely, Nikky was the least bit nervous. First of all he was teaching the boy deception. "But why don't they treat him like a human being?" he demanded of himself. Naturally there was no answer. Maria Menrad's son had a number of birthdays in his mind, real birthdays with much indulgence connected with them.

Second, suppose it really had a germ or two on it? Anxiously, having unwrapped it, he examined it in the sunlight of a window of the ring. Certainly, thus closely inspected, it looked odd. There were small granules over it.

The Crown Prince waited patiently. "Miss Braithwaite says that if you look at them under a glass, there are bugs on them," he observed, with interest.

"Perhaps, after all, you'd better not have it."

"They are very small bugs," said Prince Ferdinand William Otto anxiously. "I don't object to them at all."

So, after all, Nikky uneasily presented his gift; and nothing untoward happened. He was rewarded, however, by such a glow of pleasure and gratitude from the boy that his scruples faded.

No Hedwig again, to distract Nikky's mind. The lesson went on; trot, canter, low jumps. And then what Nikky called "stunts," an American word which delighted the Crown Prince.

But, Nikky, like the big child he was himself, had kept his real news to the last.

Already, he was offering himself on the altar of the child's safety. Behind his smiles lay something of the glow of the martyr. His eyes were sunken, his lips drawn. He had not slept at all, nor eaten. But to the boy he meant to show no failing, to be the prince of playmates, the brother of joy. Perhaps in this way, he felt, lay his justification.

So now, with the Crown Prince facing toward the Palace again, toward luncheon with his aunt and a meeting with the delegation, Nikky, like an epicure of sensations, said: "By the way, Otto, I found that dog you saw yesterday. What was his name? Toto?"

"Where did you find him? Yes, Toto!"

"I looked him up," said Nikky modestly. "You see, it's like this: He's a pretty nice dog. There aren't many dogs like him. And I thought-well, nobody can say I can't have a dog."

"You've got him? You, yourself?"

"I, myself. I dare say he has fleas, and they will get in the carpet, but —I tell you what I thought: He will be really your dog, do you see? I'll take care of him, and keep him for you, and bring him out to walk where you can see him. Then, when they say you may have a dog, you've got one, already. All I have to do is to bring him to you."

Wise Nikky, of the understanding boy's heart. He had brought into the little Prince's life its first real interest, something vital, living. And something of the soreness and hurt of the last few hours died in Nikky before Prince Ferdinand William Otto's smile.

"Oh, Nikky!" was all the child said at first, and grew silent for very happiness. Then: "We can talk about him. You can tell me all the things he does, and I can send him bones, can't I? Unless you don't care to carry them."

This, in passing, explains the reason why, to the eyes of astonished servants, from that day forth the Crown Prince of Livonia apparently devoured his chop, bone and all. And why Nikky resembled, at times, a well-setup, trig, and soldierly appearing charnel-house. "If I am ever arrested," he once demurred, "and searched, Highness, I shall be consigned to a madhouse."

Luncheon was extremely unsuccessful. His Cousin Hedwig looked as though she had been crying, and Hilda, eating her soup too fast, was sent from the table. The Crown Prince, trying to make conversation, chose Nikky as his best subject, and met an icy silence. Also, attempting to put the bone from a chicken leg in his pocket, he was discovered.

"What in the world!" exclaimed the Archduchess. "What do you want of a chicken bone?"

"I just wanted it, Tante."

"It is greasy. Look at your fingers!"

"Mother," Hedwig said quietly, "it is his birthday."

"I do not need you to remind me of that. Have I not been up since the middle of the night, for that reason?"

But she said no more, and was a trifle more agreeable during the remainder of the meal. She was just a bit uneasy before Hedwig those days. She did not like the look in her eyes.

That afternoon, attired in his uniform of the Guards, the Crown Prince received the delegation of citizens in the great audience, chamber of the Palace, a solitary little figure, standing on the red carpet before the dais at the end. Behind him, stately with velvet hangings, was the tall gilt chair which some day would be his. Afternoon sunlight, coming through the long windows along the side, shone on the prisms of the heavy chandeliers, lighted up the paintings of dead and gone kings of his line, gleamed in great mirrors and on the polished floor.

On each side of his small figure the Council grouped itself, fat Friese, rat-faced Marschall, Bayerl, with his soft voice and white cheeks lighted by hot eyes, and the others. They stood very stiff, in their white gloves. Behind them were grouped the gentlemen of the Court, in full dress and decorated with orders. At the door stood the Lord Chamberlain, very gorgeous in scarlet and gold.

The Chancellor stood near the boy, resplendent in his dress uniform, a blue ribbon across his shirt front, over which Mathilde had taken hours. He was the Mettlich of the public eye now, hard of features, impassive, inflexible.

In ordinary times less state would have been observed, a smaller room, Mettlich only, or but one or two others, an informal ceremony. But the Chancellor shrewdly intended to do the delegation all honor, the Palace to give its best, that the city, in need, might do likewise.

And he had staged the affair well. The Crown Prince, standing alone, so small, so appealing, against his magnificent background, was a picture to touch the hardest. Not for nothing had Mettlich studied the people, read their essential simplicity, their answer to any appeal to the heart. These men were men of family. Surely no father of a son could see that lonely child and not offer him loyalty.

With the same wisdom, he had given the boy small instruction, and no speech of thanks. "Let him say what comes into his head," Mettlich had reasoned. "It will at least be spontaneous and boyish."

The Crown Prince was somewhat nervous. He blinked rapidly as the delegation entered and proceeded up the room. However, happening at that moment to remember Nikky with the brass inkwell, he forgot himself in amusement. He took a good look at the gold casket, as it approached, reverently borne, and rather liked its appearance. It would have been, he reflected, extremely convenient to keep things in, pencils and erasers, on his desk. But, of course, he would not have it to keep. Quite a number of things passed into his possession and out again with the same lightning-like rapidity.

The first formalities over, and the Crown Prince having shaken hands nine times, the spokesman stepped forward. He had brought a long, written speech, which had already been given to the newspapers. But after a moment's hesitation he folded it up.

"Your Royal Highness," he said, looking down, "I have here a long speech, but all that it contains I can say briefly. It is your birthday, Highness. We come, representing many others, to present to you our congratulations, and-the love of your people. It is our hope" —He paused. Emotion and excitement were getting the better of him —"our hope, Highness, that you will have many happy years. To further that hope, we are here to-day to say that we, representing all classes, are your most loyal subjects. We have fought for His Majesty the King, and if necessary we will fight for you." He glanced beyond the child at the Council, and his tone was strong and impassioned: "But to-day we are here, not to speak of war, but to present to you our congratulations, our devotion, and our loyalty."

Also a casket. He had forgotten that. He stepped back, was nudged, and recollected.

"Also a gift," he said, and ruined a fine speech among smiles. But the presentation took place in due order, and Otto cleared his throat.

"Thank you all very much," he said. "It is a very beautiful gift. I admire it very much. I should like to keep it on my desk, but I suppose it is too valuable. Thank you very much."

The spokesman hoped that it might be arranged that he keep it on his desk, an ever-present reminder of the love of his city. To this the Chancellor observed that it would be arranged, and the affair was over. To obviate the difficulty of having the delegation back down the long room, it was the Crown Prince who departed first, with the Chancellor.

Altogether, it was comfortably over, and the Chancellor reflected grimly that the boy had done well. He had made friends of the delegation at a time when he needed friends. As they walked along the long corridors of the Palace together, the Chancellor was visualizing another scene, which must come soon, pray God with as good result: the time when, the old King dead and the solemn bell of the cathedral tolling, this boy would step out on to the balcony overlooking the Place, and show himself to the great throng below the windows.

To offset violence and anarchy itself, only that one small figure on the balcony!

Late in the afternoon the King sent for Prince Ferdinand William Otto. He had not left his bed since the day he had placed the matter of Hedwig's marriage before the Council, and now he knew he would never leave it. There were times between sleeping and waking when he fancied he had already gone, and that only his weary body on the bed remained. At such times he saw Hubert, only, strangely enough, not as a man grown, but as a small boy again; and his Queen, but as she had looked many years before, when he married her, and when at last, after months of married wooing, she had crept willing into his arms.

So, awakening from a doze, he saw the boy there, and called him Hubert. Prince Ferdinand William Otto, feeling rather worried, did the only thing he could think of. He thrust his warm hand into his grandfather's groping one, and the touch of his soft flesh roused the King.

The Sister left them together, and in her small room dropped on her knees before the holy image. There, until he left, she prayed for the King's soul, for the safety and heavenly guidance of the boy. The wind stirred her black habit and touched gently her white coif. She prayed, her pale lips moving silently.

In the King's bedchamber Prince Ferdinand William Otto sat on a high chair, and talked. He was extremely relieved that his exile was over, but he viewed his grandfather, with alarm. His aunt had certainly intimated that his running away had made the King worse. And he looked very ill.

"I'm awfully sorry, grandfather," he said.

"For what?"

"That I went away the other day, sir."

"It was, after all, a natural thing to do."

The Crown Prince could hardly believe his ears.

"If it could only be arranged safely — a little freedom —" The King lay still with closed eyes.

Prince Ferdinand William Otto felt uneasy. "But I am very comfortable, and-and happy," he hastened to say. "You are, please, not to worry about me, sir. And about the paper I threw at Monsieur Puaux the other day, I am sorry about that too. I don't know exactly why I did it."

The King still held his hand, but he said nothing. There were many things he wanted to say. He had gone crooked where this boy must go straight. He had erred, and the boy must avoid his errors. He had cherished enmities, and in his age they cherished him. And now —

"May I ask you a question, sir?"

"What is it?"

"Will you tell me about Abraham Lincoln?"

"Why?" The King was awake enough now. He fixed the Crown Prince with keen eyes.

"Well, Miss Braithwaite does not care for him. She says he was not a great man, not as great as Mr. Gladstone, anyhow. But Bobby-that's the boy I met; I told you about him-he says he was the greatest man who ever lived."

"And who," asked the King, "do you regard as the greatest man?"

Prince Ferdinand William Otto fidgeted, but he answered bravely, "You, sir."

"Humph!" The King lay still, smiling slightly. "Well," he observed, "there are, of course, other opinions as to that. However-Abraham Lincoln was a very great man. A dreamer, a visionary, but a great man. You might ask Miss Braithwaite to teach you his 'Gettysburg Address.' It is rather a model as to speech-making, although it contains doctrines that-well, you'd better learn it."

He smiled again, to himself. It touched his ironic sense of humor that he, who had devoted his life to maintaining that all men are not free and equal, when on that very day that same doctrine of liberty was undermining his throne-that he should be discussing it with the small heir to that throne.

"Yes, sir," said Prince Ferdinand William Otto. He hoped it was not very long.

"Otto," said the King suddenly, "do you ever look at your father's picture?"

"Not always."

"You might-look at it now and then. I'd like you to do it."

"Yes, sir."

Chapter XXV
The Gate of the Moon

A curious friendship had sprung up between old Adelbert and Bobby Thorpe. In off hours, after school, the boy hung about the ticket-taker's booth, swept now to a wonderful cleanliness and adorned within with pictures cut from the illustrated papers. The small charcoal fire was Bobby's particular care. He fed and watched it, and having heard of the baleful effects of charcoal fumes, insisted on more fresh air than old Adelbert had ever breathed before.

"You see," Bobby would say earnestly, as he brushed away at the floor beneath the burner, "you don't know that you are being asphyxiated. You just feel drowsy, and then, poof! —you're dead."

Adelbert, dozing between tickets, was liable to be roused by a vigorous shaking, to a pair of anxious eyes gazing at him, and to a draft of chill spring air from the open door.

"I but dozed," he would explain, without anger. "All my life have I breathed the fumes and nothing untoward has happened."

Outwardly he was peaceful. The daughter now received his pension in full, and wrote comforting letters. But his resentment and bitterness at the loss of his position at the Opera continued, even grew.

For while he had now even a greater wage, and could eat three meals, besides second breakfast and afternoon coffee, down deep in his heart old Adelbert felt that he had lost caste. The Opera-that was a setting! Great staircases of marble, velvet hangings, the hush before the overture, and over all the magic and dignity of music. And before his stall had passed and repassed the world-royalties, the aristocracy, the army. Hoi polloi had used another entrance by which to climb to the upper galleries. He had been, then, of the elect. Aristocrats who had forgotten their own opera-glasses had requested him to give them of his best, had through long years learned to know him there, and had nodded to him as they swept by. The flash of jewels on beautiful necks, the glittering of decorations on uniformed chests, had been his life.

And now, to what had he fallen! To selling tickets for an American catch-penny scheme, patronized by butchers, by housemaids, by the common people a noisy, uproarious crowd, that nevertheless counted their change with suspicious eyes, and brought lunches in paper boxes, which they scattered about.

"Riff-raff!" he said to himself scornfully.

There was, however, a consolation. He had ordered a new uniform. Not for twenty years had he ventured the extravagance, and even now his cautious soul quailed at the price. For the last half-dozen years he had stumped through the streets, painfully aware of shabbiness, of a shiny back, of patches, when, on the anniversary of the great battle to which he had sacrificed a leg, the veterans marched between lines of cheering people.

Now, on this approaching anniversary, he could go peacefully, nay, even proudly. The uniform was of the best cloth, and on its second fitting showed already its marvel of tailoring. The news of it had gone around the neighborhood. The tailor reported visits from those who would feel of the cloth, and figure its expensiveness. In the evening-for he worked only until seven-he had his other preparations: polishing his sword, cleaning his accouterments.

On an evening a week before the parade would occur, he got out his boots. He bought always large boots with straight soles, the right not much different from the left in shape. Thus he managed thriftily to wear, on his one leg, first one of the pair, then the other. But they were both worn now, and because of the cost of the new uniform, he could not buy others.

Armed with the better of the two he visited the cobbler's shop, and there met with bitter news.

"A patch here, and a new heel, comrade," he said. "With that and a polishing, it will do well enough for marching."

The usual group was in the shop, mostly young men, a scattering of gray heads. The advocates of strange doctrines, most of them. Old Adelbert disapproved of them, regarded them with a sort of contempt.

Now he felt that they smiled behind his back. It was his clothing, he felt. He shrugged his shoulders disdainfully. He no longer felt ashamed before them. Already, although the tailor still pressed its seams and marked upon it with chalk, he was clad in the dignity of the new uniform.

He turned and nodded to them. "A fine evening," he said. "If this weather holds, we will have —a good day for the marching." He squinted a faded eye at the sky outside.

"What marching?"

Old Adelbert turned on the speaker sharply. "Probably you have forgotten," he said scornfully, "but in a week comes an anniversary there are many who will remember. The day of a great battle. Perhaps," he added, "if you do not know of what I speak, there are some here who will tell you."

Unexpectedly the crowd laughed.

Old Adelbert flushed a dusky red and drew himself up. "Since when," he demanded, "does such a speech bring laughter? It was no laughing matter then."

"It is the way of the old to live in the past," a student said. Then, imitating old Adelbert's majestic tone: "We, we live in the future. Eh, comrades?" He turned to the old soldier: "You have not seen the bulletins?"

"Bulletins?"

"There will be no marching, my friend. The uniform now-that is a pity. Perhaps the tailor —" His eyes mocked.

"No marching?"

"An order of the Council. It seems that the city is bored by these ancient-reminders. It is for peace, and would forget wars. And processions are costly. We grow thrifty. Bands and fireworks cost money, and money, my hero, is scarce-very scarce."

Again the group laughed.

After a time he grasped the truth. There was such an order. The cause was given as the King's illness.

"Since when," demanded old Adelbert angrily, "has the sound of his soldiers' marching disturbed the King?"

"The sound of wooden legs annoys him," observed the mocking student, lighting a cigarette. "He would hear only pleasant sounds, such as the noise of tax-money pouring into his vaults. Me —I can think of a pleasanter: the tolling of the cathedral bell, at a certain time, will be music to my ears!"

Old Adelbert stood, staring blindly ahead. At last he went out into the street, muttering. "They shame us before the people," he said thickly.

The order of the Council had indeed been issued, a painful business over which Mettlich and the Council had pondered long. For, in the state of things, it was deemed unwise to permit any gathering of the populace en masse. Mobs lead to riots, and riots again to mobs. Five thousand armed men, veterans, but many of them in their prime, were in themselves a danger. And on these days of anniversary it had been the custom of the University to march also, a guard of honor. Sedition was rife among the students.

The order was finally issued...

Old Adelbert was not keen, but he did not lack understanding. And one thing he knew, and knew well. The concierge, downstairs was no patriot. Time had been when, over coffee and bread, he had tried to instill in the old soldier his own discontent, his new theories of a land where all were equal and no man king. He had hinted of many who believed as he did. Only hints, because old Adelbert had raised a trembling hand and proclaimed treason.

But now?

Late in the evening he made his resolve, and visited the bureau of the concierge. He was away, however, and his niece spoke through the barred window.

"Two days, or perhaps three," she said. "He is inspecting a farm in the country, with a view to purchase."

The old soldier had walked by the Palace that night, and had again shaken his fist at its looming shadow. "You will see," he said, "there be other sounds more painful than the thump of a wooden leg."

He was ill that night. He tossed about in a fever. His body ached, even the leg which so long ago had mouldered in its shallow grave on a battle-field. For these things happen. By morning he was better, but he was a different man. His eyes glowed. His body twitched. He was stronger, too, for now he broke his sword across his knee, and flung the pieces out of the window. And with them went the last fragment of his old loyalty to his King.

Old Adelbert was now, potentially, a traitor.

The spring came early that year. The last of February saw the parks green. Snowdrops appeared in the borders of paths. The swans left their wooden houses and drifted about in water much colder than the air. Bobby abandoned the aeroplane for a kite and threw it aloft from Pike's Peak. At night, when he undressed, marbles spilled out of his pockets and rolled under the most difficult furniture. Although it was still cold at nights and in the early mornings, he abandoned the white sweater and took to looking for birds and nests in the trees of the park. It was, of course, much too early for nests, but nevertheless he searched, convinced that even if grown-ups talked wisely of more cold weather, he and the birds knew it was spring. And, of course, the snow-drops.

On the morning after old Adelbert had turned his back on his King, Bobby Thorpe rose early, so early, indeed, that even Pepy still slept in her narrow bed, and the milk-sellers had not started on their rounds. The early rising was a mistake, owing to a watch which had strangely gained an hour.

Somewhat disconsolately, he wandered about. Heavy quiet reigned. From a window he watched the meat-seller hang out a freshly killed deer, just brought from the mountains He went downstairs and out on the street, past the niece of the concierge, who was scrubbing the stairs.

"I'm going for a walk," he told her. "If they send Pepy down you might tell her I'll be back for breakfast."

He stood for a time surveying the deer. Then he decided to go hunting himself. The meat-seller obligingly gave him the handle of a floor-brush, and with this improvised gun Bobby went deer-stalking. He turned into the Park, going stealthily, and searching the landscape with keen hunter's eyes. Once or twice he leveled his weapon, killed a deer, cut off the head, and went on. His dog trotted, at his heels. When a particularly good shot presented itself, Bobby said, "Down, Tucker," and Tucker, who played extremely well, would lie down, ears cocked, until the quarry was secured.

Around the old city gate, still standing although the wall of which it had been a part was gone, there was excellent hunting. Here they killed and skinned a bear, took fine ivory tusks from a dead elephant, and searched for the trail of a tiger.

The gate was an excellent place for a tiger. Around it was planted an almost impenetrable screen of evergreens, so thick that the ground beneath was quite bare of grass. Here the two hunters crawled on stomachs that began to feel a trifle empty, and here they happened on the trail.

Tucker found it first. His stumpy tail grew rigid. Nose to the ground, he crawled and wriggled through the undergrowth, Bobby at his heels. And now Bobby saw the trail, footprints. It is true that they resembled those of heavy boots with nails. But on the other hand, no one could say surely that the nail-marks were not those of claws.

Tucker circled about. The trail grew more exciting. Bobby had to crawl on hands and feet under and through thickets. Branches had been broken as by the passage of some large body. The sportsman clutched his weapon and went on.

An hour later the two hunters returned for breakfast. Washing did something to restore the leader to a normal appearance, but a wondering family discovered him covered with wounds and strangely silent.

"Why, Bob, where have you been?" his mother demanded. "Why, I never saw so many scratches!"

"I've been hunting," he replied briefly. "They don't hurt anyhow."

Then he relapsed into absorbed silence. His mother, putting cream on his cereal, placed an experienced hand on his forehead. "Are you sure you feel well, dear?" she asked. "I think your head is a little hot."

"I'm all right, mother."

She was wisely silent, but she ran over in her mind the spring treatment for children at home. The blood, she felt, should be thinned after a winter of sausages and rich cocoa. She mentally searched her medicine case.

A strange thing happened that day. A broken plate disappeared from the upper shelf of a closet, where Pepy had hidden it; also a cup with a nick in it, similarly concealed; also the heel of a loaf of bread. Nor was that the end. For three days a sort of magic reigned in Pepy's kitchen. Ten potatoes, laid out to peel, became eight. Matches and two ends of candle walked out, as it were, on their own feet. A tin pan with a hole in it left the kitchen-table and was discovered hiding in Bobby's bureau, when the Fraulein put away the washing.

On the third day Mrs. Thorpe took her husband into their room and closed the door.

"Bob," she said, "I don't want to alarm you. But there is something wrong with Bobby."

"Sick, you mean?"

"I don't know." Her voice was worried. "He's not a bit like himself. He is always away, for one thing. And he hardly eats at all."

"He looks well enough nourished!"

"And he comes home covered with mud. I have never seen his clothes in such condition. And last night, when he was bathing, I went into the bathroom. He is covered with scratches."

"Now see here, mother," the hunter's father protested, "you're the parent of a son, a perfectly hardy, healthy, and normal youngster, with an imagination. Probably he's hunting Indians. I saw him in the Park yesterday with his air-rifle. Any how, just stop worrying and let him alone. A scratch or two won't hurt him. And as to his not eating,—well, if he's not eating at home he's getting food somewhere, I'll bet you a hat."

So Bobby was undisturbed, save that the governess protested that he heard nothing she told him, and was absent-minded at his lessons. But as she was always protesting about something, no one paid any attention. Bobby drew ahead on his pocket allowance without question, and as his birthday was not far off, asked for "the dollar to grow on" in advance. He always received a dollar for each year, which went into the bank, and a dollar to grow on, which was his own to spend.

With the dollar he made a number of purchases candles and candlestick, a toy pistol and caps, one of the masks for the Carnival, now displayed in all the windows, a kitchen-knife, wooden plates, and a piece of bacon.

Now and then he appeared at the Scenic Railway, abstracted and viewing with a calculating eye the furnishings of the engine-room and workshop. From there disappeared a broken chair, a piece of old carpet, discarded from a car, and a large padlock, but the latter he asked for and obtained.

His occasional visits to the Railway, however, found him in old Adelbert's shack. He filled his pockets with charcoal from the pail beside the stove, and made cautious inquiries as to methods of cooking potatoes. But the pall of old Adelbert's gloom penetrated at last even through the boy's abstraction.

"I hope your daughter is not worse," he said politely, during one of his visits to the ticket-booth.

"She is well. She recovers strength rapidly."

"And the new uniform-does it fit, you?"

"I do not know," said old Adelbert grimly. "I have not seen it recently."

"On the day of the procession we are all going to watch for you. I'll tell you where we twill be, so you can look for us."

"There will be no procession."

Then to the boy old Adelbert poured out the bitterness of his soul. He showed where he had torn down the King's picture, and replaced it with one of a dying stag. He reviewed his days in the hospital, and the hardships through which he had passed, to come to this. The King had forgotten his brave men.

Bobby listened. "Pretty soon there won't be any kings," he observed. "My father says so. They're out of date."

"Aye," said old Adelbert.

"It would be kind of nice if you had a president. Then, if he acted up, you could put him out."

"Aye," said old Adelbert again.

During the rest of the day Bobby considered. No less a matter than the sharing of a certain secret occupied his mind. Now; half the pleasure of a secret is sharing it, naturally, but it should be with the right person. And his old playfellow was changed. Bobby, reflecting, wondered whether old Adelbert would really care to join his pirate crew, consisting of Tucker and himself. On the next day, however, he put the matter to the test, having resolved that old Adelbert needed distraction and cheering.

"You know," he said, talking through the window of the booth, "I think when I grow up I'll be a pirate."

"There be worse trades," said old Adelbert, whose hand was now against every man.

"And hide treasure," Bobby went on. "In a —in a cave, you know. Did you ever read 'Treasure Island'?"

"I may have forgotten it. I have read many things."

"You'd hardly forget it. You know —

    'Fifteen men on a dead man's chest
    Yo-ho-ho and a bottle of rum.'"

Old Adelbert rather doubted the possibility of fifteen men on one dead man's chest, but he nodded gravely. "A spirited song," he observed.

Bobby edged closer to the window. "I've got the cave already."

"So!"

"Here, in the Park. It is a great secret. I'd like to show it to you. Only it's rather hard to get to. I don't know whether you'd care to crawl through the bushes to it."

"A cave-here in the Park?"

"I'll take you, if you'd like to see it."

Old Adelbert was puzzled. The Park offered, so far as he knew, no place for a cave. It was a plain, the site of the old wall; and now planted in grass and flowers. He himself had seen it graded and sown. A cave!

"Where?"

"That's a secret. But I'll show it to you, if you won't tell."

Old Adelbert agreed to silence. In fact, he repeated after the boy, in English he did not understand, a most blood-curdling oath of secrecy, and made the pirate sign-which, as every one knows, is a skull and crossbones-in the air with his forefinger.

"This cave," he said, half smiling, "must be a most momentous matter!"

Until midday, when the Railway opened for business, the old soldier was free. So the next morning, due precautions having been taken, the two conspirators set off. Three, rather, for Tucker, too, was now of the band of the black flag, having been taken in with due formality a day or two before, and behaving well and bravely during the rather trying rites of initiation.

Outside the thicket Bobby hesitated. "I ought to blindfold you," he said. "But I guess you'll need your eyes. It's a hard place to get to."

Perhaps, had he known the difficulties ahead, old Adelbert would not have gone on. And; had he turned back then, the history of a certain kingdom of Europe would have been changed. Maps, too, and schoolbooks, and the life-story of a small Prince. But he went on. Stronger than his young guide, he did not crawl, but bent aside the stiff and ungainly branches of the firs. He battled with the thicket, and came out victorious.. He was not so old, then, or so feeble. His arm would have been strong for the King, had not — "There it is!" cried Bobby.

Not a cave, it appeared at first. A low doorway, barred with an iron grating, and padlocked. A doorway in the base of a side wall of the gate, and so heaped with leaves that its lower half was covered.

Bobby produced a key. "I broke the padlock that was on it," he explained. "I smashed it with a stone. But I got another. I always lock it."

Prolonged search produced the key. Old Adelbert's face was set hard. On what dungeon had this boy stumbled? He himself had lived there many years, and of no such aperture had he heard mention. It was strange.

Bobby was removing the leaf-mould with his hands. "It was almost all covered when I found it," he said, industriously scraping. "I generally close it up like this when I leave. It's a good place for pirates, don't you think?"

"Excellent!"

"I've brought some things already. The lock's rusty. There it goes. There are rats. I hope you don't mind rats."

The door swung in, silently, as though the hinges had been recently oiled; as indeed they had, but not by the boy.

"It's rather dirty," he explained. "You go down steps first. Be very careful."

He extended an earthy hand and led the old man down. "It's dark here, but there's a room below; quite a good room. And I have candles."

Truly a room. Built of old brick, and damp, but with a free circulation of air. Old Adelbert stared about him. It was not entirely dark. A bit of light entered from the aperture at the head of the steps. By it, even before Bobby had lighted his candle, he saw the broken chair, the piece of old carpet, and the odds and ends the child had brought.

"I cook down here sometimes," said Bobby, struggling with matches that had felt the damp. "But it is very smoky. I should like to have a stove. You don't know where I can get a secondhand stove, do you? with a long pipe?"

Old Adelbert felt curiously shaken. "None have visited this place since you have been here?" he asked.

"I don't suppose any one knows about it. Do you?"

"Those who built it, perhaps. But it is old, very old. It is possible —"

He stopped, lost in speculation. There had been a story once of a passageway under the wall, but he recollected nothing clearly. A passageway leading out beyond the wall, through which, in a great siege, a messenger had been sent for help. But that was of a passage; while this was a dungeon.

The candle was at last lighted. It burned fitfully, illuminating only a tiny zone in the darkness.

"I need a lantern," Bobby observed. "There's a draft here. It comes from the other grating. Sometime, when you have time, I'd like to see what's beyond it. I was kind of nervous about going alone."

It was the old passage, then, of course. Old Adelbert stared as Bobby took the candle and held it toward a second grated door, like the first, but taller.

"There are rats there," he said. "I can hear them; about a million, I guess. They ate all the bread and bacon I left. Tucker can get through. He must have killed a lot of them."

"Lend me your candle."

A close examination revealed to old Adelbert two things: First, that a brick-lined passage, apparently in good repair, led beyond the grating. Second, that it had been recently put in order. A spade and wheelbarrow, both unmistakably of recent make, stood just beyond, the barrow full of bricks, as though fallen ones had been gathered up. Further, the padlock had been freshly oiled, and the hinges of the grating. No unused passage this, but one kept in order and repair. For what?

Bobby had adjusted the mask and thrust the knife through the belt of his Norfolk jacket. Now, folding his arms, he recited fiercely,

> "'Fifteen men on a dead man's chest.
> Yo-ho-ho and a bottle of rum!'"

"A spirited song," observed old Adelbert, as before. But his eyes were on the grating.

That evening Adelbert called to see his friend, the locksmith in the University Place. He possessed, he said, a padlock of which he had lost the key, and which, being fastened to a chest, he was unable to bring with him. A large and heavy padlock, perhaps the size of his palm.

When he left, he carried with him a bundle of keys, tied in a brown paper.

But he did not go back to his chest. He went instead to the thicket around the old gate, which was still termed the "Gate of the Moon," and there, armed with a lantern, pursued his investigations during a portion of the night.

When he had finished, old Adelbert, veteran of many wars, one-time patriot and newly turned traitor, held in his shaking hands the fate of the kingdom.

Chapter XXVI
At the Inn

The Countess Loschek was on her way across the border. The arrangements were not of her making. Her plan, which had been to go afoot across the mountain to the town of Ar-on-ar, and there to hire a motor, had been altered by the arrival at the castle, shortly after the permission was given, of a machine. So short an interval, indeed, had elapsed that she concluded, with reason, that this car now placed at her disposal was the one which had brought that permission.

"The matter of passports for the border is arranged, madame," Black Humbert told her.

"I have my own passports," she said proudly.

"They will not be necessary."

"I will have this interview at my destination alone; or not at all."

He drew himself to his great height and regarded her with cold eyes. "As you wish," he said. "But it is probably not necessary to remind madame that, whatever is discussed at this meeting, no word must be mentioned of the Committee, or its plans."

Although he made no threat, she had shivered. No, there must be no word of the Committee, or of the terror that drove her to Karl. For, if the worst happened, if he failed her, and she must do the thing they had set her to do, Karl must never know. That card she must play alone.

So she was not even to use her own passports! Making her hasty preparations, again the Countess marveled. Was there no limit to the powers of the Committee of Ten? Apparently the whole machinery of the Government was theirs to command. Who were they, these men who had sat there immobile behind their masks? Did she meet any of them daily in the Palace? Were the eyes that had regarded her with unfriendly steadiness that night in the catacombs, eyes that smiled at her day by day, in the very halls of the King? Had any of those shrouded and menacing figures bent over her hand with mocking suavity? She wondered.

A hasty preparation at the last it was, indeed, but a careful toilet had preceded it. Now that she was about to see Karl again, after months of separation, he must find no flaw in her. She searched her mirror for the ravages of the past few days, and found them. Yet, appraising herself with cold eyes, she felt she was still beautiful. The shadows about her eyes did not dim them.

Everything hung on the result of her visit. If Karl persisted, if he would marry Hedwig in spite of the trouble it would precipitate, then indeed she was lost. If, on the other hand, he was inclined to peace, if her story of a tottering throne held his hand, she would defy the Committee of Ten. Karl himself would help her to escape, might indeed hide her. It would not be for long. Without Karl's support the King's death would bring the Terrorists into control. They would have other things to do than to hunt her out. Their end would be gained without her. Let them steal the Crown Prince, then. Let Hedwig fight for her throne and lose it. Let the streets run, deep with blood and all the pandemonium of hell break loose.

But if Karl failed her?

Even here was the possibility of further mischance. Suppose the boy gone, and the people yet did not rise? Suppose then that Hedwig, by her very agency, gained the throne and held it. Hedwig, Queen of Livonia in her own right, and Karl's wife!

She clenched her teeth.

Over country roads the machine jolted and bumped. At daybreak they had not yet reached the border. In a narrow lane they encountered a pilgrimage of mountain folk, bent for the shrine at Etzel.

The peasants drew aside to let the Machine pass, and stared at it. They had been traveling afoot all night, and yet another day and a night would elapse before they could kneel in the church.

"A great lady," said one, a man who carried a sleeping child in his arms.

"Perhaps," said a young girl, "she too has made a pilgrimage. All go to Etzel, the poor and the rich. And all receive grace."

The Countess did not sleep. She was, with every fiber of her keen brain, summoning her arguments. She would need them, for she knew-none better-how great a handicap was hers. She loved Karl, and he knew it. What had been her strength had become her weakness.

Yet she was composed enough when, before the sun was well up, the machine drew up in the village before the inn where Mettlich had spent his uneasy hours.

Her heavy veils aroused the curiosity of the landlord. When, shortly after, his daughter brought down a letter to be sent at once to the royal hunting-lodge, he shrugged his shoulders. It was not the first time a veiled woman had come to his inn under similar circumstances. After all, great people are but human. One cannot always be a king.

The Countess breakfasted in her room. The landlord served her himself, and narrowly inspected her. She was not so young as he had hoped, but she was beautiful. And haughty. A very great person, he decided, incognito.

The King was hunting, he volunteered. There were great doings at the lodge. Perhaps Her Excellency would be proceeding there.

She eyed him stonily, and then sent him off about his business.

So all the day she ate her heart out in her bare room. Now and then the clear sound of bugles reached her, but she saw no hunters. Karl followed the chase late that day. It was evening before she saw the tired horses straggling through the village streets. Her courage was oozing by that time. What more could she say than what he already knew? Many agencies other than hers kept him informed of the state of affairs in Livonia. A bitter thought, this, for it showed Karl actuated by love of Hedwig, and not by greed of power. She feared that more than she feared death.

She had expected to go to the lodge, but at nine o'clock that night Karl came to her, knocking at the door of her room and entering without waiting for permission.

The room was small and cozy with firelight. Her scarlet cloak, flung over a chair, made a dash of brilliant color. Two lighted candles on a high carved chest, and between them a plaster figure of the Mother and Child, a built-in bed with white curtains-that was the room.

Before the open fire Olga Loschek sat in her low chair. She wore still her dark traveling dress; and a veil, ready to be donned at the summons of a message from Karl, trailed across her knee. In the firelight she looked very young-young and weary. Karl, who had come hardened to a scene, found her appealing, almost pathetic.

She rose at his entrance and, after a moment of surprise, smiled faintly. But she said nothing, nor did Karl, until he had lifted one of her cold hands and brushed it with his lips.

"Well!" he said. "And again, Olga!"

"Once again." She looked up at him. Yes, he was changed. The old Karl would have taken her in his arms. This new Karl was urbane, smiling, uneasy.

He said nothing. He was apparently waiting for her to make the first move. But she did not help him. She sat down and he drew a small chair to the fire.

"There is nothing wrong, is there?" he said. "Your note alarmed me. Not the note, but your coming here."

"Nothing-and everything." She felt suddenly very tired. Her very voice was weary. "I sent you a letter asking you to come to the castle. There were things to discuss, and I did not care to take this risk of coming here."

"I received no letter."

"No!" She knew it, of course, but she pretended surprise, a carefully suppressed alarm.

"I have what I am afraid is bad news, Olga. The letter was taken. I received only a sheet of blank paper."

"Karl!" She leaped to her feet.

She was no mean actress. And behind it all was her real terror, greater, much greater, than he could know. Whatever design she had on Karl's pity, she was only acting at the beginning. Deadly peril was clutching her, a double peril, of the body and of the soul.

"Taken! By whom?"

"By some one you know-young Larisch."

"Larisch!" No acting there. In sheer amazement she dropped back from him, staring with wide eyes. Nikky Larisch! Then how had the Terrorists got it? Was all the world in their employ?

"But-it is impossible!"

"I'm sorry, Olga. But even then there is something to be explained. We imprisoned him-we got him in a trap, rather by accident. He maintained that he had not made away with the papers. A mystery, all of it. Only your man, Niburg, could explain, and he —"

"Yes?"

"I am afraid he will never explain, Olga."

Then indeed horror had its way with her. Niburg executed as a spy, after making who knew what confession! What then awaited her at the old castle above the church at Etzel? Karl, seeing her whitening lips, felt a stirring of pity. His passion for her was dead, but for a long time he had loved her, and now, in sheer regret, he drew her to him.

"Poor girl," he said softly. "Poor girl!" And drew his hand gently over her hair.

She shivered at his touch. "I can never go back," she said brokenly.

But at that he freed her. "That would be to confess before you are accused," he reminded her. "We do not know that Niburg told. He was doomed anyhow. To tell would help nothing. The letter, of course, was in code?"

"Yes."

She sat down again, fighting for composure.

"I am not very brave," she said. "It was unexpected. In a moment I shall be calmer. You must not think that I regret the risk. I have always been proud to do my best for you."

That touched him. In the firelight, smiling wanly at him, she was very like the girl who had attracted him years before. Her usual smiling assurance was gone. She looked sad, appealing. And she was right. She had always done her best for him. But he was cautious, too.

"I owe you more than I can tell you," he said. "It is the sort of debt that can never be paid. Your coming here was a terrible risk. Something urgent must have brought you."

She pushed back her heavy hair restlessly.

"I was anxious. And there were things I felt you should know."

"What things?"

"The truth about the King's condition, for one. He is dying. The bulletins lie. He is no better."

"Why should the bulletins lie?"

"Because there is a crisis. You know it. But you cannot know what we know-the living in fear, the precautions, everything."

"So!" said Karl uneasily. "But the Chancellor assured me —" He stopped. It was not yet time to speak of the Chancellor's visit.

"The Chancellor! He lies, of course. How bad things are you may judge when I tell you that a hidden passage from the Palace has been opened and cleared, ready for instant flight."

It was Karl's turn to be startled. He rose, and stood staring down at her. "Are you certain of that?"

"Certain!" She laughed bitterly. "The Terrorists Revolutionists, they call themselves-are everywhere. They know everything, see everything. Mettlich's agents are disappearing one by one. No one knows where, but all suspect. Student meetings are prohibited. The yearly procession of veterans is forbidden, for they trust none, even their old soldiers. The Council meets day after day in secret session."

"But the army —"

"They do not trust the army."

Karl's face was grave. Something of the trouble in Livonia he had known. But this argued an immediate crisis.

"On the King's death," the Countess said, "a republic will be declared. The Republic of Livonia! The Crown Prince will never reign."

She shivered, but Karl was absorbed in the situation.

"Incredible!" he commented. "These fears are sometimes hysterias, but what you say of the preparations for flight —I thought the boy was very popular."

"With some. But when has a child stood between the mob and the thing it wants? And the thing they cry for is liberty. Down with the royal house! Down with the aristocracy!"

She was calm enough now. Karl was listening, was considering, looked uneasy. She had been right. He was not for acquiring trouble, even by marriage.

But, if she had read Karl, he also knew her. In all the years he had known her she had never been reckless. Daring enough, but with a calculating daring that took no chances. And yet she had done a reckless thing by coming to him. From under lowered eyelids he considered her. Why had she done it? The situation was serious enough, but even then — "So you came to-day to tell me this?"

She glanced up, and catching his eyes, colored faintly. "These are things you should know."

He knew her very well. A jealous woman would go far. He knew now that she was jealous. When he spoke it was with calculating brutality. "You mean, in view of my impending marriage?"

So it was arranged! Finally arranged. Well, she had done her best. He knew the truth. She had told it fairly. If, knowing it, he persisted, it would be because her power over him was dead at last.

"Yes. I do not know how far your arrangements have gone. You have at least been warned."

But she saw, by the very way he drew himself up and smiled, that he understood. More than that, he doubted her. He questioned what she had said.

The very fact that she had told him only the truth added to her resentment.

"You will see," she said sullenly.

Because he thought he already saw, and because she had given him a bad moment, Karl chose to be deliberately cruel. "Perhaps!" he said. "But even then if this marriage were purely one of expediency, Olga, I might hesitate. Frankly, I want peace. I am tired of war, tired of bickering, tired of watching and being watched. But it is not one of expediency. Not, at least, only that. You leave out of this discussion the one element that I consider important, Hedwig herself. If the Princess Hedwig were to-morrow to be without a country, I should still hope to marry her."

She had done well up to now, had kept her courage and her temper, had taken her cue from him and been quiet and poised. But more than his words, his cruel voice, silky with friendship, drove her to the breaking point. Karl, who hated a scene, found himself the victim of one, and was none the happier that she who had so long held him off was now herself at arm's length, and struggling.

Bitterly, and with reckless passion, she flung at him Hedwig's infatuation for young Larisch, and prophesied his dishonor as a result of it. That leaving him cold and rather sneering, she reviewed their old intimacy, to be reminded that in that there had been no question of marriage, or hope of it.

"I am only human, Olga," he said, in an interval when she had fallen to quiet weeping. "I loved you very sincerely, and for a long time. Marriage between us was impossible. You always knew that."

In the end she grew quiet and sat looking into the fire with eyes full of stony despair. She had tried and failed. There was one way left, only one, and even that would not bring him back to her. Let Hedwig escape and marry Nikky Larisch-still where was she? Let the Terrorists strike their blow and steal the Crown Prince. Again-where was she?

Her emotions were deadened, all save one, and that was her hatred of Hedwig. The humiliation of that moment was due to her. Somehow, some day, she would be even with Hedwig. Karl left her there at last, huddled in her chair, left full of resentment, the ashes of his old love cold and gray. There was little reminder of the girl of the mountains in the stony-eyed woman he had left sagged low by the fire.

Once out in the open air, the King of Karnia drew a long breath. The affair was over. It had been unpleasant. It was always unpleasant to break with a woman. But it was time. He neither loved her nor needed her. Friendly relations between the two countries were established; and soon, very soon, would be ratified by his marriage.

It was not of Olga Loschek, but of Hedwig that he thought, as his car climbed swiftly to the lodge.

Chapter XXVII
The Little Door

Hedwig had given up. She went through her days with a set face, white and drawn, but she knew now that the thing she was to do must be done. The King, in that stormy scene when the Sister prayed in the next room, had been sufficiently explicit. They had come on bad times, and could no longer trust to their own strength. Proud Livonia must ask for help, and that from beyond her border.

"We are rotten at the core," he said bitterly. "An old rot that has eaten deep. God knows, we have tried to cut it away, but it has gone too far. Times are, indeed, changed when we must ask a woman to save us!"

She had thrown her arms over the bed and buried her face in them. "And I am to be sacrificed," she had said, in a flat voice. "I am to go through my life like mother, soured and unhappy. Without any love at all."

The King was stirred. His thin, old body had sunk in the bed until it seemed no body at all. "Why without love?" he asked, almost gently. "Karl knows our condition-not all of it, but he is well aware that things are unstable here. Yet he is eager for the marriage. I am inclined to believe that he follows his inclinations, rather than a political policy."

The thought that Karl might love her had not entered her mind. That made things worse, if anything—a situation unfair to him and horrible to herself. In the silence of her own room, afterward, she pondered over that. If it were true, then a certain hope she had must be relinquished-none other than to throw herself on his mercy, and beg for a nominal marriage, one that would satisfy the political alliance, but leave both of them free. Horror filled her. She sat for long periods, dry-eyed and rigid.

The bronze statue of the late Queen, in the Place, fascinated her in those days. She, too, had been only a pawn in the game of empires; but her face, as Hedwig remembered it, had been calm and without bitterness. The King had mourned her sincerely. What lay behind that placid, rather austere old face? Dead dreams? Or were the others right, that after a time it made no difference, that one marriage was the same as another?

She had not seen Nikky save once or twice, and that in the presence of others. On these occasions he had bowed low, and passed on. But once she had caught his eyes on her, and had glowed for hours at what she saw in them. It braced her somewhat for the impending ordeal of a visit from Karl.

The days went on. Dressmakers came and went. In the mountains lace-makers were already working on the veil, and the brocade of white and gold for her wedding-gown was on the loom. She was the pale center of a riot of finery. Dressmakers stood back and raised delighted hands as, one by one; their models were adjusted to her listless figure.

In the general excitement the Crown Prince was almost forgotten. Only Nikky remained faithful; but his playing those days was mechanical, and one day he was even severe. This was when he found Prince Ferdinand William Otto hanging a cigarette out of a window overlooking the courtyard, and the line of soldiers underneath in most surprising confusion. The officer of the day was not in sight.

Nikky, entering the stone-paved court, and feeling extremely glum, had been amazed to see the line of guards, who usually sat on a bench, with a sentry or picket, or whatever they called him, parading up and down before them-Nikky was amazed to see them one by one leaping into the air, in the most undignified manner. Nikky watched the performance. Then he stalked over. They subsided sheepishly. In the air was the cause of the excitement, a cigarette dangling at the end of a silk thread, and bobbing up and down. No one was to be seen at the window above.

Nikky was very tall. He caught the offending atom on its next leap, and jerked it off. As he had suspected, it was one of his own, bearing an "N" and his coat of arms.

The Crown Prince received that day, with the cigarette as an excuse, a considerable amount of Nikky's general unhappiness and rage at the world.

"Well," said Prince Ferdinand William Otto, when it was over, "I have to do something, don't I?"

It was Miss Braithwaite's conviction that this prank, and several other things, such as sauntering about with his hands in his pockets, and referring to his hat as a "lid," were all the result of his meeting that American boy.

"He is really not the same child," she finished. "Oskar found him the other day with a rolled-up piece of paper lighted at the end, pretending he was smoking."

The Chancellor came now and then, but not often. And his visits were not cheering. The Niburg affair had left its mark on him. The incident of the beggar on the quay was another scar. The most extreme precautions were being taken, but a bad time was coming, and must be got over somehow.

That bad time was Karl's visit.

No public announcement of the marriage had yet been made. It was bound to be unpopular. Certainly the revolutionary party would make capital of it. To put it through by force, if necessary, and, that accomplished, to hold the scourge of Karnia's anger over a refractory people, was his plan. To soothe them with the news of the cession of the seaport strip was his hope.

Sometimes, in the early morning, when the King lay awake, and was clearer mentally than later in the day, he wondered. He would not live to see the result of all this planning. But one contingency presented itself constantly. Suppose the Crown Prince did not live? He was sturdy enough, but it was possible. Then Hedwig, Queen of Karnia, would be Queen of Livonia. A dual kingdom then, with Karl as Hedwig's consort, in control, undoubtedly. It would be the end of many dreams.

It seemed to him in those early hours, that they were, indeed, paying a price. Preparations were making for Karl's visit. Prince Hubert's rooms were opened at last, and redecorated as well as possible in the short time at command, under the supervision of the Archduchess. The result was a crowding that was neither dignified nor cheerful. Much as she trimmed her own lean body, she decorated. But she was busy, at least, and she let Hedwig alone.

It was not unusual, those days, to find Annunciata, flushed with exertion, in the great suite on an upper floor, in the center of a chaos of furniture, shoving chairs about with her own royal arms, or standing, head on one side, to judge what she termed the composition of a corner. Indignant footmen pushed and carried, and got their wigs crooked and their dignified noses dirty, and held rancorous meetings in secluded places.

But Annunciata kept on. It gave her something to think of in place of the fear, that filled her, made her weary enough to sleep at night.

And there was something else that comforted her.

Beyond the windows of the suite was a flat roof, beneath which was the ballroom of the Palace. When the apartment was in use, the roof was made into a garden, the ugly old walls hidden with plants in tubs and boxes, the parapet edged with flowers. It was still early, so spring tulips were planted now on the parapet, early primroses and hyacinths. In the center an empty fountain was cleared, its upper basins filled with water vines, its borders a riot of color. When the water was turned on, it would be quite lovely.

But it was not the garden on the roof which cheered Annunciata. It had, indeed, rather sad memories. Here had Hubert's young wife kept her cages of birds, fed with her own hands, and here, before Otto was born, she had taken the air in a long chintz-covered chair.

Annunciata, overseeing the roof as she had overseen the apartment, watched the gardeners bringing in their great loads of plants from the summer palace, and saw that a small door, in a turret, was kept free of access. To that door, everything else failing, the Archduchess pinned her faith. She carried everywhere with her a key that would open it.

Long ago had the door been built, long ago, when attacking forces, battering in the doors below, might swarm through the lower floors, held back on staircases by fighting men who retreated, step by step, until, driven at last to the very top, they were apparently lost. More than once; in bygone times the royal family had escaped by that upper door, and the guard after them. It was known to few.

The staircase in the wall had passed into legend, and the underground passage with it. But they still existed, and had recently been put in order. The Chancellor had given the command; and because there were few to be trusted, two monks from the monastery attached to the cathedral had done the work.

So the gardeners set out their potted evergreens, and covered the primroses on the balustrade against frost, and went away. And the roof had become by magic a garden, the walls were miniature forests, but the door remained —a door.

On a desperate morning Hedwig threw caution to the winds and went to the riding-school. She wore her old habit, and was in the ring, but riding listlessly, when Nikky and Otto appeared.

"And eat." Nikky was saying. "He always eats. And when I take him for a walk in the park, he digs up bones that other dogs have buried, and carries them home with him. We look very disreputable." The Crown Prince laughed with delight, but just then Nikky saw Hedwig, and his own smile died.

"There's Hedwig!" said Prince Ferdinand William Otto. "I'm rather glad to see her. Aren't you?"

"Very glad, indeed."

"You don't look glad."

"I'm feeling very glad inside."

They rode together, around and around the long oval, with its whitewashed railing, its attendant grooms, its watchful eyes overhead. Between Nikky and Hedwig Prince Ferdinand William Otto laughed and chattered, and Hedwig talked a great deal about nothing, with bright spots of red burning in her face.

Nikky was very silent. He rode with his eyes set ahead; and had to be spoken to twice before he heard.

"You are not having a very good time, are you?" Prince Ferdinand William Otto inquired anxiously. To tell the truth, he had been worried about Nikky for some days. Nikky had been his one gleam of cheerfulness in a Palace where all was bustle and excitement and every one seemed uneasy. But Nikky's cheerfulness had been forced lately. His smile never reached his eyes. "I haven't done anything, have I?" he persisted.

"Bless you, no!" said Nikky heartily. "I—well, I didn't sleep well last night. That's all."

He met Hedwig's glance squarely over the head of the Crown Prince.

"Nor did I," Hedwig said.

Later, when the boy was jumping, they had a moment together. The Crown Prince was very absorbed. He was just a little nervous about jumping. First he examined his stirrups and thrust his feet well into them. Then he jammed his cap down on his head and settled himself, in the saddle, his small knees gripping hard.

"It's higher than usual, isn't it?" he inquired, squinting at the hurdle.

The riding-master examined it. "It is an inch lower than yesterday, Your Royal Highness."

"Perhaps we'd better have it the same as yesterday," said the boy, who was terribly afraid of being afraid.

Then, all being adjusted, and his mouth set very tight, indeed, Prince Ferdinand William Otto took the first jump, and sailed over it comfortably.

"I don't mind at all, after the first," he confided to the riding-master.

"Are you angry that I came?" asked Hedwig.

"Angry? You know better."

"You don't say anything."

"Hedwig," said Nikky desperately, "do you remember what I said to you the other day? That is in my heart now. I shall never change. That, and much more. But I cannot say it to you. I have given my word."

"Of course they would make you promise. They tried with me, but I refused." She held her chin very high. "Why did you promise? They could not have forced you. They can do many things, but they cannot control what you may say."

"There are reasons. Even those I cannot tell you. It would be easier, Hedwig, for me to die than to live on and see what I must see. But I cannot even die." He smiled faintly. "You see, I am not keeping my promise."

"I think you will not die," said Hedwig cruelly. "You are too cautious."

"Yes, I am too cautious," he agreed heavily.

"You do not know the meaning of love."

"Then God grant I may never know, if it is worse than this:"

"If I were a man, and loved a woman, I would think less of myself and more of her. When I saw her unhappy and being forced to a terrible thing, I would move heaven and earth to save her."

"How would you do it?" said Nikky in a low tone.

Hedwig shrugged her shoulders. "I would find a way. The world is large. Surely, if one really cared, it could be managed. I should consider my first duty to her."

"I am a soldier, Highness. My first duty is to my country."

"You?" said Hedwig, now very white. "I was not speaking of you. I was speaking of a man who truly loved a woman."

She rode away, and left him there. And because she was hurt and reckless, and not quite sane, she gave him a very bad half-hour. She jumped again, higher each time, silencing the protests of the riding-master with an imperious gesture. Her horse tired. His sides heaved, his delicate nostrils dilated. She beat him with her crop, and flung him again at the hurdle.

Prince Ferdinand William Otto was delighted, a trifle envious. "She jumps better than I do," he observed to Nikky, "but she is in a very bad humor."

At last, his patience exhausted and fear in his heart, Nikky went to her. "Hedwig," he said sternly. "I want you to stop this childishness. You will kill yourself."

"I am trying very hard to."

"You will kill your horse. Look at him."

For answer she raised her crop, but Nikky bent forward and caught the reins.

"How dare you!" she said furiously.

For answer Nikky turned and, riding beside her, led her weary horse out of the ring. And long training asserted itself. Hedwig dared not make a scene before the waiting grooms. She rode in speechless rage, as white as Nikky, and trembling with fury. She gave him no time to assist her to dismount, but slipped off herself and left him, her slim, black-habited figure held very straight.

"I'm afraid she's very angry with you," said the Crown Prince, as they walked back to the Palace. "She looked more furious than she did about the fruitcake."

That afternoon Nikky went for a walk. He took Toto with him, and they made the circuit of the Park, which formed an irregular circle about the narrow streets of the old citadel where the wall had once stood. He walked, as he had done before, because he was in trouble, but with this difference, that then, he had walked in order to think, and now he walked to forget.

In that remote part where the Gate of the Moon stood, and where, outside, in mediaeval times had been the jousting-ground, the Park widened. Here was now the city playground, the lake where in winter the people held ice carnivals, and where, now that spring was on the way, they rode in the little cars of the Scenic Railway.

An old soldier with a wooden leg, and a child, were walking together by the lake, and conversing seriously. A dog was burying a bone under a near-by tree. Toto, true to his instincts, waited until the bone was covered, and then, with calm proprietorship, dug it up and carried it off. Having learned that Nikky now and then carried bones in his pockets, he sat up and presented it to him. Nikky paying no attention at first, Toto flung it up in the air, caught it on his nose, balanced it a second, and dropped it. Then followed a sudden explosion of dog-rage and a mix-up of two dogs, an old soldier, a young one, a boy, and a wooden leg. In the end the wooden leg emerged triumphant, Toto clinging to it under the impression that he had something quite different. The bone was flung into the lake, and a snarling truce established.

But there had been a casualty. Bobby had suffered a severe nip on the forearm, and was surveying it with rather dazed eyes.

"Gee, it's bleeding!" he said.

Nikky looked worried, but old Adelbert, who had seen many wounds, recommended tying it up with garlic, and then forgetting it. "It is the first quarter of the moon," he said. "No dog's bite is injurious at that time."

Nikky, who had had a sniff of the bone of contention, was not so easy in his mind. First quarter of the moon it might be, but the bone was not in its first quarter. "I could walk home with the boy," he suggested, "and get something at a chemist's on the way."

"Will it hurt?" demanded Bobby.

"We will ask for something that will not hurt."

So it happened that Bobby and Tucker, the two pirates, returned that day to their home under the escort of a tall young man who carried a bottle wrapped in pink paper in his hand, and looked serious. Old Pepy was at home. She ran about getting basins, and because Nikky had had his first-aid training, in a very short time everything was shipshape, and no one the worse.

"Do you suppose it will leave a scar?" Bobby demanded.

"Well, a little one, probably."

"I've got two pretty good ones already," Bobby boasted, "not counting my vaccination. Gee! I bet mother'll be surprised."

"The Americans," said Pepy, with admiring eyes fixed on their visitor, "are very peculiar about injuries. They speak always of small animals that crawl about in wounds and bring poison."

"Germs!" Bobby explained. "But they know about germs here, too. I, played with a boy one, afternoon at the Scenic Railway-my father is the manager, you know. If you like, I can give you some tickets. And the boy said a fig lady he had was covered with germs. We ate it anyhow."

Nikky looked down smilingly. So this was the American lad! Of course. He could understand Otto's warm feeling now. They were not unlike, the two children. This boy was more sturdy, not so fine, perhaps, but eminently likable. He was courageous, too. The iodine had not been pleasant, but he had only whistled.

"And nothing happened to the other boy, because of the germs?"

"I don't know. He never came back. He was a funny boy. He had a hat like father's. Gee!"

Nikky took his departure, followed by Pepy's eyes. As long as he was in sight she watched him from the window. "He is some great person," she said to Bobby. "Of the aristocracy. I know the manner."

"A prince, maybe?"

"Perhaps. You in America, you have no such men, I think, such fine soldiers, aristocrats, and yet gentle. The uniform is considered the handsomest in Europe."

"Humph!" said Bobby aggressively. "You ought to see my uncle dressed for a Knight Templar parade. You'd see something."

Nikky went down the stairs, with Toto at his heels, a valiant and triumphant Toto, as becomes a dog who has recently vanquished a wooden leg.

At the foot of the staircase a man was working replacing a loosened tile in the passage; a huge man, clad in a smock and with a bushy black beard tucked in his neck out of the way. Nikky nodded to him, and went out. Like a cat Black Humbert was on his feet, and peering after him from the street door. It was he, then, the blond devil who, had fallen on them that night, and had fought as one who fights for the love of it! The concierge went back to the door of his room.

Herman Spier sat inside. He had fortified his position by that trip to the mountains, and now spent his days in Black Humbert's dirty kitchen, or in errand-running. He was broiling a sausage on the end of a fork.

"Quick!" cried Black Humbert. "Along the street, with a black dog at his heels, goes one you will recognize. Follow him, and find out what you can."

Herman Spier put the sausage in his pocket-he had paid for it himself, and meant to have it-and started out. It was late when he returned.

He gave Nikky's name and position, where his lodgings were, or had been until now. He was about to remove to the Palace, having been made aide-de-camp to the Crown Prince.

"So!" said Black Humbert.

"It is also," observed Herman Spier, eating his sausage, "this same one who led the police to Niburg's room. I have the word of the woman who keeps the house."

The concierge rose, and struck the table with his fist. "And now he comes here!" he said. "The boy upstairs was a blind. He has followed us." He struck the sausage furiously out of Herman's hand. "Tonight the police will come. And what then?"

"If you had taken my advice," said the clerk, "you would have got rid of that fellow upstairs long ago." He picked up the sausage and dusted it with his hand. "But I do not believe the police will come. The child was bitten. I saw them enter."

Nevertheless, that night, while Herman Spier kept watch at the street door, the concierge labored in the little yard behind the house. He moved a rabbit hutch and, wedging his huge body behind it, loosened a board or two in the high wooden fence.

More than the Palace prepared for flight.

Still later, old Adelbert roused from sleep. There were footsteps in the passage outside, the opening of a door. He reflected that the concierge was an owl and, the sounds persisting, called out an irritable order for quiet.

Then he slept again, and while he slept the sounds recommenced. Had he glanced out into the passage, then, he would have seen two men, half supporting a third, who tottered between them. Thus was the student Haeckel, patriot and Royalist, led forth to die.

And he did not die.

Chapter XXVIII
Tee Crown Prince's Pilgrimage

The day when Olga Loschek should have returned to the city found her too ill to travel. No feigned sickness this, but real enough, a matter of fever and burning eyes, and of mutterings in troubled sleep.

Minna was alarmed. She was fond of her mistress, in spite of her occasional cruelties, and lately the Countess had been strangely gentle. She required little attention, wished to be alone, and lay in her great bed, looking out steadily at the bleak mountain-tops, to which spring never climbed.

"She eats nothing," Minna said despairingly to the caretaker. "And her eyes frighten me. They are always open, even in the night, but they seem to see nothing."

On the day when she should have returned, the Countess roused herself enough to send for Black Humbert, fretting in the kitchen below. He had believed that she was malingering until he saw her, but her flushed and hollow cheeks showed her condition.

"You must return and explain," she said. "I shall need more time, after all." When he hesitated, she added: "There are plenty to watch that I do not escape. I could not, if I would. I have not the strength."

"Time is passing," he said gruffly, "and we get nowhere."

"As soon as I can travel, I will come."

"If madame wishes, I can take a letter."

She pondered over that, interlacing her fingers nervously as she reflected.

"I will send no letter," she decided, "but I will give you a message, which you can deliver."

"Yes, madame."

"Say to the Committee," she began, and paused. She had thought and thought until her brain burned with thinking, but she had found no way out. And yet she could not at once bring herself to speech. But at last she said it: "Say to the Committee that I have reflected and that I will do what they ask. As far," she added, "as lies in my power. I can only —"

"That is all the Committee expects," he said civilly, and with a relief that was not lost on her. "With madame's intelligence, to try is to succeed."

Nevertheless, he left her well guarded. Even Minna, slipping off for an evening hour with a village sweetheart, was stealthily shadowed. Before this, fine ladies had changed garments with their maids and escaped from divers unpleasantnesses.

Olga Loschek lay in her bed, and always there were bells. The cattle were being driven up into the mountains for the summer grazing, great, soft-eyed herds, their bells tinkling slowly as they made their deliberate, soft-footed progress along the valley; the silvery bells for mass; the clock striking the hour with its heavy, vibrating clamor of bronze.

When she sank into the light sleep of fever, they roused her, or she slept on; hearing in their tones the great bell of St. Stefan's announcing the King's death. Bells, always bells.

At the end of two days she was able to be up again. She moved languidly about her room, still too weak to plan. There were times when she contemplated suicide, but she knew herself to be too cowardly to do more than dream of it.

And on the fourth day came the Crown Prince of Livonia on a pilgrimage.

The manner of his coming was this:

There are more ways than one of reaching the hearts of an uneasy people. Remission of taxes is a bad one. It argues a mistake in the past, in exacting such tithes. Governments may make errors, but must not acknowledge them. There is the freeing of political prisoners, but that, too, is dangerous, when such prisoners breathe sedition to the very prison walls.

And there is the appeal to sentiment. The Government, pinning all its hopes to one small boy, would further endear him to the people. Wily statesman that he was, the Chancellor had hit on this to offset the rumors of Hedwig's marriage.

But the idea was not his, although he adopted it. It had had its birth in the little room with the Prie-dieu and the stand covered with bottles, had been born of the Sister's belief in the miracles of Etzel.

However, he appropriated it, and took it to the King.

"A pilgrimage!" said the King, when the mater was broached to him. "For what? My recovery? Cannot you let your servant depart in peace?"

"Pilgrimages," observed the Chancellor, "have had marvelous results, sire. I do not insist that they perform miracles, as some believe," —he smiled faintly, —"but as a matter of public feeling and a remedy for discord, they are sometimes efficacious."

"I see," said the King. And lay still, looking at the ceiling.

"Can it be done safely?" he asked at last.

"The maddest traitor would not threaten the Crown Prince on a pilgrimage. The people would tear him limb from limb."

"Nevertheless, I should take all precautions," he said dryly. "A madman might not recognize the-er-religious nature of the affair."

The same day the Chancellor visited Prince Ferdinand William Otto, and found him returned from his drive and busy over Hedwig's photograph frame.

"It is almost done," he said. "I slipped over in one or two places, but it is not very noticeable, is it?"

The Chancellor observed it judicially, and decided that the slipping over was not noticeable at all. Except during school hours Miss Braithwaite always retired during the Chancellor's visits, and so now the two were alone.

"Otto," said the Chancellor gravely, "I want to talk to you very seriously."

"Have I done anything?"

"No." He smiled. "It is about something I would like you to do. For your grandfather."

"I'll do anything for him, sir."

"We know that. This is the point. He has been ill for along time. Very ill."

The boy watched him with a troubled face. "He looks very thin," he said. "I get quite worried when I see him."

"Exactly. You have heard of Etzel?"

Prince Ferdinand William Otto's religious instruction was of the best. He had, indeed, heard of Etzel. He knew the famous pilgrimages in order, and could say them rapidly, beginning, the year of Our Lord 915 —the Emperor Otto and Adelheid, his spouse; the year of Our Lord 1100, Ulrich, Count of Ruburg; and so on.

"When people are ill," he said sagely, "they go to Etzel to be cured."

"Precisely. But when they cannot go, they send some one else, to pray for them. And some-times, if they have faith enough, the holy miracle happens, and they are cured."

The Chancellor was deeply religious, and although he had planned the pilgrimage for political reasons, for the moment he lost sight of them. What if, after all, this clear-eyed, clean-hearted child could bring this miracle of the King's recovery? It was a famous shrine, and stranger things had been brought about by less worthy agencies.

"I thought," he said, "that if you would go to Etzel, Otto, and there pray for your grandfather's recovery, it-it would be a good thing."

The meaning of such a pilgrimage dawned suddenly on the boy. His eyes filled, and because he considered it unmanly to weep, he slid from his chair and went to the window. There he got out his pocket-handkerchief and blew his nose.

"I'm afraid he's going to die," he said, in a smothered voice.

The Chancellor followed him to the window, and put an arm around his shoulders. "Even that would not be so terrible, Otto," he said. "Death, to the old, is not terrible. It is an open door, through which they go gladly, because-because those who have gone ahead are waiting just beyond it."

"Are my mother and father waiting?"

"Yes, Otto."

He considered. "And my grandmother?"

"Yes."

"He'll be very glad to see them all again."

"Very happy, indeed. But we need him here, too, for a while. You need him and —I. So we will go and pray to have him wait a little longer before he goes away. Hour about it?"

"I'll try. I'm not very good. I do a good many things, you know."

Here, strangely enough, it was the Chancellor who fumbled for his handkerchief. A vision had come to him of the two of them kneeling side by side at Etzel, the little lad who was "not very good," and he himself with his long years behind him of such things as fill a man's life. And because the open door was not so far ahead for him either, and because he believed implicitly in the great Record within the Gate, he shook his shaggy head.

So the pilgrimage was arranged. With due publicity, of course, and due precaution for safety. By train to the foot of the mountains, and then on foot for the ten miles to Etzel.

On the next day the Crown Prince fasted, taking nothing but bread and a cup of milk. On the day of the pilgrimage, however, having been duly prepared, and mass having been said at daybreak in the chapel, with all the Court present, he was given a substantial breakfast. His small legs had a toilsome journey before them.

He went through his preparation in a sort of rapt solemnity. So must the boy crusaders have looked as, starting on their long journey, they faced south and east, toward the far-distant Sepulcher of Our Lord.

The King's Council went, the Chancellor, the Mayor of the city, wearing the great gold chain of his office around his neck, and a handful of soldiers, —a simple pilgrimage and the more affecting. There were no streaming banners, no magnificent vestments. The Archbishop accompanied them; and a flag-bearer.

They went on foot to the railway station through lines of kneeling people, the boy still rapt; and looking straight ahead, the Chancellor seemingly also absorbed, but keenly alive to the crowds. As he went on, his face relaxed. It was as if the miracle had already happened. Not the miracle for which the boy would pray, but a greater one. Surely these kneeling people, gazing with moist and kindly eyes at the Crown Prince, could not, at the hot words of demagogues, turn into the mob he feared. But it had happened before. The people who had, one moment, adored the Dauphin of France on his balcony at Versailles, had lived to scream for his life.

On and on, through the silent, crowded streets. No drums; no heralds, no bugles. First the standard-bearer; then the Archbishop, walking with his head bent; then the boy, alone and bareheaded, holding his small hat in moist; excited fingers; then the others, the Chancellor and the Mayor together, the Council, the guard. So they moved along, without speech, grave, reverent, earnest.

At the railway station a man stepped out of the crowd and proffered a paper to the Crown Prince. But he was too absorbed to see it, and a moment later the Chancellor had it, and was staring with hard eyes at the individual who had presented it. A moment later, without sound, or breach of decorum, the man was between two agents, a prisoner. The paper, which the Chancellor read on the train and carefully preserved, was a highly seditious document attacking the Government and ending with threats.

The Chancellor, who had started in an exalted frame of mind, sat scowling and thoughtful during the journey. How many of those who had knelt on the street had had similar seditious papers in their pockets? A people who could kneel, and, kneeling, plot!

The Countess, standing on her balcony and staring down into the valley, beheld the pilgrimage and had thus her first knowledge of it. She was incredulous at first, and stood gazing, gripping the stone railing with tense hands. She watched, horror-stricken. The Crown Prince, himself, come to Etzel to pray! For his grandfather, of course. Then, indeed, must things be bad with the King, as bad as they could be.

The Crown Prince was very warm. She could see the gleam of his handkerchief as he wiped his damp face. She could see the effort of his tired legs to keep step with the standard-bearer.

The bells again. How she hated them! They rang out now to welcome the pilgrims, and a procession issued from the church door, a lay brother first, carrying a banner, then the fathers, two by two; the boys from the church school in long procession. The royal party halted at the foot of the street. The fathers advanced. She could make out Father Gregory's portly figure among them. The bell tolled. The villagers stood in excited but quiet groups, and watched.

Then the two banners touched, the schoolboys turned, followed by the priests. Thus led, went the Crown Prince of Livonia to pray for his grandfather's life.

The church doors closed behind them.

Olga Loschek fell on her knees. She was shaking from head to foot. And because the religious training of her early life near the shrine had given her faith in miracles, she prayed for one. Rather, she made a bargain with God: — If any word came to her from Karl, any, no matter, to what it pertained, she would take it for a sign, and attempt flight. If she was captured, she would kill herself.

But, if no word came from Karl by the hour of her departure the next morning, then she would do the thing she had set out to do, and let him beware! The King dead, there would be no King. Only over the dead bodies of the Livonians would they let him marry Hedwig and the throne. It would be war.

Curiously, while she was still on her knees, her bargain made, the plan came to her by which, when the time came, the Terrorists were to rouse the people to even greater fury. Still kneeling, she turned it over in her mind. It was possible. More, it could be made plausible, with her assistance. And at the vision it evoked, —Mettlich's horror and rage, Hedwig's puling tears, her own triumph, —she took a deep breath. Revenge with a vengeance, retaliation for old hurts and fresh injuries, these were what she found on her knees, while the bell in the valley commenced the mass, and a small boy; very rapt and very earnest, prayed for his grandfather's life.

Yet the bargain came very close to being made the other way that day, and by Karl himself.

Preparations were being made for his visit to Livonia. Ostensibly this visit was made because of the King's illness. Much political capital was being made of Karl's going to see, for the last time, the long-time enemy of his house. While rumor was busy, Karnia was more than satisfied.

Even the Socialist Party approved, and their papers, being more frank than the others, spoke openly of the chances of a dual kingdom, the only bar being a small boy.

On the day of the pilgrimage Karl found himself strangely restless and uneasy. He had returned to his capital the day before, and had busied himself until late that night with matters of state. He had slept well, and wakened to a sense of well-being. But, during the afternoon, he became uneasy. Olga Loschek haunted him, her face when he had told her about the letter, her sagging figure when he had left her.

Something like remorse stirred in him. She had taken great risks for him. Of all the women he had known, she had most truly and unselfishly loved him. And for her years of service he had given her contempt. He reflected, too, that he had, perhaps, made an enemy where he needed a friend. How easy, by innuendo and suggestion, to turn Hedwig against him, Hedwig who already fancied herself interested elsewhere.

Very nearly did he swing the scale in which Olga Loschek had hung her bargain with God-so nearly that in the intervals of affixing his sprawling signature to various documents, he drew a sheet of note-paper toward him. Then, with a shrug, he pushed it away. So Olga Loschek lost her bargain.

At dawn the next morning the Countess, still pale with illness and burning with fever, went back to the city.

Chapter XXIX
Old Adelbert the Traitor

"Thus," said the concierge, frying onions over his stove; "thus have they always done. But you have been blind. Rather, you would not see."

Old Adelbert stirred uneasily. "So long as I accept my pension —"

"Why should you not accept your pension. A trifle in exchange for what you gave. For them, who now ill-use you, you have gone through life but half a man. Women smile behind their hands when you hobble by."

"I do not hold with women," said old Adelbert, flushing. "They take all and give nothing." The onions were done, and the concierge put them, frying-pan and all, on the table. "Come, eat while the food is hot. And give nothing," he repeated, returning to the attack. "You and I ride in no carriages with gilt wheels. We work, or, failing work, we starve. Their feet are on our necks. But one use they have for us, you and me, my friend-to tax us."

"The taxes are not heavy," quoth old Adelbert.

"There are some who find them so." The concierge heaped his guest's plate with onions. And old Adelbert, who detested onions, and was besides in no mood for food, must perforce sample them.

"I can cook," boasted his host. "The daughter of my sister cannot cook. She uses milk, always milk. Feeble dishes, I call them. Strong meat for strong men, comrade."

Old Adelbert played with his steel fork. "I was a good patriot," he observed nervously, "until they made me otherwise."

"I will make you a better. A patriot is one who is zealous for his country and its welfare. That means much. It means that when the established order is bad for a country, it must be changed. Not that you and I may benefit. God knows, we may not live to benefit. But that Livonia may free her neck from the foot of the oppressor, and raise her head among nations."

From which it may be seen that old Adelbert had at last joined the revolutionary party, an uneasy and unhappy recruit, it is true, but —a recruit. "If only some half-measure would suffice," he said, giving up all pretense of eating. "This talk of rousing the mob, of rioting and violence, I do not like them."

"Then has age turned the blood in your veins to water!" said the concierge contemptuously. "Half-measures! Since when has a half-measure been useful? Did half-measures win in your boasted battles? And what half-measures would you propose?"

Old Adelbert sat silent. Now and then, because his mouth was dry, he took a sip of beer from his tankard. The concierge ate, taking huge mouthfuls of onions and bread, and surveying his feeble-hearted recruit with appraising eyes. To win him would mean honor, for old Adelbert, decorated for many braveries, was a power among the veterans. Where he led, others would follow.

"Make no mistake," said Black Humbert cunningly. "We aim at no bloodshed. A peaceful revolution, if possible. The King, being dead, will suffer not even humiliation. Let the royal family scatter where it will. We have no designs on women. The Chancellor, however, must die."

"I make no plea for him," said old Adelbert bitterly. "I wrote to him also, when I lost my position, and received no reply. We passed through the same campaigns, as I reminded him, but he did nothing."

"As for the Crown Prince," observed the concierge, eyeing the old man over the edge of his tankard, "you know our plan for him. He will be cared for as my own child, until we get him beyond the boundaries. Then he will be safely delivered to those who know nothing of his birth. A private fund of the Republic will support and educate him."

Old Adelbert's hands twitched. "He is but a child," he said, "but already he knows his rank."

"It will be wise for him to forget it." His tone was ominous. Adelbert glanced up quickly, but the Terrorist had seen his error, and masked it with a grin. "Children forget easily," he said, "and by this secret knowledge of yours, old comrade, all can be peacefully done. Until you brought it to me, we were, I confess, fearful that force would be necessary. To admit the rabble to the Palace would be dangerous. Mobs go mad at such moments. But now it may be effected with all decency and order."

"And the plan?"

"I may tell you this." The concierge shoved his plate away and bent over the table. "We have set the day as that of the Carnival. On that day all the people are on the streets. Processions are forbidden, but the usual costuming with their corps colors as pompons is allowed. Here and there will be one of us clad in red, a devil, wearing the colors of His Satanic Majesty. Those will be of our forces, leaders and speech-makers. When we secure the Crown Prince, he will be put into costume until he can be concealed. They will seek, if there be time, the Prince Ferdinand William Otto. Who will suspect a child, wearing some fantastic garb of the Carnival?"

"But the King?" inquired old Adelbert in a shaking voice. "How can you set a day, when the King may rally? I thought all hung on the King's death."

The concierge bent closer over the table. "Doctor Wiederman, the King's physician, is one of us," he whispered. "The King lives now only because of stimulants to the heart. His body is already dead. When the stimulants cease, he will die."

Old Adelbert covered his eyes. He had gone too far to retreat now. Driven by brooding and trouble, he had allied himself with the powers of darkness.

The stain, he felt, was already on his forehead. But before him, like a picture on a screen, came the scene by which he had lived for so many years, the war hospital, the King by his bed, young then and a very king in looks, pinning on the breast of his muslin shirt the decoration for bravery.

He sat silent while the concierge cleared the table, and put the dishes in a pan for his niece to wash. And throughout the evening he said little. At something before midnight he and his host were to set out on a grave matter, nothing less than to visit the Committee of Ten, and impart the old soldier's discovery. In the interval he sat waiting, and nursing his grievances to keep them warm.

Men came and went. From beneath the floor came, at intervals, a regular thudding which he had never heard before, and which he now learned was a press.

"These are days of publicity," explained the concierge. "Men are influenced much by the printed word. Already our bulletins flood the country. On the day of the Carnival the city will flame with them, printed in red. They will appear, as if by magic power, everywhere."

"A call to arms?"

"A call to liberty," evaded the concierge.

Not in months had he taken such pleasure in a recruit. He swaggered about the room, recounting in boastful tones his influence with the Committee of Ten.

"And with reason," he boasted, pausing before the old soldier. "I have served them well; here in this house is sufficient ammunition to fight a great battle. You, now, you know something of ammunition. You have lived here for a long time. Yet no portion of this house has been closed to you. Where, at a guess, is it concealed?"

"It is in this house?"

"So I tell you. Now, where?"

"In the cellar, perhaps."

"Come, I will show you." He led old Adelbert by the elbow to a window overlooking the yard. Just such an enclosure as each of the neighboring houses possessed, and surrounded by a high fence. Here was a rabbit hutch, built of old boards, and familiar enough to the veteran's eyes; and a dovecote, which loomed now but a deeper shadow among shadows.

"Carrier-pigeons," explained the concierge. "You have seen them often, but you suspected nothing, eh? They are my telegraph. Now, look again, comrade. What else?"

"Barrels," said old Adelbert, squinting. "The winter's refuse from the building. A —a most untidy spot."

His soldierly soul had revolted for months at the litter under his window. And somewhere, in the disorder, lay his broken sword. His sword broken, and he — "Truly untidy," observed the concierge complacently. "A studied untidiness, and even then better than a room I shall show you in the cellar, filled to overflowing with boxes containing the winter's ashes. Know you," he went on, dropping his voice, "that these barrels and boxes are but —a third full of rubbish. Below that in cases is-what we speak of."

"But I thought —a peaceful revolution, a —"

"We prepare for contingencies. Peace if possible. If not, war. I am telling you much because, by your oath, you are now one of us, and bound to secrecy. But, beside that, I trust you. You are a man of your word."

"Yes," said old Adelbert, drawing himself up. "I am a man of my word. But you cannot fight with cartridges alone."

"We have rifles, also, in other places. Even I do not know where all of them are concealed." The concierge chuckled in his beard. "The Committee knows men well. It trusts none too much. There are other depots throughout the city, each containing supplies of one sort and another. On the day of the uprising each patriot will be told where to go for equipment. Not before."

Old Adelbert was undoubtedly impressed. He regarded the concierge with furtive eyes. He, Adelbert, had lived in the house with this man of parts for years, and had regarded him as but one of many.

Black Humbert, waiting for the hour to start and filling his tankard repeatedly, grew loquacious. He hinted of past matters in which he had proved his value to the cause. Old Adelbert gathered that, if he had not actually murdered the late Crown Prince and his wife, he had been closely concerned in it. His thin, old flesh crept with anxiety. It was a bad business, and he could not withdraw.

"We should have had the child, too," boasted the concierge, "and saved much bother. But he had been, unknown to us, sent to the country. A matter of milk, I believe."

"But you say you do not war on children!"

"Bah! A babe of a few months. Furthermore," said the concierge, "I have a nose for the police. I scent a spy, as a dog scents a bone. Who, think you, discovered Haeckel?"

"Haeckel!" Old Adelbert sat upright in his chair.

"Aye, Haeckel, Haeckel the jovial, the archconspirator, who himself assisted to erect the press you hear beneath your feet. Who but I? I suspected him. He was too fierce. He had no caution. He was what a peaceful citizen may fancy a revolutionist to be. I watched him. He was not brave. He was reckless because he had nothing to fear. And at last I caught him."

Old Adelbert was sitting forward on the edge of his chair; his jaw dropped. "And what then?" he gasped. "He was but a boy. Perhaps you misjudged him. Boys are reckless."

"I caught him," said the concierge. "I have said it. He knew much. He had names, places, even dates. For that matter; he confessed."

"Then he is dead?" quavered old Adelbert.

The concierge shrugged his shoulders. "Of course," he said briefly. "For a time he was kept here, in an upper room. He could have saved himself, if he would. We could have used him. But he turned sulky, refused speech, did not eat. When he was taken away," he added with unction, "he was so weak that he could not walk." He rose and consulted a great silver watch. "We can go now," he said. "The Committee likes promptness."

They left together, the one striding out with long steps that were surprisingly light for his size, the other, hanging back a trifle, as one who walks because he must. Old Adelbert, who had loved his King better than his country, was a lagging "patriot" that night. His breath came short and labored. His throat was dry. As they passed the Opera, however, he threw his head up. The performance was over, but the great house was still lighted, and in the foyer, strutting about, was his successor. Old Adelbert quickened his steps.

At the edge of the Place, near the statue of the Queen, they took a car, and so reached the borders of the city. After that they walked far. The scent of the earth, fresh-turned by the plough, was in their nostrils. Cattle, turned out after the long winter, grazed or lay in the fields. Through the ooze of the road the two plodded; old Adelbert struggling through with difficulty, the concierge exhorting him impatiently to haste.

At last the leader paused, and surveyed his surroundings: "Here I must cover your eyes, comrade," he said. "It is a formality all must comply with."

Old Adelbert drew back. "I do not like your rule. I am not as other men. I must see where I go."

"I shall lead you carefully. And, if you fear, I can carry you." He chuckled at the thought. But old Adelbert knew well that he could do it, knew that he was as a child to those mighty arms. He submitted to the bandage, however, with an ill grace that caused the concierge to smile.

"It hurts your dignity, eh, old rooster!" he said jovially. "Others, of greater dignity, have felt the same. But all submit in the end."

He piloted the veteran among the graves with the ease of familiarity. Only once he spoke. "Know you where you are?"

"In a field," said Adelbert, "recently ploughed."

"Aye, in a field, right enough. But one which sows corruption, and raises nothing, until perhaps great St. Gabriel calls in his crop."

Then, realizing the meaning of the mounds over which he trod, old Adelbert crossed himself.

"Only a handful know of this meeting-place," boasted the concierge. "I, and a few others. Only we may meet with the Committee face to face."

"You must have great influence," observed old Adelbert timidly.

"I control the guilds. He who to-day can sway labor to his will is powerful, very powerful comrade. Labor is the great beast which tires of carrying burdens, and is but now learning its strength."

"Aye," said old Adelbert. "Had I been wise, I would have joined a guild. Then I might have kept my place at the Opera. As it is, I stood alone, and they put me out."

"You do not stand alone now. Stand by us, and we will support you. The Republic will not forget its friends."

Thus heartened, old Adelbert brightened up somewhat. Why should he, an old soldier, sweat at the thought of blood? Great changes required heroic measures. It was because he was old that he feared change. He stumped through the passageway without urging, and stood erect and with shoulders squared while the bandage was removed.

He was rather longer than Olga Loschek had been in comprehending his surroundings. His old eyes at first saw little but the table and its candles in their gruesome holders. But when he saw the Committee his heart failed. Here, embodied before him, was everything he had loathed during all his upright and loyal years anarchy, murder, treason. His face worked. The cords in his neck stood out like strings drawn to the breaking-point.

The concierge was speaking. For all his boasting, he was ill at ease. His voice had lost its bravado, and had taken on a fawning note.

"This is the man of whom word was sent to the Committee," he said. "I ventured to ask that he be allowed to come here, because he brings information of value."

"Step forward, comrade," said the leader. "What is your name and occupation?"

"Adelbert, Excellency. As to occupation, for years I was connected with the Opera. Twenty years, Excellency. Then I grew old, and another —" His voice broke. What with excitement and terror, he was close to tears. "Now I am reduced to selling tickets for an American contrivance, a foolish thing, but I earn my bread by it."

He paused, but the silence continued unbroken. The battery of eyes behind the masks was turned squarely on him.

Old Adelbert fidgeted. "Before that, in years gone by, I was in the army," he said, feeling that more was expected of him, and being at a loss. "I fought hard, and once, when I suffered the loss you perceive, the King himself came to my bed, and decorated me. Until lately, I have been loyal. Now, I am-here." His face worked.

"What is the information that brings you here?"

Suddenly old Adelbert wept, terrible tears that forced their way from his faded eyes, and ran down his cheeks. "I cannot, Excellencies!" he cried. "I find I cannot."

He collapsed into the chair, and throwing his arms across the table bowed his head on them. His shoulders heaved under his old uniform. The Committee stirred, and the concierge caught him brutally by the wrist.

"Up with you!" he said, from clenched teeth. "What stupidity is this? Would you play with death?"

But old Adelbert was beyond fear. He shook his head. "I cannot," he muttered, his face hidden.

Then the concierge stood erect and folded his arms across his chest. "He is terrified, that is all," he said. "If the Committee wishes, I can tell them of this matter. Later, he can be interrogated."

The leader nodded.

"By chance," said the concierge, "this-this brave veteran" —he glanced contemptuously at the huddled figure in the chair, "has come across an old passage, the one which rumor has said lay under the city wall, and for which we have at different times instituted search."

He paused, to give his words weight. That they were of supreme interest could be told by the craning forward of the Committee.

"The entrance is concealed at the base of the old Gate of the Moon. Our friend here followed it, and reports it in good condition. For a mile or thereabouts it follows the line of the destroyed wall. Then it turns and goes to the Palace itself."

"Into the Palace?"

"By a flight of stairs, inside the wall, to a door in the roof. This door, which was locked, he opened, having carried keys with him. The door he describes as in the tower. As it was night, he could not see clearly, but the roof at that point is flat."

"Stand up, Adelbert," said the leader sharply. "This that our comrade tells is true?"

"It is true, Excellency."

"Shown a diagram of the Palace, could you locate this door?"

Old Adelbert stared around him hopelessly. It was done now. Nothing that he could say or refuse to say would change that. He nodded.

When, soon after, a chart of the Palace was placed on a table, he indicated the location of the door with a trembling forefinger. "It is there," he said thickly. "And may God forgive me for the thing I have done!"

Chapter XXX
King Karl

"They love us dearly!" said King Karl.

The Chancellor, who sat beside him in the royal carriage, shrugged his shoulders. "They have had little reason to love, in the past, Majesty," he said briefly.

Karl laughed, and watched the crowd. He and the Chancellor rode alone, Karl's entourage, a very modest one, following in another carriage. There was no military escort, no pomp. It had been felt unwise. Karl, paying ostensibly a visit of sympathy, had come unofficially.

"But surely," he observed, as they passed between sullen lines of people, mostly silent, but now and then giving way to a muttering that sounded ominously like a snarl, —"surely I may make a visit of sympathy without exciting their wrath!"

"They are children," said Mettlich contemptuously. "Let one growl, and all growl. Let some one start a cheer, and they will cheer themselves hoarse."

"Then let some one cheer, for God's sake!" said Karl, and turned his mocking smile to the packed streets.

The Chancellor was not so calm as he appeared. He had lined the route from the station to the Palace with his men; had prepared for every contingency so far as he could without calling out the guard. As the carriage, drawn by its four chestnut horses, moved slowly along the streets, his eyes under their overhanging thatch were watching ahead, searching the crowd for symptoms of unrest.

Anger he saw in plenty, and suspicion. Scowling faces and frowning brows. But as yet there was no disorder. He sat with folded arms, magnificent in his uniform beside Karl, who wore civilian dress and looked less royal than perhaps he felt.

And Karl, too, watched the crowd, feeling its temper and feigning an indifference he did not feel. Olga Loschek had been right. He did not want trouble. More than that, he was of an age now to crave popularity. Many of the measures which had made him beloved in his own land had no higher purpose than this, the smiles of the crowd. So he watched and talked of indifferent things.

"It is ten years since I have been here," he observed, "but there are few changes."

"We have built no great buildings," said Mettlich bluntly. "Wars have left us no money, Majesty, for building!"

That being a closed road, so to speak, Karl tried another. "The Crown Prince must be quite a lad," he experimented. "He was a babe in arms, then, but frail, I thought."

"He is sturdy now." The Chancellor relapsed into watchfulness.

"Before I see the Princess Hedwig," Karl made another attempt, "it might be well to tell me how she feels about things. I would like to feel that the prospect is at least not disagreeable to her."

The Chancellor was not listening. There was trouble ahead. It had come, then, after all. He muttered something behind his gray mustache. The horses stopped, as the crowd suddenly closed in front of them.

"Drive on!" he said angrily, and the coachman touched his whip to the horses. But they only reared, to be grasped at the bridles by hostile hands ahead.

Karl half rose from his seat.

"Sit still, Majesty," said the Chancellor. "It is the students. They will talk, that is all."

But it came perilously near to being a riot. Led by some students, pushed by others, the crowd surrounded the two carriages, first muttering, then yelling. A stone was hurled, and struck one of the horses. Another dented the body of the carriage itself. A man with a handkerchief tied over the lower half of his face mounted the shoulders of two companions, and harangued the crowd. They wanted no friendship with Karnia. There were those who would sell them out to their neighbor and enemy. Were they to lose their national existence? He exhorted them madly through the handkerchief. Others, further back, also raised above the mob, shrieked treason, and called the citizens to arm against this thing. A Babel of noise, of swinging back and forth, of mounted police pushing through to surround the carriage, of cries and the dominating voices of the student-demagogues. Then at last a semblance of order, low muttering, an escort of police with drawn revolvers around the carriage, and it moved ahead.

Through it all the Chancellor had sat with folded arms. Only his livid face told of his fury. Karl, too, had sat impassive, picking at his small mustache. But, as the carriage moved on, he said: "A few moments ago I observed that there had been few changes. But there has been, I perceive, after all, a great change."

"One cannot judge the many by the few, Majesty."

But Karl only raised his eyebrows.

In his rooms, removing the dust of his journey, broken by the automobile trip across the mountains where the two railroads would some day meet, Karl reflected on the situation. His amour-propre was hurt. Things should have been better managed, for one thing. It was inexcusable that he had been subjected to such a demonstration. But, aside from the injury to his pride, was a deeper question. If this was the temper of the people now, what would it be when they found their suspicions justified? Had Ogla Loschek been right after all, and not merely jealous? And if she were, was the game worth the candle?

Pacing the drawing-room of his suite with a cigarette, and cursing the tables and bric-a-brac with which it was cluttered, Karl was of a mind to turn back, after all, Even the prospect which his Ministers had not failed to recognize, of the Crown Prince never reaching his maturity, was a less pleasing one than it had been. A dual monarchy, one portion of it restless and revolutionary, was less desirable than the present peace and prosperity of Karnia. And unrest was contagious. He might find himself in a difficult position.

He was, indeed, even now in a difficult position.

He glanced about his rooms. In one of them Prince Hubert had met his death. It was well enough for Mettlich to say the few could not speak for the many. It took but one man to do a murder, Karl reflected grimly.

But when he arrived for tea in the Archduchess's white drawing-room he was urbane and smiling. Hedwig, standing with cold hands and terrified eyes by the tea-table, disliked both his urbanity and his smile. He kissed the hand of the Archduchess and bent over Hedwig's with a flash of white teeth.

Then he saw Olga Loschek, and his smile stiffened. The Countess came forward, curtsied, and as he extended his hand to her, touched it lightly with her lips. They were quite cold. For just an instant their eyes met.

It was, on the surface, an amiable and quiet teaparty. Hilda, in a new frock, flirted openly with the King, and read his fortune in tea-leaves. Hedwig had taken up her position by a window, and was conspicuously silent. Behind her were the soft ring of silver against china; the Countess's gay tones; Karl's suave ones, assuming gravity, as he inquired for His Majesty; the Archduchess Annunciata pretending a solicitude she did not feel. And all forced, all artificial, Olga Loschek's heart burning in her, and Karl watching Hedwig with open admiration and some anxiety.

"Grandmother," Hedwig whispered from her window to the austere old bronze figure in the Place, "was it like this with you, at first? Did you shiver when he touched your hand? And doesn't it matter, after a year?"

"Very feeble," said the Archduchess's voice; behind her, "but so brave —a lesson to us all."

"He has had a long and conspicuous career," Karl observed. "It is sad, but we must all come to it. I hope he will be able to see me."

"Hedwig!" said her mother, sharply, "your tea is getting cold."

Hedwig turned toward the room. Listlessness gave her an added dignity, a new charm. Karl's eyes flamed as he watched her. He was a connoisseur in women; he had known many who were perhaps more regularly beautiful, but none, he felt, so lovely. Her freshness and youth made Olga, beautifully dressed, superbly easy, look sophisticated and a trifle hard. Even her coldness appealed to him. He had a feeling that the coldness was only a young girl's armor, that under it was a deeply passionate woman. The thought of seeing her come to deep, vibrant life in his arms thrilled him.

When he carried her tea to her, he bent over her. "Please!" he said. "Try to like me. I —"

"I'm sorry," Hedwig said quickly. "Mother has forgotten the lemon."

Karl smiled and, shrugging his shoulders, fetched the lemon. "Right, now?" he inquired. "And aren't we going to have a talk together?"

"If you wish it, I dare say we shall."

"Majesty," said Hilda, frowning into her teacup. "I see a marriage for you." She ignored her mother's scowl, and tilted her cup to examine it.

"A marriage!" Karl joined her, and peered with mock anxiety at the tea-grounds. "Strange that my fate should be confined in so small a compass! A happy marriage? Which am I?"

"The long yellow leaf. Yes, it looks happy. But you may be rather shocked when I tell you."

"Shocked?"

"I think," said Hilda, grinning, "that you are going to marry me."

"Delightful!"

"And we are going to have —"

"Hilda!" cried the Archduchess fretfully. "Do stop that nonsense and let us talk. I was trying to recall, this morning," she said to Karl, "when you last visited us." She knew it quite well, but she preferred having Karl think she had forgotten. "It was, I believe, just before Hubert —"

"Yes," said Karl gravely, "just before."

"Otto was a baby then."

"A very small child. I remember that I was afraid to handle him."

"He is a curious boy, old beyond his years. Rather a little prig, I think. He has an English governess, and she has made him quite a little woman."

Karl laughed, but Hedwig flushed.

"He is not that sort at all," she declared stoutly. "He is lonely and-and rather pathetic. The truth is that no one really cares for him, except —"

"Except Captain Larisch!" said the Archduchess smoothly. "You and he, Hedwig, have done your best by him, surely."

The bit of byplay was not lost on Karl-the sudden stiffening of Hedwig's back, Olga's narrowed eyes. Olga had been right, then. Trust her for knowing facts when they were disagreeable. His eyes became set and watchful, hard, too, had any noticed. There were ways to deal with such a situation, of course. They were giving him this girl to secure their own safety, and she knew it. Had he not been so mad about her he might have pitied her, but he felt no pity, only a deep and resentful determination to get rid of Nikky, and then to warm her by his own fire. He might have to break her first. After that manner had many Queens of Karnia come to the throne. He smiled behind his small mustache.

When tea was almost over, the Crown Prince was announced. He came in, rather nervously, with hie hands thrust in his trousers pockets. He was very shiny with soap and water and his hair was still damp from parting. In his tailless black jacket, his long gray trousers, and his round Eton collar, he looked like a very anxious little schoolboy, and not royal at all.

Greetings over, and having requested that his tea be half milk, with four lumps of sugar, he carried his cup over beside Hedwig, and sat down on a chair. Followed a short silence, with the

Archduchess busy with the tea-things, Olga Loschek watching Karl, and Karl intently surveying the Crown Prince. Ferdinand William Otto, who disliked a silence, broke it first.

"I've just taken off my winter flannels," he observed. "I feel very smooth and nice underneath."

Hilda giggled, but Hedwig reached over and stroked his arm. "Of course you do," she said gently.

"Nikky," continued Prince Ferdinand William Otto, stirring his tea, "does not wear any flannels. Miss Braithwaite thinks he is very careless."

King Karl's eyes gleamed with amusement. He saw the infuriated face of the Archduchess, and bent toward the Crown Prince with earnestness.

"As a matter of fact," he said, "since you have mentioned the subject, I do not wear any either. Your 'Nikky' and I seem most surprisingly to have the same tastes-about various things."

Annunciata was in the last stages of irritation. There was no mistaking the sneer in Karl's voice. His smile was forced. She guessed that he had heard of Nikky Larisch before, that, indeed, he knew probably more than she did. Just what, she wondered, was there to know? A great deal, if one could judge by Hedwig's face.

"I hope you are working hard at your lesson, Otto," she said, in the severe tone which Otto had learned that most people use when they refer to lessons.

"I'm afraid I'm not doing very well, Tante. But I've learned the 'Gettysburg Address.' Shall I say it?"

"Heavens, no!" she protested. She had not the faintest idea what the "Gettysburg Address" was. She suspected Mr. Gladstone.

The Countess had relapsed into silence. A little back from the family circle, she had watched the whole scene stonily, and knowing Karl as only a woman who loves sincerely and long can know a man, she knew the inner workings of his mind. She saw anger in the very turn of his head and set of his jaw. But she saw more, jealousy, and was herself half mad with it.

She knew him well. She had herself, for years, held him by holding herself dear, by the very difficulty of attaining her. And now this indifferent, white-faced girl, who might be his, indeed, for the taking, but who would offer or promise no love, was rousing him to the instinct of possession by her very indifference. He had told her the truth, that night in the mountain inn. It was Hedwig he wanted, Hedwig herself, her heart, all of her. And, if she knew Karl, he would move heaven and earth to get the thing he wanted.

She surveyed the group. How little they knew what was in store for them! She, Olga Loschek, by the lifting of a finger, could turn their smug superiority into tears and despair, could ruin them and send them flying for shelter to the very ends of the earth.

But when she looked at the little Crown Prince, legs dangling, eating his thin bread and butter as only a hungry small boy can eat, she shivered. By what means must she do all this! By what unspeakable means!

Karl saw the King that evening, a short visit marked by extreme formality, and, on the King's part, by the keen and frank scrutiny of one who is near the end and fears nothing but the final moment. Karl found the meeting depressing and the King's eyes disconcerting.

"It will not be easy going for Otto," said the King, at the end of the short interview. "I should like to feel that his interests will be looked after, not only here, but by you and yours. We have a certain element here that is troublesome."

And Karl, with Hedwig in his mind, had promised.

"His interests shall be mine, sir," he had said.

He had bent over the bed then, and raised the thin hand to his lips. The interview was over. In the anteroom the King's Master of the Horse, the Chamberlain, and a few other gentlemen stood waiting, talking together in low tones. But the Chancellor, who had gone in with Karl and then retired, stood by a window, with his arms folded over his chest, and waited. He put resolutely out of his mind the face of the dying man on his pillows, and thought only of this thing which he-Mettlich had brought about. There was no yielding in his face or in his heart, no doubt of his course. He saw, instead of the lovers loitering in the Place, a new and greater kingdom, anarchy held down by an ironshod heel, peace and the fruits thereof, until out of very prosperity the people grew fat and content.

He saw a boy king, carefully taught, growing into his responsibilities until, big with the vision of the country's welfare, he should finally ascend the throne. He saw the river filled with ships, carrying merchandise over the world and returning with the wealth of the world. Great buildings, too, lifted their heads on his horizon, a dream city, with order for disorder, and citizens instead of inhabitants.

When at last he stirred and sighed, it was because his old friend, in his bed in the next room, would see nothing of all this, and that he himself could not hope for more than the beginning, before his time came also.

The first large dinner for months was given that night at the Palace, to do King Karl all possible honor. The gold service which had been presented to the King by the Czar of Russia was used. The anticipatory gloom of the Court was laid aside, and jewels brought from vaults were worn for the first time in months. Uniforms of various sorts, but all gorgeous, touched fine shoulders, and came away, bearing white, powdery traces of the meeting. The greenhouses at the summer palace had been sacked for flowers and plants. The corridor from the great salon to the dining-hall; always a dreary passage, had suddenly become a fairy path of early-spring bloom. Even Annunciata, hung now with ropes of pearls, her hair dressed high for a tiara of diamonds, her cameos exchanged for pearls, looked royal. Proving conclusively that clutter, as to dress, is entirely a matter of value.

Miss Braithwaite, who had begun recently to think a palace the dreariest place in the world, and the most commonplace, found the preparations rather exciting. Being British she dearly loved the aristocracy, and shrugged her shoulders at any family which took up less than a page in the peerage. She resented deeply the intrusion of the commoner into British politics, and considered Lloyd George an upstart and an interloper.

That evening she took the Crown Prince to see the preparations for the festivities. The flowers appealed to him, and he asked for and secured a rose, which he held carefully. But the magnificence of the table only faintly impressed him, and when he heard that Nikky would not be present, he lost interest entirely. "Will they wheel my grandfather in a chair?" he inquired.

"He is too ill," Miss Braithwaite said.

"He'll be rather lonely, when they're all at the party. You don't suppose I could go and sit with him, do you?"

"It will be long after your bedtime."

Bedtime being the one rule which was never under any circumstances broken, he did not persist. To have insisted might have meant five off in Miss Braithwaite's book, and his record was very good that week. Together the elderly Englishwoman and the boy went back to the schoolroom.

The Countess Loschek, who had dressed with a heavy heart, was easily the most beautiful of the women that night. Her color was high with excitement and anger, her eyes flashed, her splendid shoulders gleamed over the blue and orchid shades of her gown. A little court paid tribute to her beauty, and bowed the deeper and flattered the more as she openly scorned and flouted them. She caught once a flicker of admiration in Karl's face, and although her head went high, her heart beat stormily under it.

Hedwig was like a flower that required the sun. Only her sun was happiness. She was in soft white chiffons, her hair and frock alike girlish and unpretentious. Her mother, coming into her dressing room, had eyed her with disfavor.

"You look like a school-girl," she said, and had sent for rouge, and with her own royal hands applied it. Hedwig stood silent, and allowed her to have her way without protest. Had submitted, too, to a diamond pin in her hair, and a string of her mother's pearls.

"There," said Annunciata, standing off and surveying her, "you look less like a baby."

She did, indeed? It took Hedwig quite five minutes to wash the rouge off her face, and there was, one might as well confess, a moment when a part of the crown jewels of the kingdom lay in a corner of the room, whence a trembling maid salvaged them, and examined them for damage.

The Princess Hedwig appeared that evening without rouge, and was the only woman in the room thus unadorned. Also she wore her coming-out string of modest pearls and a slightly defiant, somewhat frightened, expression.

The dinner was endless, which was necessary, since nothing was to follow but conversation. There could, under the circumstances, be no dancing. And the talk at the table, through course after course, was somewhat hectic, even under the constraining presence of King Karl. There were two reasons for this: Karl's presence and his purpose-as yet unannounced, but surmised, and even known-and the situation in the city.

That was bad. The papers had been ordered to make no mention of the occurrence of the afternoon, but it was well known. There were many at the table who felt the whole attempt foolhardy, the setting of a match to inflammable material. There were others who resented Karl's presence in Livonia, and all that it implied. And perhaps there were, too, among the guests, one or more who had but recently sat in less august and more awful company.

Beneath all the brilliance and chatter, the sparkle and gayety, there was, then, uneasiness, wretchedness, and even treachery. And outside the Palace, held back by the guards, there still stood a part of the sullen crowd which had watched the arrival of the carriages and automobiles, had craned forward to catch a glimpse of uniform or brilliantly shrouded figure entering the Palace, and muttered as it looked.

Dinner was over at last. The party moved back to the salon, a vast and empty place, hung with tapestries and gayly lighted. Here the semblance of gayety persisted, and Karl, affability itself, spoke a few words to each of the guests. Then it was over. The guests left, the members of the Council, each with a wife on his arm, frowsy, overdressed women most of them. The Council was chosen for ability and not for birth. At last only the suite remained, and constraint vanished.

The family withdrew shortly after-to a small salon off the large one. And there, at last, Karl cornered Hedwig and demanded speech.

"Where?" she asked, glancing around the crowded room.

"I shall have to leave that to you," he said. "Unless there is a balcony."

"But do you think it is necessary?"

"Why not?"

"Because what I have to say does not matter."

"It matters very much to me," he replied gravely.

Hedwig went first, slipping away quietly and unnoticed. Karl asked the Archduchess's permission to follow her, and found her waiting there alone, rather desperately calm now, and with a tinge of excited color in her cheeks. Because he cared a great deal, and because, as kings go, he was neither hopelessly bad nor hard, his first words were kind and genuine, and almost brought her to tears.

"Poor little girl!" he said.

He had dropped the curtain behind him, and they stood alone.

"Don't," said Hedwig. "I want to be very calm, and I am sorry for myself already."

"Then you think it is all very terrible?"

She did not reply, and he drew a chair for her to the rail. When she was seated, he took up his position beside her, one arm against a pillar.

"I wonder, Hedwig," he said, "if it is not terrible because it is new to you, and because you do not know me very well. Not," he added hastily, "that I think your knowing me well would be an advantage! I am not so idiotic. But you do not know me at all, and for a good many years I must have stood in the light of an enemy. It is not easy to readjust such things-witness the reception I had to-day!"

"I do not think of you in that way, as-as an enemy."

"Then what is it?"

"Why must we talk about it?" Hedwig demanded, looking up at him suddenly with a flash of her old spirit. "It will not change anything."

"Perhaps not. Perhaps-yes. You see, I am not quite satisfied. I do not want you, unless you are willing. It would be a poor bargain for me, and not quite fair."

A new turn, this, with a vengeance! Hedwig stared up with startled eyes. It was not enough to be sacrificed. And as she realized all that hung on the situation, the very life of the kingdom, perhaps the safety of her family, everything, she closed her eyes for fear he might see the fright in them.

Karl bent over and took one of her cold hands between his two warm ones. "Little Hedwig," he said, "I want you to come willingly because —I care a great deal. I would like you to care, too. Don't you think you would, after a time?"

"After a time!" said Hedwig drearily. "That's what they all say. After a time it doesn't matter. Marriage is always the same-after a time."

Karl rather winced at that, and released her hands, but put them down gently. "Why should marriage be always the same, after a time?" he inquired.

"This sort of marriage, without love."

"It is hardly that, is it? I love you."

"I wonder how much you love me."

Karl smiled. He was on his own ground here. The girlish question put him at ease. "Enough for us both, at first," he said. "After that —"

"But," said Hedwig desperately, "suppose I know I shall never care for you, the way you will want me to. You talk of being fair. I want to be fair to you. You have a right —" She checked herself abruptly. After all, he might have a right to know about Nikky Larisch. But there were others who had rights, too-Otto to his throne, her mother and Hilda and all the others, to safety, her grandfather to die in peace, the only gift she could give him.

"What I think you want to tell me, is something I already know," Karl said gravely. "Suppose I am willing to take that chance? Suppose I am vain enough, or fool enough, to think that I can make you forget certain things, certain people. What then?"

"I do not forget easily."

"But you would try?"

"I would try," said Hedwig, almost in a whisper.

Karl bent over and taking her hands, raised her to her feet.

"Darling," he said, and suddenly drew her to him. He covered her with hot kisses, her neck, her face, the soft angle below her ear. Then he held her away from him triumphantly. "Now," he said, "have you forgotten?"

But Hedwig, scarlet with shame, faced him steadily. "No," she said.

Later in the evening the old King received a present, a rather wilted rose, to which was pinned a card with "Best wishes from Ferdinand William Otto" printed on it in careful letters.

It was the only flower the King had received during his illness.

When, that night, he fell asleep, it was still clasped in his old hand, and there was a look of grim tenderness on the face on the pillow, turned toward his dead son's picture.

Chapter XXXI
Let Mettlich Guard His Treasure

Troubled times now, with the Carnival only a day or two off, and the shop windows gay with banners; with the press under the house of the concierge running day and night, and turning out vast quantities of flaming bulletins printed in red; with the Committee of Ten in almost constant session, and Olga Loschek summoned before it, to be told of the passage, and the thing she was to do; with the old King very close to the open door, and Hedwig being fitted for her bridal robe and for somber black at one fitting.

Troubled times, indeed. The city was smouldering, and from some strange source had come a new rumor. Nothing less than that the Royalists, headed by the Chancellor, despairing of crowning the boy Prince, would, on the King's death, make away with him, thus putting Hedwig on the throne Hedwig, Queen of Karnia perhaps already by secret marriage.

The city, which adored the boy, was seething. The rumor had originated with Olga Loschek, who had given it to the Committee as a useful weapon. Thus would she have her revenge on those of the Palace, and at the same time secure her own safety. Revenge, indeed, for she knew the way of such rumors, how they fly from house to house, street to street. How the innocent, proclaiming their innocence, look even the more guilty.

When she had placed the scheme before the Committee of Ten, had seen the eagerness with which they grasped it —"In this way," she had said, in her scornful, incisive tones, "the onus of the boy is not on you, but on them. Even those who have no sympathy with your movement will burn at such a rumor. The better the citizen, the more a lover of home and order, the more outraged he will be. Every man in the city with a child of his own will rise against the Palace."

"Madame," the leader had said, "you should be of the Committee."

But she had ignored the speech contemptuously, and gone on to other things.

Now everything was arranged. Black Humbert had put his niece to work on a Carnival dress for a small boy, and had stayed her curiosity by a hint that it was for the American lad.

"They are comfortable tenants," he had said. "Not lavish, perhaps, as rich Americans should be, but orderly, and pleasant. The boy has good manners. It would be well to please him."

So the niece, sewing in the back room, watched Bobby in and out, with pleasant mysteries in her eyes, and sewing sang the song the cathedral chimed:

> "Draw me also, Mary mild,
> To adore Thee and thy Child!
> Mary mild,
> Star in desert drear and wild."

So she sang, and sewed, and measured Bobby's height as he passed by the wainscoting in the passage, and cunningly cut a pattern.

"So high," she reflected, humming, "is his shoulder. And so, to this panel, should go the little trousers. 'Star in desert drear and wild.'"

Now and then, in the evenings, when the Americans were away, and Bobby was snug in bed, with Tucker on the tiny feather comfort at his feet, the Fraulein would come downstairs and sit in Black Humbert's room. At such times the niece would be sent on an errand, and the two would talk. The niece, who, although she had no lover, was on the lookout for love, suspected a romance of the middle-aged, and smiled in the half-darkness of the street; smiled with a touch of malice, as one who has pierced the armor of the fortress, and knows its weakness.

But it was not of love that Humbert and the Fraulein talked.

Herman Spier was busy in those days and making plans. Thus, day by day, he dined in the restaurant where the little Marie, now weary of her husband, sat in idle intervals behind the cashier's desk, and watched the grass in the Place emerge from its winter hiding place. When she turned her eyes to the room, frequently she encountered those of Herman Spier, pale yet burning, fixed on her. And at last, one day when her husband lay lame with sciatica, she left the desk and paused by Herman's table.

"You come frequently now," she observed. "It is that you like us here, or that you have risen in the shop?"

"I have left the shop," said Herman, staring at her. Flesh, in a moderate amount, suited her well. He liked plump women. They were, if you please, an armful. "And I come to see you."

"Left the shop!" Marie exclaimed. "And Peter Niburg-he has left also? I never see him."

"No," said Herman non-committally.

"He is ill, perhaps?"

"He is dead," said Herman, devouring her with his eyes.

"Dead!" She put a hand to her plump side.

"Aye. Shot as a spy." He took another piece of the excellent pigeon pie. Marie, meantime, lost all her looks, grew pasty white.

"Of the-the Terrorists?" she demanded, in a whisper.

"Terrorists! No. Of Karnia. He was no patriot."

So the little Marie went back to her desk, and to her staring out over the Place in intervals of business. And what she thought of no one can know. But that night, and thereafter, she was very tender to her spouse, and put cloths soaked in hot turpentine water on his aching thigh.

On the surface things went on as usual at the Palace. Karl's visit had been but for a day or two. He had met the Council in session, and had had, because of their growing alarm, rather his own way with them.

But although he had pointed to the King's condition and theirs-as an argument for immediate marriage-he failed. The thing would be done, but properly and in good time. They had a signed agreement to fall back upon, and were in no hurry to pay his price. Karl left them in a bad temper, well concealed, and had the pleasure of being hissed through the streets.

But he comforted himself with the thought of Hedwig. He had taken her in his arms before he left, and she had made no resistance. She had even, in view of all that was at stake, made a desperate effort to return his kiss, and found herself trembling afterward.

In two weeks he was to return to her, and he whispered that to her.

On the day after the dinner-party Otto went to a hospital with Miss Braithwaite. It was the custom of the Palace to send the flowers from its spectacular functions to the hospitals, and the Crown Prince delighted in these errands.

So they went, escorted by the functionaries of the hospital, past the military wards, where soldiers in shabby uniforms sat on benches in the spring sunshine, to the general wards beyond. The Crown Prince was almost hidden behind the armful he carried. Miss Braithwaite had all she could hold. A convalescent patient, in slippers many sizes too large for him, wheeled the remainder in a barrow, and almost upset the barrow in his excitement.

Through long corridors into wards fresh-scrubbed against his arrival, with white counterpanes exactly square, and patients forbidden to move and disturb the geometrical exactness of the beds, went Prince Ferdinand William Otto. At each bed he stopped, selected a flower, and held it out. Some there were who reached out, and took it with a smile. Others lay still, and saw neither boy nor blossom.

"They sleep, Highness," the nurse would say.

"But their eyes are open."

"They are very weary, and resting."

In such cases he placed the flower on the pillow, and went on.

One such; however, lying with vacant eyes fixed on the ceiling, turned and glanced at the boy, and into his empty gaze crept a faint intelligence. It was not much. He seemed to question with his eyes. That was all. As the little procession moved on, however, he raised himself on his elbow.

"Lie down!" said the man in the next bed sharply.

"Who was that?"

The ward, which might have been interested, was busy keeping its covers straight and in following the progress of the party. For the man had not spoken before.

"The Crown Prince."

The sick man lay back and dosed his eyes. Soon he slept. His comrade in the next bed beckoned to a Sister.

"He has spoken," he said. "Either he recovers, or-he dies."

But again Haeckel did not die. He lived to do his part in the coming crisis, to prove that even the great hands of Black Humbert on his throat were not so strong as his own young spirit; lived, indeed, to confront the Terrorist as one risen from the dead. But that day he lay and slept, by curious irony the flower from Karl's banquet in a cup of water beside him.

On the day before the Carnival, Hedwig had a visitor, none other than the Countess Loschek. Hedwig, all her color gone now, her high spirit crushed, her heart torn into fragments and neatly distributed between Nikky, who had most of it, the Crown Prince, and the old King. Hedwig, having given her permission to come, greeted her politely but without enthusiasm.

"Highness!" said the Countess, surveying her. And then, "You poor child!" using Karl's words, but without the same inflection, using, indeed, the words a good many were using to Hedwig in those days.

"I am very tired," Hedwig explained. "All this fitting, and-everything."

"I know, perhaps better than you think, Highness." Also something like Karl's words. Hedwig reflected with bitterness that everybody knew, but nobody helped her. And, as if in answer to the thought, Olga Loschek came out plainly.

"Highness," she said, "may I speak to you frankly?"

"Please do," Hedwig replied. "Everybody does, anyhow. Especially when it is something disagreeable."

Olga Loschek watched her warily. She knew the family as only the outsider could know it; knew that Hedwig, who would have disclaimed the fact, was like her mother in some things, notably in a disposition to be mild until a certain moment, submissive, even acquiescent, and then suddenly to become, as it were, a royalty and grow cold, haughty. But if Hedwig was driven in those days, so was the Countess, desperate and driven to desperate methods.

"I am presuming, Highness, on your mother's kindness to me, and your own, to speak frankly."

"Well, go on," said Hedwig resignedly. But the next words brought her up in her chair.

"Are you going to allow your life to be ruined?" was what the Countess said.

Careful! Hedwig had thrown up her head and looked at her with hostile eyes. But the next moment she had forgotten she was a princess, and the granddaughter to the King, and remembered only that she was a woman, and terror-stricken. She flung out her arms, and then buried her face in them.

"How can I help it?" she said.

"How can you do it?" Olga Loschek countered. "After all, it is you who must do this thing. No one else. It is you they are offering on the altar of their ambition."

"Ambition?"

"Ambition. What else is it? Surely you do not believe these tales they tell-old wives' tales of plot and counterplot!"

"But the Chancellor —"

"Certainly the Chancellor!" mocked Olga Loschek. "Highness, for years he has had a dream. A great dream. It is not for you and me to say it is not noble. But, to fulfill his dream to bring prosperity and greatness to the country, and naturally, to him who plans it, there is a price to pay. He would have you pay it."

Hedwig raised her face and searched the other woman's eyes.

"That is all, then?" she said. "All this other, this fright, this talk of treason and danger, that is not true?"

"Not so true as he would have you believe," replied Olga Loschek steadily. "There are malcontents everywhere, in every land. A few madmen who dream dreams, like Mettlich himself, only not the same dream. It is all ambition, one dream or another."

"But my grandfather —"

"An old man, in the hands of his Ministers!"

Hedwig rose and paced the floor, her fingers twisting nervously. "But it is too late," she cried at last. "Everything is arranged. I cannot refuse now. They would —I don't know what they would do to me!"

"Do! To the granddaughter of the King. What can they do?"

That aspect of things; to do her credit, had never occurred to Hedwig. She had seen herself, hopeless and alone, surrounded by the powerful, herself friendless. But, if there was no danger to save her family from? If her very birth, which had counted so far for so little, would bring her immunity and even safety?

She paused in front of the Countess. "What can I do?" she asked pitifully.

"That I dare not presume to say. I came because I felt —I can only say what, in your place, I should do."

"I am afraid. You would not be afraid." Hedwig shivered. "What would you do?"

"If I knew, Highness, that some one, for whom I cared, himself cared deeply enough to make any sacrifice, I should demand happiness. I rather think I should lose the world, and gain something like happiness."

"Demand!" Hedwig said hopelessly. "Yes, you would demand it. I cannot demand things. I am always too frightened."

The Countess rose. "I am afraid I have done an unwise thing," she said, "If your mother knew —" She shrugged her shoulders.

"You have only been kind. I have so few who really care."

The Countess curtsied, and made for the door. "I must go," she said, "before I go further, Highness. My apology is that I saw you unhappy, and that I resented it, because —"

"Yes?"

"Because I considered it unnecessary."

She was a very wise woman. She left then, and let the next step come from Hedwig. It followed, as a matter of record, within the hour, at least four hours sooner than she had anticipated. She was in her boudoir, not reading, not even thinking, but sitting staring ahead, as Minna had seen her do repeatedly in the past weeks. She dared not think, for that matter.

Although she was still in waiting, the Archduchess was making few demands on her. A very fever of preparation was on Annunciata. She spent hours over laces and lingerie, was having jewels reset for Hedwig, after ornate designs of her own contribution, was the center of a cyclone of boxes, tissue paper, material, furs, and fashion books, while maids scurried about and dealers and dressmakers awaited her pleasure. She was, perhaps, happier than she had been for years, visited her father, absently and with pins stuck in her bosom, and looked dowdier and busier than the lowliest of the seamstresses who, by her thrifty order, were making countless undergarments in a room on an upper floor.

Hedwig's notification that she would visit her, therefore, found the Countess at leisure and alone. She followed the announcement almost immediately, and if she had shown cowardice before, she showed none now. She disregarded the chair Olga Loschek offered, and came to the point with a directness that was like the King's.

"I have come," she said simply, "to find out what to do."

The Countess was as direct.

"I cannot tell you what to do, Highness. I can only tell you what I would do."

"Very well." Hedwig showed a touch of impatience. This was quibbling, and it annoyed her.

"I should go away, now, with the person I cared about."

"Where would you go?"

"The world is wide, Highness."

"Not wide enough to hide in, I am afraid."

"For myself," said the Countess, "the problem would not be difficult. I should go to my place in the mountains. An old priest, who knows me well, would perform the marriage. After that they might find me if they liked. It would be too late."

Emergency had given Hedwig insight. She saw that the woman before her, voicing dangerous doctrine, would protect herself by letting the initiative come from her.

"This priest-he might be difficult."

"Not to a young couple, come to him, perhaps, in peasant costume. They are glad to marry, these fathers. There is much irregularity. I fancy," she added, still with her carefully detached manner, "that a marriage could be easily arranged."

But, before long, she had dropped her pretense of aloofness, and was taking the lead. Hedwig, weary with the struggle, and now trembling with nervousness, put herself in her hands, listening while she planned, agreed eagerly to everything. Something of grim amusement came into Olga Loschek's face after a time. By doing this thing she would lose everything. It would be impossible to conceal her connivance. No one, knowing Hedwig, would for a moment imagine the plan hers. Or Nikky's, either, for that matter.

She, then, would lose everything, even Karl, who was already lost to her. But-and her face grew set and her eyes hard-she would let those plotters in their grisly catacombs do their own filthy work. Her hands would be clean of that. Hence her amusement that at this late day she, Olga Loschek, should be saving her own soul.

So it was arranged, to the last detail. For it must be done at once. Hedwig, a trifle terrified, would have postponed it a day or so, but the Countess was insistent. Only she knew how the very hours counted, had them numbered, indeed, and watched them flying by with a sinking heart.

She made a few plans herself, in those moments when Hedwig relapsed into rapturous if somewhat frightened dreams. She had some money and her jewels. She would go to England, and there live quietly until things settled down. Then, perhaps, she would go some day to Karl, and with this madness for Hedwig dead, of her marriage, perhaps —! She planned no further.

If she gave a fleeting thought to the Palace, to the Crown Prince and his impending fate, she dismissed it quickly. She had no affection for Annunciata, and as to the boy, let them look out for him. Let Mettlich guard his treasure, or lose it to his peril. The passage under the gate was not of her discovery or informing.

Chapter XXXII
Nikky and Hedwig

Nikky had gone back to his lodging, where his servant was packing his things. For Nikky was now of His Majesty's household, and must exchange his shabby old rooms for the cold magnificence of the Palace.

Toto had climbed to the chair beside him, and was inspecting his pockets, one by one. Toto was rather a problem, in the morning. But then everything was a problem now. He decided to leave the dog with the landlady, and to hope for a chance to talk the authorities over. Nikky himself considered that a small boy without a dog was as incomplete as, for instance, a buttonhole without a button.

He was very downhearted. To the Crown Prince, each day, he gave the best that was in him, played and rode, invented delightful nonsense to bring the boy's quick laughter, carried pocketfuls of bones, to the secret revolt of his soldierly soul, was boyish and tender, frivolous or thoughtful, as the occasion seemed to warrant.

And always he was watchful, his revolver always ready and in touch, his eyes keen, his body, even when it seemed most relaxed, always tense to spring. For Nikky knew the temper of the people, knew it as did Mathilde gossiping in the market, and even better; knew that a crisis was approaching, and that on this small boy in his charge hung that crisis.

The guard at the Palace had been trebled, but even in that lay weakness.

"Too many strange faces," the Chancellor had said to him, shaking his head. "Too many servants in livery, and flunkies whom no one knows. How can we prevent men, in such livery, from impersonating our own agents? One, two, a half-dozen, they could gain access to the Palace, could commit a mischief under our very eyes."

So Nikky trusted in his own right arm and in nothing else. At night the Palace guard was smaller, and could be watched. There were no servants about to complicate the situation. But in the daytime, and especially now with the procession of milliners and dressmakers, messengers and dealers, it was more difficult. Nikky watched these people, as he happened on them, with suspicion and hatred. Hatred not only of what they might be, but hatred of what they were, of the thing they typified, Hedwig's approaching marriage.

The very size of the Palace, its unused rooms, its long and rambling corridors, its rambling wings and ancient turrets, was against its safety.

Since the demonstration against Karl, the riding-school hour had been given up. There were no drives in the park. The illness of the King furnished sufficient excuse, but the truth was that the royal family was practically besieged; by it knew not what. Two police agents had been found dead the morning after Karl's departure, on the outskirts of the city, lying together in a freshly ploughed field. They bore marks of struggle, and each had been stabbed through the veins of the neck, as though they had been first subdued and then scientifically destroyed.

Nikky, summoned to the Chancellor's house that morning, had been told the facts, and had stood, rather still and tense, while Mettlich recounted them.

"Our very precautions are our danger," said the Chancellor. "And the King —" He stopped and sat, tapping his fingers on the arm of his chair.

"And the King, sir?"

"Almost at the end. A day or two."

On that day came fresh news, alarming enough. More copies of the seditious paper were in circulation in the city and the surrounding country, passing from hand to hand. The town was searched for the press which had printed them, but it was not located. Which was not surprising, since it had been lowered through a trap into a sub-cellar of the house on the Road of the Good Children, and the trapdoor covered with rubbish.

Karl, with Hedwig in his thoughts, had returned to mobilize his army not far from the border for the spring maneuvers, and at a meeting of the King's Council the matter of a mobilization in Livonia was seriously considered.

Fat Friese favored it, and made an impassioned speech, with sweat thick on his heavy face.

"I am not cowardly," he finished. "I fear nothing for myself or for those belonging to me. But the duty of this Council is to preserve the throne for the Crown Prince, at any cost. And, if we cannot trust the army, in what can we trust?"

"In God," said the Chancellor grimly.

In the end nothing was done. Mobilization might precipitate the crisis, and there was always the fear that the army, in parts, was itself disloyal.

It was Marschall, always nervous and now pallid with terror, who suggested abandoning the marriage between Hedwig and Karl.

"Until this matter came up," he said, avoiding Mettlich's eyes, "there was danger, but of a small party only, the revolutionary one. One which, by increased effort on the part of the secret police, might have been suppressed. It is this new measure which is fatal. The people detest it. They cannot forget, if we can, the many scores of hatred we still owe to Karnia. We have, by our own act, alienated the better class of citizens. Why not abandon this marriage, which, gentlemen, I believe will be fatal. It has not yet been announced. We may still withdraw with honor."

He looked around the table with anxious, haunted eyes, opened wide so that the pupils appeared small and staring in their setting of blood-shot white. The Chancellor glanced around, also.

"It is not always easy to let the people of a country know what is good for them and for it. To retreat now is to show our weakness, to make an enemy again of King Karl, and to gain us nothing, not even safety. As well abdicate, and turn the country over to the Terrorists! And, in this crisis, let me remind you of something you persistently forget. Whatever the views of the solid citizens may be as to this marriage, —and once it is effected, they will accept it without doubt, —the Crown Prince is now and will remain the idol of the country. It is on his popularity we must depend. We must capitalize it. Mobs are sentimental. Whatever the Terrorists may think, this I know: that when the bell announces His Majesty's death, when Ferdinand William Otto steps out on the balcony, a small and lonely child, they will rally to him.

That figure, on the balcony, will be more potent than a thousand demagogues, haranguing in the public streets."

The Council broke up in confusion. Nothing had been done, or would be done. Mettlich of the Iron Hand had held them, would continue to hold them. The King, meanwhile, lay dying, Doctor Wiederman in constant attendance, other physicians coming and going. His apartments were silent. Rugs covered the corridors, that no footfall disturb his quiet hours. The nursing Sisters attended him, one by his bedside, one always on her knees at the Prie-dieu in the small room beyond. He wanted little-now and then a sip of water, the cooled juice of fruit.

Injections of stimulants, given by Doctor Wiederman himself, had scarred his old arms with purplish marks, and were absorbed more and more slowly as the hours went on.

He rarely slept, but lay inert and not unhappy. Now and then one of his gentlemen, given permission, tiptoed into the room, and stood looking down at his royal master. Annunciata came, and was at last stricken by conscience to a prayer at his bedside. On one of her last visits that was. She got up to find his eyes fixed on her.

"Father," she began.

He made no motion.

"Father, can you hear me?"

"Yes."

"I —I have been a bad daughter to you. I am sorry. It is late now to tell you, but I am sorry. Can I do anything?"

"Otto," he said, with difficulty.

"You want to see him?

"No."

She knew what he meant by that. He would have the boy remember him as he had seen him last.

"You are anxious about him?"

"Very-anxious."

"Listen, father," she said, stooping over him. "I have been hard and cold. Perhaps you will grant that I have had two reasons for it. But I am going to do better. I will take care of him and I will do all I can to make him happy. I promise."

Perhaps it was relief. Perhaps even then the thought of Annunciata's tardy and certain-to-be bungling efforts to make Ferdinand William Otto happy amused him. He smiled faintly.

Nikky, watching his rooms being dismantled, rescuing an old pipe now and then, or a pair of shabby but beloved boots, —Nikky, whistling to keep up his courage, received a note from Hedwig late that afternoon. It was very brief:

> To-night at nine o'clock I shall go to the roof beyond Hubert's old rooms, for
> air.
> HEDWIG.

Nikky, who in all his incurious young life had never thought of the roof of the Palace, save as a necessary shelter from the weather, a thing of tiles and gutters, vastly large, looked rather astounded.

"The roof!" he said, surveying the note. And fell to thinking, such a mixture of rapture and despair as only twenty-three, and hopeless, can know.

Somehow or other he got through the intervening hours, and before nine he was on his way. He had the run of the Palace, of course. No one noticed him as he made his way toward the empty suite which so recently had housed its royal visitor. Annunciata's anxiety had kept the doors of the suite unlocked. Knowing nothing, but fearing everything, she slept with the key to the turret door under her pillow, and an ear opened for untoward sounds.

In the faint moonlight poor Hubert's rooms, with their refurbished furnishings covered with white linen, looked cold and almost terrifying. A long window was open, and the velvet curtain swayed as though it shielded some dismal figure. But, when he had crossed the room and drawn the curtain aside, it was to see a bit of fairyland, the roof moonlit and transformed by growing things into a garden. There was, too, the fairy.

Hedwig, in a soft white wrap over her dinner dress, was at the balustrade. The moon, which had robbed the flowers of their colors and made them ghosts of blossoms, had turned Hedwig into a pale, white fairy with extremely frightened eyes. A very dignified fairy, too, although her heart thumped disgracefully. Having taken a most brazen step forward, she was now for taking two panicky ones back.

Therefore she pretended not to hear Nikky behind her, and was completely engrossed in the city lights.

So Hedwig intended to be remote, and Nikky meant to be firm and very, very loyal. Which shows how young and inexperienced they were. Because any one who knows even the beginnings of love knows that its victims suffer from an atrophy of both reason and conscience, and a hypertrophy of the heart.

Whatever Nikky had intended-of obeying his promise to the letter, of putting his country before love, and love out of his life-failed him instantly. The Nikky, ardent-eyed and tender-armed, who crossed the roof and took her almost fiercely in his arms, was all lover-and twenty-three.

"Sweetheart!" he said. "Sweetest heart!"

When, having kissed her, he drew back a trifle for the sheer joy of again catching her to him, it was Hedwig who held out her arms to him.

"I couldn't bear it," she said simply. "I love you. I had to see you again. Just once."

If he had not entirely lost his head before, he lost it then. He stopped thinking, was content for a time that her arms were about his neck, and his arms about her, holding her close. They were tense, those arms of his, as though he would defy the world to take her away.

But, although he had stopped thinking, Hedwig had not. It is, at such times, always the woman who thinks. Hedwig, plotting against his honor and for his happiness and hers, was already, with her head on his breast, planning the attack. And, having a strategic position, she fired her first gun from there.

"Never let me go, Nikky," she whispered. "Hold me, always."

"Always!" said Nikky, valiantly and absurdly.

"Like this?"

"Like this," said Nikky, who was, like most lovers, not particularly original. He tightened his strong arms about her.

"They are planning such terrible things." Shell number two, and high explosive. "You won't let them take me from you, will you?"

"God!" said poor Nikky, and kissed her hair. "If we could only be like this always! Your arms, Hedwig, —your sweet arms!" He kissed her arms.

Gun number three now: "Tell me how much you love me."

"I —there are no words, darling. And I couldn't live long enough to tell you, if there were." Not bad that, for inarticulate Nikky.

"More than anybody else?"

He shook her a trifle, in his arms. "How can you?" he demanded huskily. "More than anything in the world. More than life, or anything life can bring. More, God help me, than my country."

But his own words brought him up short. He released her, very gently, and drew back a step.

"You heard that?" he demanded. "And I mean it. It's incredible, Hedwig, but it is true."

"I want you to mean it," Hedwig replied, moving close to him, so that her soft draperies brushed him; the very scent of the faint perfume she used was in the air he breathed. "I want you to, because Nikky, you are going to take me away, aren't you?"

Then, because she dared not give him time to think, she made her plea,—rapid, girlish, rather incoherent, but understandable enough. They would go away together and be married. She had it all planned and some of it arranged. And then they would hide somewhere, and — "And always be together," she finished, tremulous with anxiety.

And Nikky? His pulses still beating at her nearness, his eyes on her upturned, despairing young face, turned to him for hope and comfort, what could he do? He took her in his arms again and soothed her, while she cried her heart out against his tunic. He said he would do anything to keep her from unhappiness, and that he would die before he let her go to Karl's arms. But if he had stopped thinking before, he was thinking hard enough then.

"To-night?" said Hedwig, raising a tear-stained face. "It is early. If we wait something will happen. I know it. They are so powerful, they can do anything."

After all, Nikky is poor stuff to try to make a hero of. He was so human, and so loving. And he was very, very young, which may perhaps be his excuse. As well confess his weakness and his temptation. He was tempted. Almost he felt he could not let her go, could not loosen his hold of her. Almost-not quite.

He put her away from him at last, after he had kissed her eyelids and her forehead, which was by way of renunciation. And then he folded his arms, which were treacherous and might betray him. After that, not daring to look at her, but with his eyes fixed on the irregular sky-line of the city roofs, he told her many things, of his promise to the King, of the danger, imminent now and very real, of his word of honor not to make love to her, which he had broken.

Hedwig listened, growing cold and still, and drawing away a little. She was suffering too much to be just. All she could see was that, for a matter of honor, and that debatable, she was to be sacrificed. This danger that all talked of-she had heard that for a dozen years, and nothing had come of it. Nothing, that is, but her own sacrifice.

She listened, even assented, as he pleaded against his own heart, treacherous arms still folded. And if she saw his arms and not his eyes, it was because she did not look up.

Halfway through his eager speech, however, she drew her light wrap about her and turned away. Nikky could not believe that she was going like that, without a word. But when she had disappeared through the window, he knew, and followed her. He caught her in Hubert's room, and drew her savagely into his arms.

But it was a passive, quiescent, and trembling Hedwig who submitted, and then, freeing herself, went out through the door into the lights of the corridor. Nikky flung himself, face down, on a shrouded couch and lay there, his face buried in his arms.

Olga Loschek's last hope was gone.

Chapter XXXIII
The Day of the Carnival

On the day of the Carnival, which was the last day before the beginning of Lent, Prince Ferdinand William Otto wakened early. The Palace still slept, and only the street-sweepers were about the streets. Prince Ferdinand William Otto sat up in bed and yawned. This was a special day, he knew, but at first he was too drowsy to remember.

Then he knew-the Carnival! A delightful day, with the Place full of people in strange costumes-peasants, imps, jesters, who cut capers on the grass in the Park, little girls in procession, wearing costumes of fairies with gauze wings, students who paraded and blew noisy horns, even horses decorated, and now and then a dog dressed as a dancer or a soldier.

He would have enjoyed dressing Toto in something or other. He decided to mention it to Nikky, and with a child's faith he felt that Nikky would, so to speak, come up to the scratch.

He yawned again, and began to feel hungry. He decided to get up and take his own bath. There was nothing like getting a good start for a gala day. And, since with the Crown Prince to decide was to do, which is not always a royal trait, he took his own bath, being very particular about his ears, and not at all particular about the rest of him. Then, no Oskar having yet appeared with fresh garments he ducked back into bed again, quite bare as to his small body, and snuggled down in the sheets.

Lying there, he planned the day. There were to be no lessons except fencing, which could hardly be called a lesson at all, and as he now knew the "Gettysburg Address," he meant to ask permission to recite it to his grandfather. To be quite sure of it, he repeated it to himself as he lay there: —

> "'Fourscore and seven years ago our fathers brought forth on this continent a new nation, conceived in liberty, and dedicated to the proposition that all men are created equal.'

"Free and equal," he said to himself. That rather puzzled him. Of course people were free, but they did not seem to be equal. In the summer, at the summer palace, he was only allowed to see a few children, because the others were what his Aunt Annunciata called "bourgeois." And there was in his mind also something Miss Braithwaite had said, after his escapade with the American boy.

"If you must have some child to play with," she had said severely, "you could at least choose some one approximately your equal."

"But he is my equal," he had protested from the outraged depths of his small democratic heart.

"In birth," explained Miss Braithwaite.

"His father has a fine business," he had said, still rather indignant. "It makes a great deal of money. Not everybody can build a scenic railway and get it going right. Bobby said so."

Miss Braithwaite had been silent and obviously unconvinced. Yet this Mr. Lincoln, the American, had certainly said that all men were free and equal. It was very puzzling.

But, as the morning advanced, as, clothed and fed, the Crown Prince faced the new day, he began to feel a restraint in the air. People came and went, his grandfather's Equerry, the Chancellor, the Lord Chamberlain, other gentlemen, connected with the vast and intricate machinery of the Court, and even Hedwig, in a black frock, all these people came, and talked together, and eyed him when he was not looking. When they left they all bowed rather more than usual, except Hedwig, who kissed him, much to his secret annoyance.

Every one looked grave, and spoke in a low tone. Also there was something wrong with Nikky, who appeared not only grave, but rather stern and white. Considering that it was the last day before Lent, and Carnival time, Prince Ferdinand William Otto felt vaguely defrauded, rather like the time he had seen "The Flying Dutchman," which had turned out to be only a make-believe ship and did not fly at all. To add to the complications, Miss Braithwaite had a headache.

Nikky Larisch had arrived just as Hedwig departed, and even the Crown Prince had recognized something wrong. Nikky had stopped just inside the doorway, with his eyes rather desperately and hungrily on Hedwig, and Hedwig, who should have been scolded, according to Prince Otto, had passed him with the haughtiest sort of nod.

The Crown Prince witnessed the nod with wonder and alarm.

"We are all rather worried," he explained afterward to Nikky, to soothe his wounded pride. "My grandfather is not so well to-day. Hedwig is very unhappy."

"Yes," said Nikky miserably, "she does look unhappy."

"Now, when are we going out?" briskly demanded Prince Ferdinand William Otto. "I can hardly wait. I've seen the funniest people already-and dogs. Nikky, I wonder if you could dress Toto, and let me see him somewhere."

"Out! You do not want to go out in that crowd, do you?"

"Why-am I not to go?"

His voice was suddenly quite shaky. He was, in a way, so inured to disappointments that he recognized the very tones in which they were usually announced. So he eyed Nikky with a searching glance, and saw there the thing he feared.

"Well," he said resignedly, "I suppose I can see something from the windows. Only—I should like to have a really good time occasionally." He was determined not to cry. "But there are usually a lot of people in the Place."

Then, remembering that his grandfather was very ill, he tried to forget his disappointment in a gift for him. Not burnt wood this time, but the drawing of a gun, which he explained as he worked, that he had invented. He drew behind the gun a sort of trestle, with little cars, not unlike the Scenic Railway, on which ammunition was delivered into the breech by something strongly resembling a coal-chute.

There was, after all, little to see from the windows. That part of the Place near the Palace remained empty and quiet, by order of the King's physicians. And although it was Carnival, and the streets were thronged with people, there was little of Carnival in the air. The city waited.

Some loyal subjects waited and grieved that the King lay dying. For, although the Palace had carefully repressed his condition, such things leak out, and there was the empty and silent Place to bear witness.

Others waited, too, but not in sorrow. And a certain percentage, the young and light-hearted, strutted the streets in fantastic costume, blew horns and threw confetti and fresh flowers, still dewy from the mountain slopes. The Scenic Railway was crowded with merry-makers, and long lines of people stood waiting their turn at the ticket-booth, where a surly old veteran, pinched with sleepless nights, sold them tickets and ignored their badinage. Family parties, carrying baskets and wheeling babies in perambulators, took possession of the Park and littered it with paper bags. And among them, committing horrible crimes, dispatching whole families with a wooden gun from behind near-by trees and taking innumerable prisoners, went a small pirate in a black mask and a sash of scarlet ribbon, from which hung various deadly weapons, including a bread-knife, a meat-cleaver, and a hatchet.

Attempts to make Tucker wear a mask having proved abortive, he was attired in a pirate flag of black, worn as a blanket, and having on it, in white muslin, what purported to be a skull and cross-bones but which looked like the word "ox" with the "O" superimposed over the "X."

Prince Ferdinand William Otto stood at his window and looked out. Something of resentment showed itself in the lines of his figure. There was, indeed, rebellion in his heart. This was a real day, a day of days, and no one seemed to care that he was missing it. Miss Braithwaite looked drawn about the eyes, and considered carnivals rather common, and certainly silly. And Nikky looked drawn about the mouth, and did not care to play.

Rebellion was dawning in the soul of the Crown Prince, not the impassive revolt of the "Flying Dutchman" and things which only pretended to be, like the imitation ship and the women who were not really spinning. The same rebellion, indeed, which had set old Adelbert against the King and turned him traitor, a rebellion against needless disappointment, a protest for happiness.

Old Adelbert, forbidden to march in his new uniform, the Crown Prince, forbidden his liberty and shut in a gloomy palace, were blood-brothers in revolt.

Not that Prince Ferdinand William Otto knew he was in revolt. At first it consisted only of a consideration of his promise to the Chancellor. But while there had been an understanding, there had been no actual promise, had there?

Late in the morning Nikky took him to the roof. "We can't go out, old man," Nikky said to him, rather startled to discover the unhappiness in the boy's face, "but I've found a place where we can see more than we can here. Suppose we try it."

"Why can't we go out? I've always gone before."

"Well," Nikky temporized, "they've made a rule. They make a good many rules, you know. But they said nothing about the roof."

"The roof!"

"The roof. The thing that covers us and keeps out the weather. The roof, Highness." Nikky alternated between formality and the other extreme with the boy.

"It slants, doesn't it?" observed his Highness doubtfully.

"Part of it is quite flat. We can take a ball up there, and get some exercise while we're about it."

As a matter of fact, Nikky was not altogether unselfish. He would visit the roof again, where for terrible, wonderful moments he had held Hedwig in his arms. On a pilgrimage, indeed, like that of the Crown Prince to Etzel, Nikky would visit his shrine.

So they went to the roof. They went through silent corridors, past quiet rooms where the suite waited and spoke in whispers, past the very door of the chamber where the Council sat in session, and where reports were coming in, hour by hour, as to the condition of things outside. Past the apartment of the Archduchess Annunciata, where Hilda, released from lessons, was trying the effect of jet earrings against her white skin, and the Archduchess herself was sitting by her fire, and contemplating the necessity for flight. In her closet was a small bag, already packed in case of necessity. Indeed, more persons than the Archduchess Annunciata had so prepared. Miss Braithwaite, for instance, had spent a part of the night over a traveling-case containing a small boy's outfit, and had wept as she worked, which was the reason for her headache.

The roof proved quite wonderful. One could see the streets crowded with people, could hear the soft blare of distant horns.

"The Scenic Railway is in that direction," observed the Crown Prince, leaning on the balustrade. "If there were no buildings we could see it."

"Right here," Nikky was saying to himself. "At this very spot. She held out her arms, and I —"

"It looks very interesting," said Prince Ferdinand William Otto. "Of course we can't see the costumes, but it is better than nothing."

"I kissed her," Nikky was thinking, his heart swelling under his very best tunic. "Her head was on my breast, and I kissed her. Last of all, I kissed her eyes-her lovely eyes."

"If I fell off here," observed the Crown Prince in a meditative voice, "I would be smashed to a jelly, like the child at the Crystal Palace."

"But now she hates me," said Nikky's heart, and dropped about the distance of three buttons. "She hates me. I saw it in her eyes this morning. God!"

"We might as well play ball now."

Prince Ferdinand William Otto turned away from the parapet with a sigh. This strange quiet that filled the Palace seemed to have attacked Nikky too. Otto hated quiet.

They played ball, and the Crown Prince took a lesson in curves. But on his third attempt, he described such a compound-curve that the ball disappeared over an adjacent part of the roof, and although Nikky did some blood-curdling climbing along gutters, it could not be found.

It was then that the Majordomo, always a marvelous figure in crimson and gold, and never seen without white gloves-the Majordomo bowed in a window, and observed that if His Royal Highness pleased, His Royal Highness's luncheon was served.

In the shrouded room inside the windows, however, His Royal Highness paused and looked around.

"I've been here before," he observed. "These were my father's rooms. My mother lived here, too. When I am older, perhaps I can have them. It would be convenient on account of my practicing curves on the roof. But I should need a number of balls."

He was rather silent on his way back to the schoolroom. But once he looked up rather wistfully at Nikky.

"If they were living," he said, "I am pretty sure they would take me out to-day."

Olga Loschek had found the day one of terror. Annunciata had demanded her attendance all morning, had weakened strangely and demanded fretfully to be comforted.

"I have been a bad daughter," she would say. "It was my nature. I was warped and soured by wretchedness."

"But you have not been a bad daughter," the Countess would protest, for the thousandth time. "You have done your duty faithfully. You have stayed here when many another would have been traveling on the Riviera, or —"

"It was no sacrifice," said Annunciata, in her peevish voice. "I loathe traveling. And now I am being made to suffer for all I have done. He will die, and the rest of us-what will happen to us?" She shivered.

The Countess would take the cue, would enlarge on the precautions for safety, on the uselessness of fear, on the popularity of the Crown Prince. And Annunciata, for a time at least, would relax. In her new remorse she made frequent visits to the sickroom, passing, a long, thin figure, clad in black, through lines of bowing gentlemen, to stand by the bed and wring her hands. But the old King did not even know she was there.

The failure of her plan as to Nikky and Hedwig was known to the Countess the night before. Hedwig had sent for her and faced her in her boudoir, very white and calm.

"He refuses," she said. "There is nothing more to do."

"Refuses!"

"He has promised not to leave Otto."

Olga Loschek had been incredulous, at first. It was not possible. Men in love did not do these things. It was not possible, that, after all, she had failed. When she realized it, she would have broken out in bitter protest, but Hedwig's face warned her. "He is right, of course," Hedwig had said. "You and I were wrong, Countess. There is nothing to do-or say."

And the Countess had taken her defeat quietly, with burning eyes and a throat dry with excitement. "I am sorry, Highness," she said from the doorway. "I had only hoped to save you from unhappiness. That is all. And, as you say, there is nothing to be done." So she had gone away and faced the night, and the day which was to follow.

The plot was arranged, to the smallest detail. The King, living now only so long as it was decreed he should live; would, in mid-afternoon, commence to sink. The entire Court would be gathered in anterooms and salons near his apartments. In his rooms the Crown Prince would be kept, awaiting the summons to the throne-room, where, on the King's death, the regency would be declared, and the Court would swear fealty to the new King, Otto the Ninth. By arrangement with the captain of the Palace guard, who was one of the Committee of Ten, the sentries before the Crown Prince's door were to be of the revolutionary party. Mettlich would undoubtedly be with the King. Remained then to be reckoned with only the Prince's personal servants, Miss Braithwaite, and Nikky Larisch.

The servants offered little difficulty. At that hour, four o'clock, probably only the valet Oskar would be on duty, and his station was at the end of a corridor, separated by two doors from the schoolroom. It was planned that the two men who were to secure the Crown Prince were to wear the Palace livery, and to come with a message that the Crown Prince was to accompany them. Then, instead of going to the wing where the Court was gathered, they would go up to Hubert's rooms, and from there to the roof and the secret passage.

Two obstacles were left for the Countess to cope with, and this was her part of the work. She had already a plan for Miss Braithwaite. But Nikky Larisch?

Over that problem, during the long night hours, Olga Loschek worked. It would be possible to overcome Nikky, of course. There would be four men, with the sentries, against him. But that would mean struggle and an alarm. It was the plan to achieve the abduction quietly, so quietly that for perhaps an hour-they hoped for an hour-there would be no alarm. Some time they must have, enough to make the long journey through the underground passage. Otherwise the opening at the gate would be closed, and the party caught like rats in a hole.

The necessity for planning served one purpose, at least. It kept her from thinking. Possibly it saved her reason, for there were times during that last night when Olga Loschek was not far from madness. At dawn, long after Hedwig had forgotten her unhappiness in sleep, the Countess went wearily to bed. She had dismissed Minna hours before, and as she stood before her mirror, loosening her heavy hair, she saw that all that was of youth and loveliness in her had died in the night. A determined, scornful, and hard-eyed woman, she went drearily to bed.

During the early afternoon the Chancellor visited the Crown Prince. Waiting and watching had made inroads on him, too, but he assumed a sort of heavy jocularity for the boy's benefit.

"No lessons, eh?" he said. "Then there have been no paper balls for the tutors' eyes, eh?"

"I never did that but once, sir," said Prince Ferdinand William Otto gravely.

"So! Once only!"

"And I did that because he was always looking at Hedwig's picture."

The Chancellor eyed the picture. "I should be the last to condemn him for that," he said, and glanced at Nikky.

"We must get the lad out somewhere for some air," he observed. "It is not good to keep him shut up like this." He turned to the Crown Prince. "In a day or so," he said, "we shall all go to the summer palace. You would like that, eh?"

"Will my grandfather be able to go?"

The Chancellor sighed. "Yes," he said, "I—he will go to the country also. He has loved it very dearly."

He went, shortly after three o'clock. And, because he was restless and uneasy, he made a round of the Palace, and of the guards. Before he returned to his vigil outside the King's bedroom, he stood for a moment by a window and looked out. Evidently rumors of the King's condition had crept out, in spite of their caution. The Place, kept free of murmurs by the police, was filling slowly with people; people who took up positions on benches, under the trees, and even sitting on the curb of the street. An orderly and silent crowd it seemed, of the better class. Here and there he saw police agents in plain clothes, impassive but watchful, on the lookout for the first cry of treason.

An hour or two, or three-three at the most and the fate of the Palace would lie in the hands of that crowd. He could but lead the boy to the balcony, and await the result.

Chapter XXXIV
The Pirate's Den

Miss Braithwaite was asleep on the couch in her sitting-room, deeply asleep, so that when Prince Ferdinand William Otto changed the cold cloth on her head, she did not even move. The Countess Loschek had brought her some medicine.

"It cured her very quickly," said the Crown Prince, shuffling the cards with clumsy fingers. He and Nikky were playing a game in which matches represented money. The Crown Prince had won nearly all of them and was quite pink with excitement. "It's my deal, it? When she goes to sleep like that, she nearly always wakens up much better. She's very sound asleep."

Nikky played absently, and lost the game. The Crown Prince triumphantly scooped up the rest of the matches. "We've had rather a nice day," he observed, "even if we didn't go out. Shall we divide them again, and start all over?"

Nikky, however, proclaimed himself hopelessly beaten and a bad loser. So the Crown Prince put away the cards, which belonged to Miss Braithwaite, and with which she played solitaire in the evenings. Then he lounged to the window, his hands in his pockets. There was something on his mind which the Chancellor's reference to Hedwig's picture had recalled. Something he wished to say to Nikky, without looking at him.

So he clearer throat, and looked out the window, and said, very casually:

"Hilda says that Hedwig is going to get married."

"So I hear, Highness."

"She doesn't seem to be very happy about it. She's crying, most of the time."

It was Nikky's turn to clear his throat. "Marriage is a serious matter," he said. "It is not to be gone into lightly."

"Once, when I asked you about marriage, you said marriage was when two people loved each other, and wanted to be together the rest of their lives."

"Well," hedged Nikky, "that is the idea, rather."

"I should think," said Prince Ferdinand William Otto, slightly red, "that you would marry her yourself."

Nikky, being beyond speech for an instant and looking, had His Royal Highness but seen him, very tragic and somewhat rigid, the Crown Prince went on:

"She's a very nice girl," he said; "I think she would make a good wife."

There was something of reproach in his tone. He had confidently planned that Nikky would marry Hedwig, and that they could all live on forever in the Palace. But, the way things were going, Nikky might marry anybody, and go away to live, and he would lose him.

"Yes," said Nikky, in a strange voice, "she —I am sure she would make a good wife."

At which Prince Ferdinand William Otto turned and looked at him. "I wish you would marry her yourself," he said with his nearest approach to impatience. "I think she'd be willing. I'll ask her, if you want me to."

Half-past three, then, and Nikky trying to explain, within the limits of the boy's understanding of life, his position. Members of royal families, he said, looking far away, over the child's head, had to do many things for the good of the country. And marrying was one of them. Something of old Mettlich's creed of prosperity for the land he gave, something of his own hopelessness, too, without knowing it. He sat, bent forward, his hands swung between his knees, and tried to visualize, for Otto's understanding and his own heartache, the results of such a marriage.

Some of it the boy grasped. A navy, ships, a railroad to the sea-those he could understand. Treaties were beyond his comprehension. And, with a child's singleness of idea, he returned to the marriage.

"I'm sure she doesn't care about it," he said at last. "If I were King I would not let her do it. And" —he sat very erect and swung his short legs —"when I grow up, I shall fight for a navy, if I want one, and I shall marry whoever I like."

At a quarter to four Olga Loschek was announced. She made the curtsy inside the door that Palace ceremonial demanded and inquired for the governess. Prince Ferdinand William Otto, who had risen at her entrance, offered to see if she still slept.

"I think you are a very good doctor," he said, smiling, and went out to Miss Braithwaite's sitting room.

It was then that Olga Loschek played the last card, and won. She moved quickly to Nikky's side.

"I have a message for you," she said.

A light leaped into Nikky's eyes. "For me?"

"Do you know where my boudoir is?"

"I —yes, Countess."

"If you will go there at once and wait, some one will see you there as soon as possible." She put her hand on his arm. "Don't be foolish and proud," she said. "She is sorry about last night, and she is very unhappy."

The light faded out of Nikky's eyes. She was unhappy and he could do nothing. They had a way, in the Palace, of binding one's hands and leaving one helpless. He could not even go to her.

"I cannot go, Countess," he said. "She must understand. To-day, of all days —"

"You mean that you cannot leave the Crown Prince?" She shrugged her shoulders. "You, too! Never have I seen so many faint hearts, such rolling eyes, such shaking knees! And for what! Because a few timid souls see a danger that does not exist."

"I think it does exist," said Nikky obstinately.

"I am to take the word to her, then, that you will not come?"

"That I cannot."

"You are a very foolish boy," said the Countess, watching him. "And since you are so fearful, I myself will remain here. There are sentries at the doors, and a double guard everywhere. What, in the name of all that is absurd, can possibly happen?"

That was when she won. For Nikky, who has never been, in all this history, anything of a hero, and all of the romantic and loving boy, —Nikky wavered and fell.

When Prince Ferdinand William Otto returned, it was with the word that Miss Braithwaite still slept, and that she looked very comfortable, Nikky was gone, and the Countess stood by a window, holding to the sill to support her shaking body.

It was done. The boy was in her hands. There was left only to deliver him to those who, even now, were on the way. Nikky was safe. He would wait in her boudoir, and Hedwig would not come. She had sent no message. She was, indeed, at that moment a part of one of those melancholy family groups which, the world over, in palace or peasant's hut, await the coming of death.

Prince Ferdinand William Otto chatted. He got out the picture-frame for Hedwig, which was finished now, with the exception of burning his initials in the lower left-hand corner. After inquiring politely if the smell of burning would annoy her, the Crown Prince drew a rather broken-backed "F," a weak-kneed "W," and an irregular "O" in the corner and proceeded to burn them in. He sat bent over the desk, the very tip of his tongue protruding, and worked conscientiously and carefully. Between each letter he burned a dot.

Suddenly, Olga Loschek became panic-stricken. She could not stay, and see this thing out. Let them follow her and punish her. She could not. She had done her part. The governess lay in, a drugged sleep. A turn of the key, and the door to the passage beyond which Oskar waited would be closed off. Let follow what must, she would not see it.

The boy still bent over his work. She wandered about the room, casually, as if examining the pictures on the wall. She stopped, for a bitter moment, before Hedwig's photograph, and, for a shaken one, before those of Prince Hubert and his wife. Then she turned the key, and shut Oskar safely away.

"Highness," she said, "Lieutenant Larisch will be here in a moment. Will you permit me to go?"

Otto was off his chair in an instant. "Certainly," he said, his mind still on the "O" which he was shading.

Old habit was strong in the Countess. Although the boy's rank was numbered by moments, although his life was possibly to be counted by hours, she turned at the doorway and swept him a curtsy. Then she went out, and closed the door behind her.

The two sentries stood outside. They were of the Terrorists. She knew, and they knew she knew. But neither one made a sign. They stared ahead, and Olga Loschek went out between them.

Now the psychology of the small boy is a curious thing. It is, for one thing, retentive. Ideas become, given time, obsessions. And obsessions are likely to lead to action.

The Crown Prince Ferdinand William Otto was only a small boy, for all his title and dignity. And suddenly he felt lonely. Left alone, he returned to his expectations for the day, and compared them with the facts. He remembered other carnivals, with his carriage moving through the streets, and people showering him with fresh flowers. He rather glowed at the memory. Then he recalled that the Chancellor had said he needed fresh air.

Something occurred to him, something which combined fresh air with action, yet kept to the letter of his promise-or was there a promise? —not to leave the Palace.

The idea pleased him. It set him to smiling, and his bright hair to quivering with excitement. It was nothing less than to go up on the roof and find the ball. Nikky would be surprised, having failed himself. He would have to be very careful, having in mind the fate of that unlucky child at the Crystal Palace. And he would have to hurry. Nikky would be sure to return soon.

He opened the door on to the great corridor, and stepped out, saluting the sentries, as he always did.

"I'll be back in a moment," he informed them. He was always on terms of great friendliness with the guard, and he knew these men by sight. "Are you going to be stationed here now?" he inquired pleasantly.

The two guards were at a loss. But one of them, who had a son of his own, and hated the whole business, saluted and replied that he knew not.

"I hope you are," said Ferdinand William Otto, and went on.

The sentries regarded one another. "Let him go!" said the one who was a father.

The other one moved uneasily. "Our orders cover no such contingency," he muttered. "And, besides, he will come back." He bore a strong resemblance to the boy, who, in the riding-school, had dusted the royal hearse. "I hope to God he does not come back," he said stonily.

Five minutes to four.

The Crown Prince hurried. The corridors were almost empty. Here and there he met servants, who stood stiff against the wall until he had passed. On the marble staircase, leading up, he met no one, nor on the upper floor. He was quite warm with running and he paused in his father's suite to mop his face. Then he opened a window and went out on the roof. It seemed very large and empty now, and the afternoon sun, sinking low, threw shadows across it.

Also, from the balustrade, it looked extremely far to the ground.

Nevertheless, although his heart beat a trifle fast, he was still determined. A climb which Nikky with his long legs had achieved in a leap, took him up to a chimney. Below-it seemed a long way below was the gutter. There was a very considerable slant. If one sat down, like Nikky, and slid, and did not slide over the edge, one should fetch up in the gutter.

He felt a trifle dizzy. But Nikky's theory was, that if one is afraid to do a thing, better to do it and get over being afraid.

"I was terribly afraid of a bayonet attack," Nikky had observed, "until I was in one. The next one I rather enjoyed!"

So the Crown Prince sat down on the sloping roof behind the chimney, and gathered his legs under him for a slide.

Then he heard a door open, and footsteps. Very careful footsteps. He was quite certain Nikky had followed him. But there were cautious voices, too, and neither was Nikky's. It occurred to Prince Ferdinand William Otto that a good many people, certainly including Miss Braithwaite, would not approve of either his situation or his position. Miss Braithwaite was particularly particular about positions.

So he sat still beside the chimney, well shielded by the evergreens in tubs, until the voices and the footsteps were gone. Then he took all his courage in his hands, and slid. Well for him that the ancient builders of the Palace had been reckless with lead, that the gutter was both wide and deep. Well for Nikky, too, waiting in the boudoir below and hard-driven between love and anxiety.

The Crown Prince, unaccustomed to tiles, turned over halfway down, and rolled. He brought up with a jerk in the gutter, quite safe, but extremely frightened. And the horrid memory of the Crystal Palace child filled his mind, to the exclusion of everything else. He sat there for quite a few minutes. There was no ball in sight, and the roof looked even steeper from this point.

Being completely self-engrossed, therefore, he did not see that the roof had another visitor. Had two visitors, as a matter of fact. One of them wore a blanket with a white "O" over a white "X" on it, and the other wore a mask, and considerable kitchen cutlery fastened to his belt. They had come out of a small door in the turret and were very much at ease. They leaned over the parapet and admired the view. They strutted about the flat roof, and sang, at least one of them sang a very strange refrain, which was something about

> "Fifteen men on a dead man's chest;
> Yo-ho-ho and a bottle of rum."

And then they climbed on one of the garden chairs and looked over the expanse of the roof, which was when they saw Prince Ferdinand William Otto, and gazed at him.

"Gee whiz!" said the larger pirate, through his mask. "What are you doing there?"

The Crown Prince started, and stared. "I am sitting here," explained the Crown Prince, trying to look as though he usually sat in lead gutters. "I am looking for a ball."

"You're looking for a fall, I guess," observed the pirate. "You don't remember me, kid, do you?"

"I can't see your face, but I know your voice." His voice trembled with excitement.

"Lemme give you a hand," said the pirate, whipping off his mask. "You make me nervous, sitting there. You've got a nerve, you have."

The Crown Prince looked gratified. "I don't need any assistance, thank you," he said. "Perhaps, now I'm here, I'd better look for the ball."

"I wouldn't bother about the old ball," said the pirate, rather nervously for an old sea-dog. "You better get back to a safe place. Say, what made you pretend that our Railway made you nervous?"

Prince Ferdinand William Otto climbed up the tiles, trying to look as though tiles were his native habitat. The pirates both regarded him with admiration, as he dropped beside them.

"How did you happen to come here?" asked the Crown Prince. "Did you lose your aeroplane up here?"

"We came on business," said the pirate importantly. "Two of the enemy entered our cave. We were guarding it from the underbrush, and saw them go in. We trailed them. They must die!"

"Really-die?"

"Of course. Death to those who defy us."

"Death to those who defy us!" repeated the Crown Prince, enjoying himself hugely, and quite ready for bloodshed.

"Look here, Dick Deadeye," said the larger pirate to the smaller, who stood gravely at attention, "I think he belongs to our crew. What say, old pal?"

Dick Deadeye wagged his tail.

Some two minutes later, the Crown Prince of Livonia, having sworn the pirate oath of no quarter, except to women and children, was on his way to the pirate cave.

He was not running away. He was not disobedient. He was breaking no promises. Because, from the moment he saw the two confederates, and particularly from the moment he swore the delightful oath, his past was wiped away. There was, in his consciousness, no Palace, no grandfather, no Miss Braithwaite, even no Nikky. There was only a boy and a dog, and a pirate den awaiting him.

Chapter XXXV
The Paper Crown

Strange that the old Palace roof should, in close succession; have seen Nikky forgetting his promise to the Chancellor, and Otto forgetting that he was not to run away. Strange places, roofs, abiding places, since long ago, of witches.

"How'd you happen to be in that gutter?" Bobby demanded, as they started down the staircase in the wall. "Watch out, son, it's pretty steep."

"I was getting a ball."

"Is this your house?"

"Well, I live here," temporized Prince Ferdinand William Otto. A terrible thought came to him. Suppose this American boy, who detested kings and princes, should learn who he was!

"It looks like a big place. Is it a barracks?"

"No." He hesitated. "But there are a good many soldiers here. I—I never saw these steps before."

"I should think not," boasted Bobby. "I discovered them. I guess nobody else in the world knows about them. I put up a flag at the bottom and took possession. They're mine."

"Really!" said Prince Ferdinand William Otto, quite delighted. He would never have thought of such a thing.

A door of iron bars at the foot of the long flight of steps-there were four of them-stood open. Here daylight, which had been growing fainter, entirely ceased. And here Bobby, having replaced his mask, placed an air-rifle over his shoulder, and lighted a candle and held it out to the Crown Prince.

"You can carry it," he said. "Only don't let it drip on you. You'll spoil your clothes." There was a faintly scornful note in his voice, and Ferdinand William Otto was quick to hear it.

"I don't care at all about my clothes," he protested. And to prove it he deliberately tilted the candle and let a thin stream of paraffin run down his short jacket.

"You're a pretty good sport," Bobby observed. And from that time on he addressed His Royal Highness as "old sport."

"Walk faster, old sport," he would say. "That candle's pretty short, and we've got a long way to go." Or —"Say, old sport, I'll make you a mask like this, if you like. I made this one."

When they reached the old dungeon the candle was about done. There was only time to fashion another black mask out of a piece of cloth that bore a strange resemblance to a black waistcoat. The Crown Prince donned this with a wildly beating heart. Never in all his life had he been so excited. Even Dick Deadeye was interested, and gave up his scenting of the strange footsteps that he had followed through the passage, to watch the proceedings.

"We can get another candle, and come back and cook something," said the senior pirate, tying the mask on with Pieces of brown string. "It gets pretty smoky, but I can cook, you'd better believe."

So this wonderful boy could cook, also! The Crown Prince had never met any one with so many varied attainments. He gazed through the eyeholes, which were rather too far apart, in rapt admiration.

"As you haven't got a belt," Bobby said generously, "I'll give you the rifle. Ever hold a gun?"

"Oh, yes," said the Crown Prince. He did not explain that he had been taught to shoot on the rifle-range of his own regiment, and had won quite a number of medals. He possessed, indeed, quite a number of small but very perfect guns.

With the last gasp of the candle, the children prepared to depart. The senior pirate had already forgotten the two men he had trailed through the passage, and was eager to get outdoors.

"Ready!" he said. "Now, remember, old sport, we are pirates. No quarter, except to women and children. Shoot every man."

"Even if he is unarmed?" inquired the Crown Prince, who had also studied strategy and tactics, and felt that an unarmed man should be taken prisoner.

"Sure. We don't really shoot them, silly. Now. Get in step.

> "'Fifteen men on a dead man's chest
> Yo-ho-ho and a bottle of rum.'"

They marched up the steps and out through the opening at the top. If there were any who watched, outside the encircling growth of evergreens, they were not on the lookout for two small boys and a dog. And, as became pirates, the children made a stealthy exit.

Then began, for the Crown Prince, such a day of joy as he had never known before. Even the Land of Delight faded before this new bliss of stalking from tree to tree, of killing unsuspecting citizens who sat on rugs on the ground and ate sausages and little cakes. Here and there, where a party had moved on, they salvaged a bit of food-the heel of a loaf, one of the small country apples. Shades of the Court Physicians, under whose direction the Crown Prince was daily fed a carefully balanced ration!

When they were weary, they stretched out on the ground, and the Crown Prince, whose bed was nightly dried with a warming-pan for fear of dampness, wallowed blissfully on earth still soft with the melting frosts of the winter. He grew muddy and dirty. He had had no hat, of course, and his bright hair hung over his forehead in moist strands. Now and then he drew a long breath of sheer happiness.

Around them circled the gayety of the Carnival, bands of students in white, with the tall peaked caps of Pierrots. Here and there was a scarlet figure, a devil with horns, who watched the crowd warily. A dog, with the tulle petticoats of a dancer tied around it and a great bow on its neck, made friends with Dick Deadeye, alias Tucker, and joined the group.

But, as dusk descended, the crowd gradually dispersed, some to supper, but some to gather in the Place and in the streets around the Palace. For the rumor that the King was dying would not down.

At last the senior pirate consulted a large nickel watch.

"Gee! it's almost supper time," he said.

Prince Ferdinand William Otto consulted his own watch, the one with the inscription: "To Ferdinand William Otto, from his grandfather, on the occasion of his taking his first communion."

"Why can't you come home to supper with me?" asked the senior pirate. "Would your folks kick up a row?"

"I beg your pardon?"

"Would your family object?"

"There is only one person who would mind," reflected the Crown Prince, aloud, "and she will be angry anyhow. I —do you think your mother will be willing?"

"Willing? Sure she will! My governess-but I'll fix her. She's a German, and they're always cranky. Anyhow, it's my birthday. I'm always allowed a guest on birthdays."

So home together, gayly chatting, went the two children, along the cobble-paved streets of the ancient town, past old churches that had been sacked and pillaged by the very ancestors of one of them, taking short cuts through narrow passages that twisted and wormed their way between, and sometimes beneath, century-old stone houses; across the flower-market, where faint odors of dying violets and crushed lilies-of-the-valley still clung to the bare wooden booths; and so, finally, to the door of a tall building where, from the concierge's room beside the entrance, came a reek of stewing garlic.

Neither of the children had noticed the unwonted silence of the streets, which had, almost suddenly, succeeded the noise of the Carnival. What few passers-by they had seen had been hurrying in the direction of the Palace. Twice they had passed soldiers, with lanterns, and once one had stopped and flashed a light on them.

"Well, old sport!" said Bobby in English, "anything you can do for me?"

The soldier had passed on, muttering at the insolence of American children. The two youngsters laughed consumedly at the witticism. They were very happy, the lonely little American boy and the lonely little Prince-happy from sheer gregariousness, from the satisfaction of that strongest of human inclinations, next to love-the social instinct.

The concierge was out. His niece admitted them, and went back to her interrupted cooking. The children hurried up the winding stone staircase, with its iron rail and its gas lantern, to the second floor.

In the sitting-room, the sour-faced governess was darning a hole in a small stocking. She was as close as possible to the green-tile stove, and she was looking very unpleasant; for the egg-shaped darner only slipped through the hole, which was a large one. With an irritable gesture she took off her slipper, and, putting one coarse-stockinged foot on the fender, proceeded to darn by putting the slipper into the stocking and working over it.

Things looked unpropitious. The Crown Prince ducked behind Bobby.

The Fraulein looked at the clock.

"You are fifteen minutes late," she snapped, and bit the darning thread-not with rage, but because she had forgotten her scissors.

"I'm sorry, but you see —"

"Whom have you there?"

The Prince cowered. She looked quite like his grandfather when his tutor's reports had been unfavorable.

"A friend of mine," said Bobby, not a whit daunted.

The governess put down the stocking and rose. In so doing, she caught her first real glimpse of Ferdinand William Otto, and she staggered back.

"Holy Saints!" she said, and went white. Then she stared at the boy, and her color came back. "For a moment," she muttered " —but no. He is not so tall, nor has he the manner. Yes, he is much smaller!"

Which proves that, whether it wears it or not, royalty is always measured to the top of a crown.

In the next room Bobby's mother was arranging candles on a birthday cake in the center of the table. Pepy had iced the cake herself, and had forgotten one of the "b's" in "Bobby" so that the cake really read: "Boby-XII."

However, it looked delicious, and inside had been baked a tiny black china doll and a new American penny, with Abraham Lincoln's head on it. The penny was for good fortune, but the doll was a joke of Pepy's, Bobby being aggressively masculine.

Bobby, having passed the outpost, carried the rest of the situation by assault. He rushed into the dining-room and kissed his mother, with one eye on the cake.

"Mother, here's company to supper! Oh, look at the cake! B-O-B-Y'! Mother! That's awful!"

Mrs. Thorpe looked at the cake. "Poor Pepy," she said. "Suppose she had made it 'Booby'?" Then she saw Ferdinand William Otto, and went over, somewhat puzzled, with her hand out. "I am very glad Bobby brought you," she said. "He has so few little friends —"

Then she stopped, for the Prince had brought his heels together sharply, and, bending over her hand, had kissed it, exactly as he kissed his Aunt Annunciata's when he went to have tea with her. Mrs. Thorpe was fairly startled, not at the kiss, but at the grace with which the tribute was rendered.

Then she looked down, and it restored her composure to find that Ferdinand William Otto, too, had turned eyes toward the cake. He was, after all, only a hungry small boy. With quick tenderness she stooped and kissed him gravely on the forehead. Caresses were strange to Ferdinand William Otto. His warm little heart leaped and pounded. At that moment, he would have died for her!

Mr. Thorpe came home a little late. He kissed Bobby twelve times, and one to grow on. He shook hands absently with the visitor, and gave the Fraulein the evening paper-an extravagance on which he insisted, although one could read the news for nothing by going to the cafe on the corner. Then he drew his wife aside.

"Look here!" he said. "Don't tell Bobby-no use exciting him, and of course it's not our funeral anyhow but there's a report that the Crown Prince has been kidnapped. And that's not all. The old King is dying!"

"How terrible!"

"Worse than that. The old King gone and no Crown Prince! It may mean almost any sort of trouble! I've closed up at the Park for the night." His arm around his wife, he looked through the doorway to where Bobby and Ferdinand were counting the candles. "It's made me think pretty hard," he said. "Bobby mustn't go around alone the way he's been doing. All Americans here are considered millionaires. If the Crown Prince could go, think how easy —"

His arm tightened around his wife, and together they went in to the birthday feast. Ferdinand William Otto was hungry. He ate eagerly-chicken, fruit compote, potato salad-again shades of the Court physicians, who fed him at night a balanced ration of milk, egg, and zwieback! Bobby also ate busily, and conversation languished.

Then the moment came when, the first cravings appeased, they sat back in their chairs while Pepy cleared the table and brought in a knife to cut the cake. Mr. Thorpe had excused himself for a moment. Now he came back, with a bottle wrapped in a newspaper, and sat down again.

"I thought," he said, "as this is a real occasion, not exactly Robert's coming of age, but marking his arrival at years of discretion, the period when he ceases to be a small boy and becomes a big one, we might drink a toast to it."

"Robert!" objected the big boy's mother.

"A teaspoonful each, honey," he begged. "It changes it from a mere supper to a festivity."

He poured a few drops of wine into the children's glasses, and filled them up with water. Then he filled the others, and sat smiling, this big young man, who had brought his loved ones across the sea, and was trying to make them happy up a flight of stone stairs, above a concierge's bureau that smelled of garlic.

"First," he said, "I believe it is customary to toast the King. Friends, I give you the good King and brave soldier, Ferdinand of Livonia."

They stood up to drink it, and even Pepy had a glass.

Ferdinand William Otto was on his feet first. He held his glass up in his right hand, and his eyes shone. He knew what to do. He had seen the King's health drunk any number of times.

"To His Majesty, Ferdinand of Livonia," he said solemnly. "God keep the King!"

Over their glasses Mrs. Thorpe's eyes met her husband's. How they trained their children here!

But Ferdinand William Otto had not finished. "I give you," he said, in his clear young treble, holding his glass, "the President of the United States-The President!"

"The President!" said Mr. Thorpe.

They drank again, except the Fraulein, who disapproved of children being made much of, and only pretended to sip her wine.

"Bobby," said his mother, with a catch in her voice, "haven't you something to suggest-as a toast?"

Bobby's eyes were on the cake; he came back with difficulty.

"Well," he meditated, "I guess-would 'Home' be all right?"

"Home!" they all said, a little shakily, and drank to it.

Home! To the Thorpes, a little house on a shady street in America; to the Fraulein, a thatched cottage in the mountains of Germany and an old mother; to Pepy, the room in a tenement where she went at night; to Ferdinand William Otto, a formal suite of apartments in the Palace, surrounded by pomp, ordered by rule and precedent, hardened by military discipline, and unsoftened by family love, save for the grim affection of the old King.

Home!

After all, Pepy's plan went astray, for the Fraulein got the china baby, and Ferdinand William Otto the Lincoln penny.

"That," said Bobby's father, "is a Lincoln penny, young man. It bears the portrait of Abraham Lincoln. Have you ever heard of him?"

The Prince looked up. Did he not know the "Gettysburg Address" by heart?

"Yes, sir," he said. "The-my grandfather thinks that President Lincoln was a very great man."

"One of the world's greatest. I hardly thought, over here —" Mr. Thorpe paused and looked speculatively at the boy. "You'd better keep that penny where you won't lose it," he said soberly. "It doesn't hurt us to try to be good. If you're in trouble, think of the difficulties Abraham Lincoln surmounted. If you want to be great, think how great he was." He was a trifle ashamed of his own earnestness. "All that for a penny, young man!"

The festivities were taking a serious turn. There was a little packet at each plate, and now Bobby's mother reached over and opened hers.

"Oh!" she said, and exhibited a gaudy tissue paper bonnet. Everybody had one. Mr. Thorpe's was a dunce's cap, and Fraulein's a giddy Pierrette of black and white. Bobby had a military cap. With eager fingers Ferdinand William Otto opened his; he had never tasted this delicious paper-cap joy before.

It was a crown, a sturdy bit of gold paper, cut into points and set with red paste jewels —a gem of a crown. He was charmed. He put it on his head, with the unconsciousness of childhood, and posed delightedly.

The Fraulein looked at Prince Ferdinand William Otto, and slowly the color left her lean face. She stared. It was he, then, and none other. Stupid, not to have known at the beginning! He, the Crown Prince, here in the home of these barbarous Americans, when, by every plan that had been made, he should now be in the hands of those who would dispose of him.

"I give you," said Mr. Thorpe, raising his glass toward his wife, "the giver of the feast. Boys, up with you!"

It was then that the Fraulein, making an excuse, slipped out of the room.

Chapter XXXVI
The King is Dead

Now at last the old King's hour had come. Mostly he slept, as though his body, eager for its long rest, had already given up the struggle. Stimulants, given by his devoted physician, had no effect. Other physicians there were, a group of them, but it was Doctor Wiederman who stood by the bed and waited.

Father Gregory, his friend of many years, had come again from Etzel, and it was he who had administered the sacrament. The King had roused for it, and had smiled at the father.

"So!" he said, almost in a whisper, "you would send me clean! It is hard to scour an old kettle."

Doctor Wiederman bent over the bed. "Majesty," he implored, "if there is anything we can do to make you comfortable —"

"Give me Hubert's picture," said the King. When his fingers refused to hold it, Annunciata came forward swiftly and held it before him. But his heavy eyes closed. With more intuition than might have been expected of her, the Archduchess laid it on the white coverlet, and placed her father's hand on it.

The physicians consulted in an alcove. Annunciata went back to her restless, noiseless pacing of the room. Father Gregory went to a window, and stared out. He saw, not the silent crowd in the Place, but many other things; the King, as a boy, chafing under the restraint of Court ceremonial; the King, as a young man, taking a wife who did not love him. He saw the King madly in love with his wife, and turning to excesses to forget her. Then, and for this the old priest thanked the God who was so real to him, he saw the Queen bear children, and turning to her husband because he was their father. They had lived to love deeply and' truly.

Then had come the inevitable griefs. The Queen had died, and had been saved a tragedy, for Hubert had been violently done to death. And now again a tragedy had come, but one the King would never know.

The two Sisters of Mercy stood beside the bed, and looked down at the quiet figure.

"I should wish to die so," whispered the elder. "A long life, filled with many deeds, and then to sleep away!"

"A long life, full of many sorrows!" observed the younger one, her eyes full of tears. "He has outlived all that he loved."

"Except the little Otto."

Their glances met, for even here there was a question.

As if their thought had penetrated the haze which is, perhaps, the mist that hides from us the gates of heaven, the old King opened his eyes.

"Otto!" he said. "I —wish —"

Annunciata bent over him. "He is coming, father," she told him, with white lips.

She slipped to her knees beside the bed, and looked up to Doctor Wiederman with appealing eyes.

"I am afraid," she whispered. "Can you not —?"

He shook his head. She had asked a question in her glance, and he had answered. The Crown Prince was gone. Perhaps the search would be successful. Could he not be held, then, until the boy was found? And Doctor Wiederman had answered "No."

In the antechamber the Council waited, standing and without speech. But in an armchair beside the door to the King's room the Chancellor sat, his face buried in his hands. In spite of precautions, in spite of everything, the blow had fallen. The Crown Prince, to him at once son and sovereign, the little Crown Prince, was gone. And his old friend, his comrade of many years, lay at his last hour.

Another regiment left the Palace, to break ranks beyond the crowd, and add to the searchers. They marched to a muffled drum. As the sound reached him, the old warrior stirred. He had come to this, he who had planned, not for himself, but for his country. And because he was thinking clearly, in spite of his grief, he saw that his very ambition for the boy had been his undoing. In the alliance with Karnia he had given the Terrorists a scourge to flay the people to revolt.

Now he waited for the King's death. Waited numbly. For, with the tolling of St. Stefan's bell would rise the cry for the new King.

And there was no King.

In the little room where the Sisters kept their medicines, so useless now, Hedwig knelt at the Prie-dieu and prayed.

She tried to pray for her grandfather's soul, but she could not. Her one cry was for Otto, that he be saved and brought back. In the study she had found the burntwood frame, and she held it hugged close to her with its broken-backed "F," its tottering "W," and wavering "O", with its fat Cupids in sashes, and the places where an over-earnest small hand had slipped.

Hilda stood by the stand, and fingered the bottles. Her nose was swollen with crying, but she was stealthily removing corks and sniffing at the contents of the bottles with the automatic curiosity of the young.

The King roused again. "Mettlich?" he asked.

The elder Sister tiptoed to the door and opened it. The Council turned, dread on their faces. She placed a hand on the Chancellor's shoulder.

"His Majesty has asked for you."

When he looked up, dazed, she bent down and took his hand.

"Courage!" she said quietly.

The Chancellor stood a second inside the door. Then he went to the side of the bed, and knelt, his lips to the cold, white hand on the counterpane.

"Sire!" he choked. "It is I —Mettlich."

The King looked at him, and placed his hand on the bowed gray head. Then his eyes turned to Annunciata and rested there. It was as if he saw her, not as the embittered woman of late years, but as the child of the woman he had loved.

"A good friend, and a good daughter," he said clearly. "Few men die so fortunate, and fewer sovereigns." His hand moved from Mettlich's head, and rested on the photograph.

The elder Sister leaned forward and touched his wrist. "Doctor!" she said sharply.

Doctor Wiederman came first, the others following. They grouped around the bed. Then the oldest of them, who had brought Annunciata into the world, touched her on the shoulder.

"Madame!" he said. "Madame, I —His Majesty has passed away."

Mettlich staggered to his feet, and took a long look at the face of his old sovereign and king.

In the mean time, things had been happening in the room where the Council waited. The Council, free of the restraint of the Chancellor's presence, had fallen into low-voiced consultation. What was to be done? They knew already the rumors of the streets, and were helpless before them. They had done what they could. But the boy was gone, and the city rising. Already the garrison of the fortress had been ordered to the Palace, but it could not arrive before midnight. Friese had questioned the wisdom of it, at that, and was for flight as soon as the

King died. Bayerl, on the other hand, urged a stand, in the hope that the Crown Prince would be found.

Their voices, lowered at first, rose acrimoniously; almost they penetrated to the silent room beyond. On to the discussion came Nikky Larisch, covered with dust and spotted with froth from his horse. He entered without ceremony, his boyish face drawn and white, his cap gone, his eyes staring.

"The Chancellor?" he said.

Some one pointed to the room beyond.

Nikky hesitated. Then, being young and dramatic, even in tragedy, he unbuckled his sword-belt and took it off, placing it on a table.

"Gentlemen," he said, "I have come to surrender myself."

The Council stared.

"For what reason?" demanded Marschall coldly.

"I believe it is called high treason." He closed his eyes for a moment. "It is because of my negligence that this thing has happened. He was in my charge, and I left him."

No one said anything. The Council looked at a loss, rather like a flock of sheep confronting some strange animal.

"I would have shot myself," said Nikky Larisch, "but it was too easy."

Then, rather at a loss as to the exact etiquette of arresting one's self, he bowed slightly and waited.

The door into the King's bedchamber opened.

The Chancellor came through, his face working. It closed behind him.

"Gentlemen of the Council," he said. "It is my duty my duty-to announce —" His voice broke; his grizzled chin quivered; tears rolled down his cheeks. "Friends," he said pitifully, "our good King-my old comrade-is dead!"

The birthday supper was over. It had ended with an American ice-cream, brought in carefully by Pepy, because of its expensiveness. They had cut the cake with Boby on the top, and the Crown Prince had eaten far more than was good for him.

He sat, fingering the Lincoln penny and feeling extremely full and very contented.

Then, suddenly, from a far-off church a deep-toned bell began to toll slowly.

Prince Ferdinand William Otto caught it. St. Stefan's bell! He sat up and listened. The sound was faint; one felt it rather than heard it, but the slow booming was unmistakable. He got up and pushed his chair back.

Other bells had taken it up, and now the whole city seemed alive with bells-bells that swung sadly from side to side, as if they said over and over: "Alas, alas!"

Something like panic seized Ferdinand William Otto. Some calamity had happened. Some one was perhaps his grandfather.

He turned an appealing face to Mrs. Thorpe. "I must go," he said: "I do not wish to appear rude, but something is wrong. The bells —"

Pepy had beet listening, too. Her broad face worked. "They mean but one thing," she said slowly. "I have heard it said many times. When St. Stefan's tolls life that, the King is dead!"

"No! No!" cried Ferdinand William Otto and ran madly out of the door.

Chapter XXXVII
Long Live the King!

While the birthday supper was at its height, in the bureau of the concierge sat old Adelbert, heavy and despairing. That very day had he learned to what use the Committee would put the information he had given them, and his old heart was dead within him. One may not be loyal for seventy years, and then easily become a traitor.

He had surveyed stonily the costume in which the little Prince was to be taken away. He had watched while the boxes of ammunition were uncovered in their barrels, he had seen the cobbler's shop become a seething hive of activity, where all day men had come and gone. He had heard the press beneath his feet fall silent because its work was done, and at dusk he had with his own eyes beheld men who carried forth, under their arms, blazing placards for the walls of the town.

Then, at seven o'clock, something had happened.

The concierge's niece had gone, leaving the supper ready cooked on the back of the stove. Old Adelbert sat alone, and watched the red bars of the stove fade to black. By that time it was done, and he was of the damned. The Crown Prince, who was of an age with the American lad upstairs, the Crown Prince was in the hands of his enemies. He, old Adelbert, had done it.

And now it was forever too late. Terrible thoughts filled his mind. He could not live thus, yet he could not die. The daughter must have the pension. He must live, a traitor, he on whose breast the King himself had pinned a decoration.

He wore his new uniform, in honor of the day. Suddenly he felt that he could not wear it any longer. He had no right to any uniform. He who had sold his country was of no country.

He went slowly out and up the staircase, dragging his wooden leg painfully from step to step. He heard the concierge come in below, his heavy footsteps reechoed through the building. Inside the door he called furiously to his niece. Old Adelbert heard him strike a match to light the gas.

On the staircase he met the Fraulein hurrying down. Her face was strained and her eyes glittering. She hesitated, as though she would speak, then she went on past him. He could hear her running. It reminded the old man of that day in the Opera, when a child ran down the staircase, and, as is the way of the old, he repeated himself: "One would think new legs grew in place of old ones, like the claws of sea-creatures," he said fretfully. And went on up the staircase.

In his room he sat down on a straight chair inside the door, and stared ahead. Then, slowly and mechanically, he took off his new uniform and donned the old one. He would have put on civilian clothes, had he possessed any. For by the deeds of that day he had forfeited the right to the King's garb.

It was there that Black Humbert, hurrying up, found him. The concierge was livid, his massive frame shook with excitement.

"Quick!" he said, and swore a great oath. "To the shop of the cobbler Heinz, and tell him this word. Here in the building is the boy."

"What boy?"

The concierge closed a great hand on the veteran's shoulder. "Who but the Crown Prince himself!" he said.

"But I thought-how can he be here?"

"Here is he, in our very hands. It is no time to ask questions."

"If he is here —"

"He is with the Americans," hissed the concierge, the veins on his forehead swollen with excitement. "Now, go, and quickly. I shall watch. Say that when I have secured the lad, I shall take him there. Let all be ready. An hour ago," he said, raising his great fists on high, "and everything lost. Now hurry, old wooden leg. It is a great night."

"But —I cannot. Already I have done too much. I am damned. I have lost my soul. I who am soon to die."

"YOU WILL GO."

And, at last, he went, hobbling down the staircase recklessly, because the looming figure at the stair head was listening. He reached the street. There, only a block away, was the cobbler's shop, lighted, but with the dirty curtains drawn across the window.

Old Adelbert gazed at it. Then he commended his soul to God, and turned toward the Palace.

He passed the Opera. On Carnival night it should have been open and in gala array, with lines of carriages and machines before it. It was closed, and dreary. But old Adelbert saw it not at all. He stumped along, panting with haste and exhaustion, to do the thing he had set himself to do.

Here was the Palace. Before it were packed dense throngs of silent people. Now and then a man put down a box, and rising on it, addressed the crowd, attempting to rouse them. Each time angry hands pulled him down, and hisses greeted him as he slunk away.

Had old Adelbert been alive to anything but his mission, he would have seen that this was no mob of revolutionists, but a throng of grieving people, awaiting the great bell of St. Stefan's with its dire news.

Then, above their heads, it rang out, slow, ominous, terrible. A sob ran through the crowd. In groups, and at last as a whole, the throng knelt. Men uncovered and women wept.

The bell rang on. At its first notes old Adelbert stopped, staggered, almost fell. Then he uncovered his head.

"Gone!" he said. "The old King! My old King!"

His face twitched. But the horror behind him drove him on through the kneeling crowd. Where it refused to yield, he drove the iron point of his wooden leg into yielding flesh, and so made his way.

Here, in the throng, Olga of the garderobe met him, and laid a trembling hand on his arm. He shook her off, but she clung to him.

"Know you what they are saying?" she whispered. "That the Crown Prince is stolen. And it is true. Soldiers scour the city everywhere."

"Let me go," said old Adelbert, fiercely.

"They say," she persisted, "that the Chancellor has made away with him, to sell us to Karnia."

"Fools!" cried old Adelbert, and pushed her off. When she refused to release him, he planted his iron toe on her shapely one and worked his way forward. The crowd had risen, and now stood expectantly facing the Palace. Some one raised a cry and others took it up.

"The King!" they cried. "Show us the little King!"

But the balcony outside the dead King's apartments remained empty. The curtains at the long windows were drawn, save at one, opened for air. The breeze shook its curtains to and fro, but no small, childish figure emerged. The cries kept up, but there was a snarl in the note now.

"The King! Long live the King! Where is he?"

A man in a red costume, near old Adelbert, leaped on a box and lighted a flaming torch. "Aye!" he yelled, "call for the little King. Where is he? What have they done with him?"

Old Adelbert pushed on. The voice of the revolutionist died behind him, in a chorus of fury. From nowhere, apparently, came lighted box-banners proclaiming the Chancellor's treason, and demanding a Republic. Some of them instructed the people to gather around the Parliament, where, it was stated, leading citizens were already forming a Republic. Some, more violent, suggested an advance on the Palace.

The crowd at first ignored them, but as time went on, it grew ugly. By all precedent, the new King should be now before them. What, then, if this rumor was true? Where was the little King?

Revolution, now, in the making. A flame ready to blaze. Hastily, on the outskirts of the throng, a delegation formed to visit the Palace, and learn the truth. Orderly citizens these, braving the terror of that forbidding and guarded pile in the interests of the land they loved.

Drums were now beating steadily, filling the air with their throbbing, almost drowning out the solemn tolling of the bell. Around them were rallying angry groups. As the groups grew large, each drum led its followers toward the Government House, where, on the steps; the revolutionary party harangued the crowd. Bonfires sprang up, built of no one knew what, in the public squares. Red fire burned. The drums throbbed.

The city had not yet risen. It was large and slow to move. Slow, too, to believe in treason, or that it had no king. But it was a matter of moments now, not of hours.

The noise penetrated into the very wards of the hospital. Red fires bathed pale faces on their pillows in a feverish glow. Nurses gathered at the windows, their uniforms and faces alike scarlet in the glare, and whispered together.

One such group gathered near the bedside of the student Haeckel, still in his lethargy. His body had gained strength, so that he was clothed at times, to wander aimlessly about the ward. But he had remained dazed. Now and then the curtain of the past lifted, but for a moment only. He had forgotten his name. He spent long hours struggling to pierce the mist.

But mostly he lay, or sat, as now, beside his bed, a bandage still on his head, clad in shirt and trousers, bare feet thrust into worn hospital slippers. The red glare had not roused him, nor yet the beat of the drums. But a word or two that one of the nurses spoke caught his ear and held him. He looked up, and slowly rose to his feet. Unsteadily he made his way to a window, holding to the sill to steady himself.

Old Adelbert had been working his way impatiently. The temper of the mob was growing ugly. It was suspicious, frightened, potentially dangerous.

The cry of "To the Palace!" greeted his ears he finally emerged breathless from the throng.

He stepped boldly to the old stone archway, and faced a line of soldiers there. "I would see the Chancellor!" he gasped, and saluted.

The captain of the guard stepped out. "What is it you want?" he demanded.

"The Chancellor," he lowered his voice. "I have news of the Crown Prince."

Magic words, indeed. Doors opened swiftly before them. But time was flying, too. In his confusion the old man had only one thought, to reach the Chancellor. It would have been better to have told his news at once. The climbing of stairs takes time when one is old and fatigued, and has but one leg.

However, at last it way done. Past a room where sat Nikky Larisch, swordless and self-convicted of treason, past a great salon where a terrified Court waited, and waiting, listened to the cries outside, the beating of many drums, the sound of multitudinous feet, old Adelbert stumped to the door of the room where the Council sat debating and the Chancellor paced the floor.

Small ceremony tow. Led by soldiers, who retired and left him to enter alone, old Adelbert stumbled into the room. He was out of breath and dizzy; his heart beat to suffocation. There was not air enough in all the world to breathe. He clutched at the velvet hangings of the door, and swayed, but he saw the Chancellor.

"The Crown Prince," he said thickly, "is at the home of the Americans." He stared about him. Strange that the room should suddenly be filled with a mist. "But there be those-who wait-there-to capture him."

He caught desperately at the curtains, with their royal arms embroidered in blue and gold. Shameful, in such company, to stagger so!

"Make-haste," he said, and slid stiffly to the ground. He lay without moving.

The Council roused then. Mettlich was the first to get to him. But it was too late.

Old Adelbert had followed the mist to the gates it concealed. More than that, sham traitor that he was, he had followed his King.

Chapter XXXVIII
In the Road of the Good Children

Haeckel crept to a window and looked out. Bonfires were springing up in the open square in front of the Government House. Mixed with the red glare came leaping yellow flames. The wooden benches were piled together and fired, and by each such pyre stood a gesticulating, shouting red demon.

Guns were appearing now. Wagons loaded with them drove into the Square, to be surrounded by a howling mob. The percentage of sober citizens was growing-sober citizens no longer. For the little King had not been shown to them. Obviously he could not be shown to them. Therefore rumor was right, and the boy was gone.

Against the Palace, therefore, their rage was turned. The shouts for the little King turned to threats. The Archbishop had come out on the balcony accompanied by Father Gregory. The Archbishop had raised his hands, but had not obtained silence. Instead, to his horror and dismay, a few stones had been thrown.

He retired, breathing hard. But Father Gregory had remained, facing the crowd fearlessly, his arms not raised in benediction, but folded across his chest. Stones rattled about him, but he did not flinch, and at last he gained the ears of the crowd. His great voice, stern and fearless; held them.

"My friends," he said, "there is work to be done, and you lose time. We cannot show you the King, because he is not here. While you stand there shrieking, his enemies have their will of him. The little King has been stolen from the Palace."

He might have swayed them, even then. He tried to move them to a search of the city. But a pallid man, sweating with excitement, climbed on the shoulders of two companions, and faced the crowd.

"Aye, he is stolen," he cried. "But who stole him? Not the city. We are loyal. Ask the Palace where he is. Ask those who have allied themselves with Karnia. Ask Mettlich."

There was more, of course. The cries of "To the Palace!" increased. Those behind pushed forward, shoving the ones ahead toward the archway, where a line of soldiers with fixed bayonets stood waiting.

The Archduchess and Hilda with a handful of women, had fled to the roof, and from there saw the advance of the mob. Hedwig had haughtily refused to go.

It had seemed to Hedwig that life itself was over. She did not care very much. When the Archbishop had been driven back from the balcony, she foresaw the end. She knew of Nikky's treason now, knew it in all its bitterness, but not all its truth. And, because she had loved him, although she told herself her love was dead, she sought him out in the room where he sat and waited.

She was there when old Adelbert had brought his news and had fallen, before he could finish, Nikky had risen; and looked at her, rather stonily. Then had followed such a scene as leaves scars, Hedwig blaming him and forgiving him, and then breaking down and begging him to flight. And Nikky, with the din of the Place in his ears, and forbidden to confront the mob, listening patiently and shaking his head. How little she knew him; after all, to think that he would even try to save himself. He had earned death. Let it come.

He was not very clear himself as to how it happened. He had been tricked. But that was no excuse. And in the midst of her appeal to him to save himself, he broke in to ask where Olga Loschek was.

Hedwig drew herself up. "I do not know," she said, rather coldly.

"But after all," Nikky muttered, thinking of the lady-in-waiting, "escape is cut off. The Palace is surrounded."

For a moment Hedwig thought she had won. "It is not cut off," she said. And spoke of the turret door, and whither it led. All at once he saw it all. He looked at her with eyes that dilated with excitement, and then to her anger, shot by her and to the room where the Council waited. He was just in time to hear old Adelbert's broken speech, and to see him reel and fall.

At the hospital, Haeckel, the student, stood by his window, and little by little the veil lifted. His slow blood stirred first. The beating of drums, the shrieks of the crowd, the fires, all played their part. Another patient joined him, and together they looked out.

"Bad work!" said the other man.

"Aye!" said Haeckel. Then, speaking very slowly, and with difficulty, "I do not understand."

"The King is dead." The man watched him. He had been of interest to the ward.

"Aye," observed, Haeckel, still uncomprehending. And then, "Dead-the King?"

"Dead. Hear the bell."

"Then —" But he could not at once formulate the thought in his mind. Speech came hard. He was still in a cloud.

"They say," said the other man, "that the Crown Prince is missing, that he has been stolen. The people are frenzied."

He went on, dilating on the rumors. Still Haeckel labored. The King! The Crown Prince! There was something that he was to do. It was just beyond him, but he could not remember. Then, by accident, the other man touched the hidden spring of his memory.

"There are some who think that Mettlich —"

"Mettlich!" That was the word. With it the curtain split, as it were, the cloud was gone. Haeckel put a hand to his head.

A few minutes later, a strange figure dashed out of the hospital. The night watchman had joined the mob, and was at that moment selecting a rifle from a cart. Around the cart were students, still in their Carnival finery, wearing the colors of his own corps. Haeckel, desperate of eye, pallid and gaunt, clad still in his hospital shirt and trousers; Haeckel climbed on to the wagon, and mounted to the seat, a strange, swaying figure, with a bandage on his head. In spite of that, there were some who knew him.

"Haeckel!" they cried. The word spread. The crowd of students pressed close.

"What would you do?" he cried to them. "You know me. You see me now. I have been done almost to death by those you would aid. Aye, arm yourselves, but not against your King. We have sworn to stand together. I call on you, men of my corps, to follow me. There are those who to-night will murder the little King and put King Mob on the throne. And they be those who have tortured roe. Look at me! This they have done to me." He tore the bandage off and showed his scarred head. "'Quick!" he cried. "I know where they hide, these spawn of hell. Who will follow me? To the King!"

"To the King!"

They took up the cry, a few at first, then all of them. More than his words, the gaunt and wounded figure of Haeckel in the cart fought for him. He reeled before them. Two leaped up and steadied him, finally, indeed, took him on their shoulders, and led the way. They made a wedge of men, and pushed through the mob.

"To the little King!" was the cry they raised, and ran, a flying wedge of white, fantastic figures. Those who were unarmed seized weapons from the crowd as they passed. Urged by Haeckel, they ran through the streets.

Haeckel knew. It was because he had known that they had done away with him. His mind, working now with almost unnatural activity, flew ahead to the house in the Road of the Good Children, and to what might be enacting there. His eyes burned. Now at last he would thwart them, unless — Just before they turned into the street, a horseman had dashed out of it and flung himself out of the saddle. The door was bolted, but it opened to his ring, and Nikky faced the concierge, Nikky, with a drawn revolver in his hand, and a face deathly white.

He had had no time to fire, no time even to speak. The revolver flew out of his hand at one blow from the flail-like arms of the concierge. Behind him somewhere was coming, Nikky knew, a detachment of cavalry. But he had outdistanced them, riding frenziedly, had leaped hedges and ditches across the Park. He must hold this man until they came.

Struggling in the grasp of the concierge, he yet listened for them. From the first he knew it was a losing battle. He had lost before. But he fought fiercely, with the strength of a dozen. His frenzy was equaled by that of the other man, and his weight was less by a half. He went down finally and lay still, a battered, twisted figure.

The cavalry, in the mean time, had lost the way, was riding its foam-flecked horses along another street, and losing, time when every second counted.

But Black Humbert, breathing hard, had heard sounds in the street, and put up the chain. He stood at bay, a huge, shaken figure at the foot of the stone staircase. He was for flight now. But surely-outside at the door some one gave the secret knock of the tribunal, and followed it by the pass-word. He breathed again. Friends, of course, come for the ammunition. But, to be certain, he went to the window of his bureau, and looked out through the bars. Students!

"Coming!" he called. And kicked at Nikky's quiet figure as he passed it. Then he unbolted the door, dropped the chain, and opened the door.

Standing before him, backed by a great crowd of fantastic figures, was Haeckel.

They did not kill him at once. At the points of a dozen bayonets, intended for vastly different work, they forced him up the staircase, flight after flight. At first he cried pitifully that he knew nothing of the royal child, then he tried to barter what he knew for his life. They jeered at him, pricked him shamefully from behind with daggers.

At the top of the last flight he turnery and faced them. "Gentlemen, friends!" he implored. "I have done him no harm. It was never in my mind to do him an injury. I —"

"He is in the room where you kept me?" asked Haeckel, in a low voice.

"He is there, and safe."

Then Haeckel killed him. He struck him with a dagger, and his great body fell on the stairs. He was still moving and groaning, as they swarmed over him.

Haeckel faced the crowd. "There are others," he said. "I know them all. When we have finished here, we will go on."

They were fearful of frightening the little King, and only two went back, with the key that Haeckel had taken from the body of Black Humbert. They unlocked the door of the back room, to find His Majesty sitting on a chair, with a rather moist handkerchief in his hand. He was not at all frightened, however, and was weeping for his grandfather.

"Has the carriage come?" he demanded. "I am waiting for a carriage."

They assured him that a carriage was on the way, and were very much at a loss.

"I would like to go quickly," he said. "I am afraid my grandfather-Nikky!"

For there stood Nikky in the doorway, a staggering, white-lipped Nikky. He was not too weak to pick the child up, however, and carry him to the head of the stairs. They had moved the body of the concierge, by his order. So he stood there, the boy in his arms, and the students, only an hour before in revolt against him, cheered mightily.

They met the detachment of cavalry at the door, and thus, in state, rode back to the Palace where he was to rule, King Otto the Ninth. A very sad little King, for Nikky had answered his question honestly. A King who mopped his eyes with a very dirty handkerchief. A weary little King, too, with already a touch of indigestion!

Behind them, in the house on the Road of the Good Children, Haeckel, in an access of fury, ordered the body of the concierge flung from a window. It lay below, a twisted and shapeless thing, beside the pieces of old Adelbert's broken sword.

Chapter XXXIX
The Lincoln Penny

And so, at last, King Otto the Ninth reached his Palace, and was hurried up the stairs to the room where the Council waited. Not at all a royal figure, but a tired little boy in gray trousers, a short black Eton coat, and a rolling collar which had once been white.

He gave one glance around the room. "My grandfather!" he said. And fell to crying into his dirty pocket-handkerchief.

The Chancellor eyed grimly from under his shaggy brows the disreputable figure of his sovereign. Then he went toward him, and put his hand on his head.

"He was very eager for this rest, Otto,", he said.

Then he knelt, and very solemnly and with infinite tenderness, he kissed the small, not over-clean, hand.

One by one the Council did the same thing.

King Otto straightened his shoulders and put away the handkerchief. It had occurred to him that he was a man now and must act a man's part in the world.

"May I see him?" he asked. "I—didn't see him before."

"Your people are waiting, sire," the Chancellor said gravely. "To a ruler, his people must come first."

And so, in the clear light from the room behind him, Otto the Ninth first stood before his people. They looked up, and hard eyes grew soft, tense muscles relaxed. They saw the erectness of the small figure, the steadiness of the blue eyes that had fought back their tears, the honesty and fire and courage of this small boy who was their King.

Let such of the revolutionists as remained scream before the Parliament House. Let the flames burn and the drums beat. The solid citizens, the great mass of the people, looked up at the King and cheered mightily. Revolution had that night received its death-blow, at the hands of a child. The mob prepared to go home to bed.

While King Otto stood on the balcony, down below in the crowd an American woman looked up, and suddenly caught her husband by the arm.

"Robert," she said, "Robert, it is Bobby's little friend!"

"Nonsense!" he retorted. "It's rather dramatic, isn't it? Nothing like this at home! See, they've crowned him already."

But Bobby's mother looked with the clear eyes of most women, and all mothers.

"They have not crowned him," she said, smiling, with tears in her eyes. "The absurd little King! They have forgotten to take off his paper crown!"

The dead King lay in state in the royal chapel. Tall candles burned at his head and feet, set in long black standards. His uniform lay at his feet, his cap, his sword. The flag of his country was draped across him. He looked very rested.

In a small private chapel near by lay old Adelbert. They could not do him too much honor. He, too, looked rested, and he, too, was covered by the flag, and no one would have guessed that a part of him had died long before, and lay buried on a battlefield. It was, unfortunately, his old uniform that he wore. They had added his regimental flag to the national one, and on it they had set his shabby cap. He, too, might have been a king. There were candles at his head and feet, also; but, also, he had now no sword.

Thus it happened that old Adelbert the traitor lay in state in the Palace, and that monks, in long brown robes, knelt and prayed by him. Perhaps he needed their prayers. But perhaps, in the great accounting, things are balanced up, the good against the bad. In that ease, who knows?

The Palace mourned and the Palace rejoiced. Haeckel had told what he knew and the leaders of the Terrorists were in prison. Some, in high places, would be hanged with a silken cord, as was their due. And others would be aesthetically disposed of. The way was not yet clear ahead, but the crisis was passed and safely.

Early in the evening, soon after he had appeared on the balcony, the Court had sworn fealty to Otto the Ninth. He had stood on the dais in the throne room, very much washed and brushed by that time, and the ceremony had taken place. Such a shout from relieved throats as went up, such a clatter as swords were drawn from scabbards and held upright in the air.

"Otto!" they cried. And again, "Otto."

The little King had turned quite pale with excitement.

Late in the evening Nikky Larisch went to the Council room. The Council had dispersed, and Mettlich sat alone. There were papers all about him, and a glass of milk that had once been hot stood at his elbow. Now and then, as he worked, he took a sip of it, for more than ever now he must keep up his strength.

When Nikky was announced he frowned. Then, very faintly, he smiled. But he was stern enough when the young soldier entered. Nikky came to the point at once, having saluted. Not, when you think of it, that he should have saluted. Had he not resigned from the service? Was not his sword, in token of that surrender, still on the table and partly covered with documents. Still he did. Habit, probably.

"I have come," he said, "to know what I am to do, sir."

"Do?" asked the Chancellor, coldly.

"Whether the Crown-whether the King is safe or not," said Nikky, looking dogged and not at all now like the picture of his mother. "I am guilty of-of all that happened."

The Chancellor had meant to be very hard. But he had come through a great deal, and besides, he saw something Nikky did not mean him to see. He was used to reading men. He saw that the boy had come to the breaking-point.

"Sit down," he said, "and tell me about it."

But Nikky would not sit. He stood, looking straight ahead, and told the story. He left nothing out, the scene on the roof, his broken promise.

"Although," he added, his only word of extenuation, "God knows I tried to keep it."

Then the message from the Countess Loschek, and his long wait in her boudoir, to return to the thing he had found. As he went on, the Chancellor's hand touched a button.

"Bring here at once the Countess Loschek," he said, to the servant who came. "Take two of the guard, and bring hey."

Then, remembering the work he had to do, he took another sip of milk. "These things you have done," he said to Nikky. "And weak and wicked enough they are. But, on the other hand, you found the King."

"Others found him also. Besides, that does not affect my guilt, sir," said Nikky steadily.

Suddenly the Chancellor got up and, going to Nikky, put both hands on his shoulders.

Quite to the end now, with the Countess not in her rooms or anywhere in the Palace. With the bonfires burned to cold ashes, and the streets deserted. With the police making careful search for certain men whose names Haeckel had given, and tearing frenzied placards from the walls. With Hilda sitting before her dressing-table, holding a silk stocking to her cheek, to see if she would look well in black. With Miss Braithwaite still lying in her drugged sleep, watched over by the Sisters who had cared for the dead King, and with Karl, across the mountains, dreaming of a bride who would never be his.

Quite to the end. Only a word or two now, and we may leave the little King to fulfil his splendid destiny. Not a quiet life, we may be certain. Perhaps not a very peaceful or untroubled one. But a brave and steadfast and honorable one, be sure of that.

What should we gain by following Olga Loschek, eating her heart out in England, or the Committee of Ten, cowering in its cells? They had failed, as the wicked, sooner or later, must fail. Or Karl, growing fat in a prosperous land, alike greedy for conquest and too indolent for battle?

To finish the day, then, and close with midnight.

Nikky first, a subdued and rather battered Nikky. He was possessed by a desire, not indeed unknown to lovers, to revisit the place where he and Hedwig had met before. The roof-no less. Not even then that he hoped for himself any more than he had hoped before. But at least it could not be Karl.

He felt that he could relinquish her more easily since it was not Karl. As if, poor Nikky, it would ever make any difference who it was, so it were not he!

Strangely enough, Hedwig also had had a fancy to visit the roof. She could not sleep. And, as she had not read the Chancellor's mind, her dressing-room, filled to overflowing with her trousseau, set her frantic.

So she had dismissed her maid and gone through Hubert's rooms to the roof. Nikky found her there. He stood quite still for a moment, because it was much too good to be true. Also, because he began to tremble again. He had really turned quite shaky that evening, had Nikky.

Hedwig did not turn her head. She knew his steps, had really known he must come, since she was calling him. Actually calling, with all her determined young will. Oh, she was shameless!

But now that he had come, it was Nikky who implored, and Hedwig who held off.

"My only thought in all the world," he said. "Can you ever forgive me?" This was tactless. No lover should ever remind his lady that he has withstood her.

"For what?" said Hedwig coolly.

"For loving you so." This was much better, quite strategic, indeed. A trench gained!

"Do you really love me? I wonder."

But Nikky was tired of words, and rather afraid of them. They were not his weapons. He trusted more, as has been said somewhere else, in his two strong arms.

"Too much ever to let you go," he said. Which means nothing unless we take it for granted that she was in his arms. And she was, indeed.

The King having been examined and given some digestive tablets by the Court physicians —a group which, strangely enough, did not include Doctor Wiederman-had been given a warm bath and put to bed.

There was much formality as to the process now, several gentlemen clinging to their hereditary right to hang around and be nuisances during the ceremony. But at last he was left alone with Oskar.

Alone, of course, as much as a king is ever alone, which, what with extra sentries and so on, is not exactly solitary confinement.

"Oskar!" said the King from his pillow.

"Majesty!"

Oskar was gathering the royal garments, which the physicians had ordered burned, in case of germs.

"Did you ever eat American ice-cream?"

"No, Majesty. Not that I recall."

"It is very delicious," observed the King, and settled down in his sheets. He yawned, then sat up suddenly "Oskar!"

"Yes, Majesty."

"There is something in my trousers pocket. I almost forgot it. Please bring them here."

Sitting up in bed, and under Oskar's disapproving eye, because he, too, was infected with the germ idea, King Otto the Ninth felt around in his small pockets, until at last he had found what he wanted.

"Have I a small box anywhere, a very small box?" he inquired.

"The one in which Your Majesty's seal ring came is here. Also there is one in the study which contained crayons." —"I'll have the ring box," said His Majesty.

And soon the Lincoln penny rested on a cushion of white velvet, on which were the royal arms.

King Otto looked carefully at the penny and then closed the lid.

"Whenever I am disagreeable, Oskar," he said, "or don't care to study, or-or do things that you think my grandfather would not have done, I wish you'd bring me this box. You'd better keep it near you."

He lay back and yawned again.

"Did you ever hear of Abraham Lincoln, Oskar?" he asked:

"I —I have heard the name, Majesty,", Oskar ventured cautiously.

"My grandfather thought he was a —great man." His voice trailed off. "I —should-like —"

The excitements and sorrows of the day left him gently. He stretched his small limbs luxuriously, and half turned upon his face. Oskar, who hated disorder, drew the covering in stiff and geometrical exactness across his small figure, and tiptoed out of the room.

Sometime after midnight the Chancellor passed the guard and came into the room. There, standing by the bed, he prayed a soldier's prayer, and into it went all his hopes for his country, his grief for his dead comrade and sovereign, his loyalty to his new King.

King Otto, who was, for all the digestive tablets, not sleeping well, roused and saw him there, and sat upright at once.

"Is it morning?" he asked, blinking.

"No, Majesty. Lie down and sleep again."

"Would you mind sitting down for a little while? That is, if you are not sleepy."

"I am not sleepy," said the Chancellor, and drew up a great chair. "If I stay, will you try to sleep?"

"Do you mind if I talk a little? It may make me drowsy."

"Talk if you like, Majesty," said the old man. King Otto eyed him gravely.

"Would you mind if I got on your knee?" he asked; almost timidly. In all his life no one had so held him, and yet Bobby, that very evening, had climbed on his father's knee as though it was very generally done. "I would like to try how it feels."

"Come, then," said the Chancellor.

The King climbed out of bed and up on his lap. His Chancellor reached over and dragged a blanket from the bed.

"For fear of a cold!" he said, and draped it about the little figure. "Now, how is that?"

"It is very comfortable. May I put my head back?"

Long, long years since the Chancellor had sat thus, with a child in his arms. His sturdy old arms encircled the boy closely.

"I want to tell about running away," said the King, wide-eyed in the dusk. "I am sorry. This time I am going to promise not to do it again."

"Make the promise to yourself, Majesty. It is the best way."

"I will. I intend to be a very good King."

"God grant it, Majesty."

"Like Abraham Lincoln?"

"Like Abraham Lincoln," said the Chancellor gravely.

The King, for all his boasted wakefulness, yawned again, and squirmed closer to the old man's breast.

"And like my grandfather," he added.

"God grant that, also."

This time it was the Chancellor who yawned, a yawn that was half a sigh. He was very weary, and very sad.

Suddenly, after a silence, the King spoke: "May a King do anything he wants?"

"Not at all," said the Chancellor hastily.

"But, if it will not hurt the people? I want to do two things, or have two things. They are both quite easy." His tone was anxious.

"What are they?"

"You wouldn't like to promise first, would you?"

The Chancellor smiled in the darkness.

"Good strategy, but I am an old soldier, Majesty. What are they?"

"First, I would like to have a dog; one to keep with me."

"I —probably that can be arranged."

"Thank you. I do want a dog. And —" he hesitated.

"Yes, Majesty?"

"I am very fond of Nikky," said the King. "And he is not very happy. He looks sad, sometimes. I would like him to marry Hedwig, so we can all be together the rest of our lives."

The Chancellor hesitated. But, after all, why not? He had followed ambition all his life, and where had it brought him? An old man, whose only happiness lay in this child in his arms.

"Perhaps," he said gently, "that can be arranged also."

The night air blew softly through the open windows. The little King smiled, contentedly, and closed his eyes.

"I'm getting rather sleepy," he said. "But if I'm not too heavy, I'd like you to hold me a little longer."

"You are not too heavy, Majesty."

Soon the Chancellor, worn not with one day, but with many, was nodding. His eyes closed under his fierce eyebrows. Finally they both slept. The room was silent.

Something slipped out of the little King's hand and rolled to the floor.
It was the box containing the Lincoln penny.

www.ingramcontent.com/pod-product-compliance
Lightning Source LLC
Chambersburg PA
CBHW071417300726
48976CB00004B/1157